P9-CEF-886

FACE TO FACE . . .
WITH DEATH

The sight of the corpse in its unnatural, upside-down position, dangling at the center of the crime scene, made Jessica Coran shiver uncontrollably. Boutine hadn't told her it would be so chilling. He hadn't prepared her for the ugly extent of the brutality played out on the corpse. But then, it may've been useless to try; perhaps no one could adequately prepare another person to stand here and focus on so diabolical a sight . . .

Killer Instinct

An electrifying novel of psychological suspense
by Robert W. Walker

KILLER INSTINCT

ROBERT W. WALKER

DIAMOND BOOKS, NEW YORK

This book is a Diamond original edition, and has never
been previously published.

KILLER INSTINCT

A Diamond Book / published by arrangement with
the author

PRINTING HISTORY
Diamond edition / July 1992

ISBN: 1-55773-743-6

Diamond Books are published by The Berkley Publishing Group,
200 Madison Avenue, New York, New York 10016.
The name ''DIAMOND'' and its logo are trademarks
belonging to Charter Communications, Inc.

PRINTED IN THE UNITED STATES OF AMERICA

10 9 8 7 6 5 4 3 2 1

This dedication is for she who has been with me for 25 years; it'll be a "killer" anniversary . . .

Thanks to Adele, Richard, Ralph & Co. who've worked so tirelessly on my behalf . . .

Thanks to John and Leslie who saw the potentialities and didn't hesitate turning my candle into a torch . . .

Thanks to Clive Cussler for professional courtesies, having class, taking time and being gentle . . .

As to police agencies I have only the FBI public relations office to thank for all that "gross of literature" forwarded.

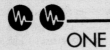

ONE

Evil is easy, and has infinite forms.
—BLAISE PASCAL
Les Provinciales (1656–57)

Something akin to a fetid spirit moved past the sheriff and his deputy when the warped cabin door creaked open, revealing a black crypt. But it was just the stale, pent up air, the closeness. Still there was the odor, heavy and solid, like a presence. The flashlight beam sluiced about the empty dark without reporting anything back.

Was the place filled with dead vermin? Had a raccoon crawled in through some hole, given birth to a litter only to die here, her starving young going unattended? Sheriff Calvin Stowell had opted to follow the lonely course of an old logging road, the terminus revealing the old Risley place. It had remained uninhabited for the last several years, the old man having died, his family scattered. Only the land held any value—the trees a mix of the finest hardwoods— but even the land seemed abandoned.

''Somepin' sure stinks, Calvin,'' said Lumley in the sheriff's ear.

The Wekosha Police had covered the territory around Baker's Road west to Three Forks, meeting up with the State Patrol moving eastward from the lake. This after repeated efforts along Old Market Road and Boyd's fishing camp and Killough Cove where the missing woman's family currently resided, all to no avail. Stowell, on a hunch, recalling the ancient, forgotten Risley place, quietly took his own direction now, and as if preordained, the weak and fading flashlight beam picked up a large shadow against one wall.

All evening long Stowell's men had fanned out along Hawk's Ridge, a massive swell of connected mounds pushing up along with the boulders here in the shape of a crescent, a giant, sleeping Gulliver in fetal position. The men had wrestled with twisted briar bush, thickets of white and jack pine, coming on ramshackle homes hidden deep in the wood, startling people in the process.

The search had begun the night before, so Stowell and the others were reluctant tonight to give up. Working far into the dark Wisconsin interior, they'd flashed pictures of the Copeland girl up and down the dismal Chippewa Creek, occasionally catching glimpses of something floating in the water that, from a distance, was easily mistaken for a swatch of clothing, or a body. All the false alarms had just added to frayed nerves and a collective frustration that threatened to explode. As frustration rose, hope waned.

Townspeople from all walks of life had joined in the search this night. The gesture had knitted them all together— *Common cloth of concern*, Stowell thought now—however, the additional manpower had netted them little else. Meanwhile time ticked on mercilessly for Annie Copeland. The cops in particular could not help but fear the worst, that "Candy," as she was known to friends and relatives, was no longer breathing, that her body was in some shallow grave in a field where she might one day, months from now, be discovered by some hunter's hound stopping to sniff at the carcass.

It had happened so often before, and Stowell had seen it firsthand in Fremont. There in the northern tier of the state, where Stowell had been a county deputy, several young women had been kidnapped, raped and mutilated by a pair of madmen who had kept their decapitated heads jammed into paint cans, using the dead orifices for sex acts too unspeakable to think of even now.

This old cabin had the same nasty feel to it, Stowell thought. He braced himself for what the odor and the shadow meant. Lumley had instinctively drawn his weapon,

the long barrel of the .45 Remington almost jabbing into
Stowell who was first through the threshold. Stowell felt as
if he'd been hit by a powerful force when it came clear that
the shadow against the wall was cast by a strangely
peaceful, dangling body—hair, head and torso turned upside
down, at the center of this small place. His throat went dry
as his eyes registered bits and pieces of this collage of
terror; so many fragmented parts: an arm lying on the floor
directly below, one breast cut away and missing, either
hidden in a dark corner or taken off by the madman.

It was unbearable, far too much for the eyes to accept or
the mind to register all at once. Stowell's insides heaved and
his head reeled, a fluttering, birdlike dizziness threatening to
overtake him. Both he and Lumley had fully seen and had
fully inhaled the death-filled room, swallowing it whole.

The disfigured face was still Candy Copeland's. There
were terrible gashes to the limbs and sex organs. Dismemberment.

Stowell rushed out past a frozen Lumley who was
stupidly pointing his big gun at the body. Outside, Stowell
fought to keep down the bile and Red Devil tobacco he'd
chewed on all evening long. Lumley ran out after him like
a kid left in a haunted house, now taking great gasps of air
as if to purge his lungs of the odor lingering inside him.

A few minutes later, Stowell returned to stand before the
body, his flashlight playing over the awful slash that had
nearly severed the head. There was a lot of blood caked
around this wound, but strangely, there was no blood on the
floor. At first, Stowell thought it was the darkness conceal-
ing the purple blood that had soaked into the ancient boards.
But when he got down on his knees and examined it closely
with the light, he saw that the only thing disturbed about the
floor boards was the layer of dirt which the killer, Lumley
and he had tracked over. He cursed the fact that they had
already compromised the crime scene, but it was the
incredible lack of blood around the body that struck him as
extremely important and startling. It reminded him of

something he had read several weeks before, something in his *True Crime* magazine, the *Police Gazette*, or was it one of those FBI bulletins he had been rummaging through? It had been an alert put out by some guy with the FBI, a big shot with one of their psychological profiling teams, a guy named Button or Buntline or Boutine. Yeah, that was it—Boutine.

The FBI had been interested in hearing from any sector in the country, but particularly the midwest, about any mutilation murder that, oddly enough, left very little in the way of blood evidence. That's what the floor beneath the dangling body made Sheriff Stowell think about now, and he was almost grateful, as it gave him something to focus on other than the horrid wounds, the decay and the waste before him.

Lumley remained at the door, only his right foot sticking through. "Want I should radio the others now, Calvin? Let 'em know?"

Lumley's voice was hollow, but Calvin Stowell was glad to hear the words just the same. "Yeah, tell 'em we've found her. . . . search is over."

Lumley had holstered his gun and was now snatching at the barking police radio dangling from his belt. It had been the only sound disturbing the absolute quiet here.

"Tell Melvin to get Chief Wright out here. It's his case."

"But we're pretty far out from Wekosha, Sheriff, and it's still in our jurisdiction, and—"

"Just get him here!" Stowell flashed his light at the other man as he shouted, creating a black silhouette of his big deputy there in the doorway.

"If you say so, sir."

"And get a message patched through to Marge to alert the FBI."

"FBI?"

"You got plugs in your ears, son?"

"No, sir, but FBI? We can nail this creep! You know it's got to be her pimp boyfriend, Scarborough."

"We don't know a fucking thing, Lumley. Now, do as I asked."

Lumley frowned, stepped out of the doorway and sauntered into the scrub out front from where he made the calls. Stowell turned his big, sad eyes once again to the dark form hanging beside him and said in a tender voice, "Nobody can ever hurt you again, Candy. And we found you . . . we found you."

A sudden gunshot outside sent Stowell racing for the door, his own gun leaping into his hand, his keen eyes scanning for the danger. All he saw was Junior Lumley standing in the clearing, his weapon pointed, saying shakily, "Something moved, Sheriff, in the bushes."

Stowell marched to where Lumley's bullet had found a stray animal, now whimpering and in much pain. The cry was not that of a dog, the keening taking on a wild, banshee screech suddenly before there was silence again.

"Careful, Sheriff . . . careful," Lumley cautioned from behind.

Stowell, flashlight in hand, kicked out at the dead opossum, its razorlike teeth clearly visible where the gums were bared in a grimace of frozen pain. Stowell gnashed his teeth together, trying to control his anger. He turned on Lumley and said firmly, "You holster that damned weapon and keep it there, Junior."

"But Sheriff—"

"Just get back to the goddamned squad car so you can direct traffic here."

"You gonna stay with the body?"

"Go, Junior, *go!*"

"I'm goin', Calvin, I'm goin'!"

Stowell called after him as Lumley disappeared down the logging trail. "And when the others get here, you call me Sheriff, Junior! *Sheriff!*" Sometimes Calvin Stowell wanted to strangle his sister's kid.

He looked back down at the dead opossum and the pool of blood in the dirt which made a stark contrast to the bloodless floor below the Copeland girl's body. It made him wonder if she had been killed elsewhere and merely brought here later. But then, why hang her by her heels and leave her body in plain view to anyone who might pass? And if she were hatcheted elsewhere, where was that location? No doubt it would be covered in blood. But the FBI bulletins had hinted at a killer who, for whatever screwed up, ritualistic or vampiristic purposes *took the blood away with him.*

Several hours later

The sight of the corpse in its unnatural, upside-down position, dangling at the center of the crime scene, made Jessica Coran shiver uncontrollably. For a moment, as the ice in her veins tried to thaw, she became angry with Otto Boutine. He hadn't told her it would be so chilling. He hadn't prepared her for the ugly extent of the brutality played out on the corpse. But then, it may've been useless to try; perhaps no one could adequately prepare another person to stand here and focus on so diabolical a sight.

But focus she must. It was her job. It was what she had come halfway across the continent for.

"You okay, Jessica?" asked Boutine in her ear.

Others in the room seemed focused on her, curiously wondering how she was going to react to something they considered unfit for feminine eyes.

"I'm . . . I'm fine, Otto," she said, consciously working at steeling herself in the face of such horror while secretly a voice was shouting inside her head: *Run! Run, girl!* Maybe she wasn't ready for such responsibility; maybe she didn't deserve Otto's confidence. But a second voice deep within, sounding very like her deceased father's, said calmly, *Stand your ground, Jess.*

She faltered, however, when she looked again at the dismembered arm, lying almost perfectly below the maimed shoulder where it had come from. The sight of the mangled breasts and vagina hit her like a body blow. She went to the wall where thick, solid cedar logs lined the cabin. She tried to take some comfort in the feel of the naked cedar, smooth and hard and clean.

Otto tentatively placed his hands on her shoulders and whispered, "I think maybe you'd better step out and come back in again, Jess. Come on, I'll do the same."

"Just give me a minute, okay?"

Otto nodded and brushed back a lock of his long, pepper-and-salt hair. "Sure . . . sure . . ."

She was glad when he looked away, so that he didn't see the next wave of disorientation rush over her, her balance shifting inside her temples like an amusement park ride. Some windows and the doors had been thrown open, but the odor of the relatively fresh corpse in the room clung to the place like a heavy blanket of fog. Decay was easier to take after the first few days of decomposition, but the initial onset, like the carcass of a deer hanging on a tree outside a hunting lodge, filled the brain with primordial stirrings about blood and death. Not even the light from the police generator could dissipate the dark horror of what had occurred here.

But it was the very freshness of the kill that had caught Otto's attention and had gotten her on a jet for Wekosha, Wisconsin, along with the best psychological profile man in the country. It was the possibility that here they had a crime scene that hadn't been completely destroyed by decay or time or the stupidity of some local authority ill-equipped to deal with sex-mutilation cases of a possible serial nature. This one was fresh enough to give Jessica and Otto hope that they might be able to actually do something about it.

Otto had some notion that this death in little Wekosha had some similarities to previous cases throughout the Midwest, cases that others had long since filed away, but which continued to disturb Boutine's sleep. All murders for which the FBI had very few clues.

Her job here was to provide a medico-legal re-creation of

the crime, a kind of "negative" of evil that had passed this way. From this a clear print of the killer might or might not be formed.

The cabin walls, the floor, the ceiling, the objects in the room, were in silent collaboration, holding secrets which she alone might translate to the world. She must pry the unseen, microscopic evidence from the larger shocking picture before them.

It was by no means the first tortured body she had ever witnessed, but somehow here, in the field, it was different. The corpse didn't arrive in a brightly lit forensics laboratory, in a neatly zipped plastic bag, and there were no water hoses or stainless-steel surgical slabs. Instead, there was a mangled body dangling from a rope by its heels, its clothing ripped and strewn about, its hair gnarled macrame, its bloodless limbs mannequinlike.

It's different when you know you're dying . . . when you die badly . . . when your suffering is prolonged . . .

She finally brought her eyes up from where they had been hiding, to look again at the body. She gritted her teeth and forced herself to be strong. She didn't know how she knew, but she knew that the victim had died slowly, fully aware of her hideous fate.

Just knowing your own death is at hand . . .

Cramped quarters. No other women in the room other than she and the corpse, lightly swaying because someone had touched or bumped it.

Whispers, garbled talk, ancient odors, dark cave . . . an awful way to die.

Amid the noise and movement of local and state lawmen, here in Wekosha, Wisconsin, Dr. Jessica Coran, medical examiner, fresh from the Quantico, Virginia, FBI laboratories, wanted to shout the dramatic order for everyone to clear the room, to take charge of the investigation, like in the movies. However, she knew this would serve little effect beyond alienating the locals, and since now that the crime scene had already been compromised, she swallowed hard and simply said, "I'll need everyone's cooperation here. Can I count on it, Otto?"

"You've got it, Dr. Coran," Boutine said with more than enough flare for the both of them. His booming voice made the others start. Chief of Division IV, Psychological Profiling of Mutilation Murderers, FBI, Otto Boutine was a hefty man with a deceptive and perpetual cat's grin. He possessed the most penetrating gray eyes that fired like steel at the heart whenever he commanded others. He poked at the door with a shiny Cross pen that he'd been nervously twirling since their arrival here. "Everyone please clear the area so Dr. Coran can work. If and when she needs assistance, she will ask."

The others began to file out with a few grunts, some of which were an octave higher than necessary. As they drifted out onto the rickety front porch, she said to Otto, "Just don't leave me completely alone, okay?"

He realized from the plea in her eyes that her request was more than a concern for procedure, that a witness be at her side at all times; the request was also quite personal.

"So what's your initial impression?" he asked awkwardly.

"Too soon to tell much beyond the fact the local medicine man is pissed."

"Yeah, I got that impression, too. Wants first call, I suppose."

"Anyone can declare her dead. No, he just wants to dress the body for burial, spare the relatives any further grief. Least, that's what he said outside."

"So where do we begin, now that it's ours?"

"The light in here stinks," she said.

"Got that right, but it's the best we can do with field generators."

"Have those guys bring up their squad cars, come through the windows and the door with their headlights. Dammit, where're those guys from Milwaukee with what we need?"

"On their way, or they better be."

She went to her black valise and began laying out the tools of her trade: slides, capsule bottles, plastic bags, labels, forceps, specialty scalpels and syringes. She took off her long beige overcoat and donned her apron, gloves and mask. From the inside pocket of the overcoat she pulled forth a scalpel in a case that she flipped open. Otto stared, wondering about the scalpel. She saw the curiosity in his eyes.

"It was my father's. I guess it's kinda superstitious, but it helps me get through times like this."

"Sure, sure," he said.

They approached the body once again and Otto asked, "It is definite, from what I see."

"What's definite?"

"We got ourselves a torture victim at the ninth level."

"A Tort 9," she said shakily.

"Next to no blood evidence, other than around the wounds."

"You've seen a few of these. I haven't. Give me time to work, okay?"

"But Jess, it's obvious, isn't it?"

"Nothing's ever obvious to me. I didn't build a reputation on reporting on the obvious. Now, let me work. It will take some time."

It had been her considerable reputation upon which Boutine had counted on. He had climbed out on a shaky limb here, a limb which could send them both tumbling should it snap. Both their careers could go down with it. But it was Boutine's bid, and so she hadn't questioned it when he had come into her lab several weeks before asking her a hundred and one questions that had begun with how many pints of blood were there in the human body and ending with how would those pints be most efficiently emptied. Meanwhile, Jessica had heard rumblings about disagreeable scenes between Boutine and his boss, Chief William Leamy, something to do with manpower, monies and time. So he had "recruited" her in an effort to enlarge his investigative powers at headquarters and to build onto his team, adding a forensics expert to his psychological profiling team. It was a maneuver, and not quite yet a *fait accompli*. She had chosen to leave such jockeying for position and strength to Otto, and to concentrate on her own chess game, which was with the killer. This game began here and now.

After an hour's examination, she began to talk to Otto once again. "She . . . the mutilation to the body was done after she was dead."

County Sheriff Stowell had drifted in, and hearing this, he remarked, "Thank God, then she didn't suffer."

"Wrong. She suffered a great deal," countered Jessica. She then said to Otto, "I'll know more about the weapons used by the killer later, after I've had a chance to examine the tissues under magnification."

"How can you be sure she was dead before the mutilation occurred?" asked Otto. "The lack of blood evidence?"

"Yes, for one."

"Killer cleaned up the place," suggested Stowell.

"Not a chance he could have cleaned it entirely from the walls, the ceiling, the floor," she said. "Besides, other than footprints, the dirt over these floors hasn't been disturbed. No, he didn't bother cleaning a damned thing."

"Then where the hell's the blood?"

She and Otto exchanged a look. Otto glared at Stowell from where he was crouched beside Jessica, and said, "This information is strictly confidential, Sheriff."

"Absolutely . . . absolutely."

She and Otto huddled together, Otto obviously excited now. "So the bastard drained her of her blood."

"A slow process and a slow death."

"What'd he use?"

"Tubes maybe . . . I can't say at this point . . . but it was controlled, very controlled."

"And the mutilation afterward? Just a cover?"

"Purely cosmetic, for our benefit."

"You can tell all that without your tests and scopes? It's that cut-and-dry?"

"No, the other way around. It's *dry* first, *cut* second."

"No doubts?"

"None. Look . . . look closely here." With forceps, she opened the awful gash to the dead woman's throat which had been smeared with blood that had dripped down to her chin and mouth, drying in an unusual pattern. "This wound is awful, but it was inflicted after she died, and the blood . . . well, it had to have been placed on—"

"Placed on?"

"Applied, smeared on, afterward."

"There's got to be prints in the blood, then."

"Not if he used surgical gloves, and I believe we're dealing with a very controlled killer here."

"You saying he's a shrewd bastard?"

"In some ways. Others, he's foolish. Like we're supposed to naively believe that she died of these wounds? Odd thing is that there is significant coloration below the facade of the blood on the throat to indicate some sort of ligature wound possibly, or something else to discolor the tissues here and here," she finished, pointing.

"So it's just as I suspected," he said, "a Tort 9."

"Think you can get me some black coffee, Otto?" she asked. "I've got a lot more to do here yet."

"Doctor, your wish is my command. This is an important step for us both."

"That coffee'll do me just fine, and maybe a hot shower later? And maybe the understanding of God?"

"I can arrange for the coffee and shower, but the other one? You're on your own there, kid."

She watched him go before turning back to the corpse, her eyes zeroing in on the whites of the dead girl's eyes where they had rolled back in her head, a natural reaction to terror. The whites were speckled with near invisible, infinitesimal red dots which would show up much better under bright light and magnification, but Jessica had seen the unmistakable telltale signs of strangulation before, and here they were. Everything pointed to the throat as the aperture through which the killer drained his victim. Below the cosmetic slash of the madman, she was certain there had to be more signs of the actual cause of death. But here, now, under these conditions, how was she to determine that? It couldn't be done.

Where was that damned coffee?

Suddenly, one of the deceased's eyes wobbled and flipped back into place, the pupil staring back at Jessica Coran, making her start. The dead girl had had lovely, deep blue eyes.

TWO

"Assuming you're right," Chief Inspector Leamy, Otto Boutine's boss, had said the day before, "that there is a serial killer making off with whole liters of blood from his victims, Otto, what in hell do you think the guy's doing with it?"

"He might be using it for any number of purposes. Case histories have people using it in ceremonies, rituals, satanic—"

"But you don't think this has anything to do with any cult? You think it's one *flippo*, right?"

Leamy leaned into the cushioned leather chair, rocking lightly, waiting for Otto's answer.

"It's my educated guess that this guy drinks the blood, but whatever he's doing with it, bathing in it or painting his walls with it, the bastard's got some warped need for it, and he wants it fresh and pumped direct from his victims."

"Whoa, you're going way out on a limb here, Otto. Nothing in the forensics reports I saw backs you on this. At every crime scenario, the locals believed the body was removed from the slaughter scene, which explains the absence of blood all over. Now you take a giant, imaginative leap and on the basis of that, the bureau's supposed to launch an all-out investigation of this guy based on possible wrong assumptions?"

"You pay me for my imagination and my intelligence, Bill. I've never let you down before, have I?"

15

Leamy hesitated, started to form words, but rolled his gums about instead.

"Well, have I?"

Leamy leaned even farther over his desk, fixing Otto with a cold stare. "You know as well as I do, Otto, that it only takes one major screw up and the organization'll find a new place for both of us to sit out our years. You remember Colin Armory? You recall where he finished up?"

Otto hated this side of Bill Leamy: the man had worked hard to get where he was, and he meant to take no risks, and what he was saying at the moment was less than veiled. There was a recession on, budget cutbacks had been brutal, and if Otto committed manpower and a small fortune on an investigation plan, it had better produce results or it was Boutine's ass and not Leamy's.

Leamy suddenly began asking Boutine about his wife's condition, a courtesy that the man had extended once too often of late, the conversation taking on a perfunctory, sterile quality. Boutine's wife was in a coma in the hospital, the victim of an aneurysm.

Otto had become convinced that a number of previously unrelated cases were in fact related, that the killer had a taste for blood, and that he was that rare breed of killer who relied on the ninth level of torture, blood draining and blood drinking, to get his kicks.

Tonight was the first time he had seen a *recent* victim of Tort 9 firsthand; he had, as a first year field operative in California, seen the results of one other such blood-sucker. And now, he knew in his soul, with every fiber of his being, that the crime scene he stared at tonight had everything to do with that awful California case, almost as if this new killer had studied under James P. Childers who died in the gas chamber in 1979 after Boutine had helped put the bastard away. But Childers left a trail so clear and obvious that it was as if he had wanted to be stopped. That seemed not to be the case with this new psychopath.

And this guy ran the torture gamut, touching almost all

the grid boxes on the FBI forms: Torture levels one and two with disfigurement of the sexual organs; dismemberment, Torts three through five. The only heinous acts the bastard seemed uninterested in performing were Torts six through eight, acts of disembowlment and cannibalism. But there was no doubt the fiend enjoyed draining his victims of their blood, slowly and with extreme caution, so as to lose not a milliliter unnecessarily. Boutine could be wrong, of course. The blood could be taken off for other than a manic feeding, and maybe the killer didn't use it as Kool-Aid, but something told him differently.

Otto believed Jessica Coran's findings would not only lend credence to his theory, but that she, like him, would soon be risking her hard-won reputation as well. As young as she was and as new to the division as she was, Dr. Coran was known for her thoroughness and her tenacity to stick by her convictions, no matter what the consequences. She was a far cry from the man who had been overlooked for the position she now held. Dr. Zachary Raynack had been blind to what Otto felt to be obvious signs of a Tort 9 killer.

"Call it a hunch," Otto had finally told Leamy the day before.

Leamy had gotten up from his seat, not a good sign. "You don't bet the ranch on a hunch, Otto. You, of all people, should know that. You sure this thing with your wife—" Leamy hesitated "—hasn't affected your reasoning on matters of—"

"You've got nothing to worry about on that score, Bill. Nothing whatsoever!" Otto hoped that his firm voice, tinged with anger, had settled Leamy's mind about him. It was obvious that Leamy's garrulous golfing buddy, Dr. Raynack, had already gotten to him.

Otto pulled his thoughts from Leamy's and Quantico's concerns about him. He concentrated instead on Jessica Coran whose orchestration of the evidence gathering must seem like science fiction to the locals. Her instruments and the procedures she followed were cutting edge, and she had taken charge as she should, sending the brawny policemen to their hands and knees to rip out linoleum just below the sink in an adjacent alcove, as well as floor boards below the victim's head. Despite what seemed a lack of any blood anywhere, she knew that trace elements, even after washing and scrubbing, could be detected under a scanning electron microscope. If the killer so much as pricked himself as he hacked away at the body, she'd find some trace of his blood from the sink, the tiles, or the boards, Otto believed. He had heard through the grapevine that she was affectionately known as the "Scavenger." Raynack, by comparison, was known as the "Rat Man" of the department.

Otto watched her intently now, finding Dr. Coran extremely easy to look at, remembering the first time he had ever seen her, and how he had felt as if his breath had been stolen. In this setting, she was of course in stark and unrelenting contrast to the male-dominated environment, but even in a roomful of vibrant women, he believed she'd stand out. Jessica had long auburn hair, which when not tied back, was just this side of wild. Her creamy complexion was flawless against a beautiful, navy-blue suit with a white chiffon blouse, but now the suit jacket was out in the car, lying atop her overcoat, replaced by a linen apron that also covered her petite skirt. Not even this could hide her slimness. Otto saw Stowell and some of the others snatching glances at her from time to time.

Terrific genes, he realized. At seventeen, she had been a tall and willowy girl, possessing a startling grace for one so young. She had her father's height, his knowing glint in the eye, and her mother's whiskey voice and high cheek bones. She had the characteristic intent-on-her-work attitude that had made her father so invaluable to the military. Boutine had known Dr. Oswald Coran as one of the finest medical examiners he had ever met, as had everyone who had dealings with the man, some of whom were the families of MIAs, senators, generals and presidents. In fact, Coran had presided over many controversial autopsies, his expertise often sought in an attempt to disprove rumors of foul play as in the plane crash deaths of two senators in a one-week period two years before.

Oswald Coran had died of a debilitating disease that first took his limbs, his muscles atrophying, leaving only his keen mind intact, imprisoned in a useless, wasted body. For such a man, it was a condemnation to hell. There was some talk that his sudden death was the result of euthanasia, but it was never pursued. Sadly for Jessica, her father's condition came on the heels of an automobile accident that had claimed her mother. Somehow Jessica persevered and had finished her residency at Bethesda Naval Hospital, where her father had once been chief of forensics.

According to Jessica's father, the Navy saw that their medical practitioners got what they needed in the way of training, as opposed to the Army. He insisted she either train under the Navy or through private medical schools. She chose the latter, but as a "navy brat" her upbringing was filled with upheaval, change and disruption, and as a result she seemed tough beneath the gentle exterior, and she hadn't a clue as to just how stunning she was. Her idea of a beauty regimen was to pull her hair back and splash on perfume, and for her, that was all it took.

She was holding back tonight, allowing Boutine to be the man in charge, and yet everyone in the place knew that she was in charge, that something had happened when she went to work. Charisma, the X-factor, whatever it was that made others respond to her, she had it. Otto knew that all he had was the ability to intimidate and frighten.

He had met her once, when she was sixteen or seventeen, at the ceremony held when her father had been made chief of forensics at Bethesda. She had come a long way.

Suddenly she stood, stretching out the cramps in her legs from the crouching she had been doing. She turned and found him staring, and almost politely asked, "Daydreaming, Otto? At a time like this?"

Not giving away anything, he fired back at her. "Defense

mechanism.'' He wondered if she had any idea that she was the subject of his thoughts.

"Give me a hand," she said. "I need a pair of tweezers I left over by the valise, and another vial, please."

He pocketed his unlit pipe, nodding, saying, "Sure, sure . . . Anything else?"

Otto felt the eyes of the other men on them, perhaps envious of him. Envious not because of his many years of service with the Bureau, nor his long record of accomplishments, but envious that he knew her personally and professionally.

"Family's got a right to put this thing to rest," said Dr. Samuel Stadtler in her ear. The gray-haired, pinch-faced local pathologist had been shuffling the periphery of the crime scene for hours muttering disturbing words to the sheriff and the others because he had not been asked by Jessica to assist in any way.

"It may be a while before I can release the body to you, Dr. Stadtler," she told him. "I'll want to be involved in the autopsy, you understand?"

"I understand more than you know," he said cryptically. "For instance, I know that murder isn't normally the concern of the Federal Bureau of Investigation. I know that Stowell called you people in, and I know how you people operate, without the slightest concern for the family."

Otto stepped in, hearing this, and seeing that all the other lawmen were anxious to see the showdown between the old country doctor and the young lady doctor. Otto said, "This is a federal affair now, Dr. Stadtler—"

But he was cut off by Jessica, who stepped into Dr. Stadtler's face. "And you can either cooperate or be removed from the case altogether. Either way, it's up to you."

"I have jurisdiction here, Doctor," snapped Stadtler.

"No, no, you don't. Not unless and until we are asked by the authorities who requested us in to leave," she countered.

"Now, I suggest, sir, that if you're so concerned about the family, then you go and sit with them and counsel them, sir."

Stadtler's face was flushed and he could not find words to express his anger. Looking around for support but finding none, he marched out. They heard his car ignition and the bump and grind of the vehicle on the weedy dirt road.

Otto turned to her and said, "You're going to find that a lot of locals are threatened by us when we come in."

"God, I hope I didn't make things worse."

"No, no, you handled him by the book."

She smiled for the first time tonight. Otto's forehead was one of his most intriguing features, being so dominant and wide at the top. His cranial size gave way to a smooth tapering jaw and firm chin, which made for a long face with a variety of expressions, all hard to read at times. He was tall, regal even; his straight-backed posture and take-charge manner never failed to impress. And now Otto's steel and ice eyes penetrated the fog of her fatigue, and for a moment she saw the pain behind those eyes, *the ghost of a demon,* perhaps two or three, demons that creased his face with concerns he could not voice.

"Better get done here," he said, drawing away from her stare as if to hide his eyes from further investigation.

"Yeah, right."

Boutine returned to the tight leash he'd held the other men on, ordering them back to work, telling them precisely what Dr. Coran wanted and needed, managing to irk them all in turn until silence blanketed the crowded little death hole. When this happened, Otto stepped outside for some air.

Everyone here had been touched by this victim; touched in a place no one wished to ever be touched. She realized only now just how badly Otto had been affected.

The idea that there was in this world someone who wanted to rob her of her blood, to drink it down and piss it away, the thought alone made the FBI woman shudder in that secret part of her soul reserved for fears she had thought long banished from her psyche.

But the psyche never did play fair, not even with itself.

Otto Boutine had seen mutilation murder in its every guise throughout his long career in the FBI Psychological Profiling Division and as an advisor before such a division existed; in fact, most of the cases he had handled dealt with some form of body mutilation. He had become the resident dean of mutilation murders, the expert, the Ben "obi-wan" Kenobi of mutilation. It sometimes concerned him that this was how he had spent his life; that he had spent more waking hours—and sometimes the hours in deep sleep—inside the minds of the most brutal killers ever brought to justice, than he had with his wife who was now slipping helplessly away from him. But from the moment he had gone into collaboration with the Bureau, he had learned how to think like a man capable of the most atrocious acts imaginable, but this, the result of the ninth level of torture, was not easily fathomed.

Intellectually, he could accept the fact there were between three and four hundred so-called real vampires roaming the country, and that while all of them had an unholy need for the taste of blood, few of them actually became serial killers, opting for other and safer means of satisfying their needs; however, emotionally, Otto had great trouble imagining the mind-set of a man capable of actually draining another human being of blood. The slow death process was so torturous, so heinous that it topped the FBI list of worst crimes of torture.

It was difficult to think like a murderer, much less a sadistic, perverted killer; now to think like a man who believed that he was a child of Satan, a descendent of zombies! That, in order to insure his survival, he must not only feed on human blood, but the rich, warm, heady mixture of a fresh kill? It was difficult even for a man of Boutine's expertise, and yet he had thrown himself into the investigation like a man bent on going over Niagara Falls in a canoe, flying in the face of Raynack, disregarding Leamy's warnings. Did it have something to do with Marilyn? Had Leamy somehow sensed his desperation for work that would take him out of Washington, away from the pale shadow of the woman who lingered on in coma, the one he could not bear to watch any longer? Or was it simply that this tort nine was what his entire career had been about? To stop a cruel and human phantom he alone believed in: a twisted creature of the dark that ingested fresh blood from another in order to accumulate—at least psychologically—supernormal power over life and death. Was it just possible that the satanic bastard believed in his own bloody immortality? The vampire complex: the fixation that gave rise to men like the Marquis de Sade, and women who believed they could stay their beauty by bathing in the blood of virgins. Human lampreys, lusting for the blood of others.

But this was the first time he'd ever seen the results of such an insane fantasy.

He stared again at the drained body hanging upside down from the rafters of the ancient log house in Wekosha, Wisconsin. The local authorities had called them in the moment they realized what they had, a bloodless mutilation scene, just as his fax had described.

Jessica Coran had been like a rock in the face of the horror. Amazing lady, terrific medical mind, incredible skill and control. He knew that he'd have to control the superlatives concerning her field performance in the report he intended to write, that he mustn't make her sound like Joan of Arc or Sister Theresa, but he was impressed, and the report would reflect a commendable job. He went to her, gripped her arm, asking, "How's it going?" She'd been at it full tilt for hours and dawn was approaching.

"Coming to an end." Her slurred voice said it all.

"You're going to need some sleep before doing the autopsy, and it's nearing light out now."

An autopsy could take hours, and a complicated one—

and this was sure to be complicated—could take eight hours.

"Don't let them do it without me, Chief."

He nodded and changed the subject. "Been some time since I've seen one quite this bad, I admit." She thought she detected a slight shudder in Boutine's voice. For a moment their eyes met, his shimmering gray darts plunging uninhibitedly into her deep blue-green pools to mesh in a silent bond of understanding. She realized for the first time that he was as profoundly wounded by the outrage committed here as she; at the same time she wondered how it could be otherwise, and how she could have thought it otherwise. Yet, Otto was Otto, so stiff, so muscular, so strongly wired together, and earlier he had seemed so *above it all,* so much in control—all useful mannerisms she had this night emulated so tenaciously, feeling like a cat with her teeth sunk deep, afraid to let go even in the least, for fear she'd lose the battle with herself.

But there it was, the hurt in his eyes.

It was just a flicker, and she was beyond fatigue, yet the flaring ember of a moment's weakness had been there. The gruesome nature of the case had struck him in his soul, just as it had hers. He tried instantly to put it out, and as must usually be the case, it was quickly extinguished, replaced with the steel again, and she half heard his directives to her.

"Time we get it wrapped up here, so you can get a few hours' sleep."

She nodded, saying nothing. But somehow, she knew that they would always hold on to a bond created here amid the carnage.

But he was suddenly all business again, throwing the mantle of chief across his brow once again, as if not interested in sharing such emotions with her. She was reminded without so much as a word of his invalid wife, who had remained now for a month in a coma at Bethesda Naval Hospital, a victim of an aneurysm. She remembered that no one got too close to Boutine, that Otto shared only the rudiments of his life and nothing of the core of his being with anyone, least of all a junior officer in the department.

The only reason he was here was to oversee her performance in fieldwork for the Bureau. He was working on a major overhaul of his profiling team, and she was central to that restructuring effort. He had held nothing back in this regard, telling her precisely what his plans for her were, and nothing about those plans said anything of sharing an emotion, even if it was spontaneous and unintentional.

Up until this morning, Dr. Jessica Coran had worked assembly-line fashion within the relatively friendly, clean and safe confines of the "store." But now she was to head up her own assembly line for the follow-through on this case. This time, she was to see the whole picture. And she did; she got it right in her face.

THREE

Jessica had given up on getting the sophisticated fingerprint equipment promised them by the Milwaukee field office. She might have had results with an ultraviolet imaging system that intensified light 700,000 times at a crime scene. But she must make do with what she had, a field generator and headlights flooding through the windows and doors. She tried to take it in stride; besides, the chances of actually capturing a print from the killer in the terribly disturbed crime scene was scarce at best. She had noticed that someone had actually picked up one of the dead girl's parts and returned it to her, laying it below the body like an offering, and it wasn't very likely that it had been the killer's doing, but someone who had been *moved* by the awful scene.

Still, she had gone through the motions, using the best technology available to her, the MAGNA brush. It was an ingenious device, small enough to carry in her breast pocket. The MAGNA made it possible to develop fingerprints on all kinds of materials, even those that once resisted processing. The locals were making their own prints with conventional tools and seemed to her in the stone age.

Everything would have to await her return to Quantico, where fluids and stains found at the scene, along with fibers, could be identified, and where DNA results might show them something. But such tests took time.

The local law guys were getting antsy now, wanting very much to cut the corpse down, close down the death house.

She couldn't blame them. It was one of those universal instincts, an urge to tidy up the helpless victim, to right the wrong so far as it could be righted, to at least put the helpless form of the victim in a more natural pose; they wanted someone to clean her wounds, not to measure and poke and take slivers of tissue from her. They wanted to put the ugliness from view.

Along with the urge to clean and tidy up came the accompanying illusion that doing so was not only helpful but the morally right thing to do.

Her father had told her about such things as this; he had been witness to it countless times, and so had she now. But he also taught her that such urges were both natural and good, despite the harm they often did in destroying evidence and the desired *sanctity* of a crime scene. Such human urges certainly served the living; they certainly served to "soften" the scene, but thankfully, and somehow, Otto's long-distance proviso that the corpse not be touched by anyone had prevailed, *amazing as it seemed*. Once again, she guessed it was the sheriff's doing, a man named Stowell. She knew that to these men she appeared hard, perhaps even perverted, to have kept them so long from releasing the body from its silent torment, its bonds and its unholy position. The kind of well-intentioned mentality that caused no end of problems at crash sites where victims of burning Boeing 707s were too soon lifted off and placed all in neat little rows, creating a nightmare of identification problems for the medical examiner.

She had been called in on such a case with the terrible fate of Pan Am flight 929. It had been her first mass-death site and it would prove a massive undertaking in more ways than one. Identifying mangled and charred bodies, fitting limbs torn and hurtled about a debris field of some hundred and fifty yards, was enough of a challenge for any forensics specialist. She had been an assistant M.E. on call at Washington Memorial when the news of the crash came over. Such an announcement is like an invitation to a frat

party, and so within the hour all roads leading to the crash
site were congested with off-duty cops, reporters, camera
crews, voyeurs of every stripe. Anyone with the remotest
excuse to be on hand converged on the site, including
politicians prepared to be interviewed.

Fire engines lined the way along with ambulances, along
with more cops than necessary. The terrible secret amid the
mayhem and confusion was the looting which was typically
blamed on the local population. At a busy airport like Dulles
International the first on scene were those whose job it was
to rescue the living and protect the bodies of those who'd
died. At the Pan Am crash the first to arrive were the Port
Authority police, followed by the WPD, the firemen and the
emergency medical supply teams, nurses, doctors, morti-
cians and then nearby residents. The amount of looting was
unforgivable.

The relatives of the dead were in an impossible situation,
Kafkaesque in its nightmarish proportions. They saw evidence of the police, the firemen and the medical teams
rushing in to save or identify their loved ones. How then
might they question a missing broach, a lost diamond, a
wallet? Without recourse, there was no way to accuse
anyone or even prove that something had been stolen.

Pan Am 929 had been a "rich" flight, coming in from
Buenos Aires, the passenger list reading like the social
register of Washington, D.C. But by the time Jessica had
arrived on scene, it looked like a planeload of paupers.
Another reason to put the bodies all in a row, she guessed,
in order to frisk them for rings and things—things that
might quickly identify the charred and mutilated remains.

She overheard one policeman say to a distraught young
woman, "You say your mother always wore this ring? But
can you say you actually saw it on her hand when she
boarded the plane in Buenos Aires?"

An archbishop on his way back to Rome via D.C. was
located, his body intact, but his gold and amethyst ring and
cross, along with a Rolex, had vanished without a trace.

Outraged, one police lieutenant ordered all wallets and jewelry removed from the bodies under the watchful eyes of his men, and these items were tagged with a number corresponding to a number given each body, and placed in plastic bags sent to the police property room so that no further thievery would occur. It was at this point that Jessica and other M.E.s had come on the scene, having battled rush-hour traffic to get there. By then there was not much personal property left, and the bodies, all neatly numbered and assembled in a row, and covered over by a green tent, had been stripped of whatever personal effects might identify them.

As a medical examiner, Jessica's main concern was to identify unrecognizable bodies. The easiest, quickest and least painful method of doing so was through the use of personal effects and the passenger list, with its seat number for every passenger. At the untouched "pristine" scene, the M.E. could see patterns of injury, relationships of body parts, enabling her to work out the exact details of what happened, and why one passenger's head was severed and another's left intact.

While she was working over the bodies at the crash site, Jessica had been painfully aware that influential people at the FBI had their eyes on her, as she was awaiting an appointment to the academy. The tragedy of Flight 929 became a litmus test for her. Two of the passengers aboard had been with the Bureau. She got the appointment, but she reserved the right to maintain a little contempt for all those who had profited in one form or another from the tragedy, including herself, all those superlatives about ambition notwithstanding.

Now in Wekosha, Wisconsin, with a single body to work with, she was expected to have all the answers, but without the necessary lab time, all she could manage was the same as Stowell or Lumley: guesswork. However, one clear fact in all of this stood out. Without a doubt the killer had literally "milked" the dead girl of her blood. She pictured an enormous vampire bat at the girl's throat, huddled there, lapping up her life with a vile tongue and incisors.

Otto returned from outdoors, looking controlled and tightly wired once again. He extended a hand to help her to her feet from her kneeling position there at the throat.

"I've got all I need," she told Otto, "and I'm ready to leave."

Lumley lost some saliva and tobacco when he blurted out, "You mean we can cut her down now?" His tone was sarcastic and brittle.

Sheriff Stowell fixed him with a stare.

Jessica said simply, "Yes, but do so very carefully and gently. We don't want any mortician wounds confusing anyone later.

"We'll be careful," said one of the Wekosha cops.

Jessica left quickly, now anxious to breathe the crisp, cold air of the Wisconsin countryside, filling her lungs with it while the car was loaded with her equipment and findings.

The night here had a silence that seemed impenetrable, the stillness like cold lead leeching into her bones. The darkness of the deep woods was complete and mysterious. It was such an isolated place, both peaceful and dangerous at once. It reminded her of a hundred hunting camps she had visited with her father on excursions for deer. The end result of their hunt was a gutted carcass, and when she heard the grunting and noise of the men inside as they released the dead girl from her bonds, she thought of the horror that she had somehow put on hold for these many hours. She could hardly blame men like Lumley who looked at her as if she were a ghoul.

"We're ready to roll, Jess," said Otto, who'd come from the car with her overcoat, placing it over her shoulders. "You're shivering," he said.

"Thank you. Didn't realize just how cold it was."

In a moment she was leaning into the soft, clean upholstery in the back of Stowell's squad car. Stowell reached into his glove compartment and offered her a pull on a Jack Daniel's bottle, which she hesitantly took only after Otto gave her a nod.

Sheriff Stowell turned the car around, nearly throwing them into a ditch, before righting the car onto the overgrown dirt road which would take them to the highway. Otto took the whiskey from her, pulling on it twice before returning it to Stowell with a "thanks."

"Sheriff Stowell has agreed to keep a lid on the more gruesome aspects of the crime, Jess," Otto was saying, while all she wanted to do was drift off with the soft slumber reaching out for her, the car gently rocking now over the dirt road.

"Good," she managed.

"But I promised something in return."

She blinked, her expression turning to curiosity, before she said, "He'll get a full report, soon as we have—"

"He wants to know if she was or was not sexually molested before the mutilation."

Stowell spoke for himself. "Candy wasn't a bad person. She didn't deserve dying like this."

"You knew her?"

"She had an arrest record."

"Prostitution?"

"Yes."

"Is that how you knew her?"

"I spent some off-duty time with her; got her a job; got her to clean up her life. Now this . . ."

Stowell filled her in on the details concerning Annie "Candy" Copeland's life. At the age of eighteen and three-quarters, she'd been a waitress for all of two months at a diner in Wekosha. Before that she had been working the streets and living with her pimp. Before this, as an idealist still in high school, she had been a volunteer at the local hospital, a candy striper, from which she had derived the nickname, Candy.

"What about her family life?" asked Jessica.

Stowell's voice had the grit of a man who had seen a

great deal of sorrow in his professional life. "She was what you'd call a *throwaway* kid. Stepfather abused her, mother looked the other way, and when she tried to fight back . . . came to me . . . they booted her onto the streets. System didn't begin to work for this kid, so I did what I could, which wasn't much."

"Stowell and I'll be talking with the pimp soon," Boutine said.

"And the stepfather."

"Co-workers at the diner, all that," Otto added.

She knew the routine. First check with those who knew her, those who came into routine contact with her; who had last seen her alive, when and where, and with whom? Suspect the relatives, the friends, the co-workers, and work from there. Question each and from each gain a new insight and a possible new lead or clue to her demise.

"So, tonight, you want me to tell you if she was sexually molested?"

"Best guesstimate, Dr. Coran," said Otto.

"My best estimate should await lab analysis, Otto, and you of all people should know that."

"Best guess, Jessica," Otto said in his most commanding voice, squeezing her hand as if to impress her as to the importance of his deal with Stowell.

She breathed deeply, allowed a sigh to escape and said, "My guess is—and it is only a guess—that this guy didn't have any interest in her sexually, that is in a normal sexual sense."

"Normal sexual sense?" asked Stowell, whose knuckles had turned white on the wheel. She could tell that he had more than just a fatherly interest in Annie Copeland. Had he been carrying on an affair with her?

"Intercourse."

"But I saw you taking a semen sample."

She knew what he was fishing for. "Yes, I found semen, but—"

"Semen's evidence of—"

"—but it hadn't penetrated beyond the cervical—"

"You can tell that from just looking?"

"It was cold in there, and the semen I found was jellied, almost as if . . ." She trailed off.

Otto squeezed her hand again and urged her on. "As if?"

"Like the blood on the wounds, smeared on, after the girl was dead, as if intended for us to *find*."

"Sonofabitch," muttered Otto.

Stowell sat in abject silence for a moment before saying, "So whoever did this wanted only one thing from her?"

"That's right, Mr. Stowell," she said. "He just wanted her blood."

"Thank you, Dr. Coran," he said before falling into a well of silence again, the green dash lights alone illuminating the wounds on his face.

Jessica looked across at Boutine where they sat in the rear. Boutine bit his upper lip before speaking. "Stowell's going to do what he can to keep the vampire aspect frozen. At least no leaks for twenty-four hours."

She realized that Boutine had bought a little time, and they both knew that the sensationalism of the case would soon overpower the small-town police force, the troopers and Stowell's county office within that time frame.

"You look like hell, Otto," she said in a whisper, not believing that the thought escaped her lips. "I'm sorry; I didn't mean to be so blunt. Guess I must look wrecked, too."

He had continued to hold onto her hand and now took both of them in his own, massaging them. "Fact is, you look fine, just fine."

"Perjury before a witness, Otto?" She pulled her hands away, glancing at Stowell's eyes in the rearview mirror.

They both needed sleep. Neither of them had had any rest for well over twenty-four hours. She leaned back into the cushioned seat again, closed her eyes and recalled the telephone call at her home that placed her on standby status. God, had that been just yesterday? At the time Otto hadn't a clue as to where they would be flying, except to say that it was likely to be a Midwest destination. He had given her a pep talk about how the Bureau wanted her to get experience in the field and that he wanted her on his team. He spoke of consolidating his team with a clinician, someone who could put the pathology back into a psychological-pathological report on a serial killer.

So he had put her into the rotation, and after hours of standing by and standing down, she was told to stand to when Boutine had called back and cryptically said, "You ever been to Wisconsin in springtime?"

"No, never," she'd replied.

"Lots of mud, what with the winter thaw."

"Is that right?"

"Got any boots?"

"Sure, I got boots."

"High-tops?"

"High-tops, low, anything that's required. Is it a go?"

"Be at the academy gates in half an hour."

An army jeep was waiting for her at the gate, and when she got in, it swung out to the airfield, where she was given help with her gear to board a sleek Learjet with engines piercing the stormy black sky, and her eardrums. In a matter of two hours they'd touched down at a remote airstrip facing a farmer's bean field. She was told they were on the outskirts of Wekosha, Wisconsin.

The entire way, Otto spent time filling her in on the case as he understood it. As it happened, however, he didn't fully understand it, primarily because it had not been reported in its entirety to him. He'd gotten it secondhand, off a fax. Anxious to prove to superiors that it would make sound sense to combine his psychological profiling team with a solid forensics team under Jessica's leadership, Otto had recklessly—*for him*—whisked her off to oversee the "trouble" in Wekosha.

On the plane with Otto, she was given the impression the case involved murder, but she wasn't told that it involved the ninth level of torture, blood-taking. She wondered how much Otto had known, and how much he had kept from her when a sudden, jarring pothole in the city's pavement brought her back to the present.

They had to first go by the city police department, where all the evidence was placed under lock and key, Otto and Stowell witnessing, as a matter of protocol. From there Stowell had a deputy drive them to the Wekosha Inn, where they had rooms awaiting them. As soon as the deputy was away, Jessica hurried inside, anxious for a shower and some well-deserved sleep, but Otto stopped her at the desk the moment she had her key in her hand, taking her aside.

"There's something you're not telling me, isn't there?" he said.

She stared into his eyes, wondering how he had ever gotten so smart at reading people. "Nothing I can prove, yet."

"What is it?"

"Aside from the bastard's having carted off most of her blood?" she asked.

"Carted off?"

"Stowell said she had been missing for two days. From the stage of rigor that I saw, I'd say she died the first night of her disappearance. Now, the guy could have hung around all night, but I don't think so. And no one can consume that much blood at one sitting. I don't care if he thinks he's a vampire or not."

"So he took the blood with him?"

"Most of it, yes."

"Some of the local idiots are trying to make a case for the Copeland girl's getting into a little B&D, or maybe auto-erotica getting out of hand."

"That's bullshit, and you know it. She was tied by her heels to the rafters and her blood syphoned off. If it had started out as some torture turn-on, there'd be whip marks, bite marks, small wounds and bruises, and like I said the sperm was smeared inside her along with the blood. She was not a party to her own death.''

''Only insomuch as the way she lived her life,'' he replied sadly.

She understood his meaning. Many a victim ''invited'' attack; many people were perfect victims.

''Stowell says they got a tire print. Not a great one, but—''

''You made sure that guy Stadtler's not to embalm her before I get a closer look at the lab?''

''Taken care of, I assure you. Meanwhile, I want you to get some solid rest. God knows, you've earned it.''

She started away with a ''good night'' trailing after, but stopped at the elevator and said, ''One thing, Otto.''

''Yes?''

''Whoever this fiend is, he showed amazing control.''

''Amazing control?''

''*Of the blood flow.* Given the body's position, there would have been tremendous pressure against the arteries leading to the cranium, the jugular in particular.''

''The kind of pressure that should have sprayed the place with her blood.''

''He knew that himself . . . has thought this thing out . . . thought about it a lot.''

''Fantasized about it, or has actually done it before, maybe,'' he suggested.

''And the bastard's come up with a way to staunch the flow, control it and contain the blood.''

''Suggest a medical background, possibly.''

''Also suggests an organized mind at work.''

They both knew the literature—if it could be called that—on the organized versus the disorganized murderer. A disorganized killer left a disorganized crime scene behind: weapons, footprints, fingerprints, personal articles and other giveaways to the police, usually in haste to run from what he had done. An organized killer only left carefully chosen clues, evidence that he *wanted* police to find, often in an attempt to send them down a blind alley; other reasons ranged from fetishes and fantasy rituals concocted in a fevered brain to a sick desire to taunt those who came in to clean up his filthy work.

If Jessica was right, they'd turn up no murder weapon, and all the suspects hauled in by the locals would likely be poor substitutes for the real thing. The local response in such killings was to chalk it up to the work of lunatic impulse. In fact, they counted on it and on moving quickly to incarcerate someone for the crime.

But they both knew that while all this would happen for the community's sake and for the newshounds, the real killer would be all but invisible. An organized killer would have returned home, gone to bed, slept the peace of the innocent, having relaxed his biting urge to take blood, and wake refreshed. He was not about to show up at Stowell's office dazed, disoriented, blood dripping from his mouth, to give himself up in order to quell a brain in turmoil over having fed on the life of another human being. Whoever this man was, he felt no remorse, pain or empathy with his victim. Instead, he likely had a place in his garage for the cutting tools he'd used on Candy Copeland, and he most likely had placed each on its respective nail or shelf before turning in for the night.

"Our guy's a tidy man," said Otto there in the dimly lit hallway, as if reading her thoughts.

"Fastidious about himself and his things," she agreed, "and I don't think he wanted to get any blood on his clothes. If he tried catching her blood in a bucket, it would still be all over that cabin, and all over him. He'd gag and wretch if he tried taking it all in at once through a hose of some sort. No, he'd have to do it in a very clean, neat way."

She was busy in her head with the image of the monster, silhouetted in the dark against his victim, working meticulously over her before tearing into her dead body with the mutilating tools in an attempt to hide his finer work.

This time neither of them said good night. Both of them knew that sleep, if it did come, would not be without disturbing images.

FOUR

When she got into her room, she turned on all the lights, and seeing the big double bed, she stretched out across it in her clothes thinking she'd just lie here for a moment. Then she was in back of Stowell's car with her hands in Otto's. She felt safe with him and she nestled in against him there in the crooning car, finding warmth in the crook of his arm, a curved, protecting cove. All around them the dismal, black Wisconsin landscape transformed into an oceanside lit bright with sunshine where they drove along a winding road above the escarpments. It was as if they were transported to Scotland, she thought, a place she had long dreamed of seeing, since her roots were there.

The ride was lovely and Otto's voice was as caring and gentle as the soft breezes coming in at the windows. He asked after her comfort. She next heard him say something about love, but it was as if he were suddenly far away and she looked up to find herself alone in the car, a roiling black cloud having turned day into night, and the car was now a hearse, and the driver was no longer Stowell, for in the rearview mirror she made out the eyes of Candy Copeland as she said, "Just sit back, missy, and enjoy the ride."

Jessica started from her sleep with a jerking motion that almost sent her off the bed. Sitting upright, panting, she surveyed her surroundings. The dream had been so real . . . so real . . .

When the bleeding had stopped, it was almost three in the morning and he was alone with the corpse and his own mind again. He hated this moment. It brought on panic and guilt and sick feelings in his head and in his stomach, and so to push it away, he relived the moments leading up to his quenching the burning thirst inside him.

He hadn't made love to her in the usual sense, yet he loved her far beyond any physical bonding, for with her life's blood literally his, literally inside of him, they had become one.

Candy, she had called herself, and she'd had the dull look of a simple schoolgirl bored with life, when he had first approached her at the bus stop. She wasn't too bright, but it wasn't brains he was after. Her speech patterns told of a meager upbringing. It was obvious she was unread, that she did very little thinking beyond what was between her legs and who was the current teen idol. She was perhaps eighteen, maybe more, and she had the hard look of a girl who liked to drink and party whenever she could find it.

She smoked fiendishly.

He must have looked strange to her, grand in a way, certainly not what she was used to. He was much older, dressed in a suit and tie, driving a nice van. He was old enough to be her father. In a sense he had made her *his*, hadn't he?

She was foul-mouthed, and she dressed like the teen idol Madonna, which made her look like a tramp. She did dope whenever she could get it.

He had certainly broken her of all her bad habits in one fell swoop . . .

When he had fooled her into taking that trip with him, she had said, "I'll help you, if you'll help me."

She'd wanted a ride and a smoke, preferably grass. She got the ride and something a great deal stronger than weed. Then she got something she never bargained for, something that would make her live forever, so long as he chose to go on living forever.

She is dead now, but still some blood trickles down the long, tapering neck, catching at the upside-down chin where it drips from the arched Adam's apple . . . and he catches the blood in his hands . . . uses it like holy water, rubs it into his face. Feels it against his skin, the smell of it—her essence—eases his tense nerves. He wants to remember the moment . . . but it's fast fading, the images weakening with every hour that passes.

He wanted to go back to that moment.

Preserve Candy and that moment in his mind.

He reached over for the Nikon shots that he had snapped of Candy—before and after shots from every angle, catching her in the pose that fed him.

Beside him, on the floor, stood the icebox and the mason jars. He went about the business now of packing the overflow away. His home freezer needed stocking, and thanks to Candy, it was looking much better.

A neighbor's dog was barking, causing an eruption of other dogs to pierce the evening sky with their howls. There was a bright moon out and the dogs saw shadows moving everywhere. His was a quiet area, peaceful really, the backyard barbecues rusty from their long winter's wait, fences crumbling with age and neglect. It was an older neighborhood, to be sure, the houses in the district erected in the late sixties. Still there weren't a lot of pestering little ones about the front yard and the street, and while the houses looked their age, only an occasional salesman showed up at the door.

Inside, he had all the comforts he required, mostly medical books and magazines. He even had a copy of *Gray's Anatomy* published before the days when such a masterpiece could have been mass-produced on flimsy paper at a reduction in print size. The book had been a prized possession of his grandfather's, a man he had never known.

He must be certain that absolutely no trace of Candy's blood be found on the tools of his trade. The blood itself, in packs in the icebox, would not long be in his possession. Melanie's was already depleted to a final pack, and Janel was soon to follow.

He was careful with his jars of blood. In the morning, he would transfer the blood into plasma packs, boxes of which he kept on hand. The stored blood would keep better that way and take up less room in his freezer.

For want of a better name, he labeled his jars *Candy,* so as not to be confused with *Melanie, Janel* or *Toni,* three earlier contributors to his supply. He kept one jar of Candy in the door of his refrigerator, some to fill his A.M. appetite, some for slides. In the morning, he'd have a microscopic look at Candy's blood, in order to determine its finer qualities, or if it possessed any unwholesome aspect. During the heat of conquest, such concerns could not be contended with.

His work was near done. He securely placed each jar atop the other with a little glass *clink,* unloading the cooler labeled *Specimens.* He had brought it in from the van. He'd waved at Jonstone down the street as he carried in the stuff. Jonstone was an insomniac, and it wasn't unusual to find him walking his dog even at three in the morning.

From the bottom of the cooler, he now lifted a small vial with a cork top. This he placed in the sink to be sterilized and reused later. Staring at the vial, it reflected the light over the sink, and he mused on its having been heated earlier by him, using his Bic lighter. He had stared through the flame at the dangling carcass. Alongside the slender tube resting in suds in his sink, he now placed an array of sullied items: a thermometer, a surgeon's scalpel, a pair of probes, a clamp, and a device he had only recently given a name to: *the spigot.*

Now he went to the case of fine steel knives and instruments gleaming in the weak light. He hadn't remembered wiping them clean, but he had. He now closed the cooler and the case, and he began to feel a little fatigued. He had driven a long way to get home.

He went into the bathroom, peeling away his shirt, revealing a broad, hairy chest and a stomach that spilled over his pants top, the navel buried within flesh, unseen. He'd been dieting, watching the fried and fatty foods whenever he was on the road, but it seemed to be doing nothing for the midsection where all his extra weight appeared one day when he woke up and examined himself closely and critically. He wasn't terribly obese, just enough to cause a bulge all around him and to strain the buttons of his shirts. He'd taken to wearing oversized ties to business meetings to cover the area at his navel, but there was only so much that could be covered.

His face, too, was overlarge, the cheeks ballooning out, his jowls inflated to the point of hiding his better features, the distinct, dark crystal-blue eyes. He'd never had so large a head before. Why now? What was he to do about it? The only parts of his anatomy that seemed untouched by his sudden weight gain were his sinewy, taut limbs. The weights he lifted helped out here. And the blood diet was helping curb his appetite, he believed.

The years had taken their toll on his complexion as well. He was ashen, the graying hair making him even more ashen in appearance. It made doing business harder, both in the daylight hours and at night. He was a colorless man, had always been a colorless man, with a low opinion of himself on account of how lowly he was regarded by just about everyone he came into contact with. Most people treated him as if he were a filing cabinet, and an empty one at that. *All his life.* But he was a great deal more interesting than anyone suspected.

Still, he must face the fact that he was at a crucial point in his life. He had read a lot about patterns and phases of growth, stages that a man went through. This was one of them, contracting the fat tummy and the fat jowls. He vowed not to let it get the best of him, and so, as tired as he was, he did his push-ups and sit-ups before showering and lying back on the bed.

In the shower, his mind had wandered back to the scene of the murder. The hot shower water was like her blood in its warmth.

In bed, his mind wandered back again to the details of the killing. He returned to survey the crumbling, filthy, odor-ridden old place in the woods miles from the main roads. He then methodically found the precise instruments that he required in the briefcase he had on hand, in order to open a vein and drain Candy of what he wanted from her. He dwelled on this, allowing the moment to cradle him to sleep. His rest was deep and peaceful, stirred only by the unpleasant flashes regarding the need for the imprecise, heavy-duty equipment he'd used on Candy.

He had had to return to the van, placing the murder weapons in a secret compartment, putting the camera filled with the negatives of the killing on the seat. From the rear now he pulled forth his battery-operated hacksaw, a nice toy. He then returned to stand before the body, deciding what touches would be best.

The hum of the hacksaw was welcome in the deafening silence of the place; he carefully sliced away the breasts before mutilating the vagina. There was next to no wasted blood. He counted on the horror of the mutilation to confound local police, send them scouring the countryside for a lunatic escaped from an asylum perhaps, or the town weirdo, or a recluse of the woods. Certainly, no one would be looking for a man like him.

When he'd done with his final cuts, he stepped back to look at the result, casting a roving, critical eye over the corpse. He started away, but at the door he stopped and returned.

"What the hell," he said aloud, touching the hacksaw almost gently to where her shoulder and arm met, severing the ligaments on all sides. With a gentle tug of his gloved hand, the bone separated neatly from its socket, and with a final flourish, he threw the arm across the room.

He was about to leave when he remembered one of his

scalpels in the kitchen. He had left it in the basin. As he passed the corpse again, he also recalled the hospital tourniquet tied tightly about her neck, and the pink ribbon in her hair which he had placed there. He snatched this away, too. He didn't want to leave any clues save those that would befuddle and misguide the authorities, like her severed arm and the mutilated genitals.

Earlier, he had fished out the vial of semen from the cooler in his van. The semen belonged to another man, someone he didn't even know. He had warmed it to room temperature, then poured some into the dead woman's vagina and the remainder in her mouth. He was then careful to put the vial and its top back into the cooler to be taken away with him.

He'd sent the authorities on the trail of a sex pervert. They'd find just what he wanted them to and nothing more, like the little surprise in her mouth and vagina.

Satisfied, the killer left. Home was far away and waiting, and yet he *was* home and in bed, his needs fulfilled, dreaming that he was coming and becoming . . . Could life be any richer? He rather doubted it.

And his dreams proved him right now . . . as before . . . and always.

He kneels on all fours like a panting animal, below her neck where she is dangling. In a frenzied, altered state of consciousness and being, he doesn't remember tying her long, loose hair back in order to have a clear path to the spigot of her throat from which her blood is about to flow, now that he has tapped into it. He has everything in place. He loosens the tourniquet with his hand held over her eyes. The blood is coming through to him in a controlled, measured flow, just as he had imagined it a thousand times. His inventiveness and imagination have not failed him.

He is in orgy at this point, and while not a religious man by anyone's standard, he knows now what fervent emotions strike like paralyzing electricity through the brain and heart of a zealot. Down on all fours, he catches the blood of her life in his mouth, swallows it warm and experiences the ethereal soul of her pass into his bowels, relinquishing to him her complete essence. Blood sacrifices . . . as old as time and man.

She does not bleed profusely or carelessly. He has taken careful steps not to squander the precious red fluid. He has covered the wound he has inflicted on her white throat with the spigot and surgical tape, turning the tourniquet, applying just enough pressure to slow the bleeding so as to catch it calmly in the mason jars he has brought with him. As each is filled, he sets it aside on the table, working by the light of an old oil lamp and a lantern flashlight he has set up on end. He doesn't want the light to draw any attention, although it is miles to the main road.

He knows his lust is insatiable and that the supply he's taken from Candy will not long last him. He knows even before he arrives home this night that he will crave the drink he craves for the rest of his life, not only because he likes the taste of blood—has liked it from childhood—but also because he likes the good feeling of the slaughter itself. He finds comfort in it; he finds reason and balance and beauty in his relationship with the body he feeds on, the woman that feeds him.

He is, after all, a vampire.

He has tried to tell people of his affliction, to get help, but that has gotten him nowhere. Most refuse to hear his cry. They don't believe that daylight hurts him, or that he sleeps by day, prowls at night, and feeds on the blood of others. He has no one. No one cares. No one but Candy, who dangles before him as his sustenance and his warm friend, forever in his mind, fulfilling him.

He thinks momentarily of home, and of taking a bath in Candy's blood. He thinks it an exciting idea and it grows. He is much closer to Candy than to Melanie or the others. Maybe a bathtub filled with *her* isn't such a crazy notion.

FIVE

The wake-up call from Otto Boutine blared in her ears, but for a moment Jessica could not recall where she was; she certainly didn't recall any sleep. It seemed that only minutes had elapsed. She woke in her clothes, sprawled on the bed. With the phone on its third, perhaps fourth ring, she made a mad dive for the thing, knocking it to the floor and catching the receiver before it dropped. Good reflexes were a blessing, something she had always possessed.

"Jess, it's me, Otto."

"What time is"—she yawned—"it?"

"Getting on toward ten, and you said you'd like to see the body in the morgue before we head back to Virginia."

"So I did."

"Stadtler isn't exactly waiting for you with bated breath."

"Fish-baited breath, maybe."

"That's why I like you so, Jess, but let's not piss anyone else off at us before we leave, okay?"

"Is that an order?"

"Consider it cheap advice. You comin'?"

"Give me ten—no—twenty minutes, Chief. I've got to shower and dress."

"Meet you in the lobby."

"Grand."

She quickly grabbed something to wear, realizing that she'd have to let her hair dry along the way, and that lately she hadn't given a thought to her appearance. She rushed

47

from bed to bath, and later when she slipped from the shower, she heard a knock at the door.

"Boutine, dammit, I'm not ready."

The knock persisted and someone was saying something on the other side, but she couldn't make it out. She threw on a robe and opened the door. A waiter stood outside holding a breakfast tray.

"Room service, compliments of 605."

Boutine could be thoughtful, she said to herself. "Oh, please, on the table." She rushed ahead of him to clear away the things she'd tossed over the table. Then she fumbled for a gratuity, but the waiter told her it was taken care of, and he promptly left.

She rushed down the toast and coffee and scrambled eggs as she continued to dress. She was a half hour getting to the lobby, where she found Boutine engrossed in the *Milwaukee Journal*.

"Anything about the case?"

"Too damned much. I swear I don't understand reporters. You politely ask 'em for cooperation and they nod and say yes, sir, anything you want, sir, and then they weasel information outta some schlock deputy P.R. officer, tack on a few innuendos, and they're practically blowing whatever careful case you might make against a suspect before you've even got the bastard in custody."

"They got the vampire angle?" She was upset now.

"No, not yet."

She sighed, pursed her lips and nodded. "Thank God for that much."

"Faxed a copy of the one good print you found to Quantico."

"And I take it, it's not on file, right?"

"Right, Sherlock."

"Stands to reason."

His quizzical stare lingered over her. "I didn't have much hope that it would check out either, but what made you think so?"

"Nature of the crime places this guy as one of the general population. Likely to be white, middle to upper class, blends in like a sci-fi horror alien who's taken over a human body. Possible dual, if not quadruple, personality, leads stellar life by day, model neighbor, belongs to the Rotary, relatives and friends think of him as just a regular guy who stays pretty much to himself. Lives with his mother or alone, and if he is married, he's a mouse, completely dominated by her. Away from home a lot; goes hunting for human blood by night. But we'll be lucky to find a parking ticket with his name on it, much less a record."

"Maybe you ought to be in psychological profiling, Doctor."

"Maybe. Any event, this case may be unsolvable."

"No one said it was going to be easy."

"Thanks for breakfast," she said. "Nice gesture."

He shrugged. "We're on expense account."

"Just the same—"

"Glad you enjoyed it."

As they went for the door, she told him, "We've got to come up with a few more details that'll stay in-house."

"That's one reason we insisted on the autopsy."

"Poor woman's suffered some very unkind cuts, and now we're going to literally open her up to more. I can see why the locals hate us."

"Something else you ought to know," he said, placing a gentle hand on her arm as he led her to the waiting car.

"Having to do with her severed arm? At the crime scene?"

"I know about that."

"What do you know about it?" He half smiled, incredulous, certain that he knew something she did not. The smile softened his granite features and she saw the boy who enjoyed puzzles and games surface in him. Word at Quantico had it that he was into sophisticated computer war games and simulations for relaxation, and that he was currently helping in the design of a software package that would simplify the work of police psychological profiling, and that this system might one day be textbook material in every criminalistics course in the country and quite possibly every police precinct in the land.

She said to his smile, "One of the cops picked up the arm from somewhere else in the room and laid it to rest beside the body."

"How the hell did you know that? This guy comes to me early this morning, says he can't sleep, saying he's scared shitless you'll find his prints on her somewhere, and that he was one of the first on scene, and that he had—"

"Picked up the arm and placed it with the body without thinking."

"And told no one, no one. So how could you know?"

"Human nature and human folly," she said, climbing into the car, leaving him to wonder and frown.

Inside, Boutine gave the driver directions, and then he turned to her. "Out with it."

She thought of the need of rescuers at crash sites and other scenes of horror and mutilation, how often they wanted to put the pieces back together, line the bodies up in neat rows. But she said, "Well, the arm was severed by some kind of cutting tool, big tool by the look of things, but in any event, it would not have fallen into place as it was, at an exact angle from where it'd come off. Whoever placed it there did so with some attention to anatomy, fitting it as closely to the socket as possible, pointing straight away. At first, I thought maybe the killer had placed it there, reset it, so to speak. But I ruled that out quickly for two reasons."

"What reasons?" He was clearly fascinated.

"First, the other missing piece, the breast, was halfway across the room, the other one dangling by a thread of skin. If the killer was obsessively interested in putting Humpty Dumpty back together again, he would have been motivated to do so for all the pieces, not just the arm."

"Good point." He understood obsessive behavior.

"As for the second reason, I saw the displaced dust where the arm had been originally thrown. It hit one of the walls, left a faint sign of fluids and left a mark at the foot of this mark on the floor. I assumed then that it had been moved.''

From the inn it took them twenty minutes to get to the hospital. It was attached to a university teaching complex. Once inside, they were led down a long corridor and a flight of steps to the morgue belowground. It looked like a hundred thousand such places tucked away in hospitals across the country, a kind of earthly perdition for the remains, until which time as cause of death could be determined, a death certificate signed and the body turned over to the family.

Boutine stopped short of the morgue door, and his booming voice seemed out of place in the silence. ''Make it quick. We have to be back in Virginia at sixteen hundred hours.''

''Understood, but I thought you were joining us.''

''No, thought I'd talk to some of the relatives, see what I might gather about the girl.''

''Good luck.''

''Same to you.'' He took her hand to shake, but he held it a bit longer, saying, ''You did excellent work last night, but you know that, don't you?''

''Doesn't hurt to hear it from you. But it's a little premature. So far we don't have a thing.''

She pushed through the door where the local coroner and an assistant stood over the body; they'd begun to run some tests already.

''Ahhhh, Dr. Coran . . . nice of you to join us,'' said Dr. Stadtler, whose forehead was discolored by age spots, as were the backs of his hands.

She replied coolly, ''I was up pretty late last night.'' Stadtler's having left the scene hours before her still rankled them both.

He pursed his lips below his mask and nodded, his eyes studying her closely. ''I do not know perhaps as much as the FBI, my dear Dr. Coran''—it grated her nerves to have someone refer to her as *my dear doctor*—''but I do know that under poor lighting conditions, we doctors miss a lot.''

He had obviously been relishing this moment, she thought. ''And what did you find, Dr. Stadler, that I overlooked? Or, rather, that you assume I overlooked.''

It was a bloodless autopsy, the first such that she had ever witnessed. She came closer to the corpse, its slashed eyes now familiar to her.

Stadler continued in a voice that overflowed with smugness, a ribbon of contempt snaking through. ''The girl's feet, below the ropes . . .'' His pause was calculated. ''Slashed.''

Despite the fact she was angry with herself for the oversight, she said, ''Achilles tendons, I know.'' The lie caught Stadler and his assistant off guard. ''But that's what autopsies are for, to be sure.'' She'd paid absolutely no attention to the feet other than to note that they had been bound.

''Yes, well,'' Stadler muttered like a chess player whose king has been cornered, ''both tendons were severed.''

''Making it impossible for her to stand, let alone run from her assailant.'' She located a frock, a cap and a mask in a nearby supply cabinet. In an autopsy room only the minimal rules of sanitation applied. It was highly unlikely that the ''patient,'' as dead as she was, was contagious. As Jessica readied herself, she thought anew of the girl's ordeal. Even if she had had a chance of escape, with her heel tendons severed, she'd have had to drag herself away, pulling herself along like a two-armed lizard. She wondered if the killer had watched her drag herself about before he hauled her up to the rafters by the rope. Doubtful. There'd been no blood trail to substantiate this. Why then cut the tendons? Another precaution against the police, to confound the issue?

There was a policeman from Wekosha in the autopsy room who hadn't said a word. She recognized him from the murder scene the day before and she guessed it was he who had replaced the arm. She gave him a cursory smile before hiding behind her mask. He volunteered something.

"Dr. Coran, I'm Captain Vaughn. Wekosha and the county sheriff's office are combining on this killing."

"Good idea." She went first to the tendons to examine the scars there. Working from the feet up on an autopsy was how she had learned her craft at Bethesda from perhaps the best man in the business, Dr. Aaron Holecraft. Holecraft was semiretired now, but he wasn't above talking to a former student about a puzzling case. She knew she'd have to see him when she got back to Quantico about the Wekosha vampire case. She knew that Holecraft had seen some Tort 9s in his day.

The wounds had been cleaned thoroughly by Stadtler's assistant. "Did you get any pictures of the tendons before you cleaned them?" she asked the assistant.

Stadtler spoke up instead. "Why? Didn't you, my dear doctor?"

"I'm not sure if the photographer last night got them, no."

"In any case, we'll be happy to provide them," said Stadtler as if he had won a small victory.

The dull-faced, heavy-set Vaughn piped in. "We're checking every MDSO file we have."

She rattled off the letters in her head as she worked and asked, "Mentally disturbed sex offenders?"

"Yes, ma'am."

"Waste of time, Captain."

"What?"

"This crime is not sex related, not in the usual sense, anyway."

"What? But she was strung up nude, and there was evidence of . . . of semen in her, wasn't there?"

"All right, all right." She realized she shouldn't have challenged him. "Go ahead with your search. Arrest everyone in your files who's ever flashed an eleven-year-old."

"But you think we'd be wasting our time?"

"Yes, I think so."

"Just the same, we've got to work on every possibility."

"Understood. Now, can we have a little quiet in here?" Jessica said in a harsher tone than she meant. "This is an autopsy, and we are taping for transcripts later, I presume, my dear Dr. Stadtler?"

Stadtler frowned at this and said, "Of course," as he flicked the recorder on.

The autopsy proceeded quickly now, and a few old track marks were found on the girl's arms, indicating drugs, but without blood, it would take very sophisticated equipment and tests to secure readings from the pancreas, the liver and other organs to show the necessary trace elements to say whether she was or was not drugged. Jessica took a sliver from each of the organs; these would go in formaldehyde-filled vials all the way to Quantico for expert eyes there. Stadtler took his own specimens, saying that he could get them examined in Milwaukee. Most of the girl's scars, other than the mutilation on the night of her death, told her biography, one of wounds and scars gathered over her lifetime. There were old, healed-over burns, stitch marks, an indication she once had had a C-section, likely giving birth or death in an unwanted pregnancy. She'd led a tortured life, and she had died a torturous death. So sad, Jessica thought.

While she couldn't yet know the identity of the monster who had killed Candy, she could see what the victim had eaten, breathed and injected. A lot of medical people became hardened like cops, having seen it all time and again, and they'd often say that the way a person died was a reflection of the way she lived. That some people lived in such a way as to attract violence; that most murder victims unintentionally courted death by placing themselves in high-risk situations. Doctors working on a dying gunshot victim frequently found remnants of other bullets in the body. Most successful suicides had scars from previous adventures. But what life-style exacted the kind of price this abused child and young woman had suffered?

Much of the autopsy was done in silence until the doctors agreed or disagreed on one thing and another. Stadtler thought the liver a bit jaundiced, while Jessica thought it had the look of pâté, indicating alcoholism and the road to cirrhosis. They agreed on the condition of the kidneys, that one was underweight—scales don't lie—and due again to alcohol abuse, it had prematurely shriveled in size. Her ovaries, like the kidneys, had become wrinkled and smaller. Rough living showed through.

There were no indications whatever that she was struck in the head, the brain sustaining no injuries other than an excessive amount of fluids, including some pockets of blood which were prized by the doctors. Now a useful blood test could be accomplished, and poisons ruled out.

They were almost finished with the autopsy when Jessica's attention was caught by some bluish coloration about the throat and neck wound. She blinked. Maybe it was the blue fluorescent lighting. The natural blue of the wound itself when blood gushed up from the severed arteries? Still, she brought a large magnifying glass on a swing arm to bear on the wound.

"What is it?" asked Stadtler, instantly curious. "Didn't you already do that?" He was asking about the depth and length measurement of the wound itself.

She replied with a question. "Have you checked the condition of the windpipe?"

"What for?"

She instantly ran her hand into the open chest cavity and up through the throat, massaging the layers of gristle that form the upper part of the windpipe, the cricoid cartilage, and she knew in an instant that the blue coloration around the throat was not due to the blue light or to the slash. She knew for a fact that the killer had also strangled his victim; but he had done so with so gentle a touch that it was not obvious, or likely provable.

Her confusion gave her away. The three men stared at her. "Just curious," she lied.

"Anyone can see she's not been strangled," said Stadtler. "May we get on with it?"

"I'm going to have to take a section here," she said, indicating the throat.

"What? What for? We were praying we'd save something of her for burial," Stadtler said sarcastically.

"Sorry, Doctor."

"Okay, I'm sorry. I was out of line on that," he replied. "But what are you getting at here?"

"I won't know until I get back to Quantico. I need electron microscopic photography on this." With her scalpel she sliced a deep square of skin around the pale jugular section, her eyes intent on the area of the clean, deep cut that was necessary. She then realized yet another hidden message below the surface. "Oh, God," she moaned.

"What is it?" Stadtler was now crazy, and he all but pushed her aside. "What?"

"Here, and here." She pointed with her scalpel, which fit neatly into the cut on either side of the jugular, and each went deep, but there were two cuts and they did not connect. The long slash that connected each was *superficial* at the center. Something else had penetrated the jugular, and the scar from this wound was near invisible below the larger throat slash that hid it.

She explained this to Stadtler.

He was shaken. "I . . . I thought you examined this last night."

"Obviously not close enough."

"What . . . does it mean?"

"It means that a second instrument was used at the jugular, and this large laceration is just a cosmetic masking of that fact."

"What other instrument?"

"I don't know, and I won't know unless I take part of her throat back with me to Virginia."

He stared long at her. "I suppose it's . . . necessary."

"Absolutely."

He stepped away and then turned. "Gets worse every

moment, doesn't it? Maybe I'm getting too old for this business. This world, perhaps.''

"Given the dismemberment, it'll be a closed casket, of course.''

"Yes, well, what's one more missing part?'' said Stadtler. "No one will miss it.''

Jessica finished removing the square cake of flesh from the throat, and Stadtler's silent, able assistant held out a small jar filled with preserving fluids for the pulpy, layered section. ''This information remains in this room, gentlemen,'' she told them. "We've got to keep this to ourselves. Not a word.''

The estimate of time of death was made the more precise by a combination of items: *livor mortis,* the dark discoloration of death, and the degree of that coloration; *algor mortis,* the cold touch of death; and *rigor mortis,* the degree of stiffness or limberness told them much. Annie ''Candy'' Copeland had died between midnight and 2 A.M., the night before her discovery. According to Stadtler, the last man to see her alive was a swinish, small-town pimp who used her and put her on the street, a man named Scarborough, known locally as Scar. The man was under arrest for suspicion of murdering Annie Copeland.

Finished with Copeland's corpse at last, Jessica stepped away from the autopsy table, the hum of the A.C. drumming in her ears. She peeled away her rubber gloves and the mask, depositing both in the bins provided at the door. ''Please have a copy of your report, along with the samples I've taken, ready to leave with me for Virginia. We'll be leaving the municipal airport sometime this afternoon. If there's a problem getting everything to me by fourteen—ah, two o'clock—please contact me, either at the inn or at the airport.

Stadtler nodded, and their eyes met, and in the silence between them, she came to realize that somewhere along the way, she'd gained his respect. He said, ''Dr. Coran, I'll see to it personally.''

She breathed deeply, licked her lips, and in a near feline expression of gratitude, she said, "Dr. Stadtler, it has been a very worthwhile experience working with you and your staff." She was grateful that she was no longer his "dear Dr. Coran."

She peeled away the green garments of her trade just outside the autopsy room in an anteroom where more bins stood, and where she could wash up. She splashed some water on her face and glanced into the mirror, taking her reflection in. She felt that she looked as if she'd been on a week's binge, and somewhere in the back of her head she heard the wafting music of a Jimmy Buffet tune strike up.

"Wasting away in Wekoshaville," she said to her reflection. Fieldwork was tough. Maybe she should've stayed in the lab.

She tamped her face with a clean, white linen, straightened her outfit, fixed her lipstick and then pushed through the door, going for the nearest exit. She needed the one thing Wekosha was good for—fresh air.

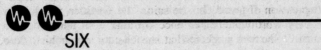

SIX

Outside the university hospital, she saw the campus filled with young people, most well dressed and energetic and rushing to someplace of importance. She wondered what had gone wrong in Candy Copeland's life, why she wasn't here, or in a similar school, working and alive and looking toward a bright future. She wondered how many of the young men rushing between classes had known Candy, and how many had used her.

A car pulled up that she recognized and Otto got out and went to the rear to help out a man in handcuffs. He cursed Otto's rough handling of him. She guessed it to be Scarborough from both his dress and his foul mouth.

"Someone I want you to meet, Thomas," he told Scarborough, towing him toward Jessica.

Boutine found a pair of stone benches, where he parked Thomas Scarborough below the warm sun and the crisp leaves of a white oak. Where he sat, the shadows creased his rough features. He was called Scar for good reason. He had three scars on his face from what looked like knife wounds suffered at an early age. She guessed him to be little older than Candy had been.

"How many times I got to tell you people, I loved Candy! I'd never harm her. She . . . she was my best girl. I loved her. We even talked about . . . about getting married someday."

"Cut the crap, Thomas, and shut up, and just tell Dr. Coran what you told me about your goddamned pig farm."

Otto stood over him like an angry father. Scarborough's head was forward, his eyes on the earth in the learned position of those beaten and intimidated all their lives. He hadn't so much as glanced at Jessica until she spoke to Otto, his eyes sneaking to one side, rolling like a snake's to take her in, all without lifting the head.

"What's this all about, Otto?" she asked.

Otto poked the kid in response.

Tommy "Scar" Scarborough spit on the ground in response. The young man was unclean, unshaven, and he smelled both of bad breath and booze, not to mention body odor. Jessica chose the bench across from him to sit, rather than get too close. Even handcuffed, he made her flesh crawl. His eyes were deep, black cinders, smoldering with rage, his complexion pockmarked from terrible years of bouts with acne and perhaps chicken pox and other diseases. His long-sleeved, unkempt shirt did little to hide the needle marks, both old and recent. It looked as if the cops had nabbed him while he was sleeping in his clothes and his own filth, and he hadn't had a bath in days.

He now lifted his square-jawed face to her and said, "You're a doctor? You saw what they . . . they did to Candy?"

"Yes," replied Jessica to both questions.

"You're the one that the cops say has found my semen in her, aren't you?"

She looked at Otto, who shrugged and said, "Tell him what you will, Dr. Coran."

"Until tests prove it, Mr. Scarborough, no one knows whose semen it is. Is it yours? You may's well tell us if it is, because with the sophisticated tests we run, we'll know in a matter of—"

"I ain't slept with her for over a month. We . . . we weren't gettin' along, you know. Started to get at each other like an old married couple. She kept pushing me for things, for this, that . . . to get married . . . that kind of shit. I cut loose on her. Left her."

Otto frowned. "Wekosha police say otherwise, Thomas. Now, if you help us, maybe we can help you. Tell the nice FBI lady what you came here to tell her."

"All right . . . all right."

Jessica was curious now. "Do you know who was last with her?"

"No, not really. He wasn't from around here."

"Then you saw him?"

"No, I didn't see him."

"What did you see?"

Otto broke in. "He says he saw the van, that the guy drove a van, and that she got in voluntarily. Got no plate numbers, but claims it might have been Illinois plates. Van was gray or beige—"

"Hard to tell colors at night. I'm color-blind."

"—and had some lettering on the side."

"Not bold lettering, just small, and I don't read good from a distance, so . . . but this guy . . . he's the one killed her."

Jessica spoke to Otto. "How many suspects have Stowell and Chief Wright placed in custody?"

"Six, working on more, all perverts."

"Hey, I'm no fuckin' pervert!" shouted Scarborough.

"Shut up! And watch your mouth around Dr. Coran."

"Just tellin' the truth."

"Just tell her about your daddy's pig farm."

"Swine farm," he corrected Otto. He looked again at Jessica, saying, "I grew up on a farm, ma'am . . . ahhhh, Doctor."

Below the grunge, she saw the farm boy in him clearly now. Perhaps some of the scars came from working around farm machinery, or at the hand of a dictatorial, Bible-thumping father with a nasty technique for disciplining an unruly child.

"Go on," she coaxed.

"Well, we slaughtered a lot of swine. My daddy'd be covered in blood by day's end . . . and so would I. My daddy would first cut the heel tendons when he'd get the pig ready—first thing—so's it couldn't get off. You know how a pig'll run at the least thing. I swear, the pig knows when you're standing there with a butcher's knife behind your back. Anyway . . . second thing my daddy'd do would tie the thing up by its hind quarters . . . and . . . and—''

He stopped, looked at Boutine, who nodded for him to go on. ''And drain out all the blood into a big caldron of boiling water. He'd drop the swine into the caldron to boil off the fine hair then. Anyhow . . . well, the way they told me I was supposed to have killed Candy . . . Christ, it sounded like something my daddy would do. Scared hell out of me.''

She caught something of the fear deep in the dark eyes. ''Your father, Thomas, he would threaten to do to you what he did to the pigs, if you didn't do what he told you to do . . . wouldn't he?''

His mouth fell open slowly. ''I . . . I never told anyone what . . . that he . . . what that man did to me.''

''See why he's such a likable suspect for Vaughn Wright and Stowell, Jessica?''

''Fits . . . all too very neatly . . .''

''They don't have anything on me. I wasn't anywhere near her when it happened!'' shouted Scarborough. ''Christ, I ain't no murderer!''

''His alibi is a boyfriend he sleeps with,'' said Otto.

Scarborough never again looked into Jessica's face, and he became belligerent and nasty again. ''Lady like you, I could do a lot with, if you ever wanted to sell it.''

Otto grabbed him up in a rage and forced him back to the car. She stared after them, her insides tugged at by the horror that a parent could create of a child's psyche, yet convinced along with Otto that this young man was not their killer. Still, she'd order specimen samples from him along with all the other suspects rounded up by Stowell and Wright, to check against what they'd found at the scene. It all might be one dead end after another, but by the same token, no rock could be left unturned, and poor Scar definitely had crawled from beneath a pretty large rock.

With Scarborough put away in the car, Otto returned to her and said, "He told us about a knot his father used on the swine, too."

"A sailor's knot?"

"Farmers use it a lot in this area, a sling knot. No way to break it so long as it is countering a . . . a dead weight."

She stared at the blindingly bright blue Wisconsin sky and fought back the fatigue and pain and memory of Candy Copeland trussed up like a swine for the slaughter. It had been an image that had come to her during the evidence gathering, and this fact was not lost on her now. In the rustle of the leaves overhead, she heard the sharp twitter of birds and she glanced a jay chase another off.

"I know this creep's as unreliable as hell, but you said something yourself the other night about how it looked, and what he said was so close to what you said . . . Well, I just thought you ought to hear it straight from the guy. Sorry if it's upset you."

She only half heard Otto's apology. She was listening to the voice in her head which had belonged to her father, saying, "You might wish to remember, child: *it doesn't matter from whom you learn, only that you do learn.*"

She repeated the favorite aphorism to Otto now and this calmed him a good deal. "You sure got mettle, Doc." Otto's compliment was, as usual, understated.

She laughed lightly. "Then why do I feel like my spine is made of Jell-O?"

"You get everything you want inside?" He indicated the hospital.

She nodded. "Yeah, all prepared to leave as soon as the results and the reports catch up to us at the airport. And you?"

"Some loose ends downtown, like this creep." He indicated Scarborough, who sat brooding in the back of the car.

"He needs psychiatric help, you know," she told him. "He was victimized and brutalized by his father."

Otto frowned and nodded. "The stuff of which murderers are made, I know."

"In his case, he seems to have stopped at degrading women and using them. I think he's too weak to kill."

"Agreed. All right, I'll meet you at the airport. You need a ride back to the inn?"

"I'll get a cab."

"Great, fine. And on the plane you can tell me all about the autopsy."

She halted him. "Not much else to add, really."

"That right?"

She didn't wish to lie outright, but without lab proof, and that would take time, she didn't want to discuss what she'd found, and she was through making half-assed guesses, even for Otto. "Yeah, 'fraid so."

"See you at the airport, then."

She waved him off. From the backseat, Scarborough waved back and winked, his grin like that of the devil, and this made her wonder how much stock she could really put in what he had said.

Well, she told herself, his DNA couldn't lie to her. She forgot about Scarborough, but she could not forget about the image of his father, covered in blood, threatening his son with mutilation and boiling in his own blood and oil.

With these thoughts swimming about her mind, she went back inside to call a cab. She was beginning to miss her apartment in Virginia, and its safe walls.

From far above it, looking through the portal of the Learjet, Wekosha, Wisconsin, looked at peace, like a quaint village nestled in the wood where nothing evil could touch. But Jessica Coran could imagine Scar in his cell still trying to convince everyone that he was innocent of any wrong-doing in the Candy Copeland affair. She imagined Sheriff Stowell, Vaughn and the other police officials desperately seeking a confession from one of the perverts dragged in under their net. She could see the child's block in the far distance that represented police headquarters, where police faced off against press and community leaders clamoring for complete disclosure. Not far away, she made out the squares and shapes of the university medical complex where she imagined Dr. Stadtler, too, was inundated by reporters trying to get the full story.

She was glad to be above it all, but she was hardly divorced from the case, her mind wandering back to the girl who called herself Candy and the awful nature of her death. The public outcry over the girl who was ignored her entire life was a little late in coming, she thought.

Still, there were other girls in the community to worry about, others who might fall prey to a terrifying predator in their midst. So the predator must be found and incarcerated or eliminated quickly. It was the predictable result of a mutilation murder; it sent a shock wave of horror through the system to discover that one so physically close had died in so brutal a scenario, with one's own community as backdrop. Now that Candy Copeland was dead, it seemed that she had gained the attention she so yearned for in life, that her murder had outraged people in the community, but that outrage failed to include an outrage against Wekosha, the outrage that Jessica felt.

Being literally above Wekosha, perhaps it was easy to judge, she decided. The jet made a pass over the city in a tight arc, the pilot having fun, coming to a southeasterly heading. The feeling for the moment was one of the plane's being like the archangel Gabriel, blowing a fiery horn across the land, screaming at the occupants of sleepy Wekosha.

She wondered momentarily if the killer lived in Wekosha or on its outskirts. She wondered if there would be more such horrible mutilations here, and if she and Otto would have to return. She prayed not.

Now that the plane was in flight, she lifted the newspapers which Boutine had slapped onto the table between them with the single command "Read," before he busied himself on the jet's computer modem and fax machine. On the front page of a special, late edition of the *Milwaukee Journal,* she found a picture of herself and before and after pictures of the victim, the glaring headlines reading: "The Ice Woman Cometh" and "FBI's M.E. Is Woman of Steel." All this according to the local authorities, some of whom were quoted directly, others indirectly. But how had they gotten her picture? Newspeople were adept at getting what they wanted, and this news foretold that they would soon know about the more grisly aspects of the crime. So far, they had not gotten this from either Stowell's people, Vaughn's or the medicine man, Stadtler. But it was only a matter of time.

She felt a little strange being characterized as a woman of steel with ice for blood just because she stood her ground and did her job. She knew that had she been a man, her demeanor and bearing at the crime scene would have been summed up differently, as professional and businesslike.

On the way to the airport from the inn, she had given a great deal of thought to the case and the part that she was now playing in it. It might be like a hundred other cases which went unsolved for years, if it were ever solved at all. Like Boutine, she didn't think the net the locals would cast out to drag in the lowlife of Wekosha was going to catch this killer. At the airport, her autopsy samples caught up with her, along with the crime-scene evidence from the evidence cage at the police department, the two couriers talking about the upcoming baseball season like old friends. Otto arrived soon after, antsy to get into the air and to learn anything new that she had as a result of the autopsy. She had told him that there was nothing new. She did so because she needed more time to think about what she had discovered; she needed to talk to J.T., to confirm her suspicions.

J.T. was John Thorpe, Jessica's second-in-command and her right arm at her Quantico laboratory. She placed complete trust in J.T. for handling medico-legal evidence, knowing that Thorpe treated it with the same reverence and care that she did. Their respect for each other was mutual, and even though John was several years her senior, he never allowed either her age or her sex to become a problem between them, unlike others under her auspices, such as Dr. Raynack, the old buzzard who once, in the heat of an argument he felt he must conduct in front of others, called her a scavenger. Behind her back, the name was still being used, and it was J.T. who made it an "acceptable" label when, on her birthday, he placed it on the cake which was shared by all in the department except Raynack.

J.T. had made a little speech over the cake, saying in his baritone voice, "We all know you're better than a bloodhound at the scene of a crime; that Sherlock Holmes would have to take a seat behind; that you don't accept anything on face value, or on the word of a man because he happens to have a Ph.D., an M.D. or even an M.E. back of his name"—a clear shot at Raynack—"or blindly accept letters printed on a death certificate. We know you leave nothing to chance or human error, that you *are* a methodical scavenger!"

She admired J.T. also because he had come up the hard way, a self-motivated orphan who had miraculously found the inner strength to set goals for himself and become a fine doctor, and then to continue on to become an M.E., when she herself had had so much help, encouragement and love from her parents and the example of her father.

Otto was suddenly standing over her with a drink in his hand, offering it to her. "Private stock," he said.

She took it gratefully. He sat across from her once more as she sipped at the bourbon and water. He seemed to know her likes, and a moment's paranoia flitted in and out of her consciousness. Otto was very perceptive, and picking up on this, he said, "I asked your friend J.T. what you liked to drink. Saw to it we had some on board."

"That's a lot of trouble to go to."

"Not if it gets me what I want."

She smiled across at him, her eyes playing a game with his. "And what's that?" Her voice crackled with a sultry edge.

"Some fast answers," he replied. "Didn't the autopsy tell you anything new?"

She told him about the severed tendons, trying to put him off.

"Anything else?"

She felt pressured. "It raised more questions than it answered. Let me put it that way."

"Then tell me about the questions it raised."

She felt they were dancing in a circle now. She was first a scientist, and he knew this, so why couldn't he accept the fact that it would take time to investigate the minutiae of this murder. "Otto, I need to get back to my lab, need J.T.'s assistance, need time—"

"Time is something we—I—don't have a lot of, Jess."

Her mouth fell open at the cryptic words. His eyes pulled from her as he laid out a stack of papers that'd come over the fax, black-and-white pictures and reports on earlier Tort 9s, the dark duplicate photos cascading across at her, photos of three other victims hanging in the air, upside down, just like Candy Copeland.

She carefully placed her now swirling drink onto the tabletop. It settled in the glass as she nervously fingered the edges of the additional information that Otto had offered.

"You made me think I was in some holding pattern," she said, staring at him now. "That this assignment was the next on docket, but it wasn't, was it?"

"Some people didn't want you on it; I did."

"You knew it was the work of the same guy all along."

"I suspected, yes."

"Then why the charade?"

He leaned back into the cushion of his seat. "I didn't want you knowing, all right? I wanted someone with no prior knowledge, someone with a fresh eye, someone who had the expertise, and I didn't want a lot of judgments predicated on this!'' He pointed to the materials lying between them.

"Is that supposed to be an apology?"

"I tell you where to go and when to go. I don't need to apologize or explain myself."

"You were hoping to get something from me to corroborate a theory or theories you're developing? Is that it?"

"Something like that, yes."

She breathed deeply and said, "You must have a hell of a lot of confidence in your theory, then."

"I do."

"That Wekosha is no isolated case."

Otto stared at her like someone caught in a lie. "That's my guess."

"And you must have had a lot of confidence in me."

He nodded firmly. "I do."

"Now you want me to review these earlier cases, see if I agree, that there's some sort of pattern here, some connection?"

"That's right; any match points you can make will add to mine, and then we can sell Leamy on it, and get my team to work on it before . . ." His voice trailed off.

"Before there's another Candy Copeland," she finished for him.

"That's right."

She nodded, sipped more from her drink and lifted one of the faxed photos. "Let me look this stuff over."

"I'll be up front if you need me," he said, getting up and going forward.

She studied each of the reports, noting the dates of each earlier blood-taking murder. She searched for patterns. One was dated November 3 of the previous year; a second, December 6. They were hundreds of miles from each other, yet both, like the third, were in the Midwest. The third report told of a bizarre death that had occurred the following March, late in the month. Why the long hiatus between the second and third killings? And now Candy Copeland on April 3. If it was the work of a single killer or a single pair of killers on a rampage, going the several months between December and March might mean a jail term was being served, or the killer had moved away for a time before returning to the area. Yet, it was such a wide-ranging area: Wisconsin, Missouri, Illinois, Iowa.

The method of murder was chillingly similar in all these cases, and it gave rise to the horrible thought that there could be far more murders committed by this madman than anyone knew, or ever might know. Other bloodless bodies buried in shallow graves and hanging in such remote locations as to have gone undiscovered.

She jotted notes from her meandering thoughts, one of which was to check with all missing persons bureaus across the Midwest, to gain a computer list of all the names and addresses of the missing and see if any lived in or around such places as Wekosha, Wisconsin, and these other small hamlets.

She also noted on the reports that all the women had not only been mutilated and drained of their blood supplies but had had their tendons severed. She noted, too, that the earlier cases had all been under the purview of Dr. Raynack, who, as acting head of the department before her appointment, had not seen fit to discuss any of these cases with her.

"The bastard," she muttered.

"Coffee?" It was Otto, returned with two cups of coffee.

"You're a lifesaver, yes."

Otto settled in again across from her in the cab. He waited expectantly for her to express herself on the faxed material. She kept him waiting until her coffee was half-consumed, and then she told him what she had found in the way of patterns, all of which he already knew.

"These were Raynack's cases, I see," she finished.

"The old doctor didn't pursue them as aggressively as I would like to have seen them pursued."

"He never left Virginia," she said. "Expected to do it all from the confines of the lab. Just took samples sent him by the local guys in every case."

"And that's only in the cases that bothered to notify us at all. I suspect there've probably been others, but we're not always notified or asked for help."

"How did you get interested in this one?" she asked.

"It was brought to my attention in a not too subtle way by John Thorpe."

"All before my appointment."

"Thorpe did the right thing, but no one, not even Raynack, knows about my having pursued the matter. As for J.T., all he knows is that he felt someone ought to investigate a little more in-depth on such cases."

"So why didn't you get John Thorpe on this flight? Instead, you have me."

"J.T.'s a good man, no doubt about that; but so are you—and I mean that in the most complimentary way. But you are also now head of your area, and I want your area to fall under my division, to be a part of my division. Raynack has fought the notion for a long time, but I'm hoping you'll see the wisdom in it."

"I can understand Raynack's reluctance."

"I've heard all of his arguments, about how scientists cannot be bullied and pressured into framing reports that *fit* a case scenario that my psych team puts together; that's not what I want to do at all."

The flight was coming to an end, a *Fasten seat belts* red light flashing now. Otto reached across and took her hand in his, a gesture she wasn't expecting. He was a handsome older man, striking with his silver-dappled head; dedicated to the work, he had shown such pain in his eyes back at that death cabin in Wekosha.

"Jess, you did a hell of a job, and I want you standing before my team with your findings up to now—"

"Whoa!"

"—tomorrow afternoon, four sharp, debriefing room 222, all right?"

"Hold on, Otto! I'd have to work my people on twenty-four-hour shifts to—"

"Just bring us what you've got to date. That's all I'm asking, Jess."

"I just don't know . . . Standing before a psychological profiling team—your team—with the paltry bits and pieces I have . . ."

"Do it for me, then, Jess."

She sighed and looked down at her hands in his. When she looked up he said, "I've got all the confidence in the world in you."

"That's . . . what I like to hear. All right," she conceded. "And thanks for the confidence."

"You earned it, measure for measure."

He released her hands and sat more calmly in his seat, the Lear descending rapidly now. He muttered almost to himself, "I'm sorry if you felt lied to, cheated or used in all this, Jess."

Part of her wanted to shout, "*Use me!*" but another part forced her to remain silent, to hear him out.

"Things're very unsettled in my life right now. Between my wife's coma taking its toll on us both, and the demands of the job . . . Leamy, Raynack, some other enemies I've managed to make . . ."

She had had no idea that he considered Leamy an enemy along with Raynack, and she wondered about the others, but she remained silent, allowing him to go on.

"Anyway, working with you has been *real*, very real and refreshing."

"Thanks, Otto, but are you sure you're not making too much of all this? Raynack's a pain in the ass, I know, but—"

"Put it this way, kid. Watch your backside with Raynack. It's people like us, you the new-kid-on-the-block and me the tired old racehorse, they screw first . . . so watch it."

She watched as he doused his coffee with a hefty helping of bourbon. She guessed he had had too much alcohol and was feeling it, and feeling sorry for himself, which was totally out of character for Boutine . . . and yet, she had heard reports about his excessive behavior of late, something about his having punched out a doctor at Bethesda.

"Hey," he began philosophically, "life and the Bureau go on, right? With or without guys like me. We're all expendable. It's what's expedient at the moment for the Bureau that ought to concern each and every one of us, right?"

"That's nonsense, Otto. Everyone knows you're the best psych team leader at Quantico, and everybody knows—"

"Nobody knows a goddamned—" He stopped himself, the old control coming back over him like a mantle.

"Your solve rate is higher than any—"

"Look, I just wanted you to understand—I mean *know*—the full extent of . . . of my . . . of my *use* for you, Dr. Coran. I may be pulling you down with me." He stared hard into her unflinching eyes now. "There! Confession, they say, is good for the soul."

She wondered if there wasn't something else he was holding back; she believed for a moment there was and that he was going to continue to confess, to say something about how he felt about *Jessica* Coran and not about *Dr.* Coran. But he lapsed into silent stoicism, staring out into the blankness of the cloud cover above Quantico.

Up front, the garbled voice of the pilot talking to the tower was the only thing that broke the silence of the cab. The revelations from Boutine, such as they were, only served to confuse her. She knew he was having difficulties with his wife's condition, that any man must, but she had not known that he was becoming paranoid, that he felt threatened here at Quantico by Leamy, Raynack and mysterious others. It must be the booze talking.

The plane touched down, the *urrrk-urrrk-urrrrrrk* of the

burning tires kissing the tarmack below a sullen, rain-soaked, dreary sky here on the outskirts of Washington, D.C. She was relieved to be returning to the Virginia facilities and to home.

SEVEN

John Thorpe met them at the airstrip the moment they touched down, wheeling out in a jeep, waving his arms, as full of enthusiasm as ever. He leaped from the backseat, rushed toward the plane and plied them with questions before they got their feet on the ground, anxious to know if the trip had panned out, or if it should have been panned.

Boutine whispered something in her ear and went by J.T. with a perfunctory hello and got into a second jeep that had come to fetch him.

The pilot called down to Jessica, asking where she wanted her bags, two forensics valises and an overnight, placed. It was a signal that he didn't do loadings and unloadings.

"You bring back any of that Wisconsin cheese?" asked J.T. jokingly. "I'll take charge of those!" he shouted up to the pilot. As he bounded up for the bags, Jessica went for the jeep, anxious for home.

"It went badly, didn't it? Waste of time, wasn't it? I could see it in Boutine's face," said J.T. when he rejoined her.

"Since when can you read Boutine's face? It's just a little premature to tell, J.T.; we'll just have to see what the lab results show. Sure, superficially, yes, it looks like it could be the work of the same guy, but that's hardly something we can set in concrete, just yet." Then her tone changed. "Why didn't you tell me you'd been talking to Boutine about the earlier cases?"

"I didn't say anything because I didn't know if he'd take any action or not, especially since Raynack was involved, and when Bountine did take action, it was so damned quick, hell . . . I didn't even know you were gone until I got to the lab this morning. I'm not the principal player here, Jess—you are."

"Well, it's . . . it's been a trip, John, a real trip."

"I imagine traveling with Boutine would be. You two get along?"

"Sure, sure we did."

"Look, I can see you're beat. I'll take charge of the goodies you brought back from Wisconsin, with your permission."

"Permission granted! I'd just like to fall into a hot tub for now."

"I'll see to everything, and you needn't worry."

She smiled at him, saying, "I know that I can count on you, J.T." She climbed into the passenger seat of the jeep as he loaded in the bags and hopped into the rear. The driver took this as his signal and he silently turned and tore away from the airstrip.

For a moment, Jessica looked for Boutine, but he had disappeared from sight too quickly for even a glance, and it hit her that now that they were back, they'd have to be more formal around each other, that she'd be calling him Chief Boutine again, and that he'd be referring to her as Dr. Coran. It made their sudden parting feel like a severing of ties, and she tried to understand why she felt so cold inside.

"I left you some instructions on where some of the samples should go for cross-checks," she told J.T., trying to sound as if her mind were on business. "MacCroone Laboratories in Chicago might tell us something more about the particles and fibers I've labeled for them. Duplicates of these samples, we'll have to share among us, but I want independent verification on everything we do where possible. If we do nail some bastard for these crimes, I don't want to leave a single stone unturned."

"Gotcha! And not to worry. I'll overnight 'em. Everything else, we'll divvy up and begin to analyze to the max."

She knew he would get the various evidence from Wekosha into the proper and expert hands required.

"Just hold on using Raynack on any of this, for the time being," she added.

He nodded. "Understood."

"I'll have to deal with him when and where necessary."

"It won't be pretty."

"Get the cloth items to—"

"Boas, I know, and latents'll have to be shared—"

"Along with the tiles and boards, taken from the scene."

"Fluid guys, I know."

"You get to keep the nail scrapings, skin, hair."

"I'll get Robertson to lend a hand on the blood and serums."

"If you can pry him loose."

"Don't worry, and as for photos, Hale's our man."

"Sounds like you're on top of it, John."

"My natural position—*on top*."

He made her laugh and he made her feel secure in the knowledge that he'd protect the sanctity of the evidence as she would herself.

"Listen, there is one vial I want for *us*. No one's to know about it but you and I, okay?"

"You found something! Didn't you? I knew it. I told Boutine you would. What is it?"

She stared him down a moment. "Take it easy. May be nothing."

"What is it?"

She reached over the seat back and dug into one of the black valises and pointed to the large beaker in which floated a square of flesh the size of a piece of Spam; it resembled Spam, too.

"From the victim?"

"Her throat."

"What do you hope to find here, Jess?"

"Won't know until we get it under the electron microscope."

"But you have a hunch?"

"I do."

"And I'll have to wait until tomorrow to find out about
it?"

"Give me three hours and I'll see you in the lab. We may
have to work all night. Boutine wants a report by sixteen-
hundred hours tomorrow."

"You're kidding. What the hell can we tell him in
twenty-four hours?"

"He's a man in a rush. We tell him what we can."

"He doesn't know about this, does he?" J.T. indicated
the throat section.

"No, just you and me for now."

As a matter of protocol, they must first get the materials
brought back with her to the lab under the eyes of a witness,
in this case the driver of the jeep, who was also a military
corporal. Once this was accomplished, the corporal drove
her on to her apartment, where she stripped off the day with
her clothes, showered and set her alarm for a few hours
hence. The peace and solitude of her apartment, the safety
she felt here, was like a soothing balm to her mind.

Four hours later she dragged herself into the Quantico
laboratories, where she was head of an investigative forensics team, one of whom was Dr. Zachary Raynack. Many of
her team were "on call" from various other divisions, but
Raynack, like J.T., was directly answerable to her, which
made tensions between the young "upstart" and the old
"fart" quite a tussle at times. For the present, she didn't
want to have to deal with Raynack, and so she purposely left
him out of the Wekosha investigation, certain that at one
point she would have to deal with the sometimes intolerable
Dr. Raynack.

For the present, however, her full concentration was on
J.T.'s work at the electron miscroscope. He was an artist
with this marvel bit of hardware. The photographs created

by the electron miscroscope meant that the photos themselves became the evidence, as the electron bombardment of
the human tissue destroyed the evidence as the photos were
being shot. J.T. made shots from every angle as the material
disintegrated under his gaze. His eyes on the tissue layer
that'd been peeled away from the larger sample, he said,
"There is a strange configuration developing here."

"I thought there could be."

J.T. gulped, his Adam's apple bobbing just below the
double eyepiece of the massive microscope that hummed
with life. "I think you've really hit on something here,
Jess."

"If what I think went on at the crime scene did go on,
we've got one cold bastard on our hands, J.T., and he's
likely to strike again. Most likely sometime around the
beginning of next month."

His eyes went from the sample to her, staring.

"Don't look at me! Get those shots in sequence."

Each layer of the throat had been put in culture and
prepared for the microscope, placed atop one another and
slipped below the eyepiece in rapid succession, making a
kind of movie of the photo process. This would then be fed
to the computer for enhancement and contour.

Death investigation required large sums of money for
personnel and for extremely expensive equipment, like the
scanning electron microscope. The SEM detected the mi-
nutest of changes in the surfaces of tissue, telltale evidence
left by, for example, a bullet, a knife or a blunt object. With
a record of patterns and through experience, Thorpe could
detect, for instance, if the section of skin he was looking at
was punctured by a screwdriver or an ice pick. This
instrument had a magnification of up to 50,000 times the
size of the specimen, and this was projected onto the
accompanying television screen in a three-dimensional
image. It could detect the difference between a burn from a
cigarette, a fire or torture; it could detect microscopic
metallic elements down to rust from an unclean knife. It

helped determine whether a knife wound was from a finely honed knife or a dull one, a scalpel or a serrated blade. It could even tell whether a cancer was caused by asbestos, and of the four kinds of asbestos, the SEM could tell which was present.

The SEM accomplished these feats because it did not work on the principle of light passing through the specimen, but bombarded the specimen instead with electrons, creating an incredibly precise image through the electromagnetic lens. Still photos could be taken as the image was sent back. These could be blown up for the nonscientist to see more clearly.

The much more portable TEM, transmission electron microscope, was an electronic version of the tried-and-true microscope. Both instruments were so sensitive to vibration that they were intentionally located in a subbasement, surrounded by solid concrete; the place sometimes made people claustrophobic, but not the scientists, whose minds were so directed on what was beneath the electron spray of the scope that hours might pass by without their realizing it.

An array of other computerized instruments that measured, sifted and otherwise separated the minutiae of a crime—the puzzle pieces—such as the gas chromatograph, or GC, machine, filled the rooms of Section IV of the Quantico labs.

Jessica was in love with the place. So, too, was J.T.

John Thorpe was a tall man, large with hands like a pair of flatirons, and yet his touch over the instruments was sensitive and light. He was aware of what she'd found now, a telltale straw hole that had punctured the dead girl's jugular but had been masked by the larger butcher's cut that had torn half her throat away, the cosmetic wound which they were supposed to have taken as the killing wound, one Raynack had possibly allowed himself to be fooled by in earlier cases.

"So tell me what you see, John."

He ran his hand through his hair. "It's peculiar, a circular cut definitely present, like . . . like a tracheotomy scar, isn't it? A catheter or tube of some sort with a beveled, sharp end, the kind used to free a blocked artery, make a circumvention in the blood or windpipe.''

''I'll check with the family physician, see if there's any record of a tracheotomy ever having been performed on the Copeland girl.''

She glanced into the miscroscope now that it was on its last frame, the tissue all but gone. ''Certainly a precision cut; sure knew what he was doing. Didn't sever the back side of the vein; knew just how deep to penetrate to the millimeter, like he'd had some practice.''

J.T. took a deep breath and let it out with his words. ''Just lodged this thing into her jugular to . . . to . . .''

''To open a vein,'' she finished for him, then saw that he had gone a bit white. ''You okay? Want to get some breakfast before taking these to the computer?''

They both knew the process of computer enhancement would take some time and that at this point a slight error could cause irreparable damage.

''You need everything you can get by sixteen-hundred hours. But this . . . this'll blow their socks off. Just how the hell did you see it at the scene?''

''Didn't. I missed the severed tendons, too. Picked up on both at autopsy yesterday.''

''Still, even at autopsy? How'd you ever know to look below the larger gash for this?'' He indicated the microscope.

''Stumbled on it when I was taking measurements of the throat gash. I took two measurements, and they didn't add up. The creep dug deep on both sides of the jugular, but he left the center almost intact. Either careless error or he's taunting us, playing games, hiding his little secret almost too well. I just got lucky.''

He lightly laughed at this. ''Nahhh, nobody just lucks onto something like this. You're a wizard, lady.''

''No, no, I'm just careful, like yourself,'' she replied

before her tone again became serious. "You do realize what this means, J.T.? That we're going to have to take another and a closer look at the earlier victims."

"Raynack's mistakes."

"Now, come on, no one made any mistakes," she corrected him. "Like I told you, if you weren't looking, or if you weren't lucky enough to stumble on it, this wound to the jugular would never surface. It just so happened that I looked for strangulation signs in the larynx and—"

"I rest my case. You thought to look more closely at the throat, ignoring the gross wounds. Raynack—"

"J.T., no more about Raynack's oversights. Regardless, we're going to have to do some exhuming."

She saw by his facial expression that his enthusiasm had taken a nosedive. No one cared to exhume a body, not even a forensics specialist. "Sure, makes sense . . . check each victim for the straw-hole mark, right?"

"It could tell us the whole story, or it could be for nothing. I'm going to put in the order, and we'll see what comes of it."

"Better not let Raynack get wind of this."

"He won't . . . not from me. So I'd appreciate complete discretion, okay?"

"You know you can trust me."

"And as for the enlargements on the electron photos, and the computer-enhanced—"

"Count on it."

"By sixteen hundred?"

"Sure . . . don't worry about the pictures. They'll be in your hands by three."

"Two-thirty."

"Don't push it."

"And J.T.?"

"Yeah, boss?"

"I'd like you to be in the meeting with—"

"Aw, come on, I hate those things."

"We've got to convince them of what we've got here,

and I may not be able to do that without you standing there corroborating everything I say.''

He shook his head over this. ''Come on, you're department head here, Jess; time to throw off that mortal coil and those chains of womanhood that—''

''No, it's no time for any bullshit, or for me to stand on principle, however good! Dammit, J.T., trust me. There can't be a man in that room that leaves with even a shadow of doubt about what kind of fiend we're dealing with.'' At the back of her mind, also, she wanted no one leaving the meeting thinking that Chief Boutine had blundered in sending her to Wisconsin. ''Please, J.T.''

''It's your show. Boutine wants you to handle it, not me.''

''I need your backing, that's all.''

''All right . . . if it means that much to you.''

''I'd kiss you if you weren't married.''

''Go ahead anyway.''

She did so on the cheek and hurried out, saying, ''Don't be late, room 222.''

''Gotcha!''

On the floor above there were six autopsy rooms, and within room A, the main autopsy room with overhead viewing seats, there were no fewer than six stainless-steel tables. A number of universities and medical centers in the area used the facilities when they were not otherwise engaged. Each autopsy room came with the appurtenances of the profession: hanging scales, sinks with running water, drains on the floor, hoses, freezing compartments, microphones and huge magnifying glasses on birdlike swivel arms. The lighting was painfully harsh. The tables were deliberately placed close together so that medical examiners could easily confer when necessary, and because of the inevitable and necessary noise of electric saws and other equipment, a soundproof booth stood in the corner for the M.E. to dictate her notes, if necessary.

Jessica wandered past room A for room C, where she stood examining the schedule, determining when she might have C, should she be able to gain access to a body in the ground since winter. Exhumation was always a big hurdle, and transportation of the body to Quantico another. She'd like to get at least one of the former victims on a table in room C under her scrutiny—preferably before the killer struck again. If her suspicions were correct, he would strike again; he *must* to feed his insatiable bloodlust.

C had only one autopsy table in it, next to a full array of X-ray equipment. The more meticulous and sometimes the more contagious cases, and cases of special medical difficulty, like exhumations, wound up in room C. A large room, it had specially designed features built into the airconditioning system, making it airtight and as safe as possible. The A.C. sucked infectious gases from the body and transferred these to an incinerator on the roof, where they were destroyed. It was perfect in cases of advanced decomposition.

She knew she was getting ahead of herself, that she'd have to get a court order, not to mention the paperwork necessary from her own sector chief, Leamy. Still, she filled in the request for the room, taking her best guess at when she'd need it and for how long. Currently, it was in use, and it'd see use off and on through the week.

She went from here to the investigation division on the same floor. Here men and women worked on color-photo processing, photo files, and in the rear were additional X-ray rooms, the offices of the dental forensics center and the neuropathology laboratory. She needed items from just about every section. She needed the photos of the scene, dental verification that the decedent was indeed Copeland, the X-rays and photos hopefully blown up by now.

She needed med reports corroborating her initial findings at the scene and during the autopsy, reports on the array of slivers she had carved from various organs from the Copeland body, from the brain to the spleen. Jessica had learned from Dr. Holecraft that there could never be enough corroborating evidence.

Jessica knew which people under her she could call and which she needed to confront in order to get what she needed for the meeting, now only an hour away. She had taken the few hours left her to conduct a few tests on her own, skipping lunch, too nervous to eat anyway. Word'd gotten round that the chief of the entire sector, William Leamy, would be at the psychological profiling session over which she and Boutine would preside. Leamy wished to see firsthand the results from Wekosha. An interest in a case from so high up could mean one of two things—promotions or firings. She thought of the small confidences that Otto had shared with her, slivers of information, innuendos. Something was in the air.

Everyone knew that Boutine had personal problems, that he had a wife at Bethesda who had succumbed to a debilitating coma and had become a financial and emotional drain on him; and some said the strain was beginning to show and tell in his work.

She had herself called for Otto to check on a fact and was unable to get him and was told that he was at Bethesda. She cringed at the thought of having to conduct a full-scale meeting with a psychological profiling team on a case of such magnitude without Otto beside her.

She'd now gathered up all her energies and every scrap of information available to her on the Copeland killing except for what J.T. had promised her, the most telling and useful information in what would be a shocking and revealing portrait of the killer. She worried that J.T. would let her down. He should have contacted her by now. Did he have everything ready yet?

Get hold of yourself, she silently scolded.

She had done all that was humanly possible, and she had run roughshod over her people, urging each to give Copeland top priority, knowing at the same time that rushing a scientist was like rushing a tortoise, that it took time to reveal so grand a thing as the grace of a tortoise, or a forensic truth.

She had been frustrated by some of her own people, however, and by the reference literature she'd consulted on blood spatters and evidence gathering. She'd thought her research would be a simple matter, drag out Helpern and Gonzales's *Legal Medicine, Pathology,* and *Toxicology,* but there was absolutely nothing on the properties of blood as it might drain from a victim's jugular when tied in the "swine" position described by Candy's pimp, Scar. She rushed to the most comprehensive volume she knew on blood characteristics, *Flight Characteristics and Stain Patterns of Human Blood,* by MacDonell and Bialousz. The slim Law Enforcement Assistance Administration volume had nothing on Tort 9s.

EIGHT

Jessica saw by her watch that it was late, and that she could no longer wait for J.T. and the enlarged SEM photos he was supposed to have met her with at the door. Inside, she could hear Boutine's booming voice, getting the meeting started, and no doubt wondering where the devil she was. Irritated, she was about to step through when she heard J.T. shout the length of the corridor, racing toward her, waving the slides in his hand. "I'm sorry, Jessie, really!"

"Forget *sorry,* just get in there and set up the shots."

He nodded sheepishly, grinning in an attempt to further apologize. "Madhouse around here," he muttered, but she pushed through to the conference room.

Boutine instantly welcomed them, his voice cordial. Around a large oak table some of the sternest-looking men and women she had ever seen gathered in one place stared at her. She knew some of them by name, others by reputation. They were all top-notch agents brought together as a think-tank team to brainstorm what had happened at Wekosha. One job they had to do was to determine if in fact the Wekosha killer was a serial killer or not.

Jessica stared back at the eyes pinned on her. Some of these people must surely resent the intrusion her presence represented. It was a break with the way things were normally done, and they must wonder why. Boutine began by introducing her, a completely unnecessary gesture, since they'd all heard that she was coming to the meeting. Earlier her presence at such a meeting was purely absentee, representation only through forensics reports. Boutine had been around for enough years to remember the time when coroners and pathologists were called in much more often, when physical evidence and psychological profiling were more closely aligned. He was speaking of that now.

"We're trying an old approach, and we're calling it psychological autopsy. Psychological autopsies have been done since Marilyn Monroe's death, to determine the psychological state of the victim by behavioral scientists, but we're going to twist that a bit and add to our behavioral scientists in this team, a medical examiner, so that the 'autopsy' in psychological autopsies isn't forgotten. Enter Dr. Coran, who, by the way, did the field forensics work we've been discussing. I trust she has more for us to ponder. Jessica," he finished, gesturing for her to take the floor.

She breathed deeply, noticing for the first time that Chief William Leamy was among those at the table. "I've brought you some items that may assist you in the Wekosha case, some slides in particular which are quite revealing."

"We've seen the photos," said Ken Schultz, one of the field agents at the table.

"You've seen nothing like these," she countered. "I assure you."

"From what we've seen, some of us are thinking ritual murder, satanism," said Stan Byrnes. "The condition of the body, the staging, the draining of blood, ropes and—"

"I think we're satanism-happy lately," said Teresa O'Rourke. O'Rourke had a quiet yet powerful style, and she'd chalked up enough wins to turn heads, make people listen. "If you read the photos and the reports closely enough, the fact the body parts were removed after death, and that a kind of 'staging' went into it all . . . well, most satanic ritual staging of one kind or another goes on *before* the actual death blow. They like to prolong the suffering of a sacrificial lamb."

"True, but—" one of the men started to counter.

"Agent O'Rourke is right," said Jessica quickly, trying to seize back control of the meeting, and to gain the other female's support in the bargain. Everyone fell silent to hear her explanation.

"You all know as well as I that all murders are not equal . . . that someone has to decide on the level of viciousness. In the past it was easy—if a jury decided you were guilty, you were executed. Now, much to our horror, there are nuances and calibrations beyond any nightmare concocted in any film or fiction. One way to measure the heinousness of a crime is by the pain and suffering of the victim."

Everyone was nodding, a good sign. Boutine signaled her with his eyes to continue.

"Was the victim conscious? For how long? What was done during that period of time to inflict pain, suffering? I can tell you this much . . ." She slowed, pausing, gathering speed. "The killer took most of her blood away with him."

"What?" asked Byrnes.

"In jars or packs or Tupperware, I don't know . . . but he carried most of it off with him. Indications and information tell us that the cabin where the murder occurred was not occupied long enough by the killer to allow him sufficient time to consume the blood before he left, and having not found it on the premises, I've assumed—"

"But to carry it away?"

"For what, future use?"

"All I know is that it'd be difficult to consume two-and-a-half liters of blood in one sitting. Given the victim's body weight, the killer would've likely taken her blood in two sittings, hours apart . . . possibly three sittings. He didn't stay long enough in the area to do that, so he had to have packed it and carried it off with him."

"This Bud's for you," said O'Rourke dryly.

There was muted, nervous laughter in response.

"But there's more," she said, "and worse information for you to swallow."

She indicated to J.T. that she was ready for the slide presentation. When the first slide came up, no one aside from Jessica Coran and John Thorpe knew what they were looking at. The super-magnified photo of the throat section she had taken from Candy Copeland looked like an enormous spongy landscape on some barren planet, pockmarked and dune-covered. The photo was three-dimensional and in color, state-of-the-art.

"What're we looking at, Dr. Coran?" Boutine asked for the others.

"A close-up of the dead girl's jugular at the exact center." She moved closer and using a pointer she located the geographic center of the jugular. "You will see here the perfectly formed circle like a Cheerio. This is not a normal aberration, but a wound, a wound that takes a great deal more precision to make than any slash to the throat such as the one you saw in the photos of the victim."

"But what does it mean?" asked O'Rourke, nearly off her seat with curiosity.

"The killer used some sort of control mechanism—a device for gauging the flow of the victim's blood from her body."

There was a long silence in the room before Byrnes said, "What kind of device?"

"I don't know."

"Christ, you don't suppose it's a . . . a fang incision, a bite?" asked Ken Schultz.

O'Rourke said, "Don't be ridiculous." Everyone else remained silent.

"You must have some idea, a guess?" persisted Byrnes.

"A valve, a tube . . . something to tap into the . . . well, her blood supply . . ." She hesitated.

"Before the bastard got around to lapping up the remainder," finished Boutine. "This guy's bad news . . . real bad news, people."

Chief William Leamy cleared his throat in the darkened room and asked, "Dr. Coran, do you know of any device used in medicine to drain away blood?"

"Certain catheters working on a syphoning principle are used to draw off unwanted liquids from the lungs, but no. This is like putting a T-section in the blood vessel and rerouting the blood flow. No such device I know of in medicine works this way."

"How long did she suffer?"

"Between twenty and thirty minutes. Lower extremities would have gone numb first, while the muscles in the head, eyes, and mouth would've continued to function, as blood was getting to these areas. Death would have ensued before all the blood was drained, but it would have been a slow death, and a death in which the victim would feel her life virtually running out of her. As to the crime scene itself, sir, a true crazy quilt of clues which were *intentionally* scattered—in more ways than one."

Will Leamy spoke for them all when he said, "We can all agree on the heinousness of the crime. We've got to locate and put this madman away, before he strikes again."

Everyone in the room knew that this was no simple task. Even if they could determine a suspect, so far they had nothing but DNA evidence from the semen to connect him to the scene. Furthermore, it had been determined that the semen possessed a virtual plethora of common elements, and so far nothing even remotely striking about it. Further analysis would be done, but Jessica was skeptical that J.T. would find anything additional, much less useful. It was like having the fingerprint but no suspect to match it with.

Jessica was pleasantly surprised by the warm looks and the nods and a few handshakes the others offered when the lights came up and Boutine called an end to the meeting. The method of proceeding from this point was to give the evidence presented time to saturate, for the PPT people to form some opinions about the kind of killer they were dealing with. Jessica had expected that the think-tank psycho-profiling team would be cooler toward her than they were. She had pictured people more interested in statistical probabilities like so many accountants over actuary tables. Boutine had tried to tell her otherwise, and it appeared he was right. They were highly intelligent, very experienced, instinctive players, this team of four that included Boutine. They would go to work now to create a profile of the most probable sort of man to do the horrendous deeds they'd only just heard about from Dr. Jessica Coran and Boutine.

Otto's team enjoyed a reputation of being the best in the PPT business. Jessica had always believed this was due to the leadership, to Otto. But the meeting had been a revelation to her as well as Otto's people, for she found them far from cautious, far from halting about making great leaps, and a great deal more curious than she'd imagined they would be. And she had gotten through to them. They had seen her worth. Hopefully, so had Chief Leamy.

The psychological profiling team appeared to have been won over by the slides J.T. had made of the wound, and her explanations to the team. She gave a smile, a nod and a twinkle in her eye to J.T. for having saved her from a tough fight. Without the slides, she doubted anyone would have believed her about the killer's modus operandi. It had given the hounds a scent and fascinated them with the cruel new twist on murder that the killer had developed.

Teresa O'Rourke, in particular, was fascinated. She held back, asking questions of Jessica. "What're your plans? What steps will you now take?"

Boutine was busy with Leamy, but he cast a wary glance in her direction. She wasn't sure how much she should share with O'Rourke beyond what was said to the group. She certainly didn't want to talk about exhumations to anyone other than Boutine. "That'll be up to Otto. Most assuredly, we'll be working day and night in the laboratory."

"The semen samples tell us anything about this guy?"

"DNA results have confirmed he's white. That's—" she

hesitated, studying O'Rourke's gaze ''—not about to help us much.''

''Bears out the statistical average.'' O'Rourke's voice suddenly took on a raspy, piratical tone when she added, ''Look, we're both women on a man's mountain here, Jessica. You mind if I call you Jessica?''

''Not at all, Teresa.''

''Good. Look, I understand you actually isolated some trace elements of blood that's most likely that of the killer's.''

''He must've nicked himself, but yes. We . . . I found trace elements of blood other than the victim's in Wekosha.''

O'Rourke smiled. ''I was told you had an eagle's eye and a deft touch.''

''Oh, really?'' She wondered who O'Rourke had been talking to. J.T.? This was cleared up with her next words.

''Thorpe tells me you got enough to run tests on.''

''That's right. Just enough, however.''

''I suggest you look for any blood deficiencies, any illnesses which might show up in the bastard's blood.''

''We are working on that already.''

''Of course. It's just that, well, you may not know that this class of killer, a bloodtaker, is usually working out of some demented need which, strangely enough, has first manifested itself in some form of physical torment—a lack of red blood corpuscles, an illness, some deformity maybe. And if we could focus in on that aspect, who knows, maybe we'd at least be able to narrow the search, halve the haystack, all that.''

Jessica had read about effects of bodily deformities and illness on the minds of murderers. She understood where O'Rourke was coming from, but she wondered why the inspector hadn't brought it up at the meeting, why the 'lobbying' for Jessica's attention?

Leamy gave O'Rourke a perfunctory hello, taking Jessica

aside. "I believe, Dr. Coran, your remarks were extremely useful. I know Otto thinks so."

"Thank you, Chief."

His eyes lingered over her just long enough to make her uncomfortable when Otto stepped between them, saying, "I told you she was remarkable, and that we need her for an early profile creation of this Wekosha vampire."

Leamy acted as if Otto was not in the room, his eyes returning to Jessica's as he asked, "You agree without reservation with Boutine? That these deaths are absolutely the work of one man with some kind of blood thirst?"

Jessica wanted to be firmer, but her words didn't sound very firm. "I . . . I'm leaning in that direction, yes sir."

"Leaning, huh? How do you account for the long delay between the killings Boutine here is trying his damndest to tie together? I mean most serial nuts of this sort may let a week or two go between slayings, but we're talking about months of elapsed time here."

Jessica didn't hesitate this time. "There may've been no delay."

"Pardon?"

"There's quite possibly many more undiscovered bodies."

Boutine nodded in agreement. "If this guy's been working his way up to his present *modus operandi*, there's no telling how many bodies he's left in shallow graves all over the heartland."

"What is our next step, Otto?" asked Leamy.

"Exhumations," she blurted out.

"Exhumations?" he asked, looking around at Otto.

Otto shrugged. "Jess, what've you got in mind?"

She shared her suspicions with the two men. "If we find the identical scar in the throats of the earlier victims, then we can be sure that we are dealing with the same man."

"Makes a lot of sense," said Otto.

"The reason for the slides," she added. "Suffice it to say, the killer is very knowledgeable and shrewd. No ordinary butcher. His efforts to appear brutal were to mask his skill with a scalpel and a specialized instrument of some kind.''

''The tube you spoke of,'' Leamy said.

''A spigot, through which he drained her blood, in a very controlled fashion.''

''Yes, well . . . a medical man, a doctor?''

''Why not?'' asked Boutine. ''Or a medic.''

''Or a nurse,'' she finished.

''Any number of people with specialized knowledge of anatomy. A medical student, a mortician.''

''Anyone who knows incisions,'' added Leamy.

''It was an incision of a very specialized kind, like . . . like a tracheotomy, except that instead of the windpipe, the killer punctured her jugular with a tubular instrument. Now, I've studied the autopsies on the earlier victims and not a word about this came out, because, I believe, the larger, superficial wound to the throat masked the truth, and in all previous cases a local man did the autopsying . . . and we all know how that goes.''

The others had to agree. The other cases hadn't been handled well. On each, the FBI had been called in long after the crime scenes had been disturbed and the pathology reports filed.

''There is one thing they all have in common,'' said Boutine. ''It's what got me going originally. And that's the geography.'' They all understood the geography of death. Most killers, even serial killers, worked within the confines of a strict geographical location, a certain area in a city, a certain town. This pattern was only broken when the killer moved away, and then it was repeated elsewhere, as in the Ted Bundy case. ''This guy, if it is one guy, really gets around.'' Boutine went to a map of the United States on the wall and he pointed out the various states where young women and one young boy had been found bound and hanging from their heels, their blood drained.

He pointed to Wisconsin, Iowa, southern Illinois and Missouri. "A midwestern kind of guy, huh?" asked Leamy.

"We've alerted every law enforcement agency in the country to be on the lookout for anything smacking of a Tort 9."

"You seem to have gotten off the mark on this rather slowly, Otto," said Leamy. "Why?"

"My people have been on it from the beginning, but we've been looking in the wrong place, in the wrong way. Now, with Dr. Coran—"

"How so, the wrong way?"

Otto sighed deeply. "The killings had all the earmarks of satanic ritual, and what with all that's been going on in the papers and the news lately . . . well, like Jess says, this guy is shrewd. So—"

"So he has the FBI, with all its manpower and equipment and communications network, wasting valuable time and personnel on running down leads to every local satanic cult in the midsection of the country. I get the picture."

"Until now, we haven't had any information pointing to one perpetrator. We knew they were taking the blood, but we had made up our collective minds that it was the work of a pack of satan worshippers. One reason is the fact we already knew that one man could not drink the blood of a full-grown person at one sitting, and these were strike-and-run slayings."

"And you're convinced now that Dr. Coran is on the right track?"

"Absolutely."

"And you, Dr. Coran . . . you wish to dig up some mottled old corpses from grave sites here, and here, and here," he said, pointing consecutively at Missouri, Illinois and Iowa."

"That is correct, sir, and it would help greatly if you could get the court orders on each."

"Now you want me to do your paperwork for you?"

"You have great influence, sir," she replied.

He frowned. "I'll see what I can do. Have the details to me before five."

"Yes, sir."

"Thank you for coming, Chief," said Otto as Leamy rushed away.

When the door closed on them, she hugged Otto and shouted, "We did it. We've got him on our side. Isn't that why you asked him to the meeting, really?"

He held onto her, enjoying the touch of the woman, savoring the moment. "You know, you're too smart for your own good. I ought to have the right to some secrets."

Her laughter filled the room and amid it both of them heard J.T.'s intentional noise with the projector. He was still puttering about with the slides. He had been in the projection room the entire time.

Otto instantly let her go, and she lightly blushed and quickly asked J.T. to get the details of time and place on the earlier deaths to Leamy's office.

J.T. said, "Sure, soon as I put these irreplaceable slides into the safe. See you both later, Chief Boutine, Dr. Coran."

There was an awkward moment between them now. Otto reached out a hesitant finger toward her cheek and said, "I'm sorry if I embarrassed you with J.T. It was—"

"No, no need to apologize . . . really."

"I'm sure he got the wrong idea."

"He has . . . well, an active imagination. It's what makes him a good lab man."

"Maybe it's more than imagination," said Otto, staring deeply into her eyes.

"Yes, perhaps . . ."

She thought he was going to take her in his arms and kiss her, but instead, he reached past her for the door, snatched it open and turned out the lights, rushing out ahead of her as if he were suddenly afraid of her. She stood in the hallway a moment wondering about her success with the P.P. team, and wondering if she had not inadvertently upset Otto, and wondering about the sudden emotions that they had shared like juggling burning knives, too hot and sharp to handle. She wondered how much J.T. had heard and seen; she wondered if J.T. had felt anything in the room. She certainly had.

Otto was vulnerable; his wife an invalid, in a coma at Bethesda. Jessica had no right to him, she told herself, and he truly had no interest in her in that direction. It was just the elation of the moment, the hours upon hours of working together. That was all, and that was all that J.T. needed to know.

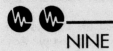

NINE

When alone, he went by the name he called himself when he took their blood: *Teach*. He often thought of himself as a teacher. Certainly, every day he taught. It was part of the job he held, to instruct. And when he killed, he taught unforgettable lessons, after all. *Teach* . . . he liked that. When he bathed, sometimes Teach used blood instead of water.

He was well read, and he had taught himself all there was to know about blood, and not just what modern medicine had to say about the substance, but what the ancients used it for, how they used it and why.

He'd read widely about the curative powers of blood, how it was a skin softener, how it restored hair. So, he lay back now in his blood-filled tub, heated by the tap water that helped to fill it. He had used up almost all of his supply, but the idea of the bath was too exciting to pass up. And it didn't fail him. He lay back, imagining the power it sent through his pores, imagining that he was inside his victim in a sense, here lying amid her, and she going through his pores, that she was her blood and her blood was her, and that it all belonged to him and him alone. Remarkable feelings rummaged about his being and his psyche, feelings of warmth and a heady feeling of belonging. He had never truly belonged anywhere . . . but here, with himself and his victim, like a circle without beginning, without end . . .

Thought was suspended, his mind arrested by the feel of her blood, the smell of it, the taste of it, for he had kept some pure, and it filled a Pepsi bottle at his side. Languid in the liquid.

He had read of great rulers like Vlad the Impaler and Genghis Khan who bathed in the blood of the people they enslaved. He supposed that he was as close to such greatness as he would ever get. The emotional impact was enough to bring a tear to his eye. He wanted no ordinary bath, and no ordinary life.

Virgin blood was hard to come by, but according to the books, it had the most curative powers. It was used as a healing agent in the diseases like leprosy and syphilis. The afflicted parts and organs had to be washed in it, and this application of blood to the skin caused it to glow with supernatural beauty. He had read of how the Hungarian countess Elizabeth Báthory in the early 1600s had murdered over six hundred girls to have them drained of their blood so that she might bathe nightly in blood and thereby remain forever beautiful and healthy. She, too, preferred virgins.

"Of course, there were a lot more of them in those days," he said, chuckling and splashing.

Blood was, after all, the source of life, he reasoned. His medical knowledge told him it was the source of two life-sustaining liquids: milk, which was blood filtered through the breasts; and semen, blood filtered through the testes.

Blood had great magnetic power, and it fascinated him. Gods and demons alike were attracted to the smell of it, just as Teach was attracted by it, especially shed blood . . . the blood of those violently slain. It was not killing and murder itself that attracted him, but the shedding of blood. The ancients who sacrificed blood to the gods were foolishly wasteful. He was not.

He had scoured occult literature for every word written on blood, and he had found that some occultists believed as he did, that the vital essence of life was actually an invisible and intangible vapor, and the medium for that vapor was blood. As far as he was concerned, modern medicine was full of shit. It was not the heart that caused the blood to

flow, but the spirit within the blood. It connected the
material and the spiritual spheres like a cosmic, astral tissue.
The Bible said it best, Teach thought: The life of the flesh
is in the blood.

"Leviticus 17:11," he said with a sigh as he dipped into
the blood with his cupped hands and poured it over his head,
laughing.

The phone rang. He cursed it, let it ring. No doubt the
office. Bastards. Hardly back from being on the road for
them, and they can't give him a few hours peace and
solitude.

"I am the blood and the life," he said.

The answering machine clicked on and he lay back to the
sound of his own voice. Then came his boss's grating voice
like a serrated knife over his brain.

"We've got orders to fill down here!" shouted his boss.
"Where the hell've you been? Time is money, mister! Want
to see your ass at HQ by three!"

Christ, he thought, if he had to go in in the middle of the
day, he'd have to cover up, wear the wide-brimmed hat, the
dark glasses. Light hurt him. Light hurt him like it hurt a
fucking vampire. It all had to do with his disorder, a
disorder he had kept hidden from everyone. But should he
get too much sun . . .

He prayed for a cloud cover, prayed for rain. He had used
up every excuse. He'd have to turn on the shower and rinse
down and get out of the tub. He hated wasting the blood, so
he decided to keep the plug in and reheat it when he
returned, after seeing Mr. Sarafian about the goddamned
orders.

"Why can't we get the body shipped here? If we
could do the work here—"

"The best we can do, Jess! Truth is we were lucky to get
this much."

She stood in the middle of Boutine's office, pacing.
"Weren't there others you were suspicious of?"

"One we can't even locate. Nobody seems to know where she was buried."

"And the other?"

"They won't let the body out of town, much less the state. Families can be very—"

"Stupid—"

"No, Jess, not stupid." His voice slurred. "Thing is, I understand exactly why they feel the way they do."

She realized he was referring to his wife. She sat down across from him and said, "I'm sorry . . . just so frustrating. If we can do some good here, stop this maniac . . . Whatever it takes, we have to do it. You know what kind of conditions we're likely to find in these rural places. It'll be like Wekosha all over again."

"You found the evidence of the tube in Wekosha, Jess. You can do it again."

"With a decomposed body? In an unsafe and poorly arranged lab?"

"You can do it."

She thought of the waste of room C upstairs. "All right, what about the second one? Which one do I go see first?"

"Afraid there's another problem there."

"Oh, no."

"The order is for the same time period. Someone else'll have to go to the second location."

She dropped her tired head forward, her long hair burying her face, all in a gesture of desperation. He came around to her and sat on the edge of his desk, as if simply wishing to get closer. "I figure J.T. is the best choice for the Illinois site. What do you think?"

"We're running multiple tests on the Copeland samples, the semen, the DNA."

"You've got capable lab people for that."

"All right, all right." She looked into his eyes, saw a glimmer of the earlier, daggerlike stare before he broke away for the window to glance over the field outside. She got up and went to him.

"Otto."

"Yes?"

"Something . . . I think we ought to talk about what happened earlier today."

"Nothing to talk about. I'll see you when you get back; army transport's the best I can do for you this time, Jess."

"That'll be fine."

"Leaves in two hours. I'll call Iowa City, have the papers waiting for you. Return trip'll have to be Greyhound if you can't work something out with the guys at the military base."

"I'll get home, don't worry. You'll do the same for J.T. so he can get to Illinois?"

"Consider it done. You really came through for me, Jess. So now you get yourself packed."

"I've felt on standby since Wekosha, expecting a call at any time, so I am pretty well packed already."

"Good."

"I'll just see that my people in the lab know what to do, and I thought I'd get some range time in before I left."

He nodded. "Behind on mine, too."

"Join me there?"

"I'd like to but . . ." He lifted a stack of files and papers and let them plop on the desk before him.

She wondered if his reasons were more complicated than the work load, but she said nothing, nodding. "I'll see you then when I get back."

"Sorry that I won't be able to see you off."

"Well, that can't be helped, I'm sure, and I am a big girl."

He laughed lightly at this. "You've certainly impressed my team and Leamy, Jess. We've made some great strides in reinstating the importance of physical evidence in psychological profiling techniques. Thanks mainly to you."

She bit her lower lip, forming a pout. "I understand why you can't see me off, Otto."

He stopped the shuffling of papers and looked deeply into her eyes. "I'm very glad that you do understand."

She closed the door to his office, understanding completely. He was feeling guilty, and he was worried about what J.T. had seen, or thought he had seen. He was worried about keeping up appearances, she decided.

As she stood there, hesitating, she realized that Otto's secretary was staring at her.

Every FBI person working as a field agent was required to log in a minimum of three hours a week at the shooting range. Unlike most people in the labs, Jessica Coran liked the firing range and enjoyed the feel of a gun in her hand, and the power it unleashed and the frustrations it exploded. For her, the shooting range was a place of catharsis, clearing her head, relaxing in its simplicity, representing as it did the ultimate solution to a problem. Even if the solution was symbolic instead of real—the target paper instead of the Wekosha fiend who had tortured Annie "Candy" Copeland—the act of imagining it so, helped her soul in the way a hot shower or a walk in the park might for someone else.

For the period of time that she concentrated on the target, putting .38 shots into the head of the black silhouette of the monster that had killed the Copeland girl, and possibly Melanie Trent in Illinois and Janel McDonell in Iowa, she felt the same kind of rush she got when closing a case. That feeling of putting an end to it was only temporary here on the firing range, but it was better than the scattered pieces that, so far, represented such a maze that no end seemed in sight.

She emptied her gun in rapid-fire succession, and after the deafening echo died down, she heard Jim Bledsoe's voice coming through her protective earphones. "Hey, hey, Dr. Coran! You're about the best shooter we got going through here these days. You going to make the contest on Saturday?"

Bledsoe was speaking from his soundproof office, a small cubicle some thirty yards away. She pressed a call button on the wall and replied, "Doubt I can make it, Jim. Things have gotten pretty heavy for me, just lately."

"Yeah, so I've heard."

She was an excellent shot, with the accompanying confidence that assured her of placing every bullet where she wanted it. She had learned to shoot as a child from her father, who had also taught her everything he knew about firearms. When she banged the switch that sent her target flying toward her, she saw that every shot had gone into the head of the silhouette, but that not all her shots could be accounted for, because several had passed through the same hole. Bledsoe's binoculars told him the same story, and his close inspection of the target would confirm this.

Her watch told her she hadn't any more time if she planned to shower and catch that transport. She had told J.T. to report to the airstrip also, that he was going to southern Illinois after the throat of Melanie Trent. She had given detailed instructions to her staff regarding the remaining Copeland evidence and the tests to run. She had expressly asked Dr. Stephen Robertson, a specialist in blood and semen analysis, to determine if the specimens displayed any disorders.

She holstered her weapon, ripped down her final target and grabbed her lab duster off the hook and made her way to the range master's office, where she turned in her target. Jim Bledsoe knew her well, and he both admired and liked her.

"Another perfect shoot, Dr. Coran. You're wasted in a laboratory. Chicago or New York could use you." He laughed lightly. "I'd like to get back into the field myself, but my leg . . . what happened in Akron . . ."

She'd heard the story many times before from Jim and did not have time to listen to it again. He had been wounded during a manhunt. Bledsoe was a big man, and even wounded, he had brought down his man, and for this act of bravery he was decorated. Now Big Jim Bledsoe logged time and targets for younger men and women on a shooting range.

He was an athletic-looking forty-six with the features of a golf pro. He kept himself in excellent health and shape, waiting for the day he would get a reassignment.

"Jim, you're just a big flatterer."

"I hear you're doing fieldwork these days, though! What gives? How'd you swing it, the Wekosha gig? Heard it was a bloody mess."

Far from bloody, she thought. "It was pretty awful, Jim."

"Heard you went as Boutine's protégé?"

She now blushed and felt the redness in her face, realizing the implication in Bledsoe's words, that she had gotten the fieldwork by sleeping with Boutine. "I earned it, Bledsoe, pure and simple."

"Hell, I know that, Dr. Coran. I didn't mean anything by . . . by . . ."

She said, "Log my time and targets, will you, Jim? And just so the rumor mill has something to grind, I've gotten *another* field assignment in Iowa. Going tonight—solo!"

"That's great, Dr. Coran. I always said you were wasted, like me, here, doing this!" He gestured to the small wooden office where he worked, overseeing the range.

"I know you mean that, Jim." She calmed. "Thanks."

"I do . . . I always say you're wasted in the lab."

She imagined what Jim meant to say, *a pretty woman like her was wasted locked away in a lab.*

"Thanks, Jim. And you might tell anyone who's even remotely interested that—"she paused—"that I'll be traveling alone."

"None of my business, Dr. Coran."

"Just . . . just log these in." She pushed the targets at him once more. As she walked off, she wondered if maybe Otto was right. Maybe Iowa City was the best place for her to be for now. Maybe there was more talk going about than she had realized.

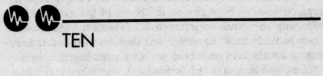

TEN

They were delayed at the airstrip, a messenger telling them that she and J.T. would both be "accompanied" by pathologists from the AFIP, the Armed Forces Institute of Pathology in Washington.

Both Jessica and J.T. were upset not only with the delay but by the obvious intrusion of the AFIP in the case. For the better part of his life, her father had been with the AFIP, carting his family all over the globe with him, going wherever he was needed. This was necessary because he was the only medical examiner in the AFIP. And things hadn't improved much since then. It was a given, and it was quite well known, that Oswald Coran was the exception to the rule, that most medical men with the AFIP were relatively helpless during an autopsy. It was like sending a boy who had learned his first finger exercises into Carnegie Hall to play a Mozart concerto.

Military pathologists knew less than hospital pathologists, and they hadn't the wide range of experience or education that she and J.T. had, and yet, here they were, coming on like a pair of "watchdogs" to oversee her work! It had been the AFIP that had so badly bungled two Kennedy assassination autopsies. Their uniforms looked a lot better than their credentials.

She tried desperately to reach Otto, to determine what this was all about, but Otto's secretary told her that Otto had been called away to Bethesda Naval Hospital to attend to his wife.

When the two AFIP men arrived, one clearly believed himself to have been placed in charge of the exhumations, directing the other to go with J.T. Captain Lyle Kaseem introduced himself to them, and then he introduced Lieutenant James Forsythe, both military pathologists. Kaseem was a thin black man, while Forsythe was white and lumpy.

"We were not briefed about your joining us," she told them flatly. "In fact, I am in charge of these exhumations, Dr. Kaseem."

"Your C.O. spoke to my C.O.," he replied. "And here we are."

The plane was idling on the strip. They wanted to arrive early enough to get some rest before the grueling work that lay ahead of them, and there were financial constraints to consider. The gravediggers would be at the cemeteries in Iowa City and Paris, Illinois, at 7:30 A.M., the normal time to dig up bodies, for if the body could be autopsied and returned to the grave the same day, the costs could be kept to a minimum. Storage space was the big expense, along with the gravedigger's labor. But it was also less harrowing on an emotional level for the families if an exhumation took no more than a single day out of their lives.

Exhuming a body, whether ten years in the earth or ten days, was a highly dramatic, supercharged situation. Most exhumations occurred a few weeks after death, during a period of time when questions about the cause of death lingered. They were proposing not only to open a grave that had been months ago sealed, but opening old hurts and wounds. They wouldn't be welcomed. The order to disturb the dead was hoisted upon the families by the powerful FBI working through the justice system. Jessica and J.T. would have a great deal to contend with, and now they would have Kaseem and Forsythe looking over their shoulders.

"We have our orders, too," shouted Captain Kaseem over the noise of the transport plane.

"You are, after all, using military equipment," shouted Forsythe, whom she chose to ignore.

"All right," she said to Kaseem, making herself heard over the noise, "but you and Dr. Forsythe *will not* forget who is in charge here, understood?"

She huddled a moment with J.T. before sending him off, telling him not to be intimidated by Forsythe, that it was an FBI matter and that he was in charge. "Christ," she moaned, "we'll have enough to do tap dancing around the local path guys, and now these clowns? Why'd Otto do this to us?"

"Doesn't trust us to do the job?" asked J.T., equally upset.

"Many hands do not make light work at an exhumation."

She left him with that thought, rushing to her transport, waving goodbye. Once settled inside, she met Kaseem's dark, brooding eyes. He had dark skin, a rogue's mustache, keen black eyes. He might be handsome if she were not so mad at him.

"What is so terribly wrong with having some assistance, Dr. Coran?" he asked.

"I don't need any more assistance. In Iowa, do you have any idea of the number of people who're going to want to be on hand to assist? No, I certainly will not need another assistant."

"How many exhumations have you done?"

"I've been involved in a few."

He nodded. "Ahh, yes, under Dr. Holecraft at Bethesda, and your father."

"That's right. And how many exhumations have you attended?" She wondered about his knowledge of her past.

"This will be my second."

"Your second? And what about Forsythe?"

"His first."

"His first!"

He shrugged. "The idea here is to get experience, and I have no intention of attempting to take over. I am here as the student."

"Then you may be terribly disappointed. There'll be no

time to hold your hand during an investigation of murder, no time to stop to instruct—''

''Just the opportunity to watch you work, Dr. Coran, will be instruction enough, I assure you.''

The gluey flattery was a bit too thick to be believed. She said, ''You may be disappointed, Doctor.''

He looked in her direction as the transport lifted from the tarmac. ''Meaning?''

''We're likely to have fifteen, maybe twenty minutes tops with the corpse. That's all it will take for me to make the determination I'm going to Iowa for.''

''But I thought it would be a full autopsy.''

''Obviously, you were misinformed.''

She fell silent, and he did likewise.

It was going to be a long flight to Iowa.

The Iowa night was complete, as if the world had fallen into a black hole, and that was how Jessica felt about being alone here. Kaseem had invited her to dine with him, but she had declined, begging off with a headache and paperwork. She'd eaten via room service, a rather dull and cold meal, and her room had begun to feel like a prison. She knew no one here. She knew nothing about the city surrounded by cornfields as far as the eye could see.

She understood that Janel McDonell, although buried here by her parents, having been reared in Iowa City, was actually found dead in a little homestead south of the city called Marshall. Her body was in the trailer house she lived in on an isolated highway, hung from the ceiling, her throat slashed. The autopsy report, signed by three men, one an M.E., said that she had died of the brutal slash to the throat and that she had died at another location and had then been placed in the trailer, since very little blood was in evidence. From her reading of the case and her knowledge of the Copeland murder, Jessica believed she'd been killed in her trailer.

She knew that the Iowa doctors would not take kindly to

her overt questioning of their findings. An exhumation on an unsolved murder case was tantamount to throwing a glove in the face. She'd have them to contend with along with Kaseem in the morning, and she needed her sleep, so she fought for it, struggling with her own troubled mind.

Before turning in she had wanted to know why the AFIP guys had been sicced on her and J.T. She'd tried Otto at his private number, but only his answering machine was replying.

She'd also tried to reach J.T. in Illinois through the authorities there, but had had no luck. A bad connection and shattering static had caused an argument with a police dispatcher in Paris, Illinois. She'd gone to bed worrying about J.T.'s situation.

Still, she had much to be thankful for. After all, she had managed to get what she wanted; she'd set up the exhumation for the early morning. It would be a difficult chore, but not impossible. Everyone who was in a need-to-know position in the city, county and state had been contacted by Boutine earlier. The local police had been polite, if stiff, and had seen to her transportation and the room. Boutine had paved the way for her. She just needed to step in, go through the motions, get what she came for and return to Quantico.

She wondered about Kaseem's motivations, and his orders. She brooded about Otto's disappearance. Then she went back to fretting about J.T. and the owl-eyed Forsythe in southern Illinois.

Even in her sleep she wondered.

In rural Paris, Illinois, John Thorpe was ready to strangle someone to death. Absolutely nothing had gone right. Boutine had not smoothed the way for him, and in fact, had somehow been misunderstood. The exhumation was in progress when he arrived, and he was whisked to the cemetery in the middle of the night. Boutine had either so frightened the locals or so angered them that they had decided to either cooperate too much or to cooperate not at all. Either way, the result was about the same.

And Forsythe was no bloody help, getting in the way at every turn.

At the grave site, lights were flashing, sending up crazy, dancing shadows against the tombstones everywhere as the noise of a backhoe was only offset by the occasional roar of thunder and an accompanying lightning bolt. A simpering, misty rain became a downpour. No one had bothered to check the weather report. And into all this came the casket with the remains of Melanie Trent encased within. Thus far, the only stroke of luck was that the casket was intact, but this luck was suddenly exploded when the vault top, held overhead by an arm of the backhoe, suddenly groaned, sending everyone racing, moments before it collapsed atop the casket.

"Son of a bitch!" shouted J.T. at the backhoe operator. "How long've you been digging graves, for Christ's sake!"

Forsythe tried to cool him down, pulling him away from the backhoe man, who had jumped from his cab, preparing to take J.T. on. Forsythe's uniform, along with the intervention of the local sheriff, brought order back to the chaos in the cemetery. J.T. shouted over Forsythe and the sheriff, "Goddamned stupid way to do a disinterment, people! Christ, if we crush the body, that'll do us a hell of a lot of good."

Men worked to remove the concrete blocks over the casket, the damaged wood coming up in large, spiked splinters, the body within soaking up the rain now seeping into a casket that had remained dry since December.

"Get her into the hearse!" the mortician shouted to his men, once the pieces of cement were cleared off.

"Wait, whoa, up there, Lem! Stanley!" shouted the sheriff. "Good God Almighty."

J.T., hearing this, rushed to the sheriff and pleaded, "What? What's wrong now? What?"

"That's not her."

"What?"

"That's not the Trent girl in that coffin."

"Oh, Christ . . . no," moaned J.T. "You people've dug up the wrong grave?"

"No, no! It's the right grave, the right marker," said the sheriff. "Just that this ain't the right body."

J.T. rushed the mortician. "Who's responsible for this? Where's the Trent girl buried, dammit?"

Again Forsythe stepped in and tried to cool J.T. down. "We'll find it. We'll look through the cemetery records. How many people could've been buried here the same day as the Trent girl? We just go to that grave and—"

The rain was pelting them so hard now that Forsythe had to talk over it, shouting.

"In the morning, Sheriff, in the light of day, dammit! No more of this blind shit. Get me the right body, and get it to the hospital morgue by nine A.M."

"I'll see what can be done," he said as calmly as if taking a breakfast order in a diner.

He had had to contend with the relatives and the local police, and no one was cooperating. J.T. had met the local coroner as well, a hospital pathologist who seemed as bitter and angry as the family at what he called the "heaping on of inhuman and awful sufferin' to the family."

John had been made to feel like the villain here, and Forsythe, jumping on this attitude of the locals, had cajoled them into believing he was here, in his capacity, to uphold all decorum in the indecorous matter. All that J.T. now wanted was to get what he came for as quickly as possible and get the hell out of Paris, Illinois.

The following day, not trusting anyone at this point, J.T. rose early after a fitful sleep, caught a cab to the cemetery, leaving Forsythe abed, to see to it that the right casket was found and lifted from the earth. He was mildly surprised to find men working. In fact, they were just then lifting out a second casket from a second enormous hole created by the monster backhoe. As the casket was lifted, there was a murmur and an unsettling undercurrent that went through the handful of people who insisted on being present. No one had telephoned to send for him, but everyone else in Paris knew what was going on at the cemetery, except now Forsythe.

The parents and other relatives had turned out in mass. They hadn't been here in the night. But now they were like a small army surrounding the scene. It was highly irregular, but it was a very small town. If anyplace on Earth might be called xenophobic, it was Paris, Illinois. They didn't cotton to strangers, and they spoke like they were all from Kentucky.

The casket was taken to a waiting hearse amid people shouting, "This ain't right! Ain't human!"

"God, man, don't you have chil-un, mister? Do you?"

John didn't have children, but he imagined that the loss of a child was assuredly the worst suffering anyone could endure . . . and then to have the remains of a buried child disturbed, the casket opened and a "piece" of the remains taken out. Little wonder they thought him a ghoul and a grave robber.

But J.T. would get what he came a thousand miles for. He'd get it for Jess and Boutine; he'd get it because their case depended upon it.

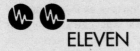

ELEVEN

There were scattered patches of lingering snow on the ground at the graveyard where Janel McDonell had rested since November of the year before below the solid Iowa earth. The snow seemed to cling about the bottoms of the headstones for cold life. Janel's headstone, ornamented with flowers and cherubs, had been removed so as not to be unintentionally hit by the giant, crablike arms of the backhoe that now sank its teeth into the grave, hefted out great mounds of rock and stone, lowered this over a growing mound and then repeated the process.

It was 9 A.M. and there was a bright Iowa sun that sent cascading shadows across the cemetery, and the trees were alive with the music of birds, some darting about the solemn group of people at the grave site. The digging had taken almost two hours, but Jessica knew she was lucky. The girl's family had not spared any expense on her in death, from the headstone to the cement vault which kept water out. Janel's parents, a well-dressed black couple who both insisted on being here, had also purchased a metal casket for her.

A silence of extreme depth blanketed the cemetery when the backhoe had finished its work and the gravediggers then had to climb in over the sealed vault and go to the laborious task of breaking the seal. This was done with hand tools, and the clinking was like that of stonecutters. It echoed about the cemetery.

When the seal was broken and the backhoe put back into

115

operation, to lift aside the enormously heavy lid, the casket was found in excellent condition, looking as it had the day it was lowered: untouched, without a crack, still very much sealed tight.

Cast-iron caskets used in the Civil War that had been opened a century later displayed remarkable preservative powers. The soldiers interred so many years before were in surprisingly good condition. Some had recognizable features, and internal organs were intact. Many of the uniforms were in such a good state of preservation that these were removed to places like the Smithsonian Institution.

Using huge, looping lengths of cloth that they stitched below and around the coffin, Janel McDonell's gravediggers tugged and pulled up her casket, and brought it to the level of the cemetery grounds, depositing it at their feet. Mrs. McDonell had long since begun an uncontrollable crying. Her husband gave her support. Old wounds ripped open wide, Jessica thought.

Jessica looked past Kaseem and asked Dr. Kevin Lewis, a pathologist at the local hospital, "Will you please direct these men to the decomposed room at the hospital?" She had been delighted to learn that Iowa City's largest university hospital had provisions for the necessary work.

The McDonells were accompanied by their lawyer, a man who kept whispering in Mr. McDonell's ear. She sensed that the lawyer was keeping close scrutiny for a future lawsuit for his clients, for the mental anguish they had been put through, despite the fact they need not be on hand. There were two policemen in uniform standing at the periphery. Along with Dr. Lewis there were two other medical men from the hospital, and there was Kaseem.

Everything now depended on Janel inside her coffin. Would the specimen she must take be in a state of preservation which might tell them what they needed? Or would decay and time have destroyed the evidence? She had been told by the local mortician that Janel had been embalmed, so there was a good chance that Jessica and

Janel had something to share about her killer. Was it the same man who had killed Copeland?

It was another half hour before the casket was transported to the University of Iowa General Hospital, the coffin coming to rest in the hospital's decomposed room, which was very like room C back at Quantico, if not quite as large or up-to-date. She knew how very fortunate she was to have such facilities, and she wondered again about J.T.'s chances of finding such niceties in Paris, Illinois. She rather doubted his chances.

The only problem with the room was that it was over-crowded—unreasonably so.

There was a toxicologist to take specimens, a stenographer, two mortuary assistants who did such work as lifting and transporting and sewing up the body after the autopsy was finished, a photographer, the county D.A., Lewis, the hospital's chief pathologist and his assistant, and of course Kaseem.

Just as the two mortuary assistants began to uncrank the lid of the coffin and slowly lift it up, a collective gasp going up with it, a last-minute arrival pushed through the door. It was the state medical examiner, an ancient fellow, who was as amazed as Jessica at the interest in the case. He blustered about the room, elbowing his way closer to the table where the men had placed Janel's body now. The old M.E. repeatedly said, "Stand back, stand back," to the others whom he deemed unnecessary. His ice-blue eyes could cut glass, she thought, if they weren't smoldering with some old venomous resentment.

In fact, Jessica felt the room was thick with old resentments. Everyone was on hand to either prove or disprove something. Young Janel's death had, apparently, been a case that had harmed some reputations, embarrassed some people and agencies, and even now she had a lot of important men scrambling and jockeying for position around her. The case was one of the biggest in Iowa City history, and it still stood on the books as an unsolved homicide. Police and the D.A.'s office had been crucified in the press.

There'd been allegations made by the black community of Iowa City that said in essence that if the murdered girl had been white instead of black, the city authorities would have acted more quickly to apprehend the killer. State law enforcement officials also came under some pretty heavy fire. And so had some of the medical men who had done the original autopsy. Now enters a woman from out of state, an FBI coroner, disinterring the almost forgotten embarrassment to the system, about to quite possibly embarrass that system and the people in it again.

The old M.E. said harshly but slowly into the stenographer's face, so that she could get every word, "Why in the fuck do we need an army in here?" His eyes surveyed Kaseem's uniform as he frowned.

"Dr. Balsam," said the D.A., "I think you know everyone here, except Captain Kaseem with the AFIP and Dr. Coran with the FBI."

"Ahh, yes, the young lady who has stirred up the hornet's nest."

She was sterile, so they did not shake hands. She thought his remark a little like President Lincoln's to Harriet Beecher Stowe, blaming the outbreak of civil war on her book.

"I am going to get on with what I came for, Doctors," said Jessica. "I intend to be out of your town by noon." She hadn't meant it to sound like the script for a bad western, but it had.

"You will have to work fast, then," said Lewis, a slim man of perhaps thirty-five.

"From the look of her, Lewis," began Balsam, "I'd say Dr. Coran's usual style is fast."

She accepted a smile from the devilish old man.

He said conspiratorially, "I was an admirer of your father's, you know."

She looked more closely at Balsam, the most seasoned

veteran of the autopsy room here. "If you know my father's reputation, then, sir, you have my admiration. But I think you know that."

"If my autopsy is to be questioned, I'd rather it was your father's assessment, or Dr. Holecraft's."

"I worked under Holecraft," she said.

"So I've heard."

"Heard?" She wondered about the source. Like Kaseem, he'd done his homework. Was there a dossier?

He quickly cleared up her confusion. "I inquired, and I have a few friends in Washington. Otto Boutine is one of them."

"Dr. Balsam, I have not come here to disprove anything."

"But an exhumation—you don't exhume a body if you trust the forensics report, and I, and some of these men in this room, we signed that report."

"Your report said that Janel died of blood loss from a severe wound to the throat, Dr. Balsam. I am here to either confirm that or introduce a new possibility."

"A new possibility. *Hmmmmmmph!* Do you hear that, Lewis? The girl's head was barely attached, the wound was so large, and this one's going to find another cause of death? Proceed, Dr. Coran."

She breathed deeply, the odor of the body filling her nostrils, despite the specially designed air-conditioned room. She said, "Thank you, one and all. Now, if you will give me some space, I accept your challenge, Dr. Balsam."

When the mortuary assistants had opened the coffin, they had found Janel McDonell remarkably well preserved. The black skin had a pink cast to it against the pink crinoline dress she had been buried in. The dress was still crisp, still clean. Over her breast lay a large silver cross and a withered rose, gifts from her grieving parents, the only people other than the doctors who had seen the gash in her throat that had ended her life. These items were now laid at the bottom of the coffin.

The dryness within the coffin had preserved everything. The organs and tissues could be analyzed. Jessica felt a great wave of relief rush over her.

Earlier, the doctors had all agreed that, despite, or because of, all the factions in the room, the tissues would be divided among the pathologists and the M.E.s to do all the toxicology tests they wished for the city, for the county, for the state. Kaseem even wanted in on the divvying up of the tissues.

The dry, metal coffin had also preserved the girl's eyes. The eyes were particularly important in looking for poisons, and some of the others wanted to take some of the eye fluid for such tests. She knew that this would appease the others, that the eye contained about a tablespoon of fluid, like a little bag of water, and that since the eye itself was a hollow organ, the fluid decomposed slowly.

She allowed the others in to collect their samples, but not before she had the photographer snap close-ups of the eyes. Only Dr. Balsam seemed curious about her attention to the eyes.

"You suspect strangulation, Doctor?" he asked her.

"Perhaps."

"Why, then, slash her throat, if he has strangled her to death?"

"She was not strangled to death," Jessica assured him.

"The day I can't see a strangulation murder, I will retire," he replied.

She smiled and carried on. The two mortuary men had had enough and were gone for a smoke. Over her shoulder was Kaseem, who was being pushed out by the D.A. There was no one in the room, including Jessica, who did not feel slighted. Some had been feeling slighted since Janel Mc-Donell had died. It was an Iowa City *city* case; it was the jurisdiction of the *county;* no, the *state.* And here come the *federals* and the *military.* Kaseem's uniform lent an air of respectability about him, and it helped to keep peace, perhaps, but it was just one more symbol of the numbers of jurisdictional levels at play in the crowded room where Janel McDonell's empty shell mocked their petty concerns.

Jessica hated such ridiculous jockeying, but she was also practical and realistic. Lewis had warned her about the situation, and he had been right. It was an election year in Iowa, and the D.A. might be running for governor. Distrust, along with the fetid corpse, turned the air in the room thick. Perhaps the only way to dispel all the distrust was to have the autopsy done in the open, in full view of everyone connected with the case, and yet she had orders not to divulge information about the condition of Janel Mc-Donell's throat to anyone but Otto.

She wasn't likely to get out of this room with that secret fully intact, she realized.

Dr. Lewis did the honors of opening up the mortician's stitches. All of the internal organs were still intact and the toxicologist and the others were anxious to get at them in order to reaffirm their original findings and put this case back to rest, back into the grave.

While they took their samples, pairing off over organs they felt particularly important, Jessica felt into the throat through the deep well of the chest for any damage done in the area of the larynx.

Dr. Balsam stared at her in deep consternation and curiosity. He said in a near whisper, "You came looking for something very specific, I see. What is that?"

She removed her hand from the location and quickly cut away that part of Janel's throat that might tell them if her killer was the same man as the Wekosha blood-taker.

"What're you doing?" asked Balsam.

"I have to take a section of the jugular back to Quantico with me," she told him.

He stared into her eyes. "Yes, I see that you do."

She realized that Balsam had accepted her among a special company of doctors—as his equal. He said nothing more, and the others knew to follow his lead.

"You can put her back away now," she told Balsam.

"I'll see to it. I'll also report what you've taken from the body in my report, send it on to Boutine. Meanwhile, you've got a plane to catch—"

"Thank you, sir."

"—*and a killer*," he added.

She'd made arrangements for a military transport back to Quantico, if she could be at the airfield by noon. She told Kaseem of her plans, but he had gotten carried away with slicing samples from the liver, stomach and other organs to pay her much mind. He definitely had not learned much either about exhumations or the FBI case she was building. He had especially not learned about the case.

On her way to the airfield in a police car, she wondered if J.T. had had any of the various problems she had faced today.

TWELVE

The news broke in Washington and all over the country, thanks to United Press International, and everyone who could read, and everyone who owned a TV or radio, knew the nasty secret of the bloodthirsty killer of Wekosha, Wisconsin: that he bled his victim to death, drank his victim's blood in a ghoulish, vampiristic manner and carried the rest of her blood off with him. The newspaper painted as lurid a tale as they could with a few powerful images and details they'd so diligently scrounged for in the Copeland girl's case.

Boutine had been right, and they had been fortunate to have the almost forty-eight hours granted them before the story went public. At least they had made some headway on the physical evidence. They had quietly gone about the two additional evidence-gathering forays into Illinois and Iowa.

J.T. was late in returning with the specimen from the Trent girl, and thus far it hadn't been analyzed; however, the McDonell specimen was a definite match. Jessica had run the tests herself, using the SEM, which destroyed the specimen but preserved on print the images necessary to compare with those made on the Copeland girl. The match was unmistakable, down to the depth of the incision, the circular "pucker" of the wound to the jugular, all of it, including the severe but cosmetic throat slash which more or less masked the true cause of death. Like Candy Copeland's, Janel McDonell's life had been syphoned off with her blood through some sort of tube that fed the vampire that had killed her, and that filled his containers for any future "brews" he might like to drain.

She wondered how many more had suffered and died at the hands of this methodical, plodding, diabolical killer who left so few signs of himself. She wondered how they were ever going to catch him, since they had nothing but microscopic clues to his identity.

She got on the phone and telephoned a doctor friend and asked him twenty questions.

"Can you get for me a sample of any and all tubes and equipment you use to drain off a patient's blood? Say from a wound."

"Suction devices, you mean, or syphoning devices."

"That, and anything else you can think of that would drain off or take away unwanted fluids."

"Hell, you've just described a dialysis machine."

"Only if they've created a hand-held model, lightweight and portable."

"Now it's *all* fluids?" he asked, a little exasperated.

"Any bodily fluid, yes, Mark."

"Like in the case of a cancer patient whose lungs have filled with fluid?"

"Yes, anything at all that would act as a catheter, a drain to release blood, urine, anything."

"That's a tall order, Dr. Coran."

"It's important. It could help save a life."

"I read about your Wisconsin vampire. This has to do with him, doesn't it?"

"Please, Mark, keep this between us . . . please."

"Sure, sure. Nice to see your name in print, I should think. *Dr. Jessica Coran!* Sounded like you're Dick Tracy, and that with you on the case, the killer's days are numbered."

"Wish it were so."

"At least they got your name spelled right."

"How soon can you get the stuff to me?"

"Tell you what."

"Yes?"

"I've got surgical equipment catalogues that're filled with all kinds of gadgets. You might save yourself some time—"

"Good idea. Send them over first, and I'll try to narrow the field from the books."

"Consider it done."

She hung up, taking a deep breath, realizing the day had disappeared and her neck was getting as stiff as a board. She'd not been contacted by Boutine or anyone else since her return, and once when she called Boutine, she was told curtly that he was out and would not be returning all day. She left a message with the secretary for him to get in touch with her as soon as possible. She then called his home number. He'd told her to call there whenever necessary. Again, she got the answering machine and her frustration with him was rising.

She had heard from J.T. at noon, grousing long distance about how he planned on never going back to Paris again. He found her now in the lab, coming as he did straight from the airstrip with the specimen from the Trent girl in a cooler. It was 8:30 P.M. by the wall clock.

"Devil of a time, Jess," he said.

"Welcome home." She went to him, taking his coat. "You look like hell."

"Murphy's law in triplicate." He told her of the frightful night he'd spent, finishing with, "And it's only through my Job-like patience that I didn't murder someone—Forsythe for one."

"Pain in the ass. So was Kaseem, but the man did lend an air of respectability and military bearing to the proceedings without even trying."

"I don't think we've seen the last of those two, Jess, really. Something fishy-smelling about the whole setup, like big brother is watching."

"Maybe . . . maybe not."

"What else could it be?"

"AFIP has been wanting to get better training in this area. Our guys stationed all over the world have a guy like Forsythe or Kaseem doing autopsies in places like Manila, Germany, Guam . . . Well, maybe anything they can learn from us—"

"Nahh, that's too simple. Besides, what can they learn on an exhumation?"

"More than you might think. Are you sure we're not just being paranoid a bit here?"

"Paranoia is a healthy emotion, despite the bad rap it gets."

She thought again of Boutine, wondering if he had known about the AFIP's involvement, wondering again where he was.

"Look," she told J.T., spreading out the new images on the McDonell SEM photos, laying them alongside the Copeland shots. "Can hardly tell them apart. You couldn't if you didn't know one of them was buried for six months. Look at the configuration, here, about the center. Big as a bull's eye. She got the killer's ugly spigot jammed into her jugular, too."

"It'd take a guy who really knew what he was doing to hit the mark twice," he replied. "Now, what about thrice?" His eyes lit up with the cooler he held to her eyes. "My damnable vacation into prairie hell best not have been for nothing."

"You've got to be bushed, John. Hell, it's almost nine and you've gone through an exhumation, an autopsy and what must've been the longest flight in history from Illinois to here—"

"Three stopovers, and when the military says stopover, you get a *real* stopover! But I won't rest until I know. You go on. I'll just see what this tells us."

"You sure?"

"*Determined* is the operative word."

She smiled and kissed him on the cheek.

''Makes it all worthwhile, and my life complete,'' he said.

This made her laugh. ''Good night, and keep all this under lock and key.''

''Now who's paranoid?''

''Better safe than sorry's all.'' She left for her office, leaving J.T. to finish up. One match was nice, but the findings could be refuted if interpreted wrongly by others, a thing that happened more often than not in forensic science. But two, if J.T. could pull it off, would be unassailable. They could then begin to search for the kind of awful weapon that the killer had used. The investigators could then see the hacksaw for what it was.

In her office she hung up her lab coat, looked about her desk, wondering if there were any reports she needed to take home with her. She lifted a couple of files she'd been meaning to rummage through, some early work on the Tort 9 killer type. She wanted to see what research had been done. It was indeed scant from the size of the files.

Suddenly, there was someone at her door. She saw the shadow cross her desk, and she was startled when she looked up to find Boutine leaning against the doorjamb, looking shaken, his clothes looking as if slept in, his hair wild, the normally focused eyes unable to look at her.

''Otto? Are you all right? I've been trying to reach you and—''

''It's Marilyn . . . my wife . . .''

She came to him, her breath coming in short gasps. ''She . . . she's gone, isn't she?''

''Odd how it happened,'' he croaked. ''She . . . she came out of her coma, just briefly . . . asking for me. When they got hold of me, I raced to Bethesda. Got there and she was gone back into coma. I stayed and stayed, trying to bring her back around, and for a brief moment, I felt her hand squeezing mine. Doctors said it was just a convulsion, a spasm, but I knew it was . . . was more than that . . . and then she just . . . just left . . . went . . . flatline.''

She took him into her arms, holding him. Over her shoulder, he said, ''Hospital staff was busy, and for a time no one noticed the flatline, no one but me, of course. I . . . I sensed she wanted to go . . . had to go. I didn't call for anyone. I just let her go.''

His frame rumbled with pent-up tears. She held onto him. After a while, she suggested, ''You shouldn't be alone tonight, Otto. Why don't you come home with me?''

He pulled away from her. He never looked confused or out of control. It was difficult for her to believe this was the same man, and yet the depth of his feeling for his wife touched her. ''Come on . . . to hell with appearances,'' she ordered him.

''I don't want to impose on you any longer.''

''Then why'd you come to me?''

He could say nothing.

''Impose. That's what friends are for, especially at times like this.''

He allowed her to lead him away.

Otto was weak with exhaustion and grief. She led him through doors, into the elevator and into her place as if guiding the blind. It wasn't the Otto Boutine she had always known. Once at her place, after he went through a half-hearted walk-through of the apartment, commenting on how it was both warm and bright all at once, he quickly found the sofa, and for the rest of the evening would remain there.

Jessica broke out a bottle of wine and they drank it and nibbled at cheese and crackers until the wine was gone and he asked if she hadn't something stronger. She returned from the kitchen with a bottle of Scotch, to which he approved, asking for it on ice, neat.

''What about something to eat?'' she asked.

''The Scotch'll do.''

''I'm going to fix myself something. Are you sure—''

"No, nothing . . . I couldn't eat."

So she settled down with him there, not eating either. He began to talk about Marilyn, about her enthusiasm for her work. She had been a civil case trial lawyer. They had met when he was on a case that took him to California. Her family was in San Diego, some of them flying to Virginia now for the wake and the funeral. As for him, it was true what she had heard—that he was without family. He'd been orphaned at the age of eighteen. Afterward he'd done a stint in the army, where he'd learned self-discipline. He had finally chosen police work at a very early age. He had come up through the system and had made of his life what it was now.

"Took me away from Marilyn a lot," he said flatly. "We'd be at a wedding, a party, some other thing—once our own anniversary—and I'd be called away. She was hurt. As understanding as she was, she was hurt."

"Otto, people like us, we're on call twenty-four hours a day. That's just the way it is. Don't beat up on yourself."

"Just . . . there was just so much I wanted to say to her," he said, the usual timbre of his voice cracking.

She went to him, her arms inviting him into her, and he buried his head in her breasts. They held, swaying in silence for some time that way.

"You've got to get some rest," she told him. "And so do I."

She got up, located some pillows and a blanket and brought these to him. She turned down the lights and the soft sound of a Strauss waltz she'd earlier placed on the CD player. She removed his shoes and made him lie down beneath the covers, his head on the pillows.

But he kept talking as if he could not stop. He told her about how he had met Marilyn, about trips they had taken together and things they had shared, from horseback riding and tennis to favorite books.

"We once went snorkeling in the Florida Keys for a week. What a place . . . what a time."

"Otto, we all feel guilty when we lose someone. We all

wonder if we said 'I love you' often enough or with enough conviction and feeling. We all regret some things we've said, done—''

"What if I did the wrong thing?" he asked point-blank. "Maybe . . . maybe I should have raced down the damned hall and screamed for help, and maybe—maybe—''

"No, Otto. You did what you felt was best for her. You didn't do anything wrong in letting her go in peace and with dignity. You know that as well as I.''

"Do I? Christ, Jess, the night before I . . . I had a dream about . . . about you, and about me.''

"Otto, that's not—''

"And before that, in Wekosha—''

"That has nothing to do with your feelings for Marilyn, or what you did, Otto. What you did, you did out of love and tenderness.''

He began to tell her more about his daily routine with Marilyn, and how he had come to miss that so much since the incident that first took her from him. Since then his life was a misery, a living medical hell of hospital waiting rooms and bills and a growing hopelessness like a cancer that had begun to overtake him and overwhelm him.

And in the meantime, he had to present himself as Otto Boutine to the rest of the world, as a man without a soft millimeter of flesh. "And now I'm reduced to what you see before you," he said apologetically.

"I see a kind and a gentle and a tender and a caring man," she replied, "and that is all I see.''

She kissed him and she thanked him.

"For what?''

"For being a good man.''

He started to protest, but she pressed her fingers to his lips. "Sleep now, rest.''

He closed his eyes and she silently left him and retreated to her bedroom, where she slipped into a nightgown and robe. From there she made her way to the bath and warmed the shower water before stepping in.

Under the gentle, pulsating water she felt herself melting, the nerves loosening their tight grip on her. The warm water, growing hotter and hotter as she turned up the tap, relaxed her almost to the point of sleep.

She didn't remember stepping from the shower or brushing her hair when she found herself climbing into bed. Her head, still damp, touching the pillow, seemed to drift off on its own, away from her body. A part of her had wanted to find Otto in her bed when she stepped from the shower; another part of her was glad that he was in the other room. He would need time. He was wounded, in much pain, feeling such guilt. If anything happened between them tonight, it would only add to his pain and guilt. She didn't want to add injury to the wound he already felt, despite her certainty that Otto had nothing whatsoever to feel guilty about.

She dreamed of Wekosha as she had every night since examining the dead Copeland girl. All the ugly details she expected to see in her dream were replaced, however, with a soft, hazy glow, shading the horror, and in the place of the horror stood Otto. Otto was reaching out to her amid the surrounding carnage, his expression like that of a little boy who had lost his way. She reached out, taking his hand and wondering what kind of a future they might have together when the hand she held, and the arm that held it, came loose from Otto with the sound of soft suction.

"He makes fools of us all," Otto's dream presence said in a resonating voice while her dream self tried desperately to replace his arm where it had come off at the socket.

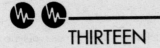

THIRTEEN

"You were right! God, you were right all along, Jess, and now we've got the killer's signature on all *three* victims!" J.T. danced about Jessica while giving her the results of the final analysis. "Same identical cut, almost invisible with the deterioration, but damned if it isn't there."

"The tube cut, like a straw mark? Show me."

He did so and they were both silent for a long time. It was like finishing a marathon. She felt as if her energies were scattered and J.T., up all night, felt spent, that he could go no further, despite the apparent victory. "We've got to show this to Boutine and his P.P. team, but it'd be a hell of a lot more effective if we could pinpoint exactly what kind of weapon the bastard used. What caused the circle cut in the jugular?"

"I've got to get some sleep," J.T. said flatly. She saw from the pallor of his skin that he truly did need some rest, and perhaps a decent meal.

"Yeah, J.T.," she offered, "you'd better get some sack time. You did great, both in Illinois and here."

"Oh, that reminds me," he countered, brushing his dirty hair from his forehead with a heavy hand, his eyelids half-closed. "Somebody's going to have to reimburse me for unexpected expenditures on the trip." He slurred the big words with his drowsy delivery.

"What expenditures?"

Yawning, he replied, "I told you about the mix-up in the

133

coffins, right? Anyhow, I had to replace the price of a casket out-of-pocket.''

''What?''

''Without going into the details, I had to use plastic money to make restitution for a damaged casket.''

''The Trent girl's?''

''That'd be too easy. No, it was for the other one they dug up by mistake.''

''That's going to take some creativity on the requisition form.''

''Just so I get it off my VISA!'' he shouted as he rushed out.

She chased a bit of the way down the hall after him. ''Can you imagine Hardy? He'll quote me chapter and verse from the agency code book of purchasing practices and—''

J.T. shouted from between closing elevator doors, ''Tell Hardy he can jam his actuary tables up his ass!''

She laughed along with anyone else in the hall who had heard. Everyone knew Hardy's reputation and so J.T.'s words were not wasted; they would likely be repeated throughout the day.

But she was the one who had to deal with the likes of Albert Hardy. She knew how very difficult it was going to be to get J.T.'s money back. The agency could tie it up forever if the bow-tied Hardy decided to question and point a finger, claiming that the gravediggers and local authorities were in error, and not the FBI agent.

Still, she found the image of Hardy exploding over a bill for a casket purchased in Illinois by John Thorpe humorous, and it cheered her, an emotion she had been in short supply of for a long time.

John had been so tired when he'd torn away his lab coat and ambled out that she wondered at his having found the elevator at all. She had not gotten much sleep herself, having talked most of the night away with Otto, mostly about the pain and difficulty he had suffered since his wife's aneurysm, and the anguish of having now lost her for good.

This morning, she had left ahead of him, jotting down a note, telling him to use the apartment for as long as he needed, and promising to be on hand at the ceremony planned for his wife. It was to be a simple, quiet affair, the body being cremated.

She tried to get her mind back onto the case. She wanted to have every conceivable angle covered for the next day when Otto would return to work. She wanted to bowl him over with their findings and blow away his team.

Aside from the results on the Iowa and Illinois exhumations, she had a mammoth stack of medical supply catalogues to crawl through. Besides the catalogues provided by Mark, there were some tubes and hard plastic items, any one of which might be the killer's tool. She'd have to narrow the field considerably, and then, selecting what proved probable, take SEM photos of the tips of these in search of a likely matchup with the strange and deadly wounds made to the throats of three small-town, midwestern women.

She went into her office and saw the stacks of calls and files, all work that needed doing, all items she had back-shelved since the night she had left for Wekosha for her first encounter with Candy Copeland and the phantom they sought to expose.

Necessary budgetary forms, charts and files that needed her attention, had fallen by the wayside, along with the departmental efficiency rating this month. This was going downhill so fast she felt as if ensnared in a California mud slide. Going the way of the toilet, she thought, and she knew she was leaving herself wide open with the Hardys of the agency. However, she reminded herself, she was now working for Boutine, one of the most influential division heads in the agency. No one, she hoped, expected her to do the work of three.

Scratch that, she thought, coming to a halt in her thinking. Yes, they did expect from her the work of three, and if she came up short, no one would shed a tear for her when they closed the door behind her.

She was no novice to the squeeze plays and maneuvering that went on in an investigatory agency. She had once been the chief medical examiner for Washington, D.C., and she lasted in the job for only as long as she could stand the political bonds that repeatedly tied her hands, making demands of her to twist and distort the truth to suit the D.A.'s office, the police or some other constituent.

She dug into the waiting morass of work. But the catalogues Mark had brought kept tugging at her.

She then put aside everything to concentrate on the hefty books.

There were indeed many strange devices that medicine put to use, but she found nothing that came close to the weapon used by the killer. Twice she thought she might have it; both times the item she was looking at was a form of the tracheotomy tube. Could the killer have used such a tube on his victim? If helpless, her hands bound, with the insertion of such a tube to the jugular, blood would stream out and leap across the room. There had been no blood trails, no trajectory patterns; instead the surge of the Copeland girl's blood was controlled from the outset. There had been the soft chokehold around the victim's neck which had almost gone undetected. Then there were the slashes to the throat, purely cosmetic, some of the blood syphoned from the dead girl, more or less painted on the wound, after death, smeared on by a pair of gloved hands or, quite possibly, a brush.

Dr. Stephen Robertson, her blood specialist, had come to her door only an hour before with news that his microscopic examination of the photos Jessica had taken of the victim's throat at close range had shown a bizarre pattern of dried lines in the blood, and in the blood itself a single sable brush hair. Robertson hadn't a doubt that the cosmetic wound had been ''touched up'' with a paintbrush.

''Three-quarter-inch, red sable,'' he had said, taking a seat as they shared the mental image of a killer so methodical as this.

"So the guy's an artist?" she replied, sounding cooler than she felt over the new revelation.

"Not too many loonies stop to paint the victim's wounds."

"To make them look ordinary, don't you see? To cover the tubular wound to the jugular. Make us miss it. But he didn't count on us; doesn't know who he's dealing with. Thinks we'll all fall for his stage tricks."

"A little of the artist, a little of the theatrical scamp."

"And a lot of medical know-how," she finished for him. "Look, I want you to go to work studying the photos made in the McDonell and Trent cases. See if we can make another point of comparison on these brush marks."

"If we ever get a suspect, he'll be nailed six ways to Sunday, sure . . . understood, Chief." But he was staring at the other files, the ones she hadn't hefted to him. "And the others?"

"Let's concentrate on the two we've managed to get on exhumation for now."

"How long, Jess? How long do you figure this creep's been getting away with this?"

"Not sure . . . no way to tell."

"But you have a suspicion?"

"A year, maybe. Maybe more."

"Good God." He seemed deflated a moment before bouncing back. "You doing any good with those catalogues?"

"So far? No."

"My guess would be some sort of glass tube, bevel-pointed. One side of the wound is a millimeter deeper than the other."

"My sentiments exactly, but how did he control the surge? Blood would have been coming through that tube like a punctured dam, given her position, upside down—the amount of pressure."

"Then you decrease the pressure."

"How?" she asked.

"Tourniquet. Valve of some sort."

"Tourniquet," she repeated. "Remember the marks to the throat that I mentioned?"

"Like a gloved strangulation."

"Fainter even than that. Could a tourniquet cause such a wound?"

He looked thoughtfully across at her. "We need to get hold of one, try it out. I should think if it was tight enough, a simple hospital tourniquet could cause such bruising below the surface."

"Get hold of one, and we'll test it out."

"On who?"

"On you."

"Me?"

"One of us!"

"We'll flip a coin."

"You're on."

He did so, saying, "You call it."

"You know, I could just order you. You know that, don't you?"

"Yeah, but you won't. Call it," he repeated.

She frowned. "Heads."

He showed her the coin. "Sorry."

Her frown deepened. "All right, you happy? You get to put me in a chokehold."

"Hey, even us married guys have our fantasies."

They laughed good-naturedly at this.

But behind her laughter, she wasn't so sure she wanted to be used as a guinea pig, no matter the cause. She'd have to submit to the test, unless she could find a stand-in. Before he could race away, she looked up tourniquets in the catalogues beside and around her, Robertson pitching in according to his nature, and they found the most portable and the most innocuous-looking hospital tourniquets, the sort that wouldn't frighten a prostitute, that might look a bit kinky in a bedroom, but just might excite anyone into autoerotic behavior. They even learned that some tourniquets were used in surgery to slow the flow of blood to an area.

It had been at this point that Robertson had seen enough and had left, and Jessica began to think about Otto. Boutine's P.P. team was scheduled to meet at two, but this may have been canceled, given Boutine's personal situation. The wake was this evening, the funeral service the following morning. Still, she had been working as if the meeting would come to pass, trying desperately to put as many of the pieces together as possible.

She was engrossed in the med tech catalogues when Albert Hardy, huffing and puffing about the costs incurred on J.T.'s trip to Paris, burst into her office. Hardy was a beefy man with red cheeks and a drinker's red nose, and when he got excited and overheated, he looked like a man about to explode. She spent ten minutes calming him down and another ten minutes explaining that she hadn't time to go into the details for the expenditures incurred in Paris, Illinois, that she had an important, high-level meeting that she had to prepare for and that he would, for the moment, have to deal with the problem on his own.

Hardy fumed. "I'll just see what Chief Leamy has to say about all this."

"Good idea," she responded coolly, "do that." She then ushered him to and through the door, but no sooner was he gone than in stepped Dr. Zachary Raynack, an M.E. with more years on the force than anyone, and a man who had been passed over when she was given direction of the forensics division. Raynack held deep-seated animosities toward her for this reason, and it hadn't been lost on her that the McDonell girl in Iowa and the Trent girl in Illinois had been his cases, and that he had done various tests on the tissues and samples forwarded to the FBI from these remote places. There had never been an opportunity for him to see the entire truth of these deaths, not long-distance.

He slammed her lab door behind him.

Raynack had dark features giving way to a gray, peppery look about both the bushy eyebrows and the head. Still, at almost fifty, he had a full head of hair. He wore thin wire-rim glasses over a wide face that was pockmarked from some childhood affliction, it seemed. He was known as one of the sharpest minds in criminal investigation. The reputation was well deserved, but in the past several years his health and his professionalism had fallen off, or so it seemed to Jessica. Zachary had always had a low tolerance for what he considered his "ignorant" colleagues, and this "professional intolerance" hadn't slacked off in the slightest, but had rather grown to cancerous proportions. And it had been for this reason that few people could work with Dr. Zach, as he was known about the building, and it was for this reason that his work had been curtailed. He had not been given anything to do with the Wekosha killing. The McDonell and Trent cases had come in as separate cases without any relation to each other; it had been Otto, tipped by J.T., who had made the connection. Meanwhile, Raynack, studying the minutiae of each case under his scope, had seen no similarities.

She had long known that even though she was his superior now, Raynack considered her one of his more ignorant colleagues, and she suspected that it didn't help her case to be female.

Raynack was a small man in stature, but his years with the department and his uncanny record of convictions gave him more clout than he may have had a right to. He was a close personal friend of Leamy's; they had been through much together over the years. While Boutine was her superior, Raynack was her elder and Leamy her commander, and it could all get very tacky and sticky quickly if Dr. Zach wished to make life hard for her. At the moment, from the look in his eye, he wanted her to shrivel up before him and die.

"You, Doctor," he said haltingly, as if he might choke before he got it out. "You go to dig up my mistakes, I hear."

There were no secrets in the department. "Not a mistake, sir," she began, but was cut off.

"No? Are you saying you don't think it a bit extreme? Exhuming not one, but two of my postmortems?"

"If you will let me explain."

"No, no, Doctor, you needn't explain. I understand Boutine is behind this. That is explanation enough. You've been charmed by Otto, quite understandable. So what do you do? Otto suggests that you awaken an old case—"

"Those two deaths are connected to a murder in Wisconsin that occurred four days ago, Dr. Raynack, and Boutine may charm *you,* sir, but he does not charm *me!*"

"Everyone knows he is using you to claw together more power. The man is an egomaniac."

"Doctor, I think your judgment is clouded by personality issues—"

"Personality issues is what the FBI is about, young woman, and if you are smart, you will learn this, and if not, you will be sucking up scum for the rest of your life."

"Do you have any interest in why I went to Iowa, Dr. Raynack? Or are you here just to lobby for your own personality? Christ," she finished with a mutter.

"I know what you went to Iowa for. To embarrass me, to send a signal to chief of operations that Boutine is right and that I should go."

"Christ, is everyone paranoid?" she asked, standing now and pacing her office. "This divisive attitude toward one another, Doctor, must go. We can't divvy up the damned department. It's all or nothing. We're all working for truth, or we're all working on building lies. What's it to be?"

"Under your direction the divvying has already started, Dr. Coran," he countered. "Forensics teams should be divvied up and placed under various other departments? As a scientist, my dear, you of all people should know what that might result in! Biased, coerced information supplied by our scientific divisions in order to fit cases *they* make! Pure science cannot work that way."

"I think you're wrong about Otto's motives and plans," she said succinctly. "And frankly, I don't agree with you.

We can't isolate ourselves with a microscope and ignore the facts—''

"Facts! Boutine doesn't give a damn about facts."

"—the facts of a case, locked away in here!" She indicated the labs with a flourish of her hands. "Never smelling the blood."

"Ahhh, yes, the blood . . . Like this vampire killer that you two have cooked up for the publicity?"

"We didn't create the psycho, Doctor!"

"But you and the press will embellish him to grand, superhuman characteristics, so that when Boutine locates this pathetic sonofabitch in some hole out there he will be the hero, and you will have placed the pedestal under his feet."

"Are you at all interested in the evidence in this case?" she shouted.

Politics and personalities, she thought with a rumbling fear welling up inside. Damn them all. Boutine included. Boutine had been smart enough and careful enough to have called it a *confession* when he told her to her face that he indeed was using her.

Now Raynack, a man who could have her job if he played his cards carefully, was making sounds like there had been some improprieties taken by Boutine where Dr. Coran was concerned. It smacked of Bledsoe's thoughtless remarks on the shooting range, but Zach was no harmless Bledsoe. Raynack could make things uncomfortable.

She tried to calm him down and she tried lies. "Dr. Raynack, it was your reports on the McDonell and Trent cases that initially stirred us up when we saw what had happened in Wekosha. You did fine work—"

"Then why're you digging up the bodies to have another go at them?"

"Something new surfaced. It had to be checked on the other two women, and there was only one way to do that."

He seemed somewhat mollified, falling into a chair, taking

a deep breath. "Then Boutine recognizes my contribution to the case?"

"Absolutely."

He thought about this for a moment. And for that moment she felt as if she were teetering on a tightrope between Boutine and Dr. Zach. Part of Raynack's concern was keeping the forensics arm of the FBI intact, and to keep it "pure," apart from the political wrangling, to keep it as an "untouchable" and unapproachable temple, forbidden to the likes of the nonscientists and the novice. He had many times said there was no place in the "service" for the armchair forensics dick; that it was the equivalent of giving a loaded .45 to a three-year-old. He considered Boutine, despite his years of training and experience in the field, just such a novice in the exacting science that went on in the crime labs.

Boutine, on the other hand, wanted the crime lab people more involved in what went on in the field and behind the closed doors of the brainstorming sessions held by the PPT.

It seemed that Raynack was the more unreasonable and unbending of the two men; Raynack with his desire to keep some kind of monastic mystery around the day-to-day of the labs. They had all played that game for a long time, and even she was guilty of it, she knew. But as policy? The days of cloaking such devices as the gas chromatograph in mystery were long gone.

So, too, perhaps, were the days of keeping people in her position in the dark about essential elements of on-scene evidence and information necessary to making a full analysis of the crime scene rather than making assumptions and long-distance guesswork do. By allowing her to work on the sum rather than the parts of the bomb, she might just have more insight than before. What harm in trying something new and bold? To hell with Zach and his *but-we've-always-done-it-that-way* mentality. It had no place in a modern crime lab.

Maybe Raynack's way was best for *his* time, through the

Eisenhower years, through the Nixon debacle and the Reagan fiasco, but now, today, the FBI must seek a better operational base, and it seemed to her that only Otto Boutine had the foresight to see this.

"If we are through, Doctor," she told him, "I do have a great deal to do."

He glanced over the scattered medical catalogues strewn about, some with dog-eared pages, others with markers sticking out. "You might at least extend me the courtesy of telling me just what it was that my reports . . . flagged."

"You had shown that the wound to the jugular in each case, from photos taken at the scene, was the work of a scalpel—sure and neat."

"Then the Wisconsin killer used a scalpel?"

"Yes."

"A particular kind of scalpel, I suppose."

"Yes." She wished to say as little as possible.

"That's the reason for the catalogues, then?"

"Searching for a match, a particular model, yes."

"Left-handed grip scalpel," he said.

"Sorry?" She was confused.

"For doctors who're left-handed. As I recall, the slash was made from right to left across the throat. The work of a lefty."

In all the information she'd absorbed over the last three days and nights, she had seen this but she had paid little heed to it. At least, for now, Raynack was mollified. And before leaving, he even said that he was sorry for having stormed in the way he had.

Jessica, who hated pettiness and whining and old-fashioned thinking, went back to scanning the catalogues for any sign of the instrument used to kill three confirmed cases of murder.

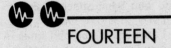

FOURTEEN

Otto Boutine stood just outside the glass partition surrounding the lab, staring at her. She'd worked straight through lunch, and she'd for a time put him and the night before out of her mind. Apparently he meant to keep in touch with his people, and obviously he would continue with the 2 P.M. meeting regardless of all that was on his mind. She waved him in to learn that he was anxious for any new results on the exhumations or any of the 101 tests being run on samples taken. He seemed agitated, as if once more he had to prove himself to Leamy, the chief of operations. She led him back into her office, where he said, "I'm sorry about last night . . . really."

"No need to apologize for being human, Otto. Christ, as much as you've been through."

"I had no right to drag you down with me."

"Otto, really, I was glad that I could be there for you. Someday, you may be able to repay the kindness."

"No, I'll never be able to quite repay you."

"Now you're getting me mad with this silliness."

"Just accept my thanks, Jess."

"Consider it done."

After a few words about the wake and how he must leave by four, he got around to the questions on his mind. "What did the exhumations prove, if anything? I just saw Zach Raynack, and he was actually civil, said something about his part in unmasking the Wekosha vampire. What did you tell him?"

She explained in some detail what the exhumations had shown, and she explained to him what she had said to Raynack, and why.

He laughed. It was the first time she'd seen him smile in several days. His laugh was genuine and strong. "I take it all back, Jess, you do know how to be tactful when you want to be."

"I think he's calmed his brain at least to a simmer."

"Ahhh, Jess, you're doing so well for me here, and you're a good friend."

She blushed in response.

"Maybe," he continued, "after a decent interval, I mean, maybe we could see each other outside of our official cloaks.

She smiled. "I'd like that, Otto."

"So, sounds like we've got something to continue our psychological autopsy with, and I think you're in for a few surprises. My people have put together a preliminary profile on our man. You're in for a treat."

She picked up all the information she needed, including a hospital tourniquet that Robertson had placed on her earlier, tightened and removed, after which he had photographed the slight discoloration about her throat. The control mechanism of the killer? Possibly. She also carried a trach tube with a razor-sharp, beveled cutting edge. "Show-and-tell time," she said.

J.T. met them at the conference room with a medical teaching tool, a see-through clinical model of a man's throat, some of the organ pieces spilling across the table when he placed it on the slick surface. Byrnes picked one up and shoved it back across at J.T. Ken Schultz examined the plastic voice box with curious fascination, asking J.T., "What gives with the dummy?"

"A little reenactment of the murder according to Dr. Coran, I assume," said Teresa O'Rourke. "This should be interesting."

And it was. The P.P. team were glued to their seats when

Jessica lowered the lights and displayed on a screen the rudiments of a tracheotomy. The trach tube was displayed in a profile view, in relation to the cricoid cartilage and the trachea. The short film explained how a tracheotomy was performed. Then the lights came up and she directed their attention to the see-through bust on the table before them. She carefully placed a tourniquet around the unwieldy shape of the see-through plastic model and after tightening it, she held up a trach tube to her eyes for them to see clearly. She then quickly and surely plunged the tube into the transparent tube that represented the see-through man's jugular, just to the right of the trachea.

The trach tube stuck and wobbled in the throat of the model, hanging there like a straw. "If there was blood passing through the jugular, it would shoot through this tube," said Jessica. "We believe the tourniquet somewhat controlled the flow, but it would have to be a hell of a tourniquet to control it all. Still . . . this is how he did it, we believe."

"Using these exact tools?" asked O'Rourke.

"Or something very similar."

The team sat below a pall of silence for a long moment. Byrnes, the heftier of the two men, said, "Looks kind of awkward. Can the tourniquet be held in place, or do you have to keep hold of it?"

"This model requires a hand be on it," said J.T., "but there are others that do not. These are calibrated and notched."

"We believe the killer used the most sophisticated equipment, and that he is very knowledgeable—"

"—of anatomy, yes," said O'Rourke. "Yes, he'd have to know exactly where the artery was located . . . precisely how deep to go with the cutting tube."

"Fits . . . all fits," said Byrnes.

Jessica showed them slides of the left-handed slash wound to the throat and pointed out the blown-up pattern that indicated that the killer had painted blood on the body after she was dead and after he had slit the throat. All these steps he took after draining all the blood he could get from the corpse.

The darkened room filled with a combined awe and a few groans.

He knew he needed more blood if he wished to continue doing blood baths. And the boss had sent him out to the Baptist Hospital in Zion, Illinois, on a special order, and there he met a mousy, bespectacled, brown-haired nurse who was left without a ride home. He gave her a ride in his van with the cooler in the back and the briefcase on the floor. He talked her into a nightcap, and before the night was over, he had capped off the night with some of her blood.

Zion was a little close to home, but the opportunity was just too perfect. The woman lived alone at the end of a street where several houses were abandoned and up for sale. He knew that no one had seen him pull into her driveway. She was so anxious for company. It was all too easy to pass on.

Her name was Renee. And now he had jars labeled *Renee*. Janel was gone forever, and so was Toni and so was Melanie.

He was home safe now, enjoying Renee. It could be days before the shell of her was found; meanwhile he had captured her essence, her soul, in his jars, syphoned out with her blood through his instruments.

He had once wanted to be a doctor, and when that dream ended, he had tried teaching for a while. The kids called him Teach, and he had allowed it. He taught biology but not for long. When he taught, he liked to use the real thing, and this upset some of the more immature of his students who preferred specimens to come in neatly wrapped, formaldehyde-soaked packages. He personally could not stand the stench of the stuff, but the odor of fresh blood—now, that was a different story.

He bullied the boys into being macho enough to be cut for

blood samples. They responded just as he expected them to. When he pushed a girl into the same kind of corner, someone came to her defense, and there was a bit of a nasty scene, and afterward he was called into the boss's office and the principal put him on notice.

By the end of the term, he knew his contract would not be renewed. Just another person with power over his life putting it to him.

He was in his late twenties, nearing thirty, and what did he have to show for it? He had been a failure at everything he did. It was just as his father had told him all his life, that everything he touched turned to shit. The old man hadn't been any help, a failure himself, dying of the hereditary disease that he had passed on to his son. He could only look to his grandfather's notebook and his collection of medical books for comfort. His father had been a fool, but his grandfather was a great man, a great doctor.

Teach sat before an old Victrola record player, which had also been his grandfather's. It was spinning in lazy whorls the strings of a Mozart concerto, the record without a scratch, but still some static chipped up from the diamond stylus. Getting parts for the old player had become near impossible, but he had found a shop in a small town on Main Street in Wekosha, Wisconsin, that was wonderful. It was like walking back into the past. The shop had some vintage 78s which he had gotten at a steal. He had also picked up some singles at Pernell's Music Emporium in Wekosha. It had cost him a month's pay, but listening to the lovely strings now made it all worthwhile. It soothed his taut nerves, this simple hobby of his, his love of music of a far-gone world, the world of Strauss, of Mozart, and sometimes he'd play music from Benny Goodman and the big-band era. He believed he had been born in the wrong time. He detested the music he heard today blaring from the radio.

The old Vic was sometimes used to listen to *Hamlet, Lear* and other Shakespearian plays, a collection of which he had gotten at a bargain rate in Paris, Illinois, where a Catholic monastic order had shut its doors and had sold off all of its library assets and holdings. He had gotten Olivier and Barrymore doing Shakespeare, along with a full production of *A Midsummer Night's Dream* by the Royal Victorian Symphony Theatre in London, England. These, along with his freezer filled with blood, were his most prized possessions, which he shared with no one.

He turned up the volume as loud as it would go and returned to his red bath. Nude, he slid into the reheated blood bath. He had had to use more jars. His supply was getting dangerously low, and he believed in the domestic truth: *one off the shelf, replace it yourself.*

In the warm crimson bath now, he resumed where he left off before they'd called him into the office that morning. He'd have to be on the road the following day early, but tonight, he had all evening to enjoy himself with Renee.

Listening to classical music and reading his favorite passage from the Bible, he heard his cat mew. The cat, a big, black tom, was left often to fend for itself, put on the street whenever he was gone. But Snuffy—so named for a chronic congestive disorder—always returned. He liked the smell of blood, too, and whenever he could get it, he'd lap it up.

"The vital essence of a living thing . . . the life of the flesh is in the blood," he read aloud to Snuffy. The cat came near enough for his extended hand to pet. But it wasn't interested in a caress, turning back on his hand and licking frantically at the bloody moisture there.

The cat knew. It somehow knew what he knew and what the Bible said was true, that the way to health, to a cure, to longer life—quality time—was through the intake of blood, orally, through the pores, any way you could get it. He rubbed the blood into the animal's thick, black coat violently and it came back for more. This made him laugh and say, "You like it, don't you . . . don't you, boy?"

After an hour's languishing in the heated bath, he pulled the plug, rinsed off under the shower head, toweled himself down and went into the next room, and down the corridor of the old house he had inherited from his father when his mother died. For sixteen years he had seen to the needs of his ailing parents, and he had watched them both wither and die, and it had both sickened and terrified him. At the end of the corridor, he went into what was once his grandfather's study, which was now his study. The old man had been a general practitioner in the days when doctors worked out of their homes, and beside his den there was a small examining room. He had wanted him to be a doctor as well, and he tried to be what he wanted to be, but it just was not to be. There were too many people in the world set against him: his teachers for one, his superiors, the doctors who made the decisions in medical school, the ones who created hurdles for him to jump over, and then there were his parents. Their illnesses had come on like a fire but then lingered for years, sapping the family of finances just as it sapped him of any compassion he might have otherwise felt for his essentially weak father and dominating mother.

So he had turned to teaching, because those who can, do; and those who can't, teach. But he learned quickly that teaching itself was yet another science—an art really—like being an actor, and only the best actors with great inward confidence and the best scripts survived teaching. His too soft approach, his too gentle demeanor and his essentially introverted nature and lack of confidence, along with the fact he had never acted, never scripted anything in his life, had failed him in this as it had failed him in medicine.

Finally, three years ago, he had turned to the want ads in the *Chicago Tribune* and in the *Sun Times,* and he searched for any jobs having to do with medicine that he might qualify for. He went through a series of such jobs before becoming a salesman for a Chicago firm specializing in medical supplies, from new pills to new forceps. The only sort of supplies they didn't supply was linens.

Into the den he carried with him his large Bible, but he now placed it aside, and below the student lamp on the oak desk, he picked up the Old World pen from the inkwell before him and now he dabbed off the feather quill in the inkwell and watched the blood drip from its end.

He had a letter to write, a response to the misrepresentations of the news coming out of Wekosha, Wisconsin, that he was some sort of vampire. He was far more than any fictional nightmare. He was quite real, and his purpose should not be confused with cinematic nonsense or lurid novels.

Using the blood of Candy, mixed with an anticoagulating agent in the inkwell, he wrote out his first line which he intended to send to a woman named Coran at FBI headquarters in Quantico, Virginia. He had already used an ordinary red Bic pen for the envelope, finding the address easily enough in the Registry of Law Enforcement Agencies at the library. He had read the feeble accounts of the so-called slash-and-drink vampire killer of Wekosha, now making the rounds of the various papers from *USA Today* to the *Enquirer*. None of them had the story right. He felt relatively secure about keeping his identity and his home safe from all the people who would enjoy getting at his throat with a scalpel.

Although careful to print, Teach wrote with a flourishing hand where once he had written with a pinched and tiny hand the words he so wanted to convey to Dr. Jessica Coran. She proposed to corner him, to bring him to what *they* called justice. We will see, he thought as he wrote:

Dear Dr. Coran,

Read Leviticus and you will understand me. I am far from a vampire, and do not consider myself one.

Candy was sweet; that is, her blood was sweet, but I am once more reduced in my supply. As you see from this note, I use blood for every little thing. Perhaps someday I will be fortunate enough to have some of your blood? Please, don't let the newspapers disparage me again. Put your mind at ease. My thirst is, from time to time, quenched. So I will not take any more than my needs dictate. I am fundamentally an environmentally conscious person, and do not squander blood. You know this from your own experience, do you not? So rest assured.

Perhaps someday we can meet, and perhaps you will give me some of your blood? I believe women have much more character than men, don't you? At any rate, you can never hope to catch me before I catch you.

Sincerely,
Teach, the one you seek.

The fools hadn't a single shred of evidence to link him to the deaths. They hadn't even placed Candy Copeland in the hospital where he had first met her in the cafeteria, sipping on a big milkshake. He had seen her in the hospital before on his trips, usually doing the scut work of mopping floors and taking out bedpans, but recently she'd been given more responsibility and she hadn't been able to cope with it. So her days were numbered, and she talked of having to go back on the streets, back to a pimp who kept her. She'd been feeling sorry for herself, and he saw his chance and he took it. He offered her some relief from her sorrows, pointing out some of the types of drugs he peddled for his company. She wanted relief from her life, her pain, and ultimately she felt no pain.

She had liked the candy cane uniform. She had liked being known as a candy striper. She took on the name "Candy" as a result, casting off "Annie."

Now that he'd finished his letter, Snuffy, who had followed him into the den and had so calmly sat over his feet for the duration of the letter, suddenly snuggled against his leg. The tom then leapt up onto the desktop in a blink and was going for the inkwell and the feather pen and the smell of blood.

He dabbed a bit on his finger and fed it to the cat.

"Reach out and touch someone, heh, kitty?" he asked.

FIFTEEN

Otto's FBI profiling team had paid microscopic attention to the autopsy reports, to maps and photographs of the various crime scenes. They had paid particular heed to how the victim was treated. A killer who takes the trouble to cover the body afterward speaks one thing, a killer who hides the body is saying something different, and a killer who displays the body like a trophy, quite another.

Byrnes said, "Our guy feels no remorse about his victims."

"But he does feel something," countered O'Rourke. "He sees them as furthering his goal; and in this sense, he cares about them."

"But not enough to cut them down, cover them over," said Schultz.

"All he's interested in is the blood. The body may's well be an empty can, a receptacle from which he has taken what they willingly gave him."

"Whoa," Jessica stepped in. "They didn't die willingly."

"Through no fault of their own, no. But in the killer's mind, *they asked for what they got.* They wanted to share in his grand design, the design to give him power over them and others."

"That's a stretch," said Byrnes.

"Well, what we know about victims—victimology—tells us that the victim unwittingly pushes the button. Something about her appearance, either dress or physical," said Schultz.

"Any rate, I agree with Teresa, this guy does not feel bad about what he's done, but good, *very good*. Which means he's likely going to strike again."

"I've put out an alert to every law enforcement agency in the nation on this one," said Otto.

Byrnes had a master's degree in educational psychology from the University of Michigan, but O'Rourke had profiled some 450 murderers, and her degree was in psychology. "If he had moved the body," she said, "even to a couch, he'd have shown some shred of human emotion. He didn't. Not in any of these instances. Now, Dr. Coran has shown that it is without a doubt the same man, I say we go with profile three."

Otto told Jessica that the team had created three profiles and that they were in the midst of narrowing it to one. "He didn't give a damn about the victims' bodies being exposed to the elements. He had no idea how soon, if ever, they'd be discovered."

"Another personality trait," said O'Rourke. "He really does not care one way or the other whether the bodies are found or not. He has a lot of rage in him, and a lot of contempt for anyone in authority."

"Didn't suckle his mother's breast enough?" asked Byrnes.

"Something like that," O'Rourke said, refusing to show any emotional response to Byrnes.

"So you don't think he stuck around for the funerals?" asked Otto.

"No way," said O'Rourke.

Schultz agreed. "He'd only have contempt for such customs."

"He'd have no desire to see them decently buried," said Teresa O'Rourke. "It would be like burying one of the canisters he used to carry off the girl's blood in. She was an object to him, an object to be emptied."

"It's the post-offensive behavior of the killer that interests me," said Schultz, lifting profile number three. "And this fits with profile three. What he did to her after she was dead, and now with this paintbrush business, Christ, it fits. The guy is a stalker."

"He brings along his own weapons," added O'Rourke.

There was no longer any argument about much of this, Jessica thought, because the autopsy information had proven so much.

"So the guy was organized and cunning," agreed Otto. "He came from a neighboring town and probably drove a van."

"Nothing impulsive or passionate about our vampire," said Byrnes. "But the facial attack, that usually means the victim knew her killer. The killer, in order to perform his terrible deeds on her, puts out her eyes so that even she can't see what he is doing."

"Maybe they had crossed paths before. We need to check on that possibility. Prelims have shown that both Janel McDonell and the Copeland girl worked in hospitals, and the way this thing is shaping up, a hospital seems a likely setting for a first meeting. Say this guy knows a lot about trach tubes and tourniquets," continued Schultz, whose degree was in sociology, "maybe our guy's a paramedic."

"Why stop at paramedic?" asked Byrnes. "Why not a doctor?"

O'Rourke quoted known dogma about murder. "The more brutal the attack—and we are talking Tort 9 here—the closer the relationship between victim and killer."

"Maybe she did bring it on herself," said Byrnes, "in a manner of speaking."

"If she did, she had no idea she was doing it," countered Schultz. "The victim might be guilty and innocent at the same time."

"Maybe she teased his sick mind at some point and he never forgot it."

"The killer showed mastery of the situation," said Otto, slowing the back-and-forth intentionally, wishing to get back to profile number three. "He killed slowly and methodically, which means he's a more sadistic personality.''

''Which places him in the probable range of late twenties or thirties,'' said O'Rourke. ''And what did he do right after the murder? Did he lounge there? Enjoy himself with the body? Necrophilia? Not so, according to Dr. Coran, who has said that the sperm did not belong to our man but was placed into the orifices—sperm brought with him in a vial. His ritual, the time gone into the act of cutting her tendons, tying her and dangling her and finally draining her . . . the other, post-offense measures were meant to fool you and me and people like Dr. Zach.''

There was some muffled laughter at this.

Schultz picked up the thread from here, clearing his throat first, his hand going habitually to his throat, as if protecting his own jugular as he spoke. ''Many killers take something of the victim's away with them—a bracelet, a ring, a watch, a mirror or compact—as a kind of artifact of the crime; to use later to excite themselves, to relive the experience, recreate the memory. This guy took blood!''

O'Rourke added to this. ''Certain kinds of killers also keep diaries, scrapbooks, other memorabilia of their deeds. With this guy, it's likely to be a freezer filled with blood in tidy packs or jars.''

''Tidy,'' said Jessica.

''What?'' asked Otto.

''Oh, nothing . . . just that I had gotten the exact same impression of the killer when we were there, in Wekosha, that he was a fastidious man. You people are remarkable,'' she said to them.

''Trust me,'' said O'Rourke, ''we rely a great deal more on statistical probability than on our deep psychological insights.''

''Ah-ahhh, Teresa,'' said Byrnes with a shake of his index finger, ''we're not to give away trade secrets.''

''Plain common sense; experience gained from sweating out hundreds of cases,'' said Schultz.

"With the Copeland case, for instance, since the victim was white, it's a good, educated guess that her killer, too, is white. But then you connected Janel McDonell to the killer, and she was black. Most black women are killed by blacks, and whites by whites," said Byrnes.

"This is especially true in the vast majority of mutilation murders," said Otto.

"We settled on white, because Trent was white. Two out of three," said Schultz.

"And the age?" Jessica asked.

O'Rourke replied. "The kind of methodical, organized killer he is points to someone who's been around a while. He's probably fantasized about these crimes for twenty years, since puberty."

"The killer's conduct with regard to the victim both before and after death," added Byrnes a bit smugly, "was quite measured, quite controlled, and this would be highly unusual in an impulsive teenager or someone in his early twenties."

"He lives alone, or if with someone else it will be an elderly parent who is dependent upon him."

"How can you possibly know that?" asked Jessica, who had remained silent, completely fascinated by the work of the profiling team.

O'Rourke half turned in her chair and crossed her shapely legs before saying, "It's virtually certain he can't carry on a lasting relationship with a woman, and if he has sustained one, it will be to a wife who is totally dominated by him, a virtual house slave. But more likely, he's a momma's boy, and is either taking care of his mother or living in her house left him when she died. This is, of course, in all probability."

"The guy did know a lot about Wekosha. He has spent a lot of time there," said Schultz.

"And Iowa City, and Paris, Illinois," added Byrnes.

"Because he knew where to take his victims. He knew how much time he had with each."

"He had to be fairly familiar with his surroundings to chance this kind of killing. He's no fool, no impulsive kid on a rampage."

"So he lives near the crime scene for a while?" asked Jessica. "People in the area had to have had dealings with him, then."

"All that's certain is that he knew the area well enough that he felt he could do whatever he wanted to do without disturbance," finished Otto. "But the distances between these cases suggests a *moving* killer, someone who may be familiar to people in Wekosha, but someone who does not stay very long, a kind of recurring, cyclical person."

"Like a deliveryman?"

"A trucker? Maybe a long-haul man?"

"Or a salesman," suggested O'Rourke.

"Hospitals on the one hand, salesmen on the other."

"Salespeople frequent hospitals every day," said Jessica.

"By the hundreds of thousands," said J.T.

Otto paced. Everyone watched him. He had an uncanny ability to come up with detailed descriptions of unknown assailants on the scantiest of information. His mind seemed to be boiling over with these new suggestions. Everyone remained silent, watching him.

Boutine began his profiling career in 1979, and at the time he taught a course in applied criminology at the FBI Academy, where students who came from all over the country brought him their cases. One story had it that when one of his former students telephoned from Oregon with a baffling case, Otto, with a handful of details about the stabbing death of a young woman, told his student he should be looking for a teenager who lived near the victim. Otto said he would be a skinny, pimply boy who spent more time with computers than people, a socially isolated individual. He said it was an impulsive act and the kid was suffering from great fear, grief and remorse, and that his guilt would give him away. "If you walk the neighborhood, knock on doors, you'll probably run into him, and when you identify yourself, just stare straight into his eyes and say, 'You know why I'm here.'" The next day the Oregon officer called back to thank Otto and to say that he had apprehended the killer, a teenager with acne whose best friend was his Tandy 2000.

Otto had made it clear that he wasn't interested in psychology for psychology's sake, that a treatise on mental disorders was of no use to the FBI, that his interest was not in *why* a killer did what he did, but *how* he did it, and how knowing that leads to his capture.

"A profile," he said now, "is supposed to point to a certain general type of person, not a certain individual—or profession. If we're not careful here, folks, we could spend the next several months following up blind leads in hospital corridors looking for a guy who sells white linen or bedpans to hospitals. I'm not sure we can stretch our profiling to that degree, at least not yet."

Without saying it, he was telling them something they all knew, that the FBI profile could be dead wrong.

"Still, Chief, don't you think we should get people in Wekosha, you know, to sniff around? More than one killer's been caught putting flowers on the grave of his victim," said Byrnes.

"Sure . . . sure," said Otto. "You want to coordinate with Milwaukee on that?"

"Will do," replied Byrnes.

"I just keep remembering the Koontz case," said Boutine.

There was a communal moan.

Otto went on. "We had the guy living alone, a possible orphan, uneducated, without a job or ties in the community, remember?"

Everyone remembered but Otto said it anyway. "He was the son of the town minister; had children and a wife and mother-in-law; was the town's most well liked, well known appliance store owner, which gave him an annual income of forty thousand plus a year. He taught Sunday school and played on the softball team, never touched a drop of alcohol and attended church regularly.'' His crimes, in fact, were an ''act'' of faith. It was a reminder that profiling was far more art than science, despite probability statistics.

''If we could pinpoint where he lived, go at this in a proactive sense,'' began Schultz. ''Put the press to work for us.''

Byrnes objected. ''That could backfire. A guy that's this nuts could kill himself.''

''Better him than another of his victims,'' said O'Rourke coldly.

''And so he's buried with what he knows, like how many others he killed,'' finished Byrnes.

The proactive technique meant utilizing the press, feeding them information selectively, the end result to smoke out the killer, taunt him, and hope that he might be foolish enough to give something of himself away. It was a deadly kind of cat-and-mouse game, a bit like Russian roulette. ''We can't use the press unless we know the guy's jumpy,'' said Boutine. ''So far, he seems quite cool.''

''How cool would he be if we put out a diagram of the kind of devices he uses in his hometown paper?'' asked O'Rourke, who seemed to favor the proactive method.

''Along with the fact he drives a gray van with lettering along the side,'' added Schultz. ''And then we leak the fact we've got some of his DNA left at the scene. Don't know about you, but that'd make me kind of jumpy.''

''Add to the list that we suspect he's some sort of a traveling pervert-salesman who combs the Midwest, possibly selling to hospitals,'' said O'Rourke.

''Call him a fag because he didn't rape the victim, some insults like that. Call him impotent, that kind of thing,'' said Byrnes. ''Yeah, maybe it would smoke him. Maybe he'd respond to insults.''

"Maybe, maybe not," said Otto.

"It's worth a shot," said Schultz.

"You want to coordinate that, then, Schultz, all the big midwestern papers get the story. Do something with the victims' families in all three cases, try to draw the bastard back to the victim psychologically. Although with this guy, I have my doubts he's going to feel the least sympathetic to the families. But start there and if that gets no results, go with the insults. Remember to stress *no bylines* on the damned stories. We don't want this psycho going after a reporter."

Otto took a deep breath before going on, pausing for everyone's complete attention. "I talked with a man in my office who claimed to be a goddamned vampire expert, who says he can help stalk this 'thing,' as he called it."

There was some muffled laughter.

"A real loon but the guy's not only the Exalted Emperor of something called the Committee for Scientific Investigation of Vampires and Werewolves in North America, he's a legitimate biologist with the Corning Corporation in Upstate New York."

This drew a few more laughs and remarks.

"Guy flew here as soon as he read about the case, insisted on seeing me and me alone—"

"You were alone with this guy?" asked O'Rourke.

"He insisted on seeing the evidence, everything we have. Of course, I showed him the door. You know how much store I put in these wackos and fringe guys, even if it is more than a goddamned weekend hobby for the man."

"So, we got 'em coming out of the woodwork," said Schultz.

"All the same, the Exalted One did say something that made sense. What sets this killer apart is his very real instinctual drives, such as his unquenchable taste for human blood. I don't go along with all the crap about superhuman gifts or reanimated beings, but this *monster* has an acquired taste for blood, whether that's due to some physiological need, a psychosexual need, or a combination of the two, that's what we must determine. What makes this bastard tick.''

''Well, from all we've researched on the subject, and there's damned little to go on, boss,'' began Byrnes. ''You've got to figure this guy is working out some twisted sexual fantasy. What is it they say: one man's garbage is another man's treasure? In sex, it's similar; what one man gags over, say menstrual blood, another man is turned on by.''

''Blood turns this bastard on for sure,'' added Jessica who had calmly listened to the discussion.

''But only eighty or ninety percent of known blood drinkers also perform deviant sex acts on their victims,'' O'Rourke interjected.

''But even the other ten percent are in it for *some* twisted psychosexual perversion,'' countered Otto, ''albeit so bloody sick that the sexual nature of the crime is overtly unapparent. I think our creep is totally screwed in the head and has, for whatever reasons, gotten blood and semen and sex and murder all balled up into one.''

''So he gets sexual pleasure from drinking the blood,'' said Jessica.

''His ultimate gratification, yes.''

The others considered this in a moment of silence.

''Maybe that's your lead, Schultz,'' suggested Byrnes.

''What lead?'' asked Schultz.

''For your story. Plaster it across the headline that the bastard we're after gets his rocks off by pouring blood down his pants.''

''Intimate that he's unable to please a woman,'' added O'Rourke.

''Intimate hell,'' replied Byrnes. ''Call him a faggot vampire.''

''Byrnes may be on the right track,'' said Schultz. ''If this thing is to work, we have to piss the bloodsucker off.''

Schultz pursed his lips, nodded and tapped a pencil before him, considering his next move. Jessica, searching the features of everyone around the room, realized that all of them were considering their next steps very carefully. None moreso than Otto.

SIXTEEN

He knew that he suffered from two rare diseases, both of which made him angry and both of which made him a blood-drinker. He had read all there was to read on his conditions. He knew that his adrenal cortex was steadily atrophying, and that only cortisone helped. It was a hormone that regulated the electrolyte balance between sodium and potassium in the body. An imbalance caused progressive fatigue, weight loss and eventual death. At one time Addison's disease was fatal, but now you took cortisone to replace the body's supply. But the damnable cortisone caused weird fatty deposits in his back, turning him into a kind of Quasimodo, bending him over. It showed up in his buttocks and his cheeks as well, giving him a John Kennedy or Jim Belushi appearance about the face. He had gone to a doctor friend who had X-rayed his pituitary gland at the base of his skull, the gland that controlled the adrenals. The pituitary was shriveled, the adrenals tiny. The disease had done its work, marking him both inside and out.

Other symptoms were anxiety, depression and an acute sensitivity to cold.

Blood, he reasoned, helped to hold the disease in check, as it warmed him both physically and spiritually.

Blood also helped combat his second disorder, *porphyria,* called by some the vampire disease, in which large amounts of white blood corpuscles were wildly manufactured in the bone marrow, leaving red corpuscles in short supply. The bone marrow defect led to a lack of heme, a pigment in the blood's

167

oxygen carrying cells as well, and this gave him a pallor. Occult historians believed that porphyrics attacked and drank the blood of others in a desperate attempt to get healthy hemoglobin into their systems. Nonsense, he thought. If that were the only reason he killed, he could stop tomorrow, go into a clinic and get all the hemoglobin he required—and he had done exactly that on more than one occasion. He knew a lot of doctors. He went to them whenever he could. He liked to watch them work, and, for the most part, he liked them.

A key symptom of his disorder was a sensitivity to sunlight, which caused scabs, scarring and sores over his skin. His gums, too, had receded as a result of the disease, exposing his teeth to such a degree that they appeared to the casual observer to be fangs.

Some people had cancer. Some were afflicted with other debilitating diseases. He counted himself lucky. His diseases could be held in check, both by cortisone, which was in plentiful and cheap supply, and by blood.

He had earlier packed the van, before the sun had come up. He had clients to see in Indiana, up and down the state, and he might get over to Ohio and down to Kentucky, if he could manage it. On the company car phone, he kept in touch, but the range wasn't as far-reaching as he and his van. He placed his heavy cases into the van, his samples, all the various brochures and catalogues provided by the company. He then stocked the rear of the van with his own, private goods, the items necessary for taking the blood from another Candy or another Renee. All he needed now was opportunity, and he would help opportunity along, knowing that it would present itself somewhere in Indiana tonight.

It was midmorning when he pulled from the driveway, waving to a few neighbors who, retired, had nothing to do beyond tending to crabgrass and their tomato plants. Somewhere a dog barked.

He pulled from the little subdivision of houses onto the main road, then took Interstate 294 in its wide arch around the sprawling city. He wanted to find a good place in Indiana to post his letter to Dr. Jessica Coran and eventually mailed it from the small post office in Hammond. People stared at him with his hat and sunglasses on, since it had become overcast. He got back into the dark interior of his van and hid behind the black-tinted windows. From there he watched a young woman pull up, get out of her car and go into the post office. She was, to him, a bucket of blood. Everyone walking before his gaze was a bucket of blood. But young girls were prettier buckets. He stayed long enough to watch the girl exit, get into her car to leave. He fell in behind her, fantasizing about doing her.

But he had a schedule to keep, and he knew that schedules could be checked, and so when the red Firebird ahead of him turned off onto a residential street, he kept pace with the traffic going back toward the interstate and Indianapolis.

At least the letter got off.

He switched on his cassette player and listened to the *Blue Danube* to combat the jackhammers and noise of busy Hammond. Hammond was bustling with sound and pollution and he hurried to the interstate. But he was careful not to go through any yellow lights, to lane-change or to cut anyone off. He certainly didn't want to be placed in Hammond, Indiana, by some stupid traffic ticket on the same day that a certain letter was mailed to the FBI's premier forensics investigator. If he was going to play games with the authorities, rub their faces in their helplessness against him, he meant to do it right.

On the seat alongside him was his brown leather briefcase. Inside the case were his special blood-tapping tools. Behind his chair was his cooler, stocked with empty jars anxious to be refilled.

Dr. Grubber was waiting for him, and following that a new client in the Indianapolis area.

The sunlight had not been harsh or glaring when he got out of the van to post the letter, and yet it still had hurt his sensitive skin and eyes; it'd bring the sores and scabs if he was not careful. Dr. Leonard Grubber would supply him with more of his concoction of proteins and carbohydrates which the man claimed was the best single source of relief from porphyria as well as Addison's disease. Grubber had been seeing to his needs since he met the man his first day on the Indiana run. Grubber was fascinated by his case and wanted to do a case study. It took a long time for the confidences and assurances to be bonded, but now he saw Grubber as a harmless medicine man who wanted to conduct his experiments. It was a trade-off, a kind of symbiotic relationship. He'd give Grubber the use of his body for study, if Grubber provided him with the medications he required to hold the diseases that ravished his body in check.

Grubber was, in fact, the closest thing he had to a friend.

Grubber's records were interesting. He had picked them up once and read about himself. Grubber had not been able to get the research and his paper published in any medical journals yet, but he kept trying.

He found his way back to the interstate and pulled into traffic. If he made good time, maybe he'd get lucky later on this evening.

Late in the day at Quantico, Teresa O'Rourke claimed that the killer lived in or around the Chicago area. This pinpointing of residence was important for several reasons, and despite her methods, everyone wanted to believe she was accurate. This would narrow the focus considerably. Records could be more easily checked, DMVs, registrations of all sorts. The Chicago FBI field offices were very professional, very good. Everyone was elated when O'Rourke demonstrated how she had arrived at Chicago. She had taken a radial scanner and had drawn circumferences of twenty, thirty, forty, fifty and one hundred miles from the kill sites, and all of them at the one-hundred-mile range intersected at or near Chicago.

It was late, however, and other than contact the bureau

offices in Chicago, there was little else they could do tonight. Besides, everyone had plans to be at the wake for Marilyn Boutine. The meeting broke up with everyone having a job to do. Byrnes was to be a catcher-in-the-rye back at Wekosha, digging deeper into the life of one Candy Copeland, and to keep a watch on her haunts for anyone who might have known her. He would even go so far as to place a recording device on her headstone, he had said.

Schultz was to work with the newspapers in an attempt to stir the killer to some foolish action that might reveal more of his identity.

O'Rourke was to fly to Chicago to give the bureau there the details of the P.P. team's work, and to share the forensics information amassed against the killer.

Boutine and Jessica would remain in Quantico to coordinate any further "troop movements." Everyone was feeling hopeful; everyone was sure that the noose was tightening, but everyone also feared the next telephone call from some law enforcement agency in need of FBI assistance on a Tort 9.

The phone call came while they were at the wake. People started disappearing early, Boutine telling them that he understood and would soon follow. Jessica stayed on with Boutine until he himself decided to put an abrupt and early end to the wake. There was too much at stake. News had come in from Zion, Illinois, of the discovery of a mutilation murder that fit the M.O. of their Tort 9 killer. Otto had put it out on every wire, and everyone in a law enforcement position in the nation, and particularly the Midwest, was watching, and while they'd had some sixty maybes, this one sounded like a certainty, down to the near spotless condition of a white to beige rug over which dangled the body from its heels from a chandelier cord. The chandelier had been torn down and cast into a heap in a corner.

"I'll fly out tonight, Otto. No need for you to go," she told him.

"How're you going to get on without me?"

"Our Chicago guy's have it. They'll be there."

He looked back at the open casket, into the face of his dead wife, nodding. "Thanks, Jess, for being here for me. Can you arrange a flight and—"

"Leave it to me. You just see to what you must here, and I'll see you when I get back."

She quickly made her way back to her place, packed and made the necessary calls. She'd be on a transport within the hour, military again. She had hoped to be able to avoid the uncomfortable military transport for the plusher Lears of the FBI, but these were all in use.

At the airfield she had another uncomfortable shock. Both Kaseem and Forsythe. They'd gotten the word on the Zion killing, and they had orders to proceed there themselves, and they had booked the same transport. She gnashed her teeth and managed a catlike grin when Kaseem extended his hand and said, "Looks as if we will be working together again."

"What is your interest in this case, Dr. Kaseem?"

Kaseem's eyes gave him away. He did hold some secret. The black orbs flashed for a millisecond, and Forsythe became uncomfortable and worked toward finding a seat.

"There is something more to your interest in these vampire killings than you've told me, isn't there? Isn't there?"

"It's a long story."

"We have a long flight ahead."

He took a deep breath. "All right, we'll talk."

During the flight, Kaseem painted a bizarre picture of a young medical technician in the marines who had a taste for blood. When caught at his peculiar addiction, the marine was removed from all medical areas, given other work to do. Stationed in West Germany in 1976, at the age of eighteen, still a private, a man named Davic Rosnich had successfully eluded military and civilian police after murdering a bunk mate in a bizarre fashion deep in a wooded area far from the base. Rosnich had convinced the other man that he was interested in him sexually, had convinced him to furlough the weekend with him and had then rendered him helpless, and finally took from the other man all of his blood.

"To this day, Rosnich has eluded capture," finished Captain Kaseem. "I . . . I was the man called in to examine the body. When I heard about your vampire killer in Wisconsin, I naturally became interested, and when I contacted my superiors, they contacted Leamy, and Leamy asked us in."

"Asked you in, I rather doubt."

"All right, so Leamy owed a favor. Nonetheless, we're here, and at least now you have a suspect."

"You should have told us about this *suspect* a long time ago."

"We did."

"Through whom?"

"I am not at liberty to say."

"God damn you, Kaseem, you'd better get at liberty to say, or I'm calling your bloody superiors and Chief Leamy and anyone else I must! Now, who?"

Kaseem sputtered a name, saying, "Teres . . ."

"Teres? Teresa? O'Rourke?"

"Yes, Teresa O'Rourke."

"O'Rourke?" she repeated, dumbfounded for the moment.

"She and I . . . we've been seeing each other for some time."

She dropped her gaze, nodding. "Your search for Rosnich, has it zeroed in on Chicago as possibly his current stamping grounds?"

"It has, yes."

"So O'Rourke is smarter than even she knows."

Kaseem became indignant at this. "Look here, what is

wrong with two law enforcement agencies working together?''

"Working together? Had you given us this information
on Rosnich, we might have already done a blood check with
military records on him, and a fingerprint check, and a—"

"O'Rourke said she would see to all of that."

"She did?"

"Yes, and it was my understanding that your forensics
people *have it*."

"Christ, then why don't I know about it?"

"I might assume you've not seen the forest for the trees."

"No, you may not. What I haven't seen has been kept
from me. That you may be sure of."

She stalked to the cockpit and demanded to use the
comlink with the ground. She asked to be patched through
to the forensics lab at Quantico, preferably John Thorpe.
Thorpe was out. She was put through and recognized Dr.
Zachary Raynack's voice on the other end asking how he
might be of service.

"You might begin by faxing every fucking thing you
have on Davic Rosnich to Chicago and being damned
certain, Doctor, that it is waiting for me there, you old
sonofabitch!"

"Now, just a minute, young woman—"

"I am not your young woman, Doctor! I'm your boss,
and if you can't live with that, if you think you can work
around me, then you've got another think coming."

"I am carrying through only on what Chief Leamy had
asked of me."

"Leamy, no. O'Rourke, yes."

He was silent at the other end and she knew she had him.
"Now, I want that information, in full, waiting for me when
I get to Chicago. Fax it to our bureau there with a request it
get to me in Zion. Do you follow, Doctor? Zach? Do you
copy that?"

"Yes, yes," he grumbled, and hung up.

"Bastard," she muttered under her breath, seeing the two

flight crewmen smiling at the show they were privy to. She stormed back to Kaseem. "Your girlfriend must want to crack this case very badly, Dr. Kaseem. She's quite an ambitious woman, isn't she?"

"Teresa has only one goal, and that is the same as yours. We were not exactly welcomed in by you and Dr. Thorpe, and so I went to her. I see no problem with working around you if you are not interested in working with the military."

"AFIP, Doctor. Not the military. I have a great deal of respect for the military usually, but the AFIP tried once to ruin my father's reputation, and no, there's no love lost between us. As for cooperating, what were you doing in Iowa City, looking over my shoulder at that dead girl we had to exhume, knowing about this man Rosnich and not saying a word to me about it?"

"Your attitude dictated my attitude, Dr. Coran."

She soothed a bit. "How old would this Rosnich be now?"

"Twenty-nine."

"The approximate age of our killer, possibly in Chicago, with some medical training. Christ, if a fingerprint or a blood sample links this man to the victims . . ." She allowed her thoughts to trail off. If O'Rourke got the killer, independent of Boutine, while Boutine was too involved with personal difficulties from being at his wife's bedside to burying her, O'Rourke would shine in Leamy's eyes. Otto had said there was some talk of his being forced into an early retirement, a rumor saying he was burned out. Had O'Rourke seen her chance and simply stepped into the breach, or had she started the rumors?

"I want to see what photographs you have of Rosnich, and anything else you have on him," she demanded of Kaseem.

"Then we are finally working together?"

She felt her jaw tighten and her chin quiver. "Yes, if that's what it takes." Uncanny was how she had felt about O'Rourke's pinpointing where the killer must live, and the other assessments she had made about him, including his age, and the reason they should go with profile three. If it was all based on Rosnich, it could well be the wrong man and the wrong profile. Otto must be told. Otto must deal with O'Rourke and patch up the shaky profile and the team itself.

She looked at the picture of the soldier turned killer in West Germany wondering how he had eluded police and had gotten to America, if indeed he was the vampire who found Annie Copeland in Wekosha, Wisconsin. The face was young and the eyes questioning in the photo that Kaseem handed her. The hair was wild, unkempt, and the mouth was set in a little, derisive half-smile at the cameraman. It was a military mug shot. Rosnich had been in the guardhouse more than once for fighting and thievery.

She tried to imagine what he would look like today. The photo almost masked a scar on his temple. Rosnich was born in a suburb of Chicago called Wheaton. Could Wheaton be the home of the blood addict?

She asked Kaseem about the details of the killing in West Germany and the investigation itself. She was trying to tie these details to what she knew about the killer.

"Was the victim hung upside down?"

"By his heels, yes. That's what first attracted us to your case."

"Were the victim's tendons cut?"

"No."

"What kind of knot was used?"

"Sling knot."

"And the slash, was it a left-handed cut or a right-handed cut?"

"Left-handed."

"Was there an unusual absence of blood?"

"The man drank his blood."

"How do you know that?"

"He was seen doing so by some children hiding in the bushes."

"All right, but was the cut to the jugular a deep penetration, and was there much pooling of blood below the corpse?"

"Sure, lots of blood, but that's only because the guy was just a kid, new at it. He hadn't thought it out. It was just a sudden, impulsive act that—"

"But not so impulsive that he didn't plan it? He did lure the other man out there," she countered.

"We still believe it could be the same man."

"So it could be. According to the experts, there are maybe three hundred blood-drinkers in the U.S. and Canada, so he could as well not be our man."

"Experts? What experts?"

"Otto Boutine. He knows more about Tort 9s than anyone."

Kaseem nodded respectfully.

"Look, we can put out an all–points on your man, get an FBI artist on this photo, touch it up, age the guy appropriately, and maybe even get a bust made of him. If he is our killer, we'll do whatever's necessary to get him. This is not a contest to see who gets him first, Dr. Kaseem; it only matters that he is stopped."

"The military wants him."

"The FBI wants him."

"The two do not have to be mutually exclusive, Dr. Coran."

"Just the same, you people play false with me again, and you can forget any cooperation whatever with the agency. And that's no threat."

Kaseem took her hand and she shook his.

"Good," he said.

"Then we understand each other."

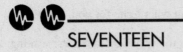

SEVENTEEN

As Jessica Coran's plane flew over Indianapolis' lights at forty thousand feet, Teach was driving up to the parking lot at Grant Memorial Hospital on the outskirts of the city. He had seen all his regular clients, and he had seen Dr. Grubber, and now his time was his. He put on his medical supply sales badge and wandered the halls of the newly constructed hospital, breathing in the hospital smells, annoyed only by the fluorescent lights, which hurt his sensitive skin. Even though it was hot, he wore long sleeves. He also wore his dark glasses, but hospital people understood the need for dark glasses to protect the eyes from the brilliance of the lights. Everything was so white.

He liked to wander about the emergency waiting room where oftentimes young people were brought in, some in need of a place to stay the night. He knew how to approach those in need.

There was a young woman in a corner by herself looking frightened and alone. He went to her and told her he was a doctor, and he asked if she was being taken care of.

"No, I've been waiting and waiting," she said, "and they won't tell me how Jimmy is."

"Jimmy? Is Jimmy your little boy?"

She laughed at this. "No, Jimmy's my boyfriend. He ran himself off the road and I was called by the police, but I've been left to sit here all this time. I got no way of knowing if he's all right."

"What's Jimmy's last name?"

"Pyles."

"Okay, good. I'll find out what I can for you, and I'll be right back," he told her.

He went straight through the door separating the waiting room from the nurses' station and found chaos inside. Everyone was busy. He gave his stay a moment longer before returning to the distraught young woman in the waiting area. The girl was instantly at him for news.

"He's stabilizing well, and it looks like he's going to be fine. Dr. Thornton said he was gotten here in time, so no serious damage was done."

She almost collapsed. "Oh, oh . . . oh, thank you . . . thank you."

"Dr. Thornton suggests you go on home; that there's nothing you can do until tomorrow. Says Jimmy'll be out of it until then; doped to the ceiling." He chuckled lightly.

"No, I don't think I could leave him. I'll just wait and—"

"No, no, child, nonsense. I have a good sedative I can prescribe for you, and once you've had some sleep—"

"I can't sleep knowing Jimmy's in pain."

"But he's not in pain. He's out of pain, thanks to Dr. Thornton and his competent staff."

"I just want to see him."

"I'm sorry, but that's out of the question. Look." He showed her some Quaalude tablets. You know what these are, don't you? These'll help you, I promise, and you'll get by this tragic time. You really do need to get your sleep, some peace of mind, and when you see him tomorrow, you'll be just fine, and when he sees you, you'll look so—"

A nurse pushed through the door and said, "Barbara, Jimmy's being X-rayed now for broken bones. He's been sedated, but he's in a lot of discomfort and there's some internal bleeding. We'll need to operate and we need the consent of his next of kin, so—"

"What? What? But Dr. Thornton said—"

"Dr. who?"

"This man, this doctor here—" She turned and found no one there.

"What man? Who're you talking about? Maybe we'd better get you a Valium."

But the girl rushed to the hallway and saw the ghost trail of the man who had been so reassuring, and she shouted, "Come back, mister! Doctor! You!"

But he was gone.

The nurse tried to console her.

It had been a close encounter and he felt his nerves rubbed raw at having lost the opportunity which had been opening up to him with each moment before the nurse stepped in and destroyed his plans. He got back into his van, feeling great frustration and anger, but the night was young, and he had a great deal of patience, and the young woman would have to come out sometime. He could use the knockout injection, or chloroform or brute force, but there was a police car parked outside the emergency entrance.

Should he wait or go? Would she wait all night inside or would she come out?

He waited for fifteen minutes and this stretched into a half hour and still she did not show. He began recalling earlier blood-takings he had performed, going through each in its every detail, reliving the events one by one. He recalled the first, Toni. She'd been a scrubwoman at a small hospital in St. Louis, Missouri. She was not particularly pretty, but her blood was good.

He recalled how a year before Toni, he had gotten his idea for the spigot; how he had drawn it up with great care, sketching it in detail in pencil. He thought the design so perfect that no one could have trouble with manufacturing the device. He took it to Maurice Lowenthal, the so-called genius in the company who had designed medical instruments on demand for doctors in the past. Lowenthal's custom-made instruments sold for large sums, making money for Balue-Stork Medical Supply.

Lowenthal wanted first to know what job the spigot was supposed to perform, saying he could not create without full knowledge of the purpose of the instrument. He understood forceps, clamps, scalpels, mirrors, visors, but this was beyond him—a tracheotomy tube with a control device? Why? To punish the poor patient by shutting off his air supply when the doctor was so moved to do so? Lowenthal understood tubes and wires and cables, anything he could fashion with his hands and his mind, but he wanted to grasp the use of the instrument.

So he took it back from Lowenthal and did nothing with it for a time. Lowenthal remained curious, however, and one day asked him who was the doctor who had asked for this strange device to be designed. He'd told Lowenthal the first name that came into his head, Grubber in Indiana.

"Ahhh, yeah, a strange bird, that Grubber."

"Yeah, strange," he had agreed.

"Did you ever find out what the thing was to be used for?"

"Grubber thought it might be the answer to relieving the pressure of any liquid buildup in the body," he had said with such confidence that he had surprised even himself. But he had been planning to come back to Lowenthal again with the design, and so he had practiced this answer. "Water on the knee, you name it."

"And water on the brain, I suppose?"

"Why not, if it can be designed accurately."

"With a thing like this, it ought to be patented, my friend, and if we patent it, it becomes the property of the company, and what do we get?"

"Yeah, I know, but those are the breaks."

"I'm up for retirement soon," said Lowenthal. "Tell you what, if we can go halfies on the rights, I'll design it at my shop at home, but it can't be used until after November, when I retire, understood? If it's a success, then everyone will want it, and we will be rich men.''

He agreed with Lowenthal, and Lowenthal had created the prototype, unaware that he had also created the perfect murder weapon.

In Zion, Illinois, Jessica found what everyone feared, another Tort 9 with the markings of the Wekosha vampire. Maybe Kaseem was right. Maybe it was his man, after all. There was an all-points bulletin released on Kaseem's man, the description going out to every cop and law enforcement agent in the city and its environs. It appeared the killer did live somewhere in the greater Chicago area, and that it could be Davic Rosnich, living under an assumed name. He would be about the right age, and he was a known blood-drinker, or so the military said.

Throughout her evidence gathering the Chicago bureau guys were very helpful, very professional. The scene was nothing like Wekosha, although Kaseem and Forsythe were forever in her way. Everything had been kept exactly as it was found and no one had been allowed to wander aimlessly around the house or the body. It was a controlled situation for a change.

She didn't have to do her own photographs, nor did she have to tell the photographer how to do his job. She had all the cooperation she required. FBI's Chicago bureau chief, Joe Brewer, was an old friend of Otto's and Otto had paved the way for her.

It was almost a carbon-copy killing of the Wekosha nightmare, with a few notable exceptions. The tendons were not cut. The rope used was the same, but the knot was a bit different. The sperm was liberally smeared about the orifices and the mutilation cuts were just as horrible, but the severed limbs were thrown across the room and lay where they had fallen. The eyes were slit, as was the jugular. And again, there was a distinct absence of blood, or even the smell of blood.

She determined first and quickly that the neck wound was once again superficial and the blood about the lips of this large wound had been smeared on, most likely with a brush. She knew instinctively that they were dealing with the same maniac.

She knew she would get no usable prints; that he worked with gloves, most likely surgical gloves. She guessed that any blood they might find would belong to the victim, that the killer hadn't so much as nicked himself.

"Found something over here," said Joe Brewer, "a capsule . . . some sort of medication."

She went to have a look. It was a red and white capsule. She asked Brewer's men to search for any matching pills, or a container, to rule if it belonged to the victim or the killer. The search turned up nothing.

"Indicating a possible connection to the killer," Jessica said. "We'll have to analyze it at the Lab."

"We can do it downtown," replied Brewer.

Jessica held her breath. She dared not hope that finally the fastidious killer had overlooked something. She would hold her prayers until the lab could tell her whether it was or was not a viable clue.

Brewer was just as anxious. He sent the capsule out immediately with strict orders that it take priority. Meanwhile, working in conjunction with Kaseem, Brewer had put together the all-points bulletin on the soldier that Kaseem sought. She was glad for this, because it kept at least one of the military guys off her back while she worked over the cadaver. Forsythe had to leave the house on two occasions, unable to hold back the meal he'd taken on the plane.

The kill was much fresher than the Copeland girl had been, and from her clothing and photos about the house, they established in a matter of minutes that the victim was a hospital nurse. Jessica felt so close to the killer now that she thought she could smell him in the room, a foul odor indeed.

She stood before the dead woman and she visualized his

movements, each in turn. He first takes control of her. He must have complete control to tie her heels and her hands and to feel the rush of superiority he requires to look upon her as an object, a container housing the fluid he wants from her. He must use an injection, possibly a powerful anesthetic. Once she is incapacitated, he ties her and rips down the chandelier and uses the naked cords to tie his rope to and hoist her up over the area where her dining room table had been before the killer pushed it over to one side. He uses a chair, but he still must be rather tall and strong to support the dangling woman while he wraps the rope round and round her heels there, pulling tight against the wire supports.

She put the chair next to the body and had Forsythe stand on it. Forsythe was six two. He had to reach to the very length of his arms to make the tie. Their killer, she reasoned, was even taller than Forsythe, perhaps six four or five. She jotted this fact down beside all the others she had learned about the killer, both from her lab work and from Otto's profiling team. The list was getting long, and for the first time, she began to see discrepancies between Kaseem's killer and her own. For one, Kaseem's man was only five nine. He'd have a near impossible time of placing the body in the position it was in, using only the chair.

She informed Kaseem of this when he returned. He was instantly dubious.

"How do you know he didn't use the table? Or a ladder?"

"Marks in the rug, here," she said, pointing. She had already had photos taken of the indentations. "They indicate the four-legged chair was used, and there are no others in the immediate area of the body."

"Just the same, my guy is very strong, a weight-lifter."

"It's not so much a matter of weight lifting as reaching." She got up on the chair, saying, "I'm over six feet up, but I could never work that rope myself."

Kaseem chose to ignore the obvious. He was convinced

that the vampire they were after was the same vampire he had encountered in West Germany. She chose then to ignore his ignorance and get on with her evidence gathering. This time, with Chicago's help, she had the latest in equipment for fingerprint finding and for dampness imaging, and the light generated by the reflective ultraviolet imager brought smudges and smears into incredible focus. The bastard's chosen the wrong place this time, she thought. Somewhere in this room he had left traces of his perspiration, and from that all she need do is establish his DNA.

She worked through the night.

At 2 A.M. she began to hear the first rumblings of another victim located in Indiana, on the outskirts of Indianapolis. Word had it that it was a young male victim, and that perhaps it had nothing whatever to do with the Zion killing; yet the victim was drained of his blood. It was yet another Tort 9, and it fell within the one-hundred-mile circumference of Chicago.

She would have to go there in the morning. Joe Brewer brought her word that Otto Boutine would catch up to her in Indiana.

Jessica wanted to strike out at the unknown, unseen assassin. She wanted to rend his tidy little world apart, threaten him as he had never been threatened before. She more and more liked O'Rourke and Schultz's suggestion to taunt him through the newspapers, and be damned with caution. She wanted to do something—*anything*—before the bastard struck again. In the space of twenty-four hours two more bodies were found. He had stepped up his killing, increased his need for victims, for blood. Why? What had changed? Or was it that he now had, along with his killing tool, a brash new attitude that he could take it when he wanted it, whenever he dared; that in fact there was no dare to it? He was feeling so far beyond capture, beyond the law and human morality, that he was flaunting his newfound power.

This is what he seemed to be saying to her. She was angry beyond words, so angry that she wanted to kill this horrible man at any cost.

Brewer drove her back toward Chicago and the Lincolnshire Inn where she was staying, fairly close to the airport. She had intended to be flying back to Virginia the following morning, but now she'd have to prevail upon Brewer's people to get her out to Indianapolis, or hire a car of her own.

She was exhausted by now and so declined Brewer's suggestion they get a bite to eat. He said he hadn't seen Otto in years, and wanted to catch up.

"You'll have plenty of time for that with Otto when he meets us in Indianapolis," she said.

"I was sorry to hear about his wife."

"Yes, so were we all."

They were just outside the inn now. "Did you know her well?"

"No, not at all, really. Except for what Otto's told me."

"Was a time I thought she was going to marry me, but she chose Otto instead."

"I didn't know."

He managed a grimacy smile that turned to a frown. "Life deals us all body blows from time to time, but this one . . . could take Otto out. He . . . well, he really loved her."

"I know that."

"Then there's nothing to the rumors . . . 'bout you and Otto?"

"Christ, Brewer, how goddamned long is the FBI grapevine?"

"I talked to Otto. He's . . . he is in love with you. You know that, don't you?"

She hadn't thought of the affection they felt for each other as love. She was unsure whether or not she wanted it to be called love, not at this time, and not with such suddenness. How did Otto know how he felt, his emotions in a complete jumble? She wasn't even sure how she felt. All she knew was that she liked it when he held her, when he had kissed her briefly, and when he had stayed overnight. She had liked how it felt to have him in the apartment. But was it love?

"Otto and I are best of friends for now . . . best of friends and we work together. Does that settle your curious mind?"

"I'm sorry if I offended you. Just wanted to tell you that I know Otto. I know he . . . that he's the kind of man who needs commitment and a real relationship and—"

"Dammit, Brewer, I thought Chicago had a Dear Abby. I don't need to stand here in the cold and listen to advice from you about my relationship with Otto." She stormed off, angry at Brewer, angry at herself, angry at Otto and the situation, but mostly angry at the Wekosha vampire, who, it appeared by the headlines in the newspapers in the lobby, had become the Chicago vampire.

She picked up a copy and took it to her room. Schultz did quite a number on the killer. He had gotten a story placed that pictured all the alleged victims of the vampire killer, along with photos of their parents where this was possible. The story told primarily of the suffering of the families left in the wake of the killer's blood letting. It was the sympathy-garnering story that Otto had approved, but as she read it, and as she thought about the vampire who slept peacefully somewhere nearby, she realized the story would gather in no sympathy from him.

Her hatred for the creature was so great that she no longer considered him human. The fact he was human—the fact he was not a freak of nature or a predatory animal—only added to the man's despicable and horrible tastes and murderous proclivities; the fact he did what he did without rage, without insanity, but with a cold, methodical and calculated process always in mind . . . this made her wish he was an animal or a mythical underworld beast.

EIGHTEEN

Even before she got to Indianapolis, Jessica learned that a task force of hundreds of law enforcement officials had been set to work on the killer of the Zion nurse. Every conceivable lead, every telephone call, every scrap of information, was being pursued tirelessly, around the clock. No call was too absurd or fantastic to respond to. The only problem was that the calls outnumbered even the hundreds upon hundreds of police officials called in on the case.

Joe Brewer had brought her up-to-date on these developments as they helicoptered to Indianapolis. He also had a lab report on the capsule found at the Zion death site. Oddly, the drug had turned out to be a potent dose of cortisone, the kind that could be had only through a prescription. Jessica knew that such a dosage was for no ordinary measure, that it meant the killer—if it belonged to him—had a serious disorder. This made her recall what Teresa O'Rourke had surmised about the killer.

"What about a print? Anything?" She knew it was unlikely.

"Not enough."

"A partial?"

"More like a smudge. A few points of reference."

She knew this fact meant an unlikely chance at any sort of computer match. Long shots seldom paid off in real life.

She returned to her thoughts about O'Rourke's uncanny assertion that the killer might well suffer from some nasty disorder of a serious physiological nature. She had to

189

consult a medical book to determine the uses for such a dose
of cortisone, and in the meantime, she asked Brewer and his
people to keep this tidbit of information in the strictest of
confidence.

"In other words," she said to Brewer point-blank, "let's
don't let it get around like the stories circulating about Otto
and me, okay?"

"Christ, Dr. Coran, I've heard nothing but the best about
you, really. I never meant to hurt you or to imply—"

"Forget about it, Inspector."

"Call me Joe."

"Fine, I'll do that. So what's the word from Otto? Will he
be waiting for us in Indianapolis, or what?"

"Something's come up that'll detain him, but he prom-
ises to make it."

"Something's come up?" She was curious, but she
doubted he knew any more than what he was told to repeat.

But Brewer volunteered, "Seems they got a letter which
he has reason to believe is from the killer."

"Really?" She tried to picture a scenario in which the
killer could have gotten the late edition of the Chicago
papers, read about himself and his heinous crimes there and
then responded as Otto had wanted him to. No, it was
impossible, given the state of the U.S. mails, and not even
Federal Express was that good. Unless the killer was
responding to stories he had read dealing with the Wekosha
killing, stories that had been wired to every newspaper
office in the country, but stories that had precious little
information in them, especially about the nature of the
brutal killings or the maniac behind them.

She shared her thoughts with Brewer, who had had his
share of dealings with brutal, sadistic killers over the years.
Brewer was almost Otto's age. Joe told her that there was no
second-guessing a madman, and that using the media to
taunt a cold-blooded killer was a lot like juggling flaming
knives, or toying with Satan, or worse, God. He did not
entirely agree on the steps that Quantico was taking, and he

flatly said that they might in effect be jeopardizing citizens in his territory. FBI headquarters was far from Chicago, and Joe feared that the Bureau sometimes forgot how easily innocent lives could be lost.

Still, the present killing spree could have nothing to do with the story placed in the Chicago papers the night before. The last two killings had been perpetrated before the story was filed, if the Indiana slaying was done by the same man.

Even before they touched down in a field across from the latest victim's house, she sensed that it was the same killer. Something about the house would have appealed to her killer. It was relatively isolated, and it had the look of a beaten-down little place. She wondered if there was something even in the homes of the victims that attracted the ''vampire.''

The view from the chopper revealed a broken-down, scavenged relic of a car in the rear, an old, tired shed, a weed patch where once there might have been a flourishing garden, some scattered barrels for burning refuse, the yard littered with trashy items, the grass in need of shearing. The house itself was a hodgepodge of construction, what had been a simple bungalow with an ill-conceived second-story addition. The Zion woman's place had had a similar, ratty appearance, old and tattered, with a porch that sagged below the men, some of whom were playing with the creaky boards as if betting on who could make the loudest squeak, when she came up the stairs, her presence silencing the talk.

Some of the local cops in tight-fitting brown outfits, and one burly biker in particular, assured Jessica that she didn't want to see what was on the inside. Others mistook her for a reporter. But she flashed her FBI badge and stepped through, asking if the coroner had been in yet.

He had, but they'd gotten word from the FBI to hold on any evidence gathering, and so they had. The coroner was busy enough that he didn't in the least mind the FBI interest, she was told.

She stepped into the dark interior, steeling herself. She

felt her backbone stiffen at the sour odors, now familiar to her. Like the Zion house, there was the distinct odor of mildew, rotten wood and decaying flesh. Walking into a corridor that had become a death trap to the young man they'd called Fowler was like walking into a gallery room created by the Devil, *and on this wall hangs the Fowler body, and beside it in the anteroom, the McDonell body, and in the drawing room, the Trent body followed by the Copeland shell.* Lovely only to the killing mind, this satanic gallery of death, filled with its awful sights and sickening odors. For a moment, she felt all alone with the black shape in the dark, silhouetted against the stairwell behind it, where it dangled: Fowler.

She could see the skinny-boy form of the body, hanging from the banister in the hallway that led to the second floor. "We got any lights?" she asked, and they instantly came up to reveal the ugly situation. The men were learning from Joe Brewer exactly who she was, about the fact she had been tracking a vampire killer since the incident in Wekosha, and that they had had another, similar case in Zion, Illinois, only the night before.

"What's known about this young man?" she asked the crowd of policemen and investigators.

"Not much," volunteered one.

"Dispatcher," said another, heavier man with a notebook that he flipped pages in, "gay, hung out at a place called Shinnola on Fourteenth and Redding in the heart of—"

"What kind of dispatcher? Trucks?"

"Trucks, ambulances—"

"Ambulances?"

"Yeah, worked at St. Luke's Hospital. Was a good worker, so everybody there says."

"Anyone see him leave the hospital with another man?"

"Negative."

She saw the familiar mutilation wounds and the lack of blood on the stairwell, the runner carpet, the wood floor and the walls. She saw the familiar hitching knot, the throat slash. It all looked on the surface like a ghastly replay, a flashback, a macabre déjà vu.

She called for Brewer who came nearer. "I'll need everything I brought in the helicopter, all the cases, all the equipment." She had borrowed Chicago's imaging system, but even with the best equipment, the search over the body and premises would take hours. Once again, the killer was far out ahead of them, still free to do this awful thing again.

Again she wondered what had precipitated the killer's sudden spree. Spree killing was not the usual serial killer's way. A spree typified the sudden snap, the leap from rational to irrational, and it typified the disorganized killer, but no amount of labeling or statistics could corner this maniac with a tracheotomy tube and a tourniquet, with his empty Pepsi bottles waiting to be refilled, with his vials of semen that he placed into his victim's orifices by hand.

She wished it were Boutine with her now instead of Brewer. She wondered what had been so important as to keep Otto. She needed his support, his strength, his nagging questions.

The place was like Wekosha in that there were too many cops freely roaming about. She had to ask Brewer to keep control of the place. She thought of what Otto had said about the killer's likely response to reading about the details of the killings in print, that it would excite him to some action which might give them a lead, however small. She silently prayed that the stories in the papers would have this effect, but some nagging doubt clung to the thought like a lamprey, sucking the life from the hope of the psychological profiling team. Whoever this guy was, she guessed that he wasn't going to "respond" as if he were a statistical symbol, that he wouldn't so easily allow them to push his buttons.

Whoever this fucking maniac was, she thought, he wasn't going to be run by any normal rules, even "normal" by deviant behavior "models." "Standards." Still, he remained a meticulous, careful bastard *before, during* and *after* he calmly took the life's blood from his victims. It made her wonder if the capsule found at the Zion murder site hadn't, after all, been planted there by the bastard, just to further confuse and confound them. Anyone who created cosmetic wounds to cover the true cause of death, anyone who intentionally faked both the sexual attack and the mutilation murder in so cool a manner, would find planting a certain drug at the scene child's play.

The Indiana victim was a male, approximate age was placed at nineteen or twenty. Her thoughts were macabre: that the killer must have read somewhere, perhaps in a medical journal, that he could get five to ten more ml./kg. of blood from a man as from a woman.

Around her she heard the investigators and Brewer discussing the matter.

"One sick puppy, this one."

"Damnedest thing I've seen in all my years."

"What's he do with the blood?"

"Could just be a copycat."

She'd know soon enough if it was a copycat killing. The straw cut to the jugular had not been in any newspaper, so if it was found in Fowler's jugular, as it had been in the Zion woman's, she knew that it was the same killer with his unique killing tool.

The men around her continued to talk and she half listened in order to keep a foot in the world of the sane as she worked in the closest of range about Fowler's throat, taking the necessary section she required for the nearest scanning electron microscope. She learned this was at the university medical complex two hours away.

Brewer was asking questions in rapid fire of the locals. "You check out all the asylums in the area?"

"Sure, first thing."

"Bring in anyone?"

"Seventeen, so far."

"Known what? Child molesters?"

"Sex offenders, deviants, cross-dressers."

Again, thought Jessica, they're looking for a sex offender. They were looking in the wrong place.

"I want you to go back to this St. Luke's and canvass the hospital, top to bottom, anyone who knew him, anyone who spoke to him yesterday, anyone who knows anything about him, even if it's just the color of his socks. Our killer picks his victims up at hospitals, we believe," Brewer told the others.

"Sure, sure . . . we'll go back over that trail."

Brewer had obviously gotten Otto to open up about the case, giving him what he needed to proceed. She went back to her evidence gathering, roping in some of Joe's men to help her set up the imaging equipment. In a matter of ten minutes the place was lit up like a white hospital corridor. The intense light made the corpse look so placidly white that it became unreal if stared at.

The meticulous work now began in earnest.

She didn't have to go to the SEM microscope to know what her senses told her, that Fowler had died at the hands of the killer they had pursued from Wekosha to here. She wanted instead to go to this hospital where Fowler worked, St. Luke's. She asked for an escort there.

Along the way, she put everything she had learned about the killer into a mental file and she scanned that file now. What kept jumping out at her was the salesman aspect, and the medical supply company possibility. Had the killer come to St. Luke's ostensibly to sell medical wares, he would have come in a van carrying his supplies and samples, possibly a gray van, but the person most likely to tell them about this was Fowler, and he was the victim.

She and Brewer, along with other FBI agents, went over the same ground as the police had earlier, pursuing any small bit of information, annoying the hospital staff, upsetting others and being asked to leave by the administrator of the hospital. The news of Fowler's tragic and horrible fate had unnerved the entire staff, and the FBI's being there only aggravated the situation, according to the officious hospital administrator, who had insisted she and Brewer be seated in his office.

"We want your records on suppliers coming into the hospital yesterday," said Brewer, not allowing the man another word.

"That would be impossible. Have you any idea how many vendors come through our doors in a given day?"

"I don't give a damn how many."

She jumped in. "You can narrow it to Chicago medical supply companies."

"That does little to help, as most of our suppliers, even those based in Indianapolis, have corporate offices in Chicago, Dr. Coran."

"Then give us a complete list."

"I don't believe there is one."

Brewer was fuming by now. "Then give us what you goddamned have!"

"Stamping about like a bull isn't going to get you anywhere with me, Inspector," said the man. "We are a hospital, and we have hospital business to conduct, and such a request—"

"Hospital business, huh? Tell me, Dr. Marchand, is it? Tell me this: Could your hospital stand an IRS audit? Could it stand an audit of credited accounts, and what about your medicine chest? Tell me, any cortisone capsules missing? Any morphine, LSD, cocaine, heroin or—"

"All right, all right," he replied shakily. "It may take some time, but I'll put my assistant to work on it immediately."

Within an hour they had a computer list that was plopped on the desk before them, as thick as a telephone book.

"You asked for them all."

NINETEEN

He was home safe now, his freezer restocked, his mind at ease, and his physical needs sated. He felt replenished by the swift taking of the boy's blood, but in those most private of private moments, in his killing mind and soul, he knew that it was not just the blood he needed, but the ritual itself, that it somehow linked him with a heritage he knew only in the innermost, deepest avenues of his psyche, a kind of traveling vampiric genetic predisposition to blood-thirst in its most primal form, and also a predisposition to administer suffering and torturous pain to his victims.

He had unloaded the van, moving from garage to house, placing all his instruments of death into the garage sink, where he routinely cleansed them of any bloody or clinging tissue. The least microscopic tissue match or blood match that might connect him with the victims could be his undoing. He knew this full well. He started the business of cleaning up, his least favorite part of the hunt for fresh prey, when fatigue overcame him.

For the first time in his killing career, he let the cleaning up go for the morning.

The office would be expecting him early tomorrow. Indiana had been trying and he had spent some desperate hours there. When the distraught young thing at the hospital did not come out of the emergency room alone, but in the company of a pair of cops who escorted her from the parking lot with flashing lights, he knew enough to not only

197

slump down in his seat there in the van where he watched them, but not to follow. He knew a curse when he saw one, and his plans for this girl had been cursed from the start.

He drove around the hospital after the police lights disappeared over a mound lined with trees. He cruised about the hospital lot like a shark surveying its waters until he saw the thin silhouette of a person draped over the front end of an I-Roc with racing stripes, the hood pointing heavenward.

His prayer was answered.

He drove up so that his window was closest to the bony, angular form in the dark, the form that held what he wanted.

"Car trouble this time of night can be a bitch," he said casually when he rolled down his window. When the young man stepped into the spray of the sodium-vapor light of the parking lot, he was instantly recognized, and so was the killer.

"Mr. Matisak? Is that you, sir?"

"Your lucky night," he said. "What do you need? A ride?"

"That's not necessary. I'll just go back inside and phone."

"You got auto club?"

"Nahhh, can't afford it when you've got payments like mine. Have to put it on my Mastercard, I guess, but where the cash'll come from, I don' know. Damned insurance is killing me."

Tommy Fowler was a fragile-looking man, effeminate in both speech and mannerism. He had long, sandy hair that cut a swath across one eye. He wore the hospital whites of an orderly, but he was too small and thin for an orderly, and so he was relegated to such duties as dispatching the shipment trucks and marking little boxes on hospital forms that indicated shipments of bed linen, towels, syringes, tubes, IV bottles, and drugs in and out of the hospital. It was on the loading dock that Tommy Fowler routinely saw Mr. Matisak, where he knew the other man as a salesman for the Balue-Stork Medical Supply out of Chicago.

There are faster ways to die, he thought but did not say. "Yeah, I know about bills," he said instead. "Look—"

"Do you know I have to work two jobs just to make—" He made a little gesture as if to pound on the hood of his shimmering white car when he stopped short, controlling the impulse, frowning. "Christ, why'm I bothering you with my troubles? Sure you got your own problems."

"Hey, Tommy, if we can't help one another out once in a while, what's it all about? You know?"

Matisak had never offered him the time of day before, Tommy was thinking. Matisak saw this behind the eyes. Matisak hurried the moment along, saying, "I've had a few setbacks lately, too." He thought of the girl in the waiting room, an hour before.

Matisak had turned up the volume a bit on the beautiful symphony that wafted from his tape deck; the strings were magnificent. He hoped that Tommy would respond to them.

Regarding him with renewed interest, Tommy said softly, "So many . . . so many slings and arrows the flesh is heir to . . . and must . . . must endure."

Matisak recognized it instantly as a flirtatious remark, and that Tommy likely got off on pain. He was playing right into his hands. He had noticed Tommy before whenever he came to the hospital, but he had never been so attracted to the kid as now. "Slings and arrows, huh? Or is it more like whips and chains the way our bosses get on our behinds?"

This made Tommy laugh lightly.

"Why don't you make your call from home, Tommy? Make it . . . easy on yourself. Hop into the van. Hell, I've got a phone in here you can use—right here."

"Hey, that'd be great."

He came around and climbed into the van as Matisak grabbed for the needle he had been holding in reserve for the girl in the waiting room. Now it was Tommy's downer. The boy would do just as well, if not better, he felt, knowing that men actually had more blood in their bodies than women.

Matthew Matisak was elated now, his heart pounding, his eyes beaming. The boy must have seen the transformation, because he put a hand out to him, taking his hand in what was ostensibly a shake but which turned into a lingering touch accompanied by a thank-you.

"It's no big thing," he replied.

"But I think it is," Tommy shot back.

He then let the boy make his phone call, allowing him to relax where he sat, allowing him to finish the call, then he pulled out the hypodermic. "You know I can get you just about anything you want, being in my line of work, Tommy. I mean stuff that'll make the world go away for a while."

Tommy grinned at this, but said, "Hey, I'm okay. I don't need anything. Life's tough, but right now, I'm clean and I . . . I sorta want to keep it that way."

"Sure, sure, I understand."

"What kinda shit you shootin' anyway?"

"New drug. Nobody's ever heard of it before."

"Cocaine base, heroin? What?"

"Can't explain its effects. Entirely new, Tommy, something developed at Balue-Stork."

"Well, I've got to be clear when those guys come for the car, or they'll take me to the cleaner's."

"Fuck the car and those guys tonight. We go to your place . . . we shoot up . . . see what develops. What do you say?"

This appealed to Tommy, but he still hesitated and finally said, "No, no, man. I'd like to but—"

Matisak saw that he was losing him. He suddenly took hold of the other man's forearm and jammed the hypo into him.

"Hey, hey, man!" shouted Tommy. "You're going to fucking pop my vein up like a balloon! I got work tomorrow! They see this and it's time to piss in a bottle and my ass is screwed! Damn you, dammit! I said no!"

"Just a little something to lift your spirits, Tommy," he told him.

"What the fuck is it? What'd you give me?" Tommy plunged out the door on his side, nearly falling. He stumbled around, a little, girlish whimper escaping him, his eyes bulging with fear and confusion. It was a look that fed Matisak, a look that made him brave and arrogant and evil all at once. He climbed down from his side of the van going through what he must do methodically in his mind when he met Tommy there in front of his car, the two men staring at each other, and Tommy coming to realize that there was something more in Matisak's interest in him than helping an acquaintance, or in going to bed with him; there was something primal in his eyes, and there was a scalpel in his hands.

"What-thaa-hell-ah-ya-doing?" Tommy's speech was slurred along with his vision. "Whaa-was-sat-stuff? Whaa-kinda-stuff-ya?" Tommy pulled away from him, but the potent drug was already coursing through his brain, spinning him like a top. He wheeled and fell between his car and the next, dragging himself along. He felt a pair of powerful hands tearing at his pants leg and shoe. Felt the shoes come off and the socks torn away, but by now it was all as unreal as a dream and he no longer felt the sensation of being held down, and he didn't feel it when the scalpel severed the tendons of both heels.

He didn't feel himself being hefted up like a potato sack by the stronger, larger man, nor the pain of an abrasion to the forehead when he was unceremoniously thrown into the rear of Matisak's recently waxed light silver-gray van. He felt only darkness as Matisak tore his wallet and keys from him. Matisak recouped the shoes and socks, leaving only the small trail of bloodstains that dotted the concrete from the I-Roc to where the back of his van had stood. He then went to the I-Roc, disengaged the alarm with the beeper on the key chain and reached inside for what he wanted, coming out with a garage door opener. This was all done to the sound of the Chicago Symphony Orchestra, the beautiful

music wafting up the side of the hospital to the windows
there.

He scanned the windows for any sign of someone's
having seen what had occurred here. He saw no one. There
were only a handful of lit windows at this hour of the night.
He looked in all directions around him. No one.

He next slid back into the driver's seat of the van, where
he popped a fresh tape into the player, looked over his
shoulder at his prize, and said, "I just want a little blood,"
and then he casually drove out of the lot.

A mile away, he turned off the road, brought up his lights
and read Tommy's ID card for his address. He hoped it
would be a suitable place for gathering up Tommy's blood;
he hoped Tommy lived alone; he hoped the rest of the night
would go with ease.

And it had, save for a little trouble finding a suitable place
to hang Tommy in the necessary position. The drugs had
worn off by then and Tommy had come around to find
himself with a tourniquet around his neck, hanging upside
down and nude. Thus far he had not been scarred or
mutilated in any other way than the cutting of the tendons—a
precaution—and the near microscopic incision to the jugular where now the spigot dangled, held firm by adhesive
tape. He could feel the spigot below his chin and just barely
see its end, but he could clearly see the mason jar filling up
before his eyes where Matt Matisak held it below the tap in
his jugular. The loss of blood further dizzied and over-
whelmed Fowler.

Matisak was halfway through filling a jar of blood when
Fowler began to thrash, spilling some of the vital juice,
staining the cheap, imitation oriental rug below the banister
of the stairs leading to the second floor. This made Matisak
curse. He then stopped the flow of blood, turning off the
thumb-tack-sized dial of the spigot and tightening the
tourniquet until Tommy choked.

Tommy began crying, blubbering incoherently. Matisak
told him, "I thought you were into pain, Tommy."

His voice choked off, his eyes alone pleading with the mad Matisak, Fowler left the killer no choice. He turned his scalpel on the young man's eyes, swiping at them, making him flinch. But he did not want to cut his eyes. Not yet, anyway. He didn't want to open another wound in this section of the body. It would reduce the powerful flow at the jugular, and it would cause a bigger loss than the spill Tommy had caused.

He just needed to calm Tommy down. He looked for the hypodermic he had prepared, found the milder dose of barbiturate and plunged this into Tommy's tied arm. It was enough of a dose to keep the other man lulled, until the blood-taking was complete. He didn't have time for games, not this time.

Afterward, he slashed the eyes, as he did with all his victims; not because he had an eye fetish, or because he didn't want the victim to see him, or as some shrink would have it, put out the eyes to save the poor victim from the sight of his own dying, but because it would confound police authorities.

With the same cold logic, with Tommy long dead now, he went to work on the genitals and limbs using his power tools. Once he was satisfied with this work, he looked into his case for the sable-hair paintbrush. To the sound of a light drizzle against the panes of the little house, Teach painted the bloodless open wounds, sucking in the odor of the blood as he dipped the brush into the jar and moved it across Tommy Fowler's throat.

It had become late by then, and he must get back to Chicago. But he mustn't rush too wildly. He mustn't leave anything of himself behind.

Now that Matisak was home from his Indiana run, he stared into a picture of Tommy Fowler, a photograph he had found in the young man's home. He smiled at the memories and placed the photo on a large board filled with the photos of his other victims on the wall in his old grandfather's and his father's den, which was now his den. He sat back and

gazed into the faces of his victims, reliving the moments at
the end that he had spent with each, the moment he literally
held their lives in his hand.

Maybe a bath before turning in would be nice, he thought.
He had enough blood now, for a while anyway.

Yes, a bath would be refreshing.

He allowed the dirty tools, for once, to sit.

TWENTY

The following day Matthew Matisak was awakened by a telephone call, and assuming that it was Mr. Sarafian at the office, he let it ring several times before answering. But it wasn't Sarafian, it was Lowenthal. Maurice Lowenthal stirred him to consciousness with a jolt when he said, "I thought you ought to know, I sent in for the patent on the spigot mechanism. It was the only safe thing to do, Matisak; otherwise, if the idea is stolen from us, we have no recourse, and with you routinely showing it about, anyone could pirate the idea."

Lowenthal was retired now, and with time on his hands he had drawn up sketches and explanations of the device that Matisak was using for his killing purposes.

"When?" he asked. "When did you send the design in for the patent."

"These things take forever—"

"When?"

"—the paperwork is impossible."

"When, damn you?"

"Six months ago, right after I retired. Balue-Stork has no claim on my genius any longer."

"You can make no reference to me in the papers, Maurice. If you do, it becomes the property of Balue-Stork. Do you understand this?"

"I couldn't use your name, so long as you're employed at the Medical Supply. It would leave us open to a lawsuit."

"Of course not." And thank God, he thought.

"You're still under contract to Balue-Stork. But they don't control me or my ideas any longer."

"You should have consulted with me first."

"I'm doing that now, partner."

You fucking Jewish idiot, he wanted to say, but he instead stifled the urge, saying nothing.

"What's wrong? I thought you would be pleased? Do you want someone to rip us off?"

There was nothing he could do about it at this point. It was done. He tried desperately to calm down. "When do you expect to hear back from the Patent Office?"

"It's impossible to say. I was hoping that by now—"

"All right."

"I'm really surprised at your attitude."

He thought fast. "You just caught me off guard, Lowenthal."

"If you wish, I could call them, ask about the delay."

"No, no! You'd probably just anger them . . . seem pushy and they'd only delay it longer."

"Have you given any idea to how we will market our little fluid drainer?"

"Through my usual accounts, at first, until we get word around." *Lowenthal must go,* he was thinking as he spoke to the man. "Are you keeping an accurate record . . . of your dealings with the Patent Office? Your designs?"

"Yes, yes, of course I am. And what about you?"

"What do you mean?"

"The prototype, of course!"

"Oh, yes."

"So how is it performing? Any complaints from Dr.— what was his name in Indiana?"

"Grubber."

"Ahhh, yes, Grubber. So?"

"It has delighted Grubber to no end."

"Excellent. Then we do stand a chance to make some money, after all?"

"Of course we do. Perhaps we should get together soon,

say tonight, go over the details. I'd like to see what you've sent on to the patent people."

"I've sent a copy of the design, of course, and an explanation of the use. There's no reason whatever we shouldn't be granted the patent."

"I'd just like to see your file on it, okay, Maurice?"

"Yes, well, of course. Tonight, about seven? You'll come here?"

"I'll see you then."

As he hung up, he reaffirmed his feelings. Lowenthal must go. But how to do it so as to cast no suspicion on himself, that was the important consideration, the one that would occupy Teach's brain all day.

Later in the day, he went into the corporate offices in suburban Elmhurst, Illinois, where he deposited new orders that he had taken in Indiana and Zion. His boss, Mr. Sarafian, caught sight of him as he was leaving with a handful of memos and orders that he must attend to. Sarafian asked after his health and told him that he looked quite pale, asked if the "road" was taking too much of a toll on him.

"No, no, sir, I love my work," he said, mustering as much enthusiasm as he could find.

"You read about that poor woman in Zion, Matt?"

Matisak stared back, his face showing complete confusion. "Woman in Zion?"

"Hell, you must've heard about it. It's on every radio station in Chicago. Sonofabitch hung her up by her heels and cut her throat and drained her of every ounce of blood, like she was a slaughter animal."

"I don't listen to the radio."

"Oh, yeah, tapes—symphonies, right. You told me before. But you must've seen the papers this morning."

He had seen the *Tribune,* which was delivered to his doorstep, and he had read the stories, but he again feigned ignorance, his shoulders hunched.

Mr. Sarafian walked with him to the office shared by the

salesmen who came and went. He asked Matisak, ''You were in Zion, and you were at the same friggin' hospital where she worked, Matisak. You really ought to read the story. He plunked down a copy of the *Sun-Times* onto the desk where Matisak sat.

Matt Matisak perused the story while his boss stood over him.

''Any chance you might've seen anything out there that night the cops'd be interested in, Matt?''

''I . . . No, nothing. I didn't know the woman. Says here she was killed at her home.''

He glanced over Renee's photo, a picture of her in her white nurse's uniform.

''Damned cops haven't got a clue. Brought in the FBI.''

He scanned for the letters F-B-I in the news account, and for the name of Dr. Jessica Coran. She was there, in the morning edition. The *Trib* hadn't had this information. The FBI broad had flown into Zion as she had Wekosha. She recognized his work. Someone recognized his hand in both killings, what the FBI would call his ''signature.'' It had been a carefully orchestrated signature, to throw them off his trail. Zion had been too close to home. He should have resisted his urges. Now here he was, sitting before his boss, who had records that showed that he was in Zion the night Renee was drained of her life.

He controlled the panic he felt welling up. How much did the FBI know? How much did Coran know? The story was not saying; the reporters didn't know what Coran knew.

What did she know?

''They'll never catch this guy,'' he said to Sarafian suddenly.

''Why do you say that?''

''They don't have a clue—not a clue! Can't you read?''

''Cops aren't going to spread out their cards in the papers, Matt.''

''Ahh, what do I care. Has nothing to do with me,'' he said, and returned to the importance of his new orders, and thoughts of Lowenthal's goddamned patent, and the problems he faced there.

He wondered if his writing to Dr. Jessica Coran had been self-destructive and foolish.

He wondered how he could cloak himself, as he was feeling naked before Sarafian, as if even a fool like Sarafian could see that he was staring at the so-called Chicago vampire.

"So, Matt . . . ah." It wasn't like Sarafian to be nervously talking.

"Yes?"

"You seeing a dermatologist? You know, for your face and hands?"

"Yes. Now, if you will please let my personal life *be* my personal life!" Matisak instinctively hid his hands, but what could he do about his face?

"Hey, Matisak, when your *appearance* begins to affect your performance, then it's no longer a personal matter, it's a business matter—and that's my only concern."

"Have you had complaints about my appearance?"

"Some, yes."

"From whom?"

"A hospital administrator in Iowa—"

"Bullshit."

"A physician in Kansas City."

"Is that all, Mr. Sarafian?"

"Just a little friendly advice, Matt. You can't be an effective salesman in dark glasses, below that hat of yours with . . . with scales on your face. You either improve in this department of grooming or you may face a firing."

"Fire me on those grounds and I'll sue this goddamned place for every dime I can get."

Sarafian stormed out, and Matisak was glad to see him go. He was all bluff and thunder and bullshit. No matter what anyone said, Matisak was Balue-Stork's top salesperson. He had proven that over and over again.

He turned his attention once more to Lowenthal and to

Dr. Jessica Coran, possibly the only two people on the globe that could conceivably place him with the murder weapon or on the scene. It was, he believed, elimination time . . . or a time for simple diversion. A little sleight of hand, a bit of smoke and mirrors. Perhaps he need only kill Lowenthal and convince Coran that he, Lowenthal, was the vampire.

With his ridiculous patent, Lowenthal had signed his own death warrant.

At seven that evening, Matthew Matisak arrived at the home of Maurice Lowenthal. It was a small bungalow filled with bric-a-brac, the lights muted, and on the shelves were hundreds of books, mostly medical and scientific books, but some fiction and biographies and histories. Lowenthal had a book on the coffee table in his little living room, a marker deep in its pages. The book was about the latest discoveries of an oceanographer, the man who had located both the sunken *Bismarck* and the *Titanic,* Robert Ballard. Matisak almost reached out for it, but remembered not to touch anything. Outside, he had used his elbow to ring the doorbell.

Lowenthal offered tea, and so he had accepted. Matisak looked about for the file containing the information on the patent. He didn't see it readily lying about as he had hoped. Once more he silently cursed Lowenthal.

Lowenthal reentered the room with two steaming cups of liquid.

"How're you enjoying retirement?" he asked, taking the cup and saucer gingerly into his possession, his mind flashing snapshot-fashion on the invisible prints forming on the porcelain dishes.

"I feared it would be a tremendous bore, and it is. But I've managed to keep busy—reading, doing some writing, even! Always wanted to do some writing."

"Really? About your experiences at the lab?"

"That, yes, but I've kind of gotten off on a tangent—

gone self-indulgent, I suppose—writing about myself, my innermost thoughts, that sort of thing. Asking questions that defy answer.''

"Careful," said Matisak, looking around, "that can prove dangerous."

"To the suicidal, perhaps, but I'm a survivor, Matt. Always have been, and when something comes along to excite my interest, say like our little invention—"

"Yes, well, that's why I'm here. Where is . . . where are the papers you've drawn up?"

"In a safe place, trust me."

"But you said we would go over them tonight." His voice rose out of control.

Lowenthal put up his hands as if he were being held at gunpoint. He got up quickly, paced the room and grimaced, saying, "We are equal partners in this, and we can have the papers drawn up. But as for me, I trust you, Matisak, regardless of whether you trust me or not." He reached for his tea, took a sip and sat back down all in one easy motion. He was comfortable with his place, his things.

Matisak guessed that the only reason he had gotten involved in the "patent" was to keep busy, to, as he had said, have something to do. Once involved, he was excited by the prospects of the instrument that he had designed. It had become for Lowenthal a shining example of how he could help suffering humanity, something he could leave behind so that his life might count for something.

"So, Maurice, are we going to go over the details tonight, or not?"

"Really, what's to go over? I've completed the technical drawings and copy, including the new materials, so that you don't get that wobbling effect, you know, when you insert the tube, so that it doesn't pull on the vessel you attach it to. You told me that was a problem; that you had to use adhesive tape, remember? All that's been worked out. And with your records, showing its usefulness, what more is there to say? Did you bring some notes?" he asked, indicating the briefcase that Matisak had brought in with him.

"Yes, a few," he lied.

"I'll be happy to go over them with you."

"You must think I'm a fool, Lowenthal."

"What?"

"You plan to take over this entire idea, gaining the patent in your name, and—"

"I only did so because I'm no longer associated with Balue-Stork. If I used your name—"

"Then my name is nowhere on the patent papers?"

"Absolutely not, but that doesn't mean we can't have papers drawn up to indicate that we are equal partners."

"Good, all right," he said, calming. "My sentiments exactly. So, where are the patent papers?"

"My safety-deposit box."

"I thought so."

"There's no safer place for them."

Matisak nodded, got to his feet and snapped open the briefcase, snatching forth a manila file folder, handing it to Lowenthal, who began to scan the typed words, flipping through. All of the information was bogus, but Lowenthal didn't know that.

"This is remarkable. It can be used then for water on the knee, fluid on the brain, fluid in the lungs. This news is wonderful! Wonderful!"

"While Lowenthal read, Matisak removed the surgical gloves, the chloroform and the scalpel from his briefcase and slowly moved around to the other side of the couch where Lowenthal sat hunched over the papers.

With Lowenthal's back to him, he poured some of the pungent liquid into a handkerchief and suddenly pressed this to Lowenthal's eyes, nose and mouth. The other man struggled and kicked, the manila folder and its contents flying like loose pigeons before his feet until he fell unconscious on the sofa.

All was going as planned. Matisak slipped on his surgical

gloves and remained behind the man now under his power. He felt a great elation come welling up from within him, and he pitied the fact he could not take Lowenthal's blood, but he quickly rationalized this away because it was an old man's blood; besides, he needed the blood to be spilt.

Holding the slumping figure up, leaning in over his shoulder, Matisak lifted the man's left forearm, and with his own right hand and scalpel, Teach Matisak taught Lowenthal a valuable lesson. He severed the arteries of the left wrist. The blood gushed from the deep wound. And now Teach lifted Lowenthal's right forearm and, using his left hand and the scalpel in it, he carved the right wrist. In so doing, no one, not even Jessica Coran, could tell that someone other than Lowenthal himself had done the cutting.

The hard part was watching the sad waste of the red fluid as it made wine stains in the man's clothing and spread over the weave of his flowered couch. The blood odor made him pant.

Matisak had some additional details to take care of. He pressed the dying man's right index finger and thumb around the handle of the scalpel, and then he repeated the process with the other hand. Some blood had smeared on the scalpel, but the dead man's prints ought to be clear.

Matisak, keeping the gloves on, retrieved his teacup and saucer as Lowenthal continued to bleed to death on the sofa where he now slumped over. In the kitchen he washed the cup and saucer, dried them and put them away. The dishwater also cleaned his gloves of blood, so he wouldn't be leaving any telltale bloody finger marks on a doorknob or door facing.

Lowenthal lived in a silent little neighborhood on the North Side of Chicago where the houses were older than Matisak. There were no children or dogs or young people strolling about, only an occasional old man with a cane. The street was tree-lined. Trash cans had been put out on the street for the next day's pickup. Matisak's van in

Lowenthal's driveway drew no attention, and most windows were lit with the shimmery blue light of TV screens. Teach stepped back out into the night and surveyed the neighborhood from the front porch, where Lowenthal had hung a little swing. He cautiously went down to his van and unloaded what he had brought with him, evidence for the authorities. He had left the cutting tools dirty in his sink the night before without reason or good cause, but now he found good cause.

He returned to the house with the box of instruments he had used on successive victims. Inside the house again, he found that Lowenthal had moved, or had fallen, his body slumped over the suicide note, his remaining tea dripping over the edge, mingling with his blood.

Still using the gloves, careful to leave no prints, he located the other man's basement door, found a light switch and calmly moved down the steps. They creaked below his weight.

He located matching tools where he could for the ones that he had brought, exchanging these, hanging his on nails and placing his on shelves where he found replaceable ones. Lowenthal's stuff was top quality, like his own. The man knew machinery. But now Lowenthal's would be caked with the blood of the Indiana boy, Fowler, still nasty with chewed flesh. And when the authorities found the old man's body, they'd also find his sketches of the spigot and the patent application papers in his safe-deposit box, and they'd find his suicide note, a note that Matisak had written in Renee's blood from the inkwell with his quill pen, all of which he had brought with him.

And so they would have their nasty old Chicago vampire in Lowenthal, and Teach could go for some time on the supply of blood that he had, allowing things to cool a bit, just so that Dr. Jessica Coran was satisfied that she had gotten the man she wanted.

It was a perfectly orchestrated plan of genius, killing two problems with one suicide. The only drawback was losing his grandfather's quill pen, but this couldn't be helped. He knew that the FBI could not be fooled by a substitute, and since he had written the earlier letter to Coran with it, he must sacrifice this.

When he returned from the basement, he saw that Lowenthal was fully dead and that the suicide could not look more authentic. The only missing ingredient was the letter, the inkwell and the pen. As far as stocking Lowenthal's refrigerator with blood, he wasn't about to give up everything for the plan. He had brought two pints. If this did not suffice, so be it. The authorities would simply decide that he had another hiding place for the blood, or that his appetite for it was completely insatiable.

He surveyed the work, ticking off each detail, going through his plan as he had a hundred times throughout the day. With the blood in the freezer compartment, he decided that his work was done, save for the letter. This he pulled from his briefcase, little blood flecks popping off it as he moved it into place, atop the coffee table amid splatters of Lowenthal's blood.

It looked perfect there.

He left with his new tools, glancing back at Lowenthal's body where it had eerily slumped over the coffee table.

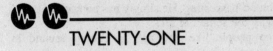

TWENTY-ONE

Jessica Coran had had to spend another day and night in Chicago, poring over the list of pharmaceutical companies and hospital supply companies in the Chicago-land area. The list was endless. Pages upon pages, and none of the names—in and of itself—was of help. Still, she narrowed the firms down to the several hundred who either distributed or made their own surgical equipment.

She had telephoned HQ in Quantico and had gotten J.T., who sounded a little strange, but when she asked him what was going on, all he said was, "Be careful out there, Jess."

She tried to get him to talk, but he dove into the case with some new twist that might have been the cause of the shakiness in his voice. "Robertson says the semen samples taken from Wekosha are definitely from a different man than those you sent from Zion."

"What about the Indiana killing? I sent the samples earlier today. You get them?"

"Just got in the door, but from first scoping, I'd have to say no connection with Wekosha. That means no DNA match. That means—"

"I know what it means, John!" She sounded more caustic than she meant to. "I think I know what it means."

"Sound tired."

"That's an understatement. Look, J.T., suppose for a moment that the guy who did the Copeland killing, the Trent and the McDonell killings was the same guy as our Zion guy. It's not a sex-lust killing in the usual sense with this

217

guy, since his lust is not to fulfill any sexual fantasy but a fantasy of blood-harvesting. He simply has no need of sex.''

"Then why the semen at all?''

"To keep people like you and me going around in circles.''

"So he gets the semen from other men? I don't get it.''

"Goddammit, he's impotent. He's in and out of hospitals until he becomes a known fixture. We know he's likely using medical apparatus—tourniquets, tubes maybe, cortisone in potent dosage, and quite possibly narcotics. He knows his way around hospitals. So he knows where the sperm bank is.''

"Ahhhh, gotcha.''

"Men.''

"What?''

"You can be so thick.''

"Thick?''

"So he doesn't like playing with girls in that way, only killing them by syphoning away their lives through a tube.'' The thought of such a killer made her feel once more for his various victims, and with the body count spiraling upward, she feared for his next victim. Her hatred of the killer grew by steady leaps.

She asked if he could transfer her to Boutine's office, complaining she'd heard nothing from him.

He said he'd transfer the call, but came on again complaining that Boutine was unavailable at the moment. She said goodbye to J.T., who seemed reluctant to hang up.

That had been at 4 P.M., some time after she and Joe Brewer had gotten back to the Chicago bureau. Now she was back at the Lincolnshire Inn, where she had a message waiting from Boutine. He was flying in. He left the number on the jet where he could be reached.

She telephoned from her room immediately.

It was wonderful to hear the strong timbre of Otto Boutine's voice again, but after the amenities, she learned why J.T. was acting so strangely, and why Otto had been kept tied up at Quantico. A letter had arrived there addressed to her, a letter which may have come from the killer. J.T. had taken receipt of the letter, and finding it odorous and suspicious, he had taken it to Boutine, who had ordered it opened. Boutine had an instant impression that it was genuine, and so he and J.T. had run it through Documents for any clues to the identity of the killer. Dried flecks of blood from the lettering had accumulated like rust in the bottom of the envelope, and these were cross-matched with those of the known victims, and the blood had been matched with Candy Copeland's after other chemical components had been separated out.

"What other chemical components?"

"Ahhh, blood had been mixed with an anticoagulating agent, so as to have more of an inky quality."

"Mixed with India ink?"

"Not quite."

"What, then?"

"Same components as in correction fluid, nail polish."

Jessica took this all in with full gulps of air. "Tell me about the paper it was written on. Any clues there?"

"Cheap, ordinary office stock."

"Copier paper?"

"Yeah, nothing special about it."

"And the handwriting?"

"Printing. Our boy's crafty."

"The pen?"

"Done with an old-style quill pen."

"Want to hear it, or wait until I get there?"

She knew the original would not leave Quantico; that he had a copy. "Go ahead," she said, although she didn't want to hear it. Over the phone, from the jet, Otto's reading of it was not enough, even verbatim. She listened intently, trying to penetrate beyond the words, to read between the lines. But she needed to see every word before her. Even so, each word took on its own chilling new meaning for her. And when the killer ended by saying that perhaps one day they might meet, that he might one day take a little of her blood, she had heard enough, and she understood why J.T. was acting as he had at the other end of the phone. He'd been ordered to say nothing of this to her, obviously by Boutine, who, as it appeared, wished to break it to her his way. He hadn't wanted her to spend the day with this additional monkey on her back; and he had wanted the letter completely analyzed before she learned about it.

He had no idea she had gotten an inkling of it through Brewer. And she kept it that way.

She had never been directly addressed by a maniac before, and this one was a level 9 torturer, a blood-drinker, Otto's Tort 9 who wanted some of *her* blood. It was like hearing his ugly voice and being touched by his ugly hand, as if she were one of his victims. The letter was a vile document, and yet it seemed to excite Boutine; for him, it was the most important single clue to finding the killer yet; for him, the killer had finally made a mistake, exposing himself for the first time.

"If he writes once, he'll write again, just as he'll kill again," said Boutine with certainty.

She didn't want to tell Boutine that she didn't want any more love letters from a human vampire. She instead told him of what they had found in Indiana and about the cortisone clue found in Zion.

"Both killings match up with our guy?"

"No doubt in my mind."

"I'll call Hector Rodriguez at the *Tribune* to print another story, and this time we'll tell the world the guy is gay, that he's a momma's boy, anything we can think of to keep him on edge."

"I'm not convinced that using the press is going to rattle this guy. He wrote that letter to me before he read anything of any substance in the *Tribune*. All they had was the useless info coming out of Wekosha, and that was pretty paltry stuff."

''The team's decided, Jess. This is the best way to go now.''

''Then why not go all the way? Really shake him up.''

''How do you mean?''

''Give it out that the killer is suffering from a rare disease—''

''Rare disease? What rare disease?''

''I've talked to several doctors here that agree with me that the level of dosage this guy's taking in the form of cortisone can be for any number of illnesses, but the one disease that would fixate our boy on a vampire obsession might be Addison's disease. This means he's very sensitive to cold, and that he's probably got large, lumpy areas on his back and buttocks. That's pretty personal shit. He's likely to have a large, oval face, big jowls.''

''Symptoms of the disease?''

''Exactly.''

''Yeah, I can see where this might shake this guy loose a bit, put a dent in his methodical armor.''

''And there's something else.''

''Shoot.''

''He really is impotent.''

''How do you know that for certain, Jessica?''

''He's stealing sperm from other men.''

''What? Say again.''

''He's using other men's semen—''

''The semen of other men? The lab tell you that?''

''In each case, the semen has been different, so there's no way we can get a DNA match on this guy's semen sample. The semen he's smearing into the orifices by hand is coming out of . . . test tubes or something. Taken from sperm banks or something.''

''He's getting drugs and semen samples from hospitals he visits,'' said Boutine. ''Then why not simply steal the blood he needs and wants from the same source?''

''It's not just blood he wants.''

''Of course not.''

"He wants power, supreme power over others. He wants to enjoy the blood-taking the old-fashioned way, and he can't do that by rifling blood banks."

"A real throwback, huh?"

"You got it. And Otto, we may's well really stick it to this creep."

"How so?"

"Give the papers the tube; the fact he plunges a nasty little straw into the victim's jugular and sucks out the blood through a tube and carries off most of the blood in jars."

"How do we know it's jars?"

"Easier to handle than packs in the situation. Mason jars, I suspect."

"Be as specific as we dare, huh?"

"The jars alone will unnerve the bastard, and possibly make him do something to flash who he is."

"But we're giving away a lot, and it'll draw the cranks like flies."

"We're holding back enough to discredit any professional confessors," she said. "Besides, stories about his manhood aren't going to bother this guy. He's sexless. His only sex is getting off on the torture and the blood he swallows, don't you see? So attacking his manhood isn't going to bother him in the least. And one more thing."

"Yeah?"

"He's targeted me, and he's going to know that I'm the one saying these things about him."

"Yeah, that worries me, Jess."

"Worries hell out of me, too, but I don't see we have much of an alternative. This guy's really stocking up for Christmas in his personal blood bank account. We've got to make an offensive move, lead with our knight."

"Suppose you're right. I'll see to it."

"How soon will you arrive?"

"Before dawn. I'll meet you there. Get some rest."

"You, too. And good night, Otto."

"Good night, Jess."

The news of the letter left Jessica shaken, but she hadn't wanted Otto to sense this, and so she covered it well. She was just relieved that he was coming to her.

In the meantime, Brewer's Chicago task force had every available law enforcement officer in the city looking into hospital records and asylum releases, and by way of the P.P. team's suggestion, all medical supply companies. Still, there were so bloody many in the area, it might take months to narrow it down to just the right one where their killer worked.

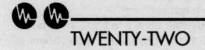

TWENTY-TWO

Otto Boutine had grown up on a weedy little farm that was aspiring to be a ranch near Bozeman, Montana. It had been a rough life, filled with hardships, but amid the difficulties there was a great affection between himself and his parents, and the life had taught him self-reliance and resourcefulness. He was raised on chores. He was responsible from a very young age for firewood, hay for the horses, the scut work around the barn, grazing the mares and helping during foldings. His memories were filled with some very good times. But they all ended in harshness.

A spate of bad luck plagued the small ranch when his mother fell ill. Diagnosed with cancer, she did not last long. It was after her passing that Otto learned just how much his father and his father's business depended upon the wisdom and guidance of his mother. The place went downhill like a California mud slide and there was nothing his father could do to help; in fact, the more Herman Boutine did, the worse his situation became. With the loss of his wife and the financial setbacks, Otto watched his father decline.

The place had had to be put up for auction, and Otto and his father watched every personal belonging go up for sale. The loss of their home was the final blow for Otto's father. All life had soured for the man, and he could see no use in the future, and no amount of talking to him seemed to matter. Otto watched him pull a cloak around himself, a

225

shroud, and in his living death he was never able to free himself from this shroud again.

He was soon in the hospital, unable to pay for the bed in which he lay. He died there within forty-eight hours of entering the hospital, hating every second of his ''welfare stay'' as he called it. Otto was not quite eighteen at the time, but he had won a scholarship to attend the University of California at Berkeley, and so, after burying his father, he left Bozeman and never looked back.

That had been in 1963, the year that John F. Kennedy was assassinated. The assassination that touched so many lives turned his attention toward law enforcement and the FBI in particular. At Berkeley he pursued a course of study that would lead him into criminal justice. Along the way he had met a young, brash lawyer named Marilyn Amesworth. They married and before them lay a beautiful life, their love for one another the great support in his life. And then she was struck down. And now he had buried his wife.

So here he was on an FBI-owned Learjet bound for Chicago as much to get to Jessica Coran as to put an end to a case which, it appeared, was shaping up to be the most important case in his career. Word about the corridors of FBI headquarters at Quantico had it that he was emotionally crippled by his latest personal bout with death; that the case should be handled by someone else, someone stronger and younger. Leamy had made it all quite clear: Boutine had twenty-four hours in which to show some break in the deadlocked case, or he was off it.

He wondered about his own deepest motives for racing to Jessica now. Ostensibly, it was to share the wording of the letter from this madman calling himself Teach, and most people would accept that. Ostensibly, his rushing away from pressing duties in Virginia to be at her side was due to the obvious threat the killer posed to Jessica. But if he were honest with himself, it was a desperate action. But was he more desperate to be with Jessica or to be nearby when she broke the case? For he had little doubt that Jess would bring about the break in the case they needed.

Still, his feelings for her were undeniable. He wondered if he should not declare them to her. He wondered if he dared.

Marilyn had been gone from him long before her actual clinical death. The lingering coma had sapped him of hope, reducing him to the little boy who watched his father's slow death. He needed someone to turn to, someone who would take the pain away, draw it off the way Jessica did, sometimes without her even knowing.

Was he acting like a fool? Would Jessica respond to him? Would she understand his needs? Or would she confuse them with motives of a different nature?

The hum of the engines was like the thinking of God, deep and resonant and peaceful but also unfathomable. He let the black-and-white copy of the letter from Teach slip from his grasp and onto the circular tabletop as his head fell back and he rested his eyes just for a moment before falling into a deep slumber.

He dreamed of Jessica.

Otto Boutine arrived at her door, and she welcomed him in. He had come alone except for the copy of the letter he had on his person, and it seemed like there was a third person in the room—the killer.

She went to the kitchenette and brewed them coffee. Otto spread the letter out on the table, saying that Documents was picking it apart, along with several shrinks and as many of his P.P. team as he was able to get back to Quantico. Byrnes was still in Wekosha, where he had uncovered very little new information, except for the fact that a guy with a medical supply company had made some purchases in the town at a music store, tapes of classical music primarily. The name of the place was Pernell's Music Emporium. A weak description of the man was of very little help, but it supported much of the theorizing that the P.P. team had done: the killer was in his late twenties or early thirties, a medical supply salesman of some sort, quiet and wallflowerlike, if not a regular shrinking violet.

With their coffee and the strange letter from Teach between them, the two FBI agents discussed its deeper meaning.

"I'm worried about this, Jess," he admitted. "It means that he's picked you from a crowd. Of all the hundreds of law enforcement people involved in this case, he has fixed his bloody attention on you. Gives me the chills, just thinking about it."

"Hasn't done much for my digestion either," she admitted. "Or my beauty sleep."

He had noticed that she'd been staring at the TV from the couch rather than in her bed when he had come in. "That's why I flew out. Christ, Jess, J.T.'s analysis of the blood scrapings—"

"What? What about them?"

"The blood on the letter matches Copeland's in every detail."

"Bastard," she muttered. "Pisses away the dead girl's blood, uses it for ink . . . God knows what other uses he makes of it."

"A real Marquis de Sade. Wouldn't be surprised if he bathed in it," he said. "So, little wonder I got worried about you out here. Called Joe Brewer personally to ask him to stick by you."

"Oh, he did that."

"That jerk didn't make a pass at you, did he?"

"Not quite."

"Meaning?"

She frowned and shrugged. "It was nothing."

"Jess?"

"He . . . he asked about our relationship."

Otto dropped his gaze. "He's not the only one asking."

"I told him we were just best of friends."

"And we are," he replied, reaching across to her hand

and covering it. "But I've had . . . hopes . . . that we might be more to one another . . . someday."

She covered his hand in hers. "I've had similar . . . hopes."

"So I came a thousand miles to be with you."

She stared at him, trying to uncover the unspoken words here. "Against orders? Not against Leamy's holy wishes, I hope."

"No, nothing like that," he said, but there seemed to be something hidden in his tone.

"What, then?"

"Someone's been spreading stories about . . . well, about you and me, Jess." He scratched nervously behind his ear, and she saw that he was exhausted.

She frowned, but leaned across to him and kissed him. "Can you blame anyone for talking? There's some fire in this smoke . . . isn't there?"

"There is . . . a fire."

"Brewer . . . some of your friends . . . are just worried it's too soon after Marilyn. Afraid I'll not be good for you or your career. And maybe, maybe they're—"

"—wrong," he finished for her, kissing her deeply, probing her mouth with his tongue.

She felt her passion for him rise like the energy above an open flame; she felt as if all her inner turmoil and emotional conflict, the horrendous nature of her long, defeating search for the killer, the stress of being in charge of a forensics division of the largest law enforcement agency in the world—all of it melted within her, turning to an invisible, yielding mist that drained off her mind, to be replaced with his touch.

She could feel, also, Otto's inner trembling as he gave into his need for her. He tenderly held her, his mouth hungrily exploring hers, until suddenly he swept her up and carried her into the bedroom, where he softly placed her against the pillows. The earlier darkness of the room had been too heavy and somber and cold, but now it was as if a ray of morning light had filtered in. She could see Otto clearly over her, his features distinct and his eyes probing. She reached up and helped him tear away his shirt, her nails going into his flesh, making him arch toward her. She lifted her mouth to his chest and suckled at him, making him groan. She lay back and opened her robe to him.

"I need you, Jess," he moaned into her ear when he eased himself over her nude form.

"And I need you," she replied, wishing that he'd said "I love you," instead. A part of Otto was still being held in check; a part of him was elsewhere. But she gave herself to him without reservation, praying that it would be enough for him, and that his coming to her like this would never be to his regret.

She pleased him.

She surprised him.

She soon realized that he would never regret tonight.

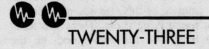

TWENTY-THREE

       The discovery of a body on Chicago's near North Side rocked the city, its police force and the FBI. From all appearances, the fearsome Chicago-Wekosha vampire was dead of his own hand, a suicide note written in blood beside him, and he had been an aged, white-haired old man, just like the original Count Dracula of Bram Stoker's novel. The man's body was found by a neighbor who often played chess with him in the evenings. Maurice Lowenthal was a retired medical instruments specialist with a firm called Balue-Stork Medical Supply of Chicago, and except for his age, he very nearly fit the PPT profile the FBI had created in its attempt to locate and end the career of this vampiristic sadist. He lived alone. He had never married. He had buried his parents. He was a man of few friends, none beyond the man in the building who enjoyed a game of chess. He had been something of a loner in his work with Balue-Stork, something of a model worker. Never complained, never a claim for workmen's compensation. Had worked steadily for over eighteen years.

    The suicide note told the whole story, and it was on the midnight news even before it was confirmed. The note read: "I cannot any longer live with my guilt and my evil inner self. I killed those poor women and boys for their blood. I now take my own."

    It was signed once more, Teach.

    It was even in the same flourishing print, and in the man's stuffy little apartment, inside the refrigerator was found a jar of blood, labeled _Renee_. The blood would test out as belonging to the Zion woman; of this, Jessica was certain. Other, empty jars were found lying about. There was amid Lowenthal's sprawled body and his own blood, on the carpeting, a saucer and a teacup. The suicide note itself was on the coffee table, glued there by a pool of blood beneath. There were additional blood splotches on the note.

The CPD swore that nothing was handled, and that nothing was moved, and that the blue coats who'd first come on scene had called it in as an FBI matter the moment they saw it. So, presumably, they had a virgin death scene.

Joe Brewer was ecstatic. "When the newspapers work for us, it is a pleasure doing business with them, isn't it?"

Otto Boutine accepted Brewer's slap on the back as tacit approval for the course they had taken. In one corner of the room a stack of _Tribunes_ and _Sun-Times_ papers told them that Lowenthal had been keeping tabs on himself through the press and media. He obviously had been "touched."

There seemed little else to do but bag the vampire and cart his body off, and that was the consensus. Everyone wanted to celebrate. Everyone but Jessica Coran. She wondered about the fact that no cortisone was found among the various drugs in the man's house, and she had come to believe the killer was a bigger, stronger man.

"Something's not entirely right here, Otto," she confided in a whisper.

He frowned but said, "I understand your misgivings. It just goes against everything we _thought_ we knew about this madman to have him suddenly feeling remorseful, sitting down over a cup of tea and guilt, to slash his wrists this way. But downstairs we've got the tools and weapons, even the goddamned spigot!"

She had herself rushed down to see the little shop of horrors, especially curious about the spigot. While in the basement, she had noticed the telltale signs of dried, stringy tissue on the teeth of one electric saw. She'd taken the matter into a cellophane bag to be matched with the body tissue of one of the vampire's victims, one of Lowenthal's victims. But now she had focused her entire attention on the suicide note where it lay in the blood, and it was not quite right.

"What is it about the note that bothers you, Jess?"

"The writing for one, exactly the same as the letter he sent to me at Quantico. He was certainly not in a suicidal mood then."

"So?"

"If he knew he was going to die, why'd he print?"

"Habit. He always prints?"

"But there's no sign of suicide in the writing."

"It's right before you, in the words."

"Yes, the words say suicide like a well-rehearsed play, but there's no tremble in the hand holding the pen."

"I lay you odds the blood he used for the note will belong to Fowler or one of his other victims."

"If not Lowenthal's."

"You're not buying into this at all, are you?"

"I may . . . after microscopic tests, and I may not, after—"

"After lab tests," he finished for her. "Don't your eyes tell you anything?"

"As a matter of fact, they do. Notice the blood *below* the paper?"

"What of it?"

"A shade darker, thicker, drier and older than that on top."

Otto looked at her queerly. "Go on, I'm listening."

"The blood below dried much earlier than the blood here on top."

He just stared back at her, not understanding.

"Don't you see? If Lowenthal had killed himself with the note here in front of him, the blood on either side of the note would be equally dry. As it is, someone placed the note on the table *after* the first pool of blood on the table had pretty much dried. After the note was placed here, additional blood accumulated on this side of the paper. It stands to reason.''

"I think you had better save this talk for the lab,'' he said curtly. "I think we've got our killer, and that's what's important here, Jess.''

"I'm not trying to make some grandstand play, Otto. I'm telling you what my experience and training suggest.''

"And I'm saying, you could be wrong . . . couldn't you?''

"I know there's a push on from Leamy to put a wrap on this thing, Otto, but I don't think we ought to let the bloody killer make the decision for us.'' She also believed Otto's job depended on closing this case.

"You're going to need a lot more than some dried blood to convince anyone that this creep isn't our man!''

"Then I'll find it,'' she insisted, promptly going to work, searching for additional information to support her gnawing suspicion that Teach was toying with them again, out to teach them all another good lesson in foolishness. She was tired of being made the fool, of being outmaneuvered by this controlled maniac. The killer was quite clever and cunning, a gamesman, perhaps a chess player like herself, and as Lowenthal had been, but a player who used deadly means to reach his ends. Perhaps Lowenthal was a helpless dupe, a pawn on the deadly chess board?

"I'm sending in a report to Chief Leamy within the hour, Jess,'' Otto told her.

She replied, "I'll need a hell of a lot more time than that, Otto.''

They both saw that Captain Lyle Kaseem had entered and had been listening to their conversation. He smiled his near perfect white teeth at them and said, "A little difference of opinion?''

"So, what's it with you, Kaseem?'' asked Otto, ticked. "Lowenthal's obviously not your man, Rosnich, so you automatically agree with her?'' he finished, indicating Jessica.

"Let's just say, I have my doubts, too.''

"Why? What possible—"

"He's an old man."

"How old do you have to be to use one of these damned devices?" Otto held up the spigot in a plastic container.

Jessica cut in. "The man would still have to truss them up, Otto, and . . . and haul them up over his—" She stopped herself, realizing that it was bad form for them to argue with Kaseem staring on.

Kaseem simply said, "I agree with Dr. Coran."

Otto looked from one to the other of the doctors, not wanting to accept any ripple in what on the surface appeared an open-and-shut case. He was tired of it, fatigued with the pressures that had been coming down on him from above. He wanted it over; and he wanted it bad enough that he was willing to deny Jessica this time.

Joe Brewer came in shouting. "We've got a safe-deposit key for Lincoln National Bank, Otto. Want to be on hand when we open it?"

"Kaseem?" asked Otto.

Kaseem chewed a bit nervously on the inner wall of his cheek, thinking it over, torn between staying—on the off chance he might learn something from Jessica Coran—and going, on the chance he might learn something from the locked box. He was like the man in the fable who had to choose between three doors to open.

"Well?" pressed Otto.

"Yeah, yeah, I'd like to be on hand."

Otto looked over his shoulder as they were exiting, giving her a wink, telling her he'd done her a favor to get Kaseem out of her way. Down deep, he must believe that if she was on to something, she'd want privacy with the scene and the corpse to determine the full extent of her suspicions.

With the others gone, she drew on some of Brewer's men to assist in the evidence gathering. During her intense investigation, she found that Lowenthal's wrists had been slashed in such a way that it did appear the man had done it to himself. This would have to stand up under more intense scrutiny, measurements and lights, but on the surface, it seemed reasonable to conclude that Lowenthal had indeed cut his own wrists. This did not help her theory.

She next looked closely at Lowenthal's body for any telltale sign of Addison's disease. Cortisone pills had not been found, nor had she seen any apparent indications that Lowenthal had the disease. She looked very closely at the skin in an effort to find symptoms of the vampire disease, porphyria. She found none whatever.

Try as she may, she could not shake the feeling that Lowenthal's death had been somehow "staged" down to the smallest detail. It would take lab time to determine and prove what even Otto was unprepared to accept. But the blood evidence alone indicated to her that there was a second party in the room who had placed the suicide note on the table after the initial blood splatters.

And given the fact the note was signed Teach, it had to be the same man who had written a letter to her in Virginia and had mailed it from Hammond, Indiana, on his way to kill Tommy Fowler in Indianapolis.

She was, by the end of her exhaustive scanning of the body and the physical evidence of the bloody note, convinced that the man calling himself Teach was still very much alive.

Then Boutine and Brewer noisily arrived, proclaiming irrefutable evidence that Lowenthal was Teach.

They had unearthed the most telling, incriminating evidence in the man's private lockbox. He was undeniably Otto's Tort 9 monster. For not only had the man designed the spigot, but here were papers of the design showing that he had recently applied for a patent with the U.S. Government Patent Office in D.C.

"Imagine that, imagine that," Brewer was saying, "to be that nuts, that you go out and get a patent on the murder weapon you use. One for the books."

Kaseem had not returned with them, perhaps accepting

this new information as the final word on the Chicago vampire.

"You can't deny what's before your eyes, Jess," Otto said to her as she scanned the schematics of the deadly little straw that Lowenthal had created.

No one, not even she, could deny that Maurice Lowenthal was indeed involved with the vampire killings, yet some nagging doubts remained. Was the vampire really dead?

TWENTY-FOUR

There was an almost perceptible, tangible sigh of relief from all of Chicago when the evening news reported an end to the vampire killings. Lowenthal's picture was flashed on every news network, and he was described as the cruel, sadistic killer that had a taste for blood. One enterprising young reporter had even learned that Lowenthal had been sent to various hospitals and places such as Wekosha, Wisconsin, as part of his job. The times of his business visits didn't entirely mesh with the time frame of the killings, but it was felt that he must have gone back to these locations on his own. A spokesperson for Balue-Stork downplayed his connection with the company, saying that he was a low-level employee who had a gift for instrument design, but that he had retired some time ago.

His retirement, Jessica had learned, was the November before the Wekosha killing. She remained skeptical, and when reporters confronted her she kept a chill distance, saying over and over, "No comment, no comment."

When pushed outside the Chicago Crime Laboratory to disclose her feelings about the case's coming to a close, she said bluntly, "It isn't closed until it's scientifically closed. The FBI does not close a case until it has the stamp of forensic proof required to close it. Is that understood?"

At his home, where he seldom watched TV, Matt Matisak glared now at the replay of events surrounding Lowenthal's death. The chief of police in Chicago had said it was the surest thing he had ever seen; that they had gotten their man.

An FBI guy named Brewer said practically the same thing, but here was this bitch holding out as if she knew something no one else knew. She was smug about it, too. So cocksure.

Teach stewed about it. He thought about it all evening long. Suppose she did find something; suppose she did know the truth? *Was she that good?* She'd been a thorn in his side since Wekosha. She alone seemed to know about him, enough so that he felt a strange bond with her, as if they had an ongoing relationship from the moment he had read about her in the newspapers. It was as if she were reaching out to him, wanting desperately to touch him, to sit down and really communicate with him.

He wondered how he could make her wish come true . . .

There were ways of finding out where she was staying.

There were ways of attracting her attention, of luring her out.

There were ways . . . and when she fell into his trap, she'd become his next victim.

But it must be done right.

And he would need an accomplice who was a fool.

He knew the perfect fool.

He knew the perfect place.

He had the perfect plan.

"Yes, yes . . . time we met, sweetheart," Teach said to the film image of Dr. Jessica Coran. "I'll make all the arrangements."

He then made a phone call, but quickly slammed the phone down. No, he mustn't contact Gamble by phone. Phone company records could give him away.

Gamble was a retarded employee at Balue-Stork's busy, cluttered mailroom. He was easily manipulated. He could be the perfect stand-in for Teach, and so if Lowenthal wasn't enough for the bastards, Lowenthal's associate in crime, Gamble, would be.

"Of course," he told himself, "the Chicago vampire is really two people. They'll love it."

He quickly dressed. His adrenaline was pumping. This

might be the best after all, doing Jessica Coran. He'd have to have some of her blood. He knew he'd be unable to walk away from her blood as he had Lowenthal's. She was classy, so sure of herself, and so very intelligent. Her blood was worth something. But he knew he'd have to leave the majority of her blood in jars all about Gamble's place, after he killed both Gamble and Coran.

The plan would take every ounce of willpower he possessed, and to help it along, he'd bring some of Fowler's blood to stave off the urges that were sure to come under the circumstances.

Fully dressed, his plan coming to full fruition, he began to locate the necessary items he must take to Gamble's place. He began packing the van in the dark. His neighbor with his damned dog stopped to chat about the pleasant breeze, about the brilliance of the stars and the clear night overhead, and then he moved on to the awful condition of some of the fences in the area and something to do with an altercation with Mrs. Philbin at the end of the street—something to do with his dog and her dog.

"I'm sorry but I can't talk just now," he told the neighbor.

"Never hardly ever see you, and when I do, it's usually when you're going out. But you usually go out early. Why so late?"

"Work . . . emergency. You know the routine."

The man's dog growled as if he smelled something foul on Matisak's pants leg.

"Stop that! Stop it, Toby. Sorry," he apologized. "Don't know what gets into him."

"Prob'ly smells the cat on me."

"Oh, yes, you're a cat person, aren't you?"

"Really have to go now."

"Sure. I'll stop in sometime for coffee, maybe."

"Sure . . . sometime."

He watched the nosy bastard move off with his terrier, glad to see them go. He quickly finished loading the van with the cooler, the briefcase and the power tools that had been Lowenthal's. If he left them with Gamble, he'd have to make some new purchases. Sears was currently running a sale on Craftsman tools.

He climbed into the van, closed the garage door with the automatic and slowly drove out into the night, the green dash lights splashing the pockmarked features of his face.

Once this Coran woman was dead, and after some time passed, he'd go back to his vampiring; until then, however, he'd feed on blood packs he might pick up from hospital banks as he did with the cortisone. Once things died down a bit, he'd return to the alluring hunt for prey and he'd get his blood the way he preferred.

"We can leave the details and cleanup to Brewer's boys," Otto was telling her over lunch at Berghoff's in downtown Chicago, "and you and I can be back at Quantico this afternoon, if you'll just accept the fact that it's over, Jess. You're going to have to sooner or later, and it may as well be—"

"I've got to be certain, Otto."

"What's that supposed to mean? That *I* don't have to be certain?"

"I didn't say that. I've got access to the Chicago Crime Lab, one of the best in the country, and given a little more time, maybe I can convince myself that you and Brewer and the rest of the country are right. I want to check that partial print from the pill we found in Zion against Lowenthal's print to—"

"You sound like Captain Ahab after the white whale, or Captain Kaseem after this Rosnich person."

"I just have to be certain. There're just too many loose ends, and the way that suicide was . . . I don't know . . . staged, like a setup. I can't bear the thought of this creep's getting away and sitting back and having a good laugh at our expense."

He almost spilled his drink when he said, "Christ, Jess! Nobody's gotten away with shit. Lowenthal *is* our man."

"Nobody's dug enough *around* Lowenthal. We don't know enough about the man, or his friends and co-workers."

"Brewer's building that evidence now. He's talking to everyone who knew him at Balue-Stork, former employers, high school teachers, you name it. By the time he's through—"

"Brewer's idea of investigating this is to nail the dead guy."

He calmed when he saw that she was getting angry. "All right . . . okay . . . how long'll you need?"

"Two days tops and maybe I can satisfy myself that Lowenthal and the Wekosha vampire are one and the same man."

Otto pulled at his face as if checking to see if he needed a shave. Then he said, "I'm going to miss you."

She breathed deeply and reached across, taking his hand in hers, squeezing. "When I get back, we'll have lots of time, Otto."

He gave her a reassuring smile. "Maybe more than you know."

Her eyes pinned his. "What're you saying?"

"I've been politely asked to retire. Nearing the age anyway, and Leamy—"

"For Christ's sake, Otto! It was your work that led to Chicago and to Lowenthal."

"No, not really. It was your work, and Leamy wants more 'fresh blood' in the department."

"Hell, Leamy's only a few years younger than you himself."

"Well, dear, it goes a lot deeper than age alone. That's just the P.R. phrase for losing *politically*."

"Who're they . . . who is Leamy replacing you with?"

"O'Rourke."

"O'Rourke? That back-stabbing bitch!"

"Whoa, hold on there. I suggested O'Rourke. She's good and—"

"She's been working behind your back, with Raynack, and—"

"I've known about that for a long time."

"And you did nothing about it?"

"She's good."

"Is that all you can say?"

"She's got the instincts of a barracuda, and that's what it takes in the department. As for me, I think I've missed out on enough living. I think I'll take the long vacation."

"That's crazy, Otto. You're the best in the FBI. We all know that. This just can't be true."

"I've weighed it all over and again, and I thank God I'm alive and that a woman like you could be interested in what I've become. But, kid, I'll understand it if you now decide that it's over between us."

"What? Dammit, Boutine, you can be insufferable."

"What did I say?"

She stood up, about to leave, but he stopped her. "I don't want to lose you, Jess, but—"

"But you think I've been chasing you because of *what* you are instead of *who* you are, that I'm no better than O'Rourke? I don't need that kind of judgment call at a time like this, Otto. Now, please, let me by."

He stood aside, staring after her, shaken by the sudden turn in their relationship. He had made a terribly wrong assumption about her. Just because O'Rourke was sleeping with Leamy . . .

He was interrupted by a waiter with a telephone, saying, "You are Inspector Boutine?"

"Yes."

"Telephone, sir."

The waiter hooked up the phone at the table and after a series of clicks, Joe Brewer came on. "Otto, you may want to cancel your flight back."

"What's that?"

"Something's come up. May be nothing, but who can tell? I'd like to hit you with it, see what you think."

"This to do with Lowenthal?"

"Yeah."

"You saying that maybe Jess is right about him?"

"Could be. Any rate, he may just be half of a duo."

"A team? He had help?"

"Maybe, Otto—it's a strict maybe."

"Comes from where?"

"Something in the apartment. Some things said by co-workers."

"At Balue-Stork?"

"Right."

"Anything concrete, or is this just backscatter?"

"He used a typewriter most of the time, but the few scraps we've found in his hand don't match the handwriting at all."

"It was printed, remember?"

"He didn't habitually print, but when he did, it was not the same."

"Anything else?"

"Some co-workers claimed he said he would one day stick it to Balue-Stork; that he was going into business with a partner to patent a new product. Sound familiar?"

"So he was talking about himself, a second personality. The guy was a split-brain! You've seen the type—signing with his other self, this Teach character."

"But he went so far as to talk to a lawyer about drawing up papers between himself and his partner, to keep his partner from exploding, he told the lawyer."

"You got the lawyer with you?"

"Can you come over?"

"Will do."

For the first time, Otto considered the fact that perhaps the wizardry of Dr. Jessica Coran had once again been right—or at least half right.

• • •

Boutine canceled his flight from Brewer's office. The jagged pieces of the puzzle had been forced to make a fit, and he had been happy with the notion that his last case would be closed with his boxing up his personal items back at Quantico, and he could leave with his head up. But the truth was, they'd dropped some of the puzzle pieces, allowing them to hide about their feet.

Everyone, that was, except Jess.

And she had touched off something in Brewer, sending him off on his own to scrounge up new, additional information, such as the fact Lowenthal's lawyer had gotten a sudden phone call only hours before his death, asking if he could arrange for papers to be drawn up between himself and a partner he had which declared them equal partners in a venture that involved some sort of medical invention that he was having patented.

"The idea," explained Jeff Eastfal, Lowenthal's lawyer, "belonged, Maurice said, to this second party; the other individual had come to Maurice with the idea. Maurice, while still under Balue-Stork's roof, began toying with the idea at night in his home lab, he said, evenings, weekends, refining it."

"Did he tell you the name of this partner?" asked Boutine.

"No."

"Did he say anything to you to indicate who this man was?"

"Nothing."

Boutine bellowed, "Christ."

"Except that they had once worked together."

"Worked together? At Balue-Stork?"

"He didn't say."

"What *did* he say?"

Eastfal put up a hand, gesturing for the FBI man to calm down, refusing to go on if he did not. Brewer muttered a few whispered words into Boutine's ear. Boutine settled into a chair.

Eastfal continued at Brewer's nod. "I got the general impression it was Balue-Stork, but honestly, he did not say. And while we're on the subject of honesty, Maurice was, so far as I knew him, an honest man, and I can't believe for a moment that he had anything whatever to do with—with murdering for blood."

"He designed the bloody murder weapon!" shouted Boutine.

"I am aware of that, but it's my considered opinion, sir, that he did not know to what uses his—his so-called partner was putting it."

Outside the lawyer's prestigious downtown offices where the halls were marbled wall and floor, with mahogany finishings and stairwells, the two FBI men stood wondering what Eastfal's story meant.

"We've got to go back to Balue-Stork, Otto," Brewer told him. "Look at this."

Brewer showed him a letter addressed to Eastfal from Maurice Lowenthal. Otto had to agree, the handwriting was light-years away from the blood letters that'd been written by Teach.

"Still, if *Teach* was a second personality—"

"I know, I know . . . wouldn't the handwriting reflect that?"

"And isn't it feasible—just feasible—that Maurice's so-called partner was his other self, this Teach? And maybe this would explain why he was afraid to give his lawyer a name."

"This case could drive me wacko," admitted Brewer. "Look, we go to Balue-Stork. Do a little snooping, say in personnel, records—"

"Sales. We hit sales records," said Boutine. "See if they've got anyone who regularly visits hospitals in Wekosha; Iowa City; Paris, Illinois; Indianapolis—"

"And Zion."

The two men stared into each other's eyes. "If there is another killer out there taking blood—" began Brewer.

"It could be Kaseem's vampire."

"It could also be the one who likes to write to Dr. Coran, too."

At that moment, Otto knew he would not be leaving Chicago without Jessica beside him. "Let's get over to this medical supply. You know the quickest route?"

"It's damned far from here; located in the suburbs. We'll have to use the siren, make it down the Eisenhower. Come on."

It was nearing 5 P.M., which was just as well. They'd go in after most of the employees were off the premises, and they'd dig all night if it was necessary.

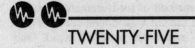

TWENTY-FIVE

Jessica Coran set up a number of tests which would separate the blood splotches on the letter both on the front and the back to determine the exact amount of time they had been on the paper. If there was a significant lag time, it would be logical to assume that the blood on top of the suicide note was different in some regard from that found below. At the crime scene she had drawn extensive diagrams for the trajectory of the blood from Lowenthal's wounds. If the suicide note had been lying on the coffee table before he cut his wrists, the splatters would be less like splotches and more like exclamation points in a series, as the vein would have spurted. The tracks on the table beneath the note had this significant shape, but the tracks on the face of the paper did not.

It was clear to her that either (1) the dead man had placed the note gently onto the table *after* he had slashed both his wrists, or (2) someone else was kind enough to do it for him. There was no doubt in her mind that the wounds inflicted were of such a brutal nature that no one could be calm under the circumstances, or clearheaded enough to locate and place that note on the table just before keeling over. She'd had Lowenthal's blood and serums checked for LSD or any other drug that might account for the unusual sequence of events surrounding his death, but the lab had found no trace of drugs, and certainly no cortisone. As for the print left on the cortisone capsule, there was simply not enough to be sure either way.

She spent hours over Lowenthal's body, his wrists to be exact, using an exacting method of measurement about the wounds, determining that the left was indeed cut by a right hand, and the right was indeed cut by a left hand. Only the most cunning, methodical of killers would think to change hands with the scalpel as he sliced each wrist, to create the illusion of suicide.

It looked rather hopeless, except for the blood evidence, and all too often, blood evidence was ignored, despite the incredible accuracy of the scientific field. To prove her point, she'd have to get a world-renowned blood specialist. Not even Robertson back at Quantico, with all of his background, would be enough to support what she was saying, and the cost factor, and the logistics of getting a man like T. Herbert Leon, or her old mentor, Holecraft, to fly to Chicago to look over the evidence . . . Well, it was not likely she'd get the okay from Otto, not in his present mood, and as for getting "permission" from O'Rourke, that'd stick in her craw like a chicken bone.

But maybe she'd have to put her personal feelings aside. She thought of all the professionals who had put in so many grueling hours on the Tort 9 case, from J.T. to Byrnes and Schultz, O'Rourke herself, even Raynack, with their *pro bono* work going to Kaseem and Forsythe. She wondered momentarily if the man who had staged the "death" of the vampire killer here in Chicago was not the same man who had eluded the military for so many years. Was it possible?

She was tired, exhausted, and while she had the killer's bloody tools to examine against what she knew of the wounds inflicted on the flesh of his victims, tests on the tissue that had come off of these blades had already confirmed a match with Tommy Fowler in Indiana.

How did Lowenthal lure his victims in? An old man who often used a cane. What Scarborough, the only so-called witness had seen was a younger man. They'd found no hairpieces or makeup kit. Yet, his spigot, under magnification, was clearly the nasty weapon used at the jugular on the Copeland girl and all the others. And if there was another vampire working with Lowenthal, he'd never give up this device.

But suppose, she stopped herself with a thought, suppose there were more than one; suppose Lowenthal had made two or three or more?

Or was she being paranoid? She had plenty of reason to be; and hadn't J.T. said that it was, after all, a healthy enough emotion if it kept you from cold, shocking surprise blows to the blind side? Like O'Rourke's sudden power grab. Like Otto's uncharacteristic tent-folding act. She wanted to scream at him for letting it all happen. The forces had been aligned against him while his wife was dying, and they said sharks lived only in oceans. And then Otto had had the audacity to say that he more or less admired O'Rourke for her cunning and her timing. Was that because Otto himself was a well-timed, cunning devil himself? Like his showing up the night before when she would never have turned him away?

She was still angry with him for implying that her interest in him had only to do with her ambition.

These thoughts crowded out her attention to her work, and she realized that she was becoming too fatigued to carry on. She'd performed the autopsy on Lowenthal as well as arranging for the various tests she'd wanted done. She now looked at her watch, and lunch felt like a distant vacation taken years before, save for the hurt she'd felt at Otto's thoughtless remark.

She peeled away her lab coat. Most of the areas of the lab were dark, the graveyard shift kept to a minimum along with the lights. She stretched and realized that a lab assistant in another room was staring through the glass at her and pointing to the phone. She only now realized the buzz in a nearby office was for her. She went to the phone and picked it up.

"Call for Dr. Coran," said a female voice.

"Yes, this is she."

"Go ahead, sir."

After a moment's hesitation and the disappearance of the operator, a raspy voice came choking through, sounding nervous.

"I saw you onnnnn TV. You . . . you are pretty."

"Who is this?"

"I . . . I'm the vampire."

"Look, I'm in no mood for a crank—"

"I take the blood in jars."

"Yes, well, thanks to the papers, everybody knows that."

"I use a modified tracheotomy tube and a tourniquet to control the blood flow, usually after severing the Achilles tendon."

She shivered from deep within her soul. "The vampire killer is dead. Maurice Lowenthal—"

"I killed Maurice. You know that . . . You're the only one who knows that."

So you want me dead, she told herself. "Why're you telling me this?"

No one outside FBI circles knew of the tourniquet or the slashed heels.

"*I want some of your blood.*"

She tried to breathe normally, but found it near impossible. Now he was quoting from the letter he had written in Copeland's blood. Either she was speaking to Candy Copeland's killer, the man who treated his victims like swine to be bled, or someone was playing the kind of cruel, sick and senseless joke that police personnel loved the most.

"I . . . I could give you some," she said, unable to know where she found the words or the nerve.

"You'll never know how happy you've made me to hear that."

"I mean . . . you could get blood from me when . . . whenever you needed, so-so"—she forced herself to control the fear-induced stuttering—"y-you wouldn't have to go on killing—"

"You'd do that for me?"

"For Teach, yes. I know you're ill, and you need help. I know you've got a disease."

"I know that you know. You know all about me."

"So we know all about each other. So where can I find you?"

"No . . . no. I'll have to give this some thought."

He hadn't expected her to react this way when he had planned the call. She could tell this from the inflection in his voice.

"Don't hang"—he was gone—"up!"

She stood in the darkened office, fear gripping her on all sides. How did he get through to her? She felt defiled just having spoken with the perverted killer, as if he had touched her in some secret place.

Her hands were trembling; every nerve in her body felt as if touched by a hot wire, she fought to remain in control. She drew on her training as an FBI agent. She had to contact someone about the phone call. It was too much to keep to herself, for any reason.

She rang for the operator, shouting her need. "The call to me just now. I need a tracer on that to determine the source. Can you do that?"

"Yes, but it will take some time."

"Do it. It's very important, very."

"I'll get on it. We've got the new system that—"

"Just do it, please."

"Yes, Dr. Coran."

She was still trembling, feeling as if she needed a stiff drink, wishing that Otto was here with her now, someone she could throw herself at; she wanted to cry and to kick all at once. The very thing she hated most in this world had just spoken to her in what his bloody mind must constitute as intimacy. She wanted to snatch her .38 from its holster and hold onto it for dear life, stretch it before her like a deadly shield of protection to ward off the evil.

People working in nearby offices were suddenly taking on evil dimensions, satanic form; everyone around her was suspect. Had the call come from within the building? Now the building itself had become a kind of evil working against her.

"Got to get hold of myself," she quietly said, trying desperately to calm her frayed nerves. It was one thing to hunt down a killer, but quite another when deadly, dangerous prey turned on you and stared you in the face. A police dispatcher called in telling her that the call was traced to a phone booth on the corner of Irving Park and Kedzie.

She next dialed long-distance for Otto, believing him most certainly back at HQ by now. She could not get him, and his fool secretary argued with her that he was still in Chicago. She became frustrated and asked to be routed to the lab in an attempt to reach J.T. But Robertson answered only to tell her that J.T. was gone for the evening.

"Anything I can do for you?" he asked.

"Yeah, as a matter of fact, there is." She proposed that he get on a plane as quickly as possible and get to Chicago. She wanted him to confirm what she had found in the Lowenthal death, giving him just enough to whet his appetite. Robertson assured her that he was on his way, and he equally assured her that Otto Boutine, so far as he knew, had not returned to Quantico.

She hung up, feeling frustrated. She dialed for the Chicago offices of the FBI, asking for Brewer, only to learn that he was unavailable, something about investigating a case. One of Brewer's men got on with her, and she briefly recounted the conversation she had had with the killer, but this man, like everyone else in the Chicago law enforcement community, had long ago decided that the killer was dead.

"Oh, you'll get hundreds of crank-heads calling, Dr. Coran, even a year from now—"

"Just tell Brewer that this guy *knew* too much!"

She slammed down the phone in anger, taking it out on the agent.

Going from the floor and through the near empty building, she felt self-conscious, and she felt like a target, and she recalled how the sadistic bastard that had killed Candy Copeland had gone about his cruel work; she recalled it in its every vivid detail.

"He's still out here somewhere," she said to the bustling city night outside the Chicago Crime Lab where she hailed a cab. She had her gun with her, and for this she was grateful. She felt for it while in the cab, reassuring as it was to the touch, even in its ankle holster below her wide-legged, billowy slacks.

In a moment, she realized that the taxi driver was staring in his rearview at her and asking, "You okay, miss?"

"Lincolnshire Inn, please," she replied coldly.

"Oh, great," he replied, snapping on the meter. Now she was a good fare, and he no longer worried about her state of mind.

God, why hadn't Otto stayed with her?

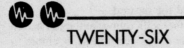

TWENTY-SIX

It was 9 P.M. when the phone woke Jessica Coran from a less than sound sleep. She at first only half heard the voice at the other end of the line, thinking it was a wrong number.

"I-I-I know you'll want ta talk to-to me," a whiny, nasally stutterer was saying. She started to protest but was stopped by his next words.

"I haf in-for-ma-tion about the vam-pire kill-kill-er."

"Who is this?"

"My name. I'm not givin' my-my name; but I-I-I think I know who-who he is."

The voice was calm save for the stutter.

"How did you get my number?"

"I've read about these ter-ter-terrible kill-killings. I've seen you in the papers, and-and to-night I got your number by—by lying. I told a lie, and they gave me this num-umberrr."

"Who gave you this number?"

"The girl with the police did it-it for me."

She inwardly cringed, believing her number was given out to a wacko who had been following the case in the papers. The man sounded like a retarded person.

"The girl at the police department? Which department?"

"Does-doesn't matter," he said impatiently.

She sat up in bed, trying to clear her mind and her eyes all at once. "What . . . what kind of lie did you tell to get my number?" she insisted.

257

"That I'm your father . . ."

She immediately resented the bastard.

". . . that, that your mother's ill, dying! and that I had to get in touch with you." There was a solidness, a timbre to the voice that kept it from being completely babyish-sounding.

"Why me? Why bring your story to me, when you've got the entire Chicago Police Department to tell it to?" Her voice was openly caustic now.

"Po-Po-Police Department? I have! I have tried them. No one will le-listen, 'cause they think I-I-I'm—well, stupid or some—all be-because I use-use-use—did-did d-d-drugs, and-and I was in the hos—"

"I see."

"No, you don't see. I see. No one but me. He lives next door. I see him comin' in with the-these things. Packin' this, this red stuff 'way in his how-how-house, you know? and he tells me once . . . once he tells me his dear old mother put up some-some tomatoes for him, and once he told me that it was jus' to-to-tomato juice, and once it was ke-ke-ketchup, but-but it's all the same. It's blood."

"Who is this other man? What is his name?"

There was a long pause at the other end, until finally, the man said, "My neighbor."

"German?"

"Kinda German, yeah. How'd you know?"

"Short, stocky man? Dark hair?" She was describing Kaseem's man.

"Yeah-yeah-yeah, that's him, but how-how-how did you know?"

Ignoring this, she asked, "Where are you located?"

"My house?"

"Yes, so we can speak. So you can show me where this man lives."

"I-I-I don't want no trouble."

"Please, just give me his address, then."

"No-no-no. I'll let you come here. You can-can-can't go there alone."

"I don't intend to, and certainly not before I've had a chance to investigate this thing further."

"All right."

"Is your neighbor home now?"

"No. Prowling. What vam-pires do this time of night. Never see him days—never. Sleeps in-in-in his how-how-house in-in-in a cof-fin, I-I bet."

"Where is your location? I'll send a car around." She wondered if this wasn't just the beginning of the crank calls.

"No! No! No cars."

"Sir, I can't help you if you don't—"

"Dr. Coran, I don't talk to no one about this no more. I-I-I quit because they were going to lock me up."

She wondered momentarily if she was not speaking this moment to the killer himself. Perhaps he was a classic dual personality, and while one side of him wallowed in the kill, another side of him abhorred it and the creature personality that had repeatedly murdered while *this personality* stood by. It was a possibility that she was talking to Davic Rosnich at this very moment, but she dared not frighten him off with such questions. She must first establish a location, a rendezvous spot with a vampire killer.

Or someone who knew the killer.

"You come alone, or not at all," insisted the stutterer.

"All right. What is the address?"

The voice said, "5234 Oak Grove. If anyone is with you, I swear, I don't talk."

"Are you sure of what you've seen?"

"Yes."

"What is the man's name you suspect."

"No, not until you come; otherwise, you won't come."

"But sir, if we had the name, we could run some checks."

"No! Just come. I'll show you. I see from my win-dow-dow some of the queer things he does. He . . . he's got all kinds of weird-looking sur-sur-gical stuff. Catheters, tubes, hypos, you-you name it.''

It was clearly a long shot, and yet something strained and pitiful in the voice made her wonder along with the mention of medical supplies and the van, not to mention tubes and catheters.

''All right, all right. I'll be there as soon as I can be.''

''I r-read the late pa-pers. Saw what you-you people said. Awful—just awful. What he did to those poor women.''

''And men,'' she added. ''He's killed at least two men, and we have good reason to suspect that there have been others,'' she added, to see what kind of response she would get.

''Men? The pa-per-pers didn't say anything 'bout men he's done? I al-always knew it—*down deep*. Such a filthy man.''

''I'm coming,'' she said, and hung up.

Jessica knew it was regulation to get backup on a net, and she fully intended to, but this wasn't a net, and she didn't have enough evidence to prove it so; she didn't have enough for a bench warrant, much less a search warrant.

Besides, she didn't believe the stutterer to be the self-assured, methodical killer she had been tracking now for so long. And going to meet with the man only constituted ''further investigation.'' Under that light, she knew she was on her own.

If only Otto had not had to fly back to D.C. Her only other choice was Brewer, a man she felt uncomfortable around.

She wasn't a complete fool to go to the address alone without some idea of what she was getting herself into. She again telephoned the field office only to find Joe Brewer still unavailable. She spoke to another agent who did some checking and who found the location of the address she wanted on a precinct map. She was given the number of the police precinct that had somehow gotten her number and had passed it along to the caller. ''If you get in touch with

Joe, tell him I'm investigating a lead that's taken me to this address.''

The agent seemed bored with the entire idea. Like Brewer and everyone else, he was convinced that the Chicago-to-Wekosha vampire was Maurice Lowenthal, and that the killer was quite dead. The fact that no more bloodless bodies had been found had lulled them all into inactivity where her case was concerned. Even Otto and the P.P. team back at Quantico had wanted to believe it ended with Lowenthal. She alone could not accept this fact.

''Sure, sure, I'll see he gets the message,'' the agent told her.

She then telephoned Precinct 13 to ask questions of the desk sergeant. She asked him if any complaint calls had come to them from the address in question.

''Ever?''

''Past year, two?''

''That might take time.''

''I'll call back in an hour?''

''Give me your number, and I'll get back to you.''

''I need to know within the hour, Sergeant.''

''Things're pretty slow here for the moment, so I think I can oblige you there, Doctor.''

''Thank you, Sergeant.''

She took the hour to dress, but in less than a half hour, the desk sergeant at 13 called back.

''Yes, there've been quite a few complaints from this man.''

''What's the name?''

''Gamble.''

''Appropriate,'' she muttered.

''What?''

''Never mind.''

''Hillary Gamble's the full name. Something of a nut case.''

Appropriate again, she thought, but kept mum. ''The name of the person he's made complaints against?''

"Practically the entire neighborhood. He's a real nuisance, this one. Goes about causing problems, it looks like."

The record check revealed a number of complaints that ranged from Peeping Toms disturbing the man's peace to a bloody nose at the hand of one neighbor. "A real pain-in-the-ass crazy, what we call in the department an asshole's asshole, if you'll pardon my language, Dr. Coran."

"What was the nature of his last complaint?"

"Claimed his neighbor had body parts in his house, that his neighbor was a murderer."

"Checks?"

"Visual turned up negative."

"Search of the interior?"

"None warranted by the visiting officers."

"How often they visit this location, Sergeant?"

"Three times since January!"

"Never searched the location?" She thought of the awful Jeffrey Dahmer case in Milwaukee, almost two years before.

"Lady, the *complainant* was arrested."

"On what charge?"

"Exposing himself to a female officer, ma'am . . . ahh, Doctor."

She inwardly moaned before hanging up.

Otto Boutine and Joe Brewer kept tripping over one name, a salesman at Balue-Stork whose route had taken him to every key location in the investigation of the Tort 9 killings, Matthew Matisak. But there were holes in the records, some showing visits of only once over a seven-month period which the personnel lady could not account for. She said they would have to talk to Matisak's immediate supervisor, a man named Sarafian.

It was past eleven, and Sarafian had to be disturbed at home and escorted in by police sent to his home to pick him up. The entire Lowenthal affair had turned the company into something of a morgue, no one wishing to be sucked into the investigation. The entire time the FBI men were thrashing through the records they requested, the Balue-Stork public relations man, a V.P. and a board member had assembled to quell the disturbances as best they could, but Otto Boutine was having none of it.

When Sarafian was brought in in an overcoat covering his pajamas, the man was outraged, shouting that he was prepared to sue the bastards responsible.

Otto Boutine interrupted him and faced him down, saying, "I'm the bastard you'll be suing, then. I'm Inspector Otto Boutine, FBI Division Chief."

Sarafian was visibly taken aback. "Well . . . FBI. Has to do with that poor bastard Lowenthal, then."

"Yes, it does. But we'd also like to talk to you about a man named Matisak."

Sarafian's eyes, a distant, dark brown, shone with a shimmery, water-and-light quality that indicated to the experienced FBI men that they had struck a chord. "Can you explain why some of his travel records and expense reports are missing from his file?"

"Backlog, maybe. We're always short of capable filing clerks. Get the worst in here from a service, and things are lost. But why're you interested in Matisak? I thought you people decided Lowenthal was the . . . the murderer?"

"What can you tell us about Matisak?"

Sarafian's shoulders raised. "Strange bird, personality-wise. Doesn't associate, but he's a good man in the field. Has some physical problems that he works hard to overcome."

"Handicapped?"

"No, wouldn't call it that."

"What, then?"

He went to a nearby wall and pulled down a photo of a group. "The sales force."

Otto picked him out of ten men immediately. Matisak fit the profile, both in age and appearance, his features scarred by some childhood disease or porphyria.

"Do you know if he is on any medication?"

"I've seen him popping pills, sure."

"What sort?"

"Couldn't say. Got it from a doctor in Indianapolis. One of our clients. The man complained that Matisak kept after him for freebies."

"We'll need the man's name."

"Grubber. Dr. Stanley Grubber."

"Where can he be reached?" pressed Brewer.

"St. Luke's Hospital."

Brewer gritted his teeth. "Sonofabitch," he muttered.

"What?" asked Sarafian.

"Never mind, Sarafian. Just get us an address on Matisak, now! And you," said Boutine, pointing to the personnel woman, "get St. Luke's in Indianapolis on the phone and get a number for this guy Grubber pronto!"

An incoming telephone call was for Brewer. He took it at a far desk, covering the mouthpiece with his hand. In a corner, he began asking questions of the caller.

"When? When did the call come in? Did she say anything else? Christ. All right. What?"

"What's going on, Joe?" Boutine asked his friend.

Joe Brewer stared at Otto, their eyes meeting.

"What the fuck is it, Joe?"

"He's . . . According to Dr. Coran, someone called her tonight at the crime lab, and she believes it was our killer."

"Matisak?"

"Maybe. Maybe just a crank call."

"Give me that phone."

Boutine hurriedly dialed the number for the crime lab, but he found that Jessica had left hours before.

He quickly dialed for the Lincolnshire Inn, getting a wrong number, cursing and asking for operator assistance. When he got through, he found no one answering Jessica's number.

"Christ, Joe, if anything's happened to her—"

"Now, don't go jumping to conclusions, Otto. We've just got to go methodical here. Get Matisak's address and—"

Otto rushed at Sarafian, who held up a card with Matisak's address on it. "I'm on my way out there, Joe. You coming?"

"Damned right, but what about a warrant?"

"Fuck the warrant. We have cause, provocation—the records showing his usual route, the fact some have been pilfered, to cover his tracks, his association with Lowenthal, Sarafian's eyes."

"Sarafian's eyes won't help us in a court of law."

"And no goddamned warrant is going to help Jess if this bastard has her."

They raced from the squat factory building of Balue-Stork with Sarafian and the others staring after them, Sarafian saying, "I always knew that Matisak was weird, but I never in a million years—"

"That's what you said about Lowenthal!" shouted Sarafian's boss. "This could destroy us in the medical community, damn! Damn! Sarafian, pack your belongings!"

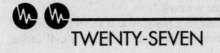

TWENTY-SEVEN

Jessica debated her options before leaving the relative safety of the Lincolnshire Inn for the address given her by Hillary Gamble. She knew he could just as well be an idiot, a fool, a member of the fringe element just out to get someone—*anyone*—to pay him a bit of attention. He may have guessed at the importance of medical supplies used by the killer, or he may have read about it in connection with the Lowenthal affair. With Lowenthal's death, the gag order on the information about the vampire killings had become too relaxed. Hell, if Brewer in Chicago could learn about Boutine and her in Virginia, anything was possible.

Still, she didn't want to meet Gamble alone, so she telephoned for Captain Lyle Kaseem, who, like her, had not felt entirely comfortable accepting Lowenthal as the vampire killer they had been stalking.

Kaseem was immediately interested in what she had to say. He was also closer to the address and said that he would meet her there.

"Fine, but hold for me. No sense in either of us stepping into a trap, Captain. Will you inform Forsythe? Will he accompany you?"

"Negative. He's left for D.C. already."

"All right. I'll get a cab and meet you at the destination."

"Will do."

It was reassuring to talk to Kaseem, and for once his military bearing seemed to bolster her confidence in him.

"And Captain—"

"Yes?"

"I suggest you arm yourself."

"I'll see you at Gamble's place. We'll see what he's got to show us, and if there's any merit to it, we'll call in the marines if necessary."

"A SWAT team at the very least."

"Tell me again what this man sounded like, the one who claimed to be the killer. Did he have a European sound, an accent at all?"

"Honestly, I was so shaken, I . . . I'm not sure."

"Well, the description given you by Gamble sounds like Rosnich."

"Only one way to find out."

"I'll see you at the location."

She had hung up, wondering if she should not try Brewer again. But now she must rush. She didn't want to keep Kaseem waiting too long. He was an impatient man. So she rushed out.

The cabdriver was collecting the fare from her when she asked if he would wait.

"Five minutes tops," he said mechanically.

She frowned in response, got out and searched for Kaseem, but he was not here. Had he gotten caught in traffic, an accident? What?

She waited to see if he would show up, and in the waiting, she lost the cab. She then decided to go the twenty yards to the door where the windows were covered in thick, heavy, paisley drapes. It was a small building with two floors, cramped into a small space between two identical two-flats. The streetlights gave the place some relief, but the shadows created by the lights were like black holes all around the steps. She thought she saw movement at one window, as if someone had been staring out all along. She felt the cool heftiness of her .38 Special strapped to her ankle below her pants leg. She could get to it quickly if she had to.

A final look around for Kaseem proved futile. She couldn't wait any longer. She rang the bell and waited.

The door swung open on an inward hinge and there stood Gamble, a short, flabby little man, balding, wearing only a pair of socks and thick-lensed glasses. His erection was the largest thing about him, she thought as she prepared to turn and walk away from the bastard, saying, "All right, Mr. Gamble, I'll be leaving now."

"No, w-wait!" He stepped out after her, pulling on a robe as he did so, pleading, "I'mmmmmm so-sorry! Really! It's—you don't unner-stand—it's a sic-sickness with me—"

She kept going down the stairs, wondering how she was going to find another cab, when he caught up to her and came around to face her. "A k-k-k-cry for help!"

She brushed him aside and the robe billowed out. She marched ahead of him.

He came alongside like a puppy trying desperately to keep up. "It doesn't change the-the fact I-I-I know who's been doin' all them aw-awful things."

There was a childish innocence about Gamble, a fat boy who never grew up. "I'm not here for fun and games, Gamble," she said curtly, moving along the street.

"He drives a-a-a van, a-a gray van," Gamble said. "N-nn likes classy music."

This made her stop.

She had half prayed that Gamble would turn out to be a crank, just another of the thousands of members of the fringe element that contacted police personnel whenever they could for any number of deep-seated reasons. She had also half prayed that he was legitimate, and now the conflict arose in her again. She was not at all sure she wanted to come face-to-face with Teach, the man she had spent so many hours and days chasing in the lab and in autopsy rooms, the same man who'd sent her a blood letter and now had telephoned her at the crime lab. If Gamble was a man with a wire loose, she could walk away with no harm done. But if she investigated with backup cars and agents, she'd come off looking like a fool, and lately, she had had enough of that. And if Gamble truly had something in this neighbor of his, she might prove that Lowenthal had not acted alone, that his death was indeed a setup to throw them off and that this final action taken by the killer was just another of his chess moves. Maybe Gamble was a big gamble, and maybe he was a pervert, but he might also possibly pinpoint the location of the madman.

If this was the case, she could then call for all the backup help she needed. She was also painfully aware of the fact that in coming here like this, alone, she was violating one of the Bureau's most sacred prime directives. But she had thought that Kaseem would have been here by now.

"'Round b-b-back is the-the van, just next door," he assured her.

A look inside that van could prove to Otto and the others that she was right, that the vampire killer was still at large.

"P-p-p-lease, you've come all this w-way. Don't let my sic-sickness stop you n-n-now. I'm sic-sick, but I'mmmmm not-not k-k-k-crazy. I kn-kn-know it's him."

"Take me to see the van," she said.

"Oh, g-g-g-g-gooood.

Brewer put out an all-points bulletin on two people, calling it in from the car that sped toward Matisak's place. He asked every law enforcement official in the city to be on the lookout for Dr. Jessica Coran, and anyone hearing from her was to report to him. He secondly gave out a description of Matthew Matisak, his address, the vehicle he drove, a light gray van bearing the markings of Balue-Stork Medical Supply along the driver's side door, down to the plates—all information gleaned from his employee record card.

They soon reached the residence of the supposed vampire killer. It looked like any other house on the block, as it was in an older district where all the brick houses were designed in identical proportions, one after another. Matisak's lawn, however, was weedy and destroyed by chinch bugs and neglect. The door was peeling and the brickwork in need of repair. The overall effect of the house was one of darkness with a tinge of despair.

The moment they pulled into the driveway, a neighbor came outside, a dog yipping at his feet at the FBI men. The neighbor shouted at them, "What're you doing there? You get away from there or I'll call the cops!"

Boutine was peering into the garage while Brewer picked the lock on the door.

"Nothing inside," Boutine said. "He appears to be gone."

"What's going on here?" the neighbor persisted.

"This is a police matter, sir!" shouted Brewer over his shoulder. And then he said to Boutine, "If he's not here, then maybe Jessica's not in harm's way after all, Otto."

"He always kills in remote locations—away from home," Boutine countered.

"So we stash the cars and stake out the place, Otto. What other choice do we have? Otto? Otto?"

"We've got to get inside, case the joint. See if there's any information whatever that might lead to his whereabouts."

"We could be blowing it, going in, Otto."

"We've got probable cause."

"That might wash if we had the CPD with us, but not as FBI men."

"You two sure you know what you're doing?" asked the neighbor, who had walked over to them in his bathrobe.

"We'll thank you to get inside your home and stay there, sir," said Brewer officiously. "We are FBI agents."

"Really? FBI? Really?"

Brewer felt like decking the bastard, but instead he flashed his badge and ID. "Satisfied?"

"What in God's name has Matisak done?"

"Please, sir, move back into your house and do not create any alarm for Mr. Matisak on his return."

"But he won't be back for days."

"How do you know that?"

"Told me so. Usually, when he packs his van, he's going back on the road, and we don't see him for days."

"We're going in," shouted Otto, smashing a window and stepping through, tearing down a set of dark blue drapes from the wall mount as he did so.

The moment Otto stepped into the dark interior he felt an almost tangible wall of oppressiveness descend upon him with the drapes that he fought off. It was the closeness of the place and the darkness, but something beyond that, an untouchable, unseeable rankness and the closeness of the den of an animal. As he moved further into the interior, he thought he sensed something else in the house with him, something alive—or something not quite alive—and for a moment, he feared the worst: he feared Jessica was hanging upside down deep within the labyrinth of this black little castle, her blood drained away like the other victims that Matisak had put through his torture chamber. He imagined that when they found the lights, Jess's body would confront him, and in her throat would be the dangling spigot used by Matisak.

Behind him he heard Brewer bitching about being unable to find the goddamned lights when suddenly he did and the house was lit, but only dimly. The bulb must be colored a strange hue, and some kind of odor was rising from it.

"What the hell is that smell?" Brewer wondered aloud.

Otto was too impatient to care. He moved along the corridors, his gun extended. Even though Otto believed the place to be empty, his gun and his hands over the gun were shaking. Brewer was right. Something about the smell of the place, like a rank, animal musk.

"Good Christ," muttered Brewer behind him.

"What is it?" he called back.

"Friggin' light bulb."

"What about it?"

"It's—it's painted red, Otto."

Otto knew instantly now what the odor was—hot blood.

The bastard used the blood to decorate his bulbs to create the red glow of the room that he apparently grooved on. Brewer's remark had made Otto look away from the corridor he was going down, but a sudden flicker of noise made him wheel and fire. A single shot plastered Matisak's big black tom cat to a back wall, blood streaking the floor to mark the trail of its having impacted with Boutine's bullet.

"Sonofabitch," moaned Boutine.

Brewer rushed to stand beside him, wondering what the sudden, high-pitched screech was. Boutine hadn't heard the screech because of the noise of the gun in his ear. The taste and smell of gunsmoke intermingled now with the odor of dried, sizzling blood on the bulb as it grew hotter and hotter.

"Think we'd better turn on some more lights," suggested Brewer.

"I want everything in this filthy place torn apart," Boutine replied.

"Where you going?" asked Brewer.

"Get in an E.T. team and to check to see if anyone's got any word on Jess."

"Sure, leave me alone in this," said Brewer, whose eyes turned toward the darkened bathroom.

TWENTY-EIGHT

Gamble led the way. It took them between two apartment buildings through a gangway with an overhead tunnel that was dark. A perfect ambush, she thought. But they arrived on the other side, staring out on a backyard with a walk and a little garden patch, a fence and a dilapidated old garage which belonged to the place next door.

It was dark and a strange wind that seemed to come from nowhere swirled in spiraling eddies about her legs. She felt the cold metal of her gun at her ankle, wondering if it was not time to yank it out, but so far there was nothing that called for a lethal weapon or a show of force. Thus far, Hillary had also managed to keep his robe on as well.

"Come on," he whispered.

"Where is the van?"

"The-the other s-s-side of the garage."

"Are you sure he's not home?"

"Y-yes. Follow m-m-me."

The only light here came from a distant streetlamp, the closest one having been broken by some child's rock.

Jessica stopped Gamble with a tug at his robe, which he seemed to be pleased with, and then she whispered back to the stubby, Truman Capote look-alike, repeating herself. "Are you absolutely certain that he is away from his place?"

"My b-b-b-bedroom w-w-window overlooks his place." His raspy voice was filled with annoyance now. "I dunno w-w-why y-y-you don't b-believe m-m-me."

How long does he usually stay out?''

"W-w-w-weeks at a t-t-t-time.''

"But that's got to be only when he has his van with him, right?''

"I . . . y-y-y-yes . . . I g-g-g-guess you're r-r-right.''

"Then you'll have to watch out for me.''

He nodded in the dark, standing before her in the robe, looking like Yoda of *Star Wars* fame. "He has a-a-a Hun-Honda Civic . . . for-for just a-a-around.''

They'd gone to the corner of the garage that abutted Gamble's fence and there it was, a light gray van with the Balue-Stork insignia so aged and peeled as to be nearly unreadable. The gray looked white to silver in the night. She recalled Candy Copeland's pimp, Scarborough, in Wekosha and sensed that he, too, had once seen this very van. She sucked in a deep breath of the warm night air, feeling her heart panting wildly beneath her blouse.

Could it be this easy? Had she finally narrowed the field down to one suspect, finding him amid the millions of people in Chicago, amid all the wackos and sickos that had confused the issues of the case? She thought of the many thousands of so-called leads that hundreds of law enforcement officials had followed, of the thousands of telephone calls and tips that had had to be checked out. Could it possibly be that she had gotten luckier than anyone had a right to be?

Or was it all just too bloody neat?

She again considered the possibility that Gamble had called her in order to lure her here, and that Teach was close enough to hear them breathing; that Teach was at this moment watching her every move. The thought sent a chill through her spine. Where was he, if he was here? In the garage? In the house, staring out from a window? In Gamble's house, waiting for them to return, waiting for her to begin to let her guard down, thinking she was safe enough with Gamble? Or was the bastard in the van that Gamble had led her to? Was the van the trap that would snap on her neck? She could be at her gun in an instant, but for now she merely checked over her shoulder to locate Gamble. He was still in the shadow of the garage.

"He unloads from here?" she asked.

"Yes."

"Why doesn't he use the garage?"

"Too-too clut-t-t-tered."

"I'm going to inspect the van."

"I-I-I'd be very k-k-k-careful."

"You just stay here, Mr. Gamble."

"D-d-don't worry 'b-bout that."

Jessica found the driver's side door locked, and so she inched her way toward the rear of the van. She had a sensation she was being watched and that Gamble had not stayed put. Glancing back, however, she found the strange, little pervert picking his ear where he stood just below the canopy of the alleyway. She watched his hand go across his mouth to cover an anxious burp, or was he trying to hide his jagged, stained teeth in an unconscious gesture? Or was he covering a leering grin? Impossible to tell, but if it was a grin, she might be in for a surprise. She readied herself for any eventuality.

She cursed when she found the rear door to the van also locked. She'd like to examine the interior, but without a warrant, what purpose would it serve? Still, if she could see inside . . . With the weak light of the streetlamp halfway down the alley, she might just see something useful. She stepped up onto the bumper and stared into the dark hole of the interior, her eyes widening, straining, when she saw a large, square, metal container, a cooler or freezer which looked very expensive, the kind seen in ambulances, used to transport donor organs and blood. Her heart skipped like a stone over frigid water. It could be the very container used to transport Candy Copeland's blood from Wekosha to Chicago.

She was without a warrant. Smashing the glass with a brick to get to the contents could only lead to problems with the evidence down the road, if this were indeed the killer's van. She tried to make out other strange objects in the van: ropes coiled like so many snakes lying in wait; a tool box and several objects that might or might not be power tools. *It had to be him,* or it was all very innocent and Gamble was the idiot that he appeared to be.

She got down from the bumper and rounded the truck, suddenly startled by Gamble, who was standing there, a sneer curling his fetid lips, saying in a whisper, "I t-t-t-tol' you s-s-so! It's him, ain't it?"

She caught her breath, having been frightened by the little runt. "Gamble, I told you to stay where you were."

"I-I-I am where I-I-I wa-was."

"I've got to use your phone. Now!"

"No problem. I-I-I'll s-sh-sh-sh-show y-you w-where it is."

His stutter seemed to be getting worse with time. Her mind was on getting a message through to Boutine and Brewer if it meant getting the entire CPD off their asses, but far to the rear of her thoughts she seemed to recall a bit of psychology that said a stutterer's stutter grew worse with stress and anxiety. Was Gamble stressed over the fact that they were so near to entrapping his neighbor? Or was he anxious about her entering his home?

She was anxious about closing a door behind them as she entered, so she asked that the front door be left ajar. He complied with a nod and a smile, pointing in the direction of the phone, which sat on a small table in the hallway. The place was darkened and she asked that he turn on some lights as she passed from the foyer to the telephone, picking it up and dialing 911.

But before the connection was made, the phone went dead and she saw the little dwarf in front of her, grinning insanely. She was grabbed suddenly from behind, her arm twisted, her neck in a chokehold and no way to get at the gun strapped to her leg. Her eyes grew wild with fear when she saw the small ugly man in front of her amble toward her with a hypodermic needle held prominently before him. The strength of the man who had her in his grasp was unbeatable, but she used this against Gamble when he got within reach, kicking out with her feet and sending Gamble tumbling toward the half-open door where a crack of light from outside revealed Gamble's bloody nose.

"Goddammit, Gamble, get it done!" cried out the man who struggled to keep hold of her. She recognized the voice as that of the man who had telephoned from a booth earlier, claiming to be Teach. She fought as best she could, at one point grabbing the phone and sending it colliding into the skull over her shoulder, bruising herself as well in the bargain. But the little one scrambled to his feet, scurried ratlike to the syringe which had cascaded into a corner and now rushed around to her and her assailant's side. The other man shouted, "You stick me with that damned thing and I'll kill you, Gamble!"

She felt the needle plunge into her thigh and she screamed, but her scream was stifled by a thick hand with a surgical glove over it. Her eyes went to the cracked door with what little light was streaming through before she was forced into the adjoining room, where only darkness reigned.

"She wanted a little light, Gamble, so give her a little light."

She somehow sensed that there was something or someone other than her two assailants in the room with them, as if the presence of evil were palpable and breathing. The drug was taking rapid effect and she wasn't sure what was real and what was imaginary any longer, but she smelled death in the darkness; she smelled an odor like that in the cabin in Wekosha and wherever else she had found the drained bodies of this madman's appetite.

Gamble was laughing, taunting her in the darkness from some distance measured in either feet or the miles created by the drug that'd made her malleable and easy to conduct. Her brain tried to fight the conductors, knowing where she was being transported to.

"A little light . . . a little light . . ." Gamble was chanting without a stutter, as if he now were calmed and relaxed, now that he had his prize within his grasp.

A pair of candles or a kerosene lamp, she could not be sure, cast shadows like demons all around her. Her own shadow melded with Gamble's stubby form against one wall, and towering behind her was that of a thing that seemed for all the world to be a giant vampire bat, the man who still held her in his grasp. But there was another black shadow also, a strange, *upset* shadow, the shadow of a dangling body, *upside down*, at the center of the room.

Her face was forced suddenly into the dead face of Lyle Kaseem's, a strange, tubular object jutting from his throat.

Gamble had not lied. It was him. It was the man she had searched for since Wekosha. It was Candy Copeland's vicious, sadistic killer; Janel McDonell's torturer; the blood-sucker who had taken the lives of so many others.

As if reading her mind, Teach said in a raspy voice, his rubber-gloved hands feeling like the touch of an alien, "And you're next, Doctor . . ."

She felt a numbness grip her body and her mind, the powerful grip of the sedative doing its work; likely the way that Kaseem had been rendered helpless. She only half heard Gamble stutter the name of the other. "M-m-mad . . . Mad M-m-mat . . . M-m-meet Mad Matt Matisak." His keening, sickening giggle followed.

"Just a little of her blood, Hillary, and you can have the body, just like I promised you."

More digusting laughter erupted from Hillary Gamble moments before she lost all sensory perception. She found herself in a dark place, somewhat shattering in its complete blackness, and yet somewhat comforting. She didn't feel anything . . . and yet the darkness into which she was thrust was surrounded by fear all about the periphery, like demons waiting to come get her . . .

• • •

Boutine and Brewer remained at Matisak's house and each moment they stayed revealed something further about the madman. Brewer, after Boutine had gone to the car to radio for assistance and news of Jessica, had inched closer and closer to the bathroom, smelling a heady, pungent odor as he did so; it was the metallic smell of blood. He had drawn his own weapon more for something to hold onto than anything else. As he neared the bathroom, he extended a hand to a hallway light, but it didn't extend into the little room at the end of the hall to do much good. Brewer felt as if he were in the haunted house at Disneyland. A chill feeling of creepiness extended along his spine to the hairs on his neck.

At the door, Brewer wheeled, but there was no one there.

He saw that the bathtub was filled with a dark, soupy mixture which looked purple. He feared the worst, got a grip on his senses and called for Boutine several times. But Boutine was still out at the car.

He gritted his teeth, placed his fingers on the light switch and closed his eyes for a moment.

He hit the switch and the room was bathed in a soft red glow, just as the living room had been. The bathwater was also a deep crimson color, almost matching the shower curtain.

"Sick bastard," muttered Brewer, who went to the sink and turned on the tap, half expecting blood to flow from it. He repeatedly threw cold water into his face, trying desperately to accept what his eyes had presented to him.

Boutine reentered with no further news on Jessica, except that she was still not answering at the hotel. Boutine's agitation was near crippling. Brewer stumbled from the bathroom, visibly quaking.

"I know how you feel about her, Otto, but we've got to believe she's okay." Brewer's voice was shaking unevenly.

"What'd you see back there?" he asked. "You're white as a ghost."

"Fucking bathtub is filled with blood."

"Christ." Otto stepped around Brewer to see for himself.

"We've got to do a top-to-bottom of this place. Find every scrap of evidence so the break-in won't be held against us. We'll need to take samples of the bath"—Joe Brewer was about to say *water,* then *blood,* but he was unable to know what to call it—"the stuff in the bathtub."

Brewer had been transfixed. Now Otto came back ashen as well. "Just imagine how many people have provided this bastard with his kicks. Imagine him using your blood for his bloody bath."

"The kitchen, Otto. Let's check the fridge."

"Be my guest."

They toured the kitchen and found the refrigerator near empty, with no jars filled with blood.

"Not much of an eater, is he?" said Brewer.

"What's down here?" asked Boutine, locating a door to a basement area. It was dark and dirty below, and once more the bulb light that flickered on did so beneath a curtain of streaked-on blood. The basement floor was dirt, the shelving laced here and there with cobwebs, but the shelves clear of dust. There were no power tools to be found, and the centerpiece of the room was a large, floor-model freezer, quite old, with the word *Philco* nearly invisible on its front.

"Must've taken the tools with him," Brewer was saying when Boutine, ahead of him, said, "The freezer."

Boutine pulled the top back and stared down at a handful of blood packs and a few jars of frozen blood. "He's cleaned out his stock. This tears it. He knows we're on to him, and he's cleared out."

"But how? How'd he know?"

"Earlier conclusion. From the papers, from something Jess said to the press, who knows? Overplayed his hand killing Lowenthal, knew we were close on his ass, panicked, rushed outta here in one hell of a hurry."

"Yeah, left his tub full of blood, left his cat, too, all locked up. I don't know. Seems to me he plans to come back."

"Should've listened to Jess. Should've known better," Otto lamented.

"Hey, the bastard had us all fooled with Lowenthal's suicide."

"Not Jess. She knew. She knew it was phony, and she tried to tell me so. And somehow he knows that she knew, that she is a threat to him."

"You're jumping to wild conclusions, Otto."

"Am I? Christ, I wish I were."

More cars arrived outside, both police and FBI, strobe lights alerting the entire neighborhood to their presence. Boutine turned to Brewer and sadly said, "If I only knew where she was."

"Sit this one out, Otto. Take my car. Get out to Lincolnshire and find her. You'll see, she'll be fine."

"I've already sent cars out there, dammit. No one can locate her."

In Matisak's den, where he had written his letter to Jessica Coran, there were blood splotches on the pad over the huge oaken desk, and a pen like the one found at Lowenthal's."

"Don't touch anything," said Otto. "Bag it all. It'll prove to be the same blood used in the letter to Jess."

"The inkwell," said Brewer, recalling the story of the blood letter. They had found the same paraphernalia at Lowenthal's.

Boutine used a handkerchief to lift it and sniff. "Blood, all right."

"Real raving maniac, this guy."

"Able to work a nine-to-five when he wasn't bloodletting." Boutine had had enough. He replaced the inkwell on the blotter and said, "Be sure our guys get it all and take complete care with everything. Get the usual—"

"We'll take care of it, Otto."

"And the telephone records. They might tell us a lot."

"Will do."

Boutine, his shoulders slumped, feeling defeated by the

vampire once more, went through the house the way he had come and out into the air where he could breathe. The house had been warm, like a Turkish bath, Matisak's disease—as Jess had said—requiring warmth. Well, now things were going to be really hot for the bastard, he thought. But the fear and worry for Jessica beat back all other thoughts, and so he found Brewer's car and called once again into central to learn if anyone anywhere in the city had heard word one from Jessica Coran.

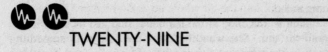

TWENTY-NINE

Jessica fought the effects of the sedative, knowing somewhere in the deep recesses of her mind that the madman would prefer a mild sedative to a strong one, that he'd prefer to see some life in her as he drained it away to no life. It would be his way.

Images of the ugly Gamble and the dark, taller figure pawing over her body now played in her fevered mind, as if flashing on a screen at the back of her retinas. She clawed her way back, back, back toward consciousness, praying against hope that they had not found and removed her gun from her.

As she did so, she began to feel something.

She felt claustrophobic; she felt a heavy weight against her chest. She felt an animal presence over her like the stifling creature in a nightmare painting that might sit upon a woman's breast and suck the breath from her mouth. She felt Gamble at her breasts, pleasing himself over her where he had torn away her blouse.

She inwardly cringed and heard the other man saying, "That's enough, Gamble."

"I'm n-n-not fin-finished with her."

She felt her slacks being undone and tugged over her hips. "Oh, Ch-Ch-Christ," moaned Gamble, "w-w-what's this?"

"It's a gun, you idiot. She's had it right along."

"I-I-I coulda been-been shot?"

285

"Get off and get the gun. Give it to me," the vampire demanded.

Gamble snatched at the leather pouch just as she tried to grab the gun. She was hit across the face with something feeling like a brick—a shoe with a foot in it—and it sent her back to the depths of confusion.

"Make her ready," said Matisak.

"I'mmmmmmm n-n-not finished w-with—"

"You're finished, damn you. Gamble? Gamble? Put the fucking gun down."

"Y-y-you pro-missssed mmm-me."

"All right, all right, but we don't have all night, Gamble."

Matisak didn't want Gamble's semen in her. He didn't want another hotshot criminalist to question why the final victim of the Chicago vampire would be raped. Matisak had worked out a neat formula. The vampire was, in fact, two men: Lowenthal and Gamble. Now, with Lowenthal gone, Gamble finds himself unable to carry on, despite a valiant effort to do so with Dr. Coran. If the little prick penetrated her and left his DNA all over her, one or more of Coran's associates might simply pick up where she left off, too nosy for his or her own good.

But now Gamble, standing nude with his disgusting shape and his even more vile erection pointed at Matisak, along with the woman's .38 Police Special, had the upper hand, and the man was downright crazy. For a moment, Matisak believed he was going to fire.

It hadn't taken much to talk the weak-minded fool into "sharing" a woman. Matisak knew all about Gamble's fantasies and proclivities and perversion. His was a sexual perversion, unlike Matisak, who had no interest in sex for sex's sake.

"All right, all right, Hillary. You're right."

"And I don't want you here when I do it!" He was asserting himself with his big guns pointed, and the stutter had suddenly disappeared. "Wait in the other room."

"Sure, sure, Hillary." Matisak turned and did as he was told. "Take whatever time you feel is necessary."

"This is going to be the best night of my life," Hillary Gamble explained. "She is beautiful."

"Yes, yes, she is."

He closed the door behind him, giving Gamble enough time to begin to feel comfortable, pacing as he did so, rubbing his chin with his gloved hands. He then found his own gun, a Beretta. He located the stubby silencer, and he screwed this onto the gun slowly.

When he reentered the room, Gamble was at the woman again like a pig over the trough. He made of himself an easy target, but it must be done exactly right. He scanned for the other gun, but it must be below the sofa beside which lay Gamble across the woman on the floor. She was beginning to fight back, coming around again, when suddenly she pulled over a lamp and it came crashing down on Gamble's head.

She then pushed him off and slithered toward a back hallway. Matisak gave pursuit, telling her to halt or he would put a bullet into her back. She turned and looked up at him from across the room, still in a dazed state of mind, yet terrified of the blood-drinker. However, somehow she managed to call his bluff.

"You won't shoot me," she said. "You don't want to waste my blood."

"I will if I must."

She took her chances, knowing that remaining inside this madhouse meant certain death; she leapt to her feet and raced for the back door, tearing it open, expecting the death shot to come any moment. She felt the cool night air on her bare legs and torso, and she screamed again and again before she felt his weight descend like a boulder over her, knocking her into the patchy, weedy grass and dirt of Gamble's backyard where she caught a momentary glance at the van used to lure her into the trap. She'd had the wind knocked from her and now she tried to catch her breath, but at the same time his gloved hand smothered her and he spit into her ear, saying, "Bitch! Damnable bitch!"

He forced her to her feet and guided her roughly back toward the maw of the death house, propelling her through the entryway, but never letting go of the grip he had on her arm, twisting it until she thought it would come off.

Inside, facing Gamble, who was still in pain, his forehead bleeding, Matisak shouted at the small man, "You stupid little bastard! Maybe you'll listen to me now! Now we do things my way! Now, get the rope. We string her up. Now!"

He then said into Jessica's ear, "You won't be doing any more running after I cut your ankle tendons." Gamble came around her with the rope, a ferret that made her skin crawl. As soon as her hands were tied, both men relaxed, and the one called Matisak, remaining in charge, shouted, "Get that black soldier out of here. It's time we went to work on her."

"Please . . . please," she pleaded uselessly.

Gamble said, "I love to hear a woman plead."

She felt the quick slashes to her ankles like bee stings when Matisak used his scalpel on her. She felt the first loss of blood trickling from her wounds and realized for the first time that she was going to die here. Her mind flashed on the horrible thoughts Candy Copeland's death had awakened in her that first night in Wekosha: *It's different when you know you are dying . . . when you die badly . . . when suffering is prolonged . . . Just knowing your own death is at hand . . .*

Worse still was knowing that Matisak could succeed with his diabolical cover-up, and no one would ever know the truth she would take to her grave . . .

She could hear them grunting as they worked to lower Kaseem's body so that she could take his place. Matisak must have had second thoughts about the police finding two bodies at the same location, for now he was ordering Gamble to help him carry the body to his van, saying, "I'll dispose of this problem later."

Gamble, like an obedient lapdog, trailed out with the

monster, an Igor to his Frankenstein. She shouted after them for Gamble to come to his senses and to realize that the other man was using him.

But they were gone and she was left to struggle against her bonds. When she did so, she came to realize that her bleeding, numb ankles had already been placed in the noose from which she would soon be dangling. Her heart raced as she fought to bring herself up to a sitting position. Tearful, dirty, all but her underclothes torn from her, she forced herself to be calm, relaxing her every muscle. She was double-jointed and she knew if she could concentrate, she could bring her arms overhead and at least get her hands out in front of her. Tied or not, they could be used as a deadly weapon, as she had learned at the academy. But her attempt was short-circuited when she heard them barging back through the kitchen, coming for her.

Gamble entered alone, coming for her, stretching his grimy hands out to her breasts as she shouted, "Dammit, Gamble, he's setting you up! Like he did Lowenthal!"

"Lowenthal k-k-killed him-s-s-self," he said to reassure himself, and she knew now that the thought had at least once been entertained by the retarded Gamble.

"Don't be a fool, Gamble. He intends to kill us both. "

Suddenly Matisak was forcing something into Gamble's hand. It was the Beretta, pointed directly at the little man's temple. Matisak stood firmly behind Gamble with complete control over the shorter man.

"Good night, Gamble," said Matisak as he pulled the trigger.

Gamble's body fell with a sound like potatoes rolling from a gunnysack. Brain matter and blood sprayed Jessica where she sat, attempting to scurry from Matisak. Her hands still behind her back, her ankles bound in the tightened noose, she could offer no resistance beyond flailing and an attempted weak-kneed kick or two. He smiled down at her before jamming a gag into her mouth, his rubber-gloved hand almost breaking her jaw. He tied a gauze bandage around the gag to hold it in place, and he spoke as he worked.

"Poor little bastard just couldn't take it any longer without his old friend and partner, Lowenthal. Gamble did his last victim, and then he did himself. Simple, neat and no guesswork. The cops'll love it. Your bosses will love it. But enough about everybody else, huh?"

He began tugging on the rope looped through a notch hole in the overhead beam and she began to feel herself being dragged toward the position that Kaseem's corpse had occupied only minutes before. Her eyes were wide with horror, the helplessness of her position making her wish for a quick and painless end.

"Yes, enough about others and the outside world, Jessica," he continued his devilish taunts. "Let's talk about us . . . about you and me, and about your blood . . ."

Otto Boutine knew the city well, having spent a number of years in the Chicago field office himself. He had sped away from Matisak's place toward the crime lab, hoping against hope that he might find Jessica curled up on a cot in an internist's room somewhere there, catching up on her sleep. Along the way, he received a patch-through from Quantico. It was the blood specialist, Robertson, telling him that Jessica had called D.C. in search of him, and that she seemed to be on to something, and had asked him to fly to Chicago tonight.

The news only added to his depression. She'd been trying to get him, and he had been unavailable to her. One of the operatives at the field office had finally come forward with a story about her having telephoned there for Brewer, claiming that the Chicago vampire had telephoned her at the crime lab. It had been this news that had sent them racing to Matisak's place. But now all leads seemed to end in a blind alley. Where on earth could she be? Would they not know until it was too late? Had she been abducted by Matisak?

The radio crackled with static and then a rough voice said

into it, "This is Sergeant Iverson, Precinct 13. Seems we got a call through dispatch from your APB—"

"Dr. Coran!" He was instantly excited. "When?"

"Well over two hours ago, sir, just before I came on shift. Just happened to be looking back over the log when I saw it."

Otto was frantic, but he tried to recall where the 13th Precinct fell, somewhere on the North Side. He had had a good friend who worked out of a decoy unit at the 13th, so he knew something of the area. He now pleaded for more information on the call. "Did Dr. Coran leave any word for me?"

"Negative, sir. Something of a strange call, actually."

"Look, do you have it transcribed? Can you read it back?"

"Sir, we have it on tape. We keep all incoming calls on tape for thirty days before we discard, and—"

"Well, for Christ's sake, Iverson, play the damned tape."

"Coming to you, Inspector Boutine."

Boutine instantly recognized and reacted to Jessica's voice, although it was going through a maze of relays from a tape not the best of quality to begin with, but it was wonderful to hear her. She was asking questions about an address that led to someone named Hillary Gamble. The name sounded familiar but he couldn't place it.

He listened to the police dispatcher's reply and waded through the ceremonies as she was then speaking to a duty sergeant. The duty sergeant pulled what they had on Gamble.

Otto racked his brain for where he had seen the name before, and then he recalled that it had been in the list of personnel folders he had shared with Brewer at Balue-Stork.

He continued to listen to the tape. Jess asked for a rundown on Gamble. It was given, and Boutine stored the address in his mind for safekeeping. He knew the area, knew that he could be there in five, ten minutes tops. He swung the car completely around, tossing the strobe light overhead as he did so, causing two other cars to collide behind him as he peeled away.

The final remark on the tape was the desk sergeant's explaining how Gamble had been arrested for indecently exposing himself on an occasion of his having called police out on a complaint against a neighbor.

Otto bore down on the neighborhood where Gamble lived. As he did so, he thought of the bizarre triangle that Lowenthal, Matisak and Gamble created. He wondered if they could all have played a part in the killings, or if Jessica had been right about Lowenthal's being an old-fashioned patsy. So how did Gamble figure into it? Hillary Gamble was male. At Balue-Stork, Otto had set his personnel file aside, thinking that a woman working in the mailroom was of no importance to the case. But Hillary was a man, and from the sound of him, a man who could be dangerous.

Otto called the precinct back. "Sergeant Iverson."

"Yes, sir?" the sergeant responded militarily.

"Check your records for any complaints filed against a Matthew Matisak."

"Have earlier done so, sir, when the APB was run on him, and sorry to say, but nothing—not so much as a parking ticket."

Otto was crossing Irving Park Road at Ashland, having come off the Kennedy, headed for Gamble's address.

Brewer's voice broke the static of the radio. "I've got your destination, Otto, and I'm behind you."

THIRTY

It was all taking too much time, Matisak thought, and he began to rush things. He lifted the trach tube and turned it to the off position. He placed the tourniquet about her neck, and finally, he kneeled below Jessica Coran's throat. With her eyes wide, the way he liked it at first, he pressed the sharp, beveled edge of the straw into her throat, but she suddenly flailed and writhed. He dropped the spigot as a trickle of blood ran down her soft, white throat, and the glass tubing crackled into jagged pieces.

"You damnable bitch!" He struck her and went back to the briefcase for a second spigot. This time he held her head so that it was immovable as he quickly jammed the straw into her jugular with the practiced hands of a physician.

She couldn't see it, but she knew that the end of the tube had just filled with her blood. He tightened the tourniquet about her throat, almost choking off her air, and then he opened the spigot.

She smelled him as he moved in closely enough to lower his head below the spigot where he lapped up her blood before it could spill to the floor.

The horror of the moment transfixed her.

She was dying.

Her life was running out of her.

There was no escape.

She was dying the way that Candy Copeland and the others had died: at the hands of a bloodsucking, human lamprey, a Tort 9 monster.

She was fast becoming another statistic for the FBI records.

And there were sure to be future victims of this madman, Matisak . . .

J.T., Boutine, Brewer, all the others, would find Gamble with his head shot off at close range, a suicide note written in blood—perhaps her blood—beside him, and Matisak would be safe from anyone's hounding him, so long as he chose to stay "on the wagon," or to gain his blood by other means. He could never again safely use the spigot.

But he *would* kill again, and again, and . . .

"Just like milking a cow," he said in her ear between gurgles and slurps.

She felt the uncaring and dizziness overtaking her; wondered how long she would be conscious. She didn't want to be conscious any longer . . .

Or was it all a terrible dream? Had the entire long nightmare of the case she had pursued since Wekosha been just that? A long, long nightmare from which she seemed unable to climb?

Was she in fact in Virginia, in her apartment, in her bed, about to wake any moment from the horror? It was a comforting alternative to which her anguished mind resorted moments before passing out.

Matisak began to enjoy himself too much. He had stopped the flow of her blood, and she had regained a weak consciousness. This excited him.

But he fought the old urges as overwhelming as they were; he must not give in. He must carry through with his plan. There was too great a push on for his capture, and even with Lowenthal's death, too much doubt cast by this woman to let her live. The search for the vampire must end with Gamble's death.

He had planned it down to the smallest detail.

But there was much to do and each moment that Dr.

Coran was here meant a moment more that someone could trace her to Gamble's place. He must hurry.

But perhaps he had time for a little indulgence, perhaps a pint.

At least a half pint.

But first he must ready everything. He lined up the jars to within reach. He positioned the briefcase and puttered about with the power tools, readying these.

It was all going so perfectly.

He could hardly believe his luck, and that she had been such a fool. In the end, he thought, they were *all* fools. And he did the same work as the trap-door spider, taking its prey in through surprise.

"It was a surprise, wasn't it, Dr. Coran?" he asked, but she wasn't replying. She just hung there upside down, like a sleeping bat.

She was pretty, this one.

Jessica thought she heard her father's voice telling her how pretty she was. She was eleven years old and somewhat gangly and very awkward. She had been teased by some insensitive lout at the new school on the army base where her father had once more been relocated, and as a child going through a difficult period, relocation was the last thing she needed. She had just gotten settled in at the school in Germany when they'd had to pack everything up for Spain. Her mother's health had started falling off as well, and she would never fully regain her strength. And so her father had been spending more time looking after her.

"You're the most beautiful girl in that school, Jessie, and when you go back, you've just got to keep telling yourself that. And then you just watch what happens . . ."

All of her life, her father had been a great morale booster, a great teacher and a wonderful friend. A flood of memories about him, and of her being with him, washed over her. It was her father who had convinced her that she had what it would take to be a medical doctor, and later what it would take to be an FBI woman.

She heard sounds around her that disturbed the memories of her and her father at their summer retreat home where the woods were alive with wind and sunshine and small creatures, and where they hunted deer. She had learned to disembowel and skin the deer at a young age, and her interest in forensic medicine began with her fascination in exploring the inner workings of the deer's body.

She had learned to overcome her initial fears and squeamishness to the point of placing her arm into the carcass up to her elbow in order to come away with the organs in her hand. Later, on many a hunting trip with men in Minnesota, Oregon and Canada, she was always told that she didn't have to watch as they cut open the carcass, hung it from a tree and proceeded to clean it of unwanted parts. More than one man who had become interested in her ran quickly away from her when she had shown them the quickest and most efficient method of disemboweling the creature.

Something dark like a void filled her mind and blotted out these thoughts now, and it sat on her chest like an evil urchin, grinning at her. It was mindless and shapeless and it, like the deer, was cut open, soaking her with blood as the deer did when she reached in to remove its insides. She strained to see what it was and then it coalesced into a form, the form of a woman. She feared going nearer, and yet her mind made the final step toward the form dangling from the tree. It was her.

The shock brought her around, making her moan, and the moan increased her consciousness.

She recalled where she was.

Recalled Gamble.

Recalled Matisak.

Recalled her escape attempt, and its having failed.

She felt her arms tied behind her back, the gag in her mouth.

She felt the pressure of the blood in her head and the pain in her ankles from her own weight.

She felt the strange, unusual weight on her throat: the spigot.

She forced herself to remain calm, telling herself she must think . . . must think . . . must think . . .

Jessica knew that Matisak didn't want her to be too conscious, and that he certainly didn't want to have her eyes pinned on him as he carried out his heinous ritual on her. It was, after all, a weakness, an addiction, and even Matisak knew that his drinking blood was an addiction, and addicts only indulged their addictions in private. He didn't like to be watched at this stage of his killing act, and not wishing her eyes to be put out by his scalpel, she held them closed against the nightmare. She thought of the mistakes she had made; how her mistakes had led her into this trap; how she had broken with FBI procedure in coming here alone; how she had gotten Kaseem killed, and how she had helped that bastard, Matisak.

Too late for regrets . . . too late, her mind told her. Or was it her father's voice? Sounded like Dad, something he'd say. She drew on the comforting thought and clung to it. It was all she had.

Within very close range of her she heard Matisak drinking her blood from a mason jar.

Some of your blood, he had written in the letter. And now he had it.

He had been clever, like a champion chess player, making his move only after a feint, using his pawns—Gamble and Lowenthal—wisely. She had been checkmated; he had won her as his final prize, a prize he meant to squeeze blood from. And like a predatory animal, he had stalked her without her knowing just how close he had crept on silent feet, to pounce when she least expected it. He held her body now with the same reverence a tiger gives its life-giving prey. She had become the slain deer and her precious life was being stripped from her by the predator.

She brought up the sheer power of the hatred she held for this monster, Matisak. She drew on her hatred for strength.

Her eyes still shut against him and his awful proceedings, she heard gas escape from him. He was burping after draining a jar of her blood. He would be coming back for more . . . and more . . . and more . . . until there was no more.

She tried to concentrate on her father, recalling his kind features, his loving manner, but his face coalesced into that of Otto Boutine. She clung to Otto's image.

Meanwhile, around her she half heard the killer stacking up the instruments that fulfilled his sick desires. She heard the rattle of bottles and the movement of heavy tools. She fought back the fear.

"Fight, Jessie. Fight and hang on," she heard her father's voice from deep within. Her father had taught her to stand up for herself, to be tough and independent; how to hunt and trap, but he had never foreseen the day when she would be in the trap.

She struggled just the same, fighting against hope to regain the strength she would need to slow Matisak down.

She forced her eyes open to the horror before her. Gamble's body still lay where it had fallen in a pool of purple blood, discolored by the lack of light. Matisak was prancing ponylike about the small, crowded space, very much pleased with himself. He was now crouching over his brown valise, staring into two vials of semen; it must not be Gamble's semen. In order for his ruse to work, Teach must use some anonymous supply, likely stolen from a sperm bank. This time, he must even leave the vial along with his tools and case, to further implicate Gamble.

His back to her, she curled her body forward at the waist, and being double-jointed, she brought her tied hands from her back to her front. At the same instant, he sensed her movement, stood and rushed at her, fearing she intended to snatch out the spigot, to destroy a second one, allowing herself to bleed to death very messily in the bargain.

She saw his charge, and with her extended fists, she madly and blindly struck out at him, creating of her fists a deadly weapon, as she had been taught at the academy.

The doubled-up fists caught Matisak in the temple, knocking him off balance, his weight grazing her as he lost his footing, tripping over Gamble. This caused her entire body to sway within inches of the gun he had used in killing Gamble, which was left now on a coffee table.

She reached for the gun, but it was just beyond her fingers. She swayed her body with as much power as she could muster, her hand extended toward the gun. Matisak kicked out at the table at the same instant her hand wrapped around the gun. She had it in her grasp. The gun slipped but she caught it by the trigger guard and held on, dangling upside down.

She heard Matisak scrambling about the floor, suddenly afraid of her, but he could not be seen. Did he have another gun? A knife? She tugged with one hand at the gag in her mouth while keeping the gun pointed ahead. As she half freed the gag, she realized that he was coming up from behind her, about to pounce. She swiveled, bringing the gun around and firing, missing him but sending him diving away into the darkness again.

She saw the scalpel gleaming in the night beside the briefcase. *Where was he?*

She opened fire, exploding the jar of blood she saw on a nearby end table, a jar of her blood.

"Damn you!" shouted Matisak, and she fired at the sound of his voice, missing him. She tugged at what remained of the gag, freeing herself of it.

"The sh-shots will bring police, Matisak! You bastard. You'd better run while you have the chance. Go on, run! Run!" Her voice was filled with venom and hatred and the wise use of her academy training which taught that intimidation was half the contest in a confrontation. "Go on, run!"

He did run, and she fired at the black shadow as it

pounced on her, ripping the gun from her. She knew he was shot, but not fatally.

She screamed as loudly as she could nonstop, trying desperately to alert someone outside the house, but even the gunshots seemed to have been ignored.

Matisak fell back from her, the gun now in his possession. He brandished the gun in her direction as if he would pull the trigger, but he failed to do so. A quick end would be welcomed, and it would be out of keeping with the vampire's modus operandi. She taunted him to shoot, saying, "Go ahead, shoot! Shoot, you bastard! Kill me, damn you! Kill me!"

But the shot did not come. Matisak stumbled, losing his balance once more, weakened by the shock of the gunshot to his side, staring at his own blood and trembling to see it running from himself.

Matisak passed out.

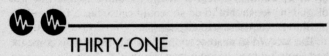

THIRTY-ONE

Using her teeth, Jessica tore at the rope holding her in bondage, knowing she hadn't fatally shot Matisak, and that her time was limited. She struggled with her bonds, animal fear motivating her. Unable to get her hands free, she curled toward her ankles where the feeling had gone dead in her feet. She tried to get her weight off the rope, remembering that so long as there was a dead weight on the knot he used, there was no way to free it.

Once she managed to lessen the pull of her body against the rope, it was not hard to remove the noose about her ankles. She was holding tight to the beam where her hands fit through the same groove as had been used to loop the rope. She carefully lowered herself so as not to jar Matisak.

The moment she was on her feet, she crumpled to the floor. She realized only now that she was unable to stand or to walk, that Matisak had severed her Archilles tendons. She knew that unless an operation was performed tonight, she'd lose the use of her legs permanently. Even if she did receive the necessary medical attention, she was certain no one would give her any guarantees she wouldn't need a cane for the rest of her life.

She lay now alongside Gamble's lifeless body, his blood matting her hair. She heard Matisak moan, disturbed from his blackout, coming around slowly.

At her throat bobbed the now heavy, disturbing object that had been the instrument of death used on all of Matisak's previous victims. She had instinctively reached up to it, wanting to tear it away, the same as she might a disgusting leech, but to do so would cause her a further loss of blood, weakness and dizziness.

The bastard so nearby, trying now desperately to come to, had crippled her, possibly for life, but he had also scarred her throat. He had also reached down into her sacred soul deep within her, and he scarred this, too, with the acid of his aberration.

She found the tattered remains of the blouse that Gamble had slit from her with his knife. She clung to it as if it might bring some measure of strength, and then she draped herself with it.

Panting, her fear rose in her like a tangible new organ that somehow took on life and welled up from the pit of her stomach; her fear had balled up within her, creating an enormous lump of palpitating tissue pushing up from her gut, trying to escape through her throat.

"Get hold of it. Get hold of yourself," she pleaded with herself, her knuckles going white where she had grabbed onto a coverlet on the couch and squeezed.

The living fear that threatened to overwhelm was fought down, and now she searched for a weapon, *anything* she might use to defend herself while in her vulnerable state. She looked everywhere for the gun but it had disappeared. Was it somewhere below Matisak's bulk? She feared going near him to investigate. One wrong move and she was certainly dead.

She debated with herself about the relative merits of using a chair, a poker, one of the bastard's power tools—anything that would end the madman's life and the nightmare she found herself in. But all of these choices necessitated dragging herself halfway across the room and back, and she wasn't sure she had the strength, or the time.

Frantic, knowing her time was running out, Jessica's eyes lit on a large, shining portion of broken glass; slick with blood—*her blood*—it was part of the jar that she'd shattered with a bullet. As if from far away, or looking through the wrong end of a telescope, her brain in a *whirr,* she watched her hand reach out for the razor's edge of the broken glass. It was hefty, a large portion of a mason jar where the bottom met the side. With this in her hands, she had the where-withal to kill the killer before he stirred. She need only slash his goddamned jugular.

She put all her effort into crawling toward Matisak now holding firm to the deadly glass. She reached his moaning form and inched along it toward his throat, trying not to disturb him further. As she got into position, within striking distance of his throat, she carefully reached around to lift his head back by the hair in order to expose the throat. It would be a fitting end, she thought, and only what the bastard deserved. She would then watch him bleed to death as he had planned to watch her.

She was about to dig into his jugular as she would a dangerous animal's with the only weapon at her disposal when he suddenly grabbed her wrist, squeezing, trying to make her drop the glass.

She screamed and tore away from him, crawling away from him, feeling like a slug, unable to walk or so much as stand without toppling over; behind her, she heard his laughter as he watched her slithering movements. An overwhelming sense of despair and helplessness pervaded her mind, threatening to weaken her resolve and sap her physical reserves, depleting her completely. She now cringed in a corner, the poor excuse for a weapon now hidden deep in the folds of a coverlet she'd found as she dragged herself as far from Matisak as she possibly could.

She wanted to scream, but that most likely would raise him sooner than it would alarm anyone outside. She could not believe that no one in the neighborhood had called the police at the sounds of shots and screaming. She thought she had faintly heard the sound of sirens earlier, but they had died away, as if racing away to another location.

But then, she was in Chicago.

Matisak came closer . . . closer . . . closer.

As they screeched into view of the house where
Gamble lived, Brewer's car slid in beside Boutine's. Brewer
hopped out and grabbed Boutine who was prepared to rush
the house. Joe repeated his earlier call for calmness and
rational thought. The FBI men had come to a halt at the end
of the block, their car motors idling hot. Brewer held both
hands against Otto's massive chest, making him hold on,
but Boutine shoved his friend aside. Brewer, like a hound on
a scent, was right back at him, standing in his face, calling
for an intelligent approach to the situation.

"Otto, we don't know anything. We can only presume
that Gamble and Jess are inside there. We have no evidence
whatever that Matisak is in that apartment house."

"Gamble works at Balue-Stork; he knows Matisak,"
countered Otto, about to strike Brewer if necessary.

Again Brewer placed a restraining hand on him. "Going
in wild eyed and shooting isn't going to cut it, *Cowboy*!"

The old nickname Brewer used for his friend seemed to
slow him even if just a little. Boutine's steely eyes bore into
Brewer like a pair of super-heated, twisting corkscrews. "If
anything's happened to Jess . . ."

"She may not even be here, Otto. Now come on."

Otto finally relented. "Whataya' have in mind?"

"The alleyway. We make our way toward the house from
the rear. Then, if it's warranted, we'll get backup."

Otto bit his lip and nodded. "All right, we do it your way,
for now. But this bastard's been yanking my chain for too
long, Joe, and I want two things to come out of this night.
We see Jess safely away and we take this creep out. And if
she is in there alone with this devil, I won't allow it a
moment longer. Come on!"

Boutine began down the alleyway at a trot.

"But we got no warrant, Otto, no juice here, no probable-
fucking-cause anymore than we had at Matisak's house."
They both knew that everything found at Matisak's would
be ruled inadmissible in a court of law. "If you charge in

here—'' But Boutine wasn't listening; instead, he was
pointing at a silver-gray, Balue-Stork van nearly invisible in
the metallic shadows behind Gamble's place.

When Brewer caught up, Otto whispered in his ear,
''There's your goddamned probable cause, Joe.''

Joe went closer to the van, inspecting it, looking into the
little square of glass at the rear, seeing only darkness inside.
''It'd still be better if we drew Matisak out,'' he whispered
back to Otto who was studying the house.

When Otto made no reply, Brewer, fidgeting with the van
door and finding it unlocked, suggested they check the interior.
He also said, ''We maybe oughta call the fire department to
the house across the street, cause a little diversion for
Matisak and his friend Gamble. Then we go in like you say,
if they don't step outside.''

Boutine just kept thinking of Jessica alone inside with a
madman. If she weren't already dead, she was suffering.
''I'm going in now, Joe.''

''That's crazy, Otto.''

''Damn it, Joe! Jess is in there. I feel it.''

Suddenly the van door came flying open and both men
whipped out their guns, almost firing at Captain Kaseem's
stiff body. ''Jesus Christ!'' said Brewer, shaken.

''Oh, God, it's Kaseem,'' said Otto, stepping around the
van for a better look. ''Think this is probable cause enough
for the court, Joe?''

''We've got to get inside there. Now.''

''Now you're talking.''

''But we need to call for backup, Otto.''

''Go ahead. I'll make my way around front and enter
from there. You come in from behind.''

Brewer raced back to the car and the radio, all the while
praying that Otto would not do anything heroic or foolish on
his own, that he'd wait a decent interval for Joe to be in
place. Brewer's mind was rocketing with images and
questions. Was Jessica inside that house, alone with Mati-

sak? Was she just as dead as Kaseem? What would it do to Otto?

Brewer tore open his car door and radioed for assistance from any and all in the area, giving Gamble's address, using the Chicago Police code for ''officer down.'' This code would send an army down on Gamble's place.

He then raced back down the alleyway for the rear of the apartment house. When he and Otto had been in the academy together, Boutine always did things the dangerous way, getting the highest marks on obstacle courses and range shooting, but also getting shot and killed more times than anyone else in the class. That propensity, along with the western flare and drawl, had earned him the moniker of Cowboy among his friends in the agency. Otto had been orphaned at an early age, had witnessed the disintegration of his family, and the loss of a small horse ranch outside Bozeman, Montana. He had come up the hard way, and for this Brewer had always admired the determination, grit, and back-bone of the man. Even in his wild youth, even while being shot dead with red dye or an electronic beam on the proving grounds at Quantico, Otto was always focused, controlled. He had now spent the better part of his life tracking the most insane of criminal minds with a sense of purpose that bordered on religious zeal.

It was what separated the Joe Brewers of the Bureau from the Otto Boutines.

So, here he was, the Cowboy still, tracking down the sinister bad guys, just as reckless and careless as the much younger man Joe had first met at the academy so many years ago.

Would he wait for backup? Would he give it the few minutes necessary? Would Otto even wait for Joe to get into place before he did a swan dive through the bay window out front? So far this night, Boutine had gone against all his training, allowing his own killer instinct to take control of him.

It was up to Joe to back him up any way he could. If Boutine would allow him that privilege.

Mad, crazed Matisak was again enjoying himself; his bloody wound seemed numb now. His facial features were contorted more with hatred for Jessica Coran than with pain.

"You've been a naughty girl, haven't you, Jessica? It will take more time now. I'll have to sedate you again, tie you by your heels again, tie your hands again . . . just as you want . . . to keep me here longer. You would die to catch me . . . give your life for the cause of stopping me. I am flattered, and I respect you . . . I do. So much character. I've never killed anyone with so much fight in her. But you leave me little choice but to do it now and be damned with how it looks."

His hand shot out for her from where he kneeled over her. With the gun in his right hand, he tore at her hair with a bloody left hand, viciously yanking her head forward, into the barrel of the gun, blackening her eye, making her screech.

"I should blow your fucking brains out now, bitch! Like I did Gamble's."

Pain was shooting through her. "But you won't." Her words were breathless.

"You think you know me?"

"Enough . . . enough to know that you want to make me suffer more, and to do that—" She tore out the trach tube at her throat and hurled it across the room. They both heard it shatter into multiple pieces.

He pistol-whipped her across the chin, knocking her back. "I have others." His assured eyes smiled wickedly at her. He put the gun into his belt and reached for her with more rope, readying to tie her up once again.

With all the strength she could put behind it, she brought up the jagged piece of glass, sinking it deep into his throat, making him scream and pull back. At the same instant the living room window burst into a thousand pieces as Otto Boutine came crashing through.

"Jess! Jess!" he was shouting as he rolled into a dark corner of the room.

"He's got a gun!" she shouted in return.

At the same instant both men opened fire, returning several shots apiece, and then silence reigned.

From the corner where she had huddled, she cried out, "Otto! Otto, are you all right?"

There was no answer and the police lights from outside sent a chilling silhouette against the window sash.

"You friend's dead," croaked Matisak. "And now it's your turn." He aimed, said, "Checkmate," and fired point-blank at her head. She heard the pathetic metal click of an empty chamber.

"Drop it! Drop it, you bastard, or you're mincemeat!" shouted Joe Brewer, who had slipped into the house from the rear. "I ought to blow you away."

Other cops swarmed in from all sides now, two in uniform taking Matisak and shoving him hard against a wall, frisking him. His side wound was still pumping blood, and the bullet had likely passed through him without hitting any vital organs. There was a cut to the throat where she had almost gotten at his jugular.

Brewer bent over Jessica, asking if she was all right. "Get me to Otto. Otto!" Her voice was choked with blood seeping into her windpipe.

Brewer helped her to where Otto was sitting upright against a wall as if simply at rest. His eyes shone only dimly in the darkness. He was bleeding from two wounds to the abdomen. He was conscious but weak.

"Get her out of here, Joe. Get her to a hospital!" Boutine began coughing and the hack made him spit up blood. It discolored his lips and his ashen-white skin. His white shirt was soaked slick with his blood.

"Get an ambulance!" she shouted, snatching at Brewer

even as the men with the stretchers were spilling into Gamble's small rat hole. "Hurry! Hurry!"

Brewer began telling the medics what to do. "Take these two. Forget the other two. One is dead and the other one is our prisoner. Now, go! Go!"

Jessica clung to Otto. She was draped in an old blanket that'd belonged to Gamble, but she, like Otto, was losing blood. The tear to her jugular and the cuts at her heels continued to bleed. She felt dizzy, light-headed, and now that she knew that Matisak was in custody, she could finally let down, and the moment she did, she went into a traumatic shock.

The medics rushed to her aid, and Boutine became agitated, yelling for them to do something for her. Brewer told Boutine to shut up and stay calm, that he was losing enough blood to kill two men. More paramedics arrived on the scene, two others taking charge of Otto while the first two worked on stabilizing Jessica.

Otto said several times as if it were a litany, "Take care of Jess . . . take care of Jess . . ."

Otto was dead before they laid him onto the stretcher.

Brewer, seeing this, became enraged. He turned to face Matisak. "You butcher! You goddamned butcher! Now you've taken—" He leapt onto Matisak, pummeling him with his fists until several other agents tore him away.

"Joe, Joe!"

"Christ's sake!"

"Cocksucking maniac kills good people, and whataya reckon'll happen to him? Fed pen for the criminally insane? Bastard oughta fry, but he won't. Oughta die here and now!"

One of the other agents grabbed for Brewer's gun in his shoulder holster just as Brewer's hand wrapped around it.

"He ain't worth your life now, Brewer . . . Brewer!"

Brewer eased his grip on the gun, and the other man took it. "Until you cool down."

"All right . . . all right," he said, pulling away. "I'm all right."

"Just the same, I'll hold on to this. You go with the woman. She'll need you when she comes out of it."

"Yeah . . . yeah . . . I suppose you're right." He stared evilly across the room at Matisak. "You better hope they fry your ass, Matisak. If they don't, I will."

Matisak looked pathetic in both size and demeanor now; he didn't look at all special, or even extraordinary in the negative sense, as of a freak in a sideshow. In fact, he looked so extremely ordinary, so close to normal and typical, that *normalcy* and *typical* and *ordinary* took on bizarre new meanings for the men standing in a circle around him. This was the vampire killer that had rocked Chicago and half a dozen midwestern states? He was neither tall nor short, neither fat nor thin, and his facial features might put him behind a desk in a bank or below a hood in a car shop. The only thing that marked him as at all different was a slight hump at the shoulders, almost like a buffalo hump, a thickness about the jowls, some scales and pock-mark discolorations over the skin. His hair was thinning and whispy, the receding hairline cutting a jagged edge in his profile. The eyes alone might seem unusual as they glowed a dark blue against the lights that were turned up on the bloody scene that Matisak had created.

In the midst of it lay Gamble's body, a bullet through the temple.

Brewer gathered himself up and shouted to his next in command. "Leonard, three things, okay?"

"You name it, boss."

"Get that bastard out of my sight and handle him as if he were Harry Houdini; and I want our best E.T. team in here and no one—*no one*—is to touch a goddamned thing—"

"Brewer! She's coming around," said one of the agents of Jessica. "She wants to talk to you."

"No way," said the medic. "She needs every ounce of energy."

Joe Brewer went to his knees over Jessica.

"Joe . . . Joe . . ."

"Yes, it's me."

"Otto . . . is he . . . ?"

"He's . . . he's going to be fine, Jess." The lie felt like lead in his throat.

She breathed deeply. "Thank God."

"Yeah . . ."

"And Joe . . ."

"Yes?"

"Nail the bastard, Joe. Promise me."

"You've got it, Dr. Coran. You've got it."

The medics carried her out.

The second set of medics lifted Boutine on his stretcher but Brewer stopped them. "Put . . . put the chief's body back against the wall where he was shot."

"What?"

"Do the fuck as I say!"

The medics shrugged at each other. Leonard conferred with Brewer. Brewer said loudly enough for all to hear, "I want photographs of everything in this room, and that includes Otto Boutine's . . . body."

"Yes, sir," replied Leonard, who turned to the other agents and said, "Come on, let's get the work done."

They all understood what it was that Brewer wanted most to happen here tonight: that they leave no stone unturned in nailing Matisak to the cross of justice. Whatever now would become of Matthew Matisak, Brewer and the other FBI men meant to avenge Boutine and Jessica Coran for the murder of one of their own and the torture of another.

Brewer finally left, leaving Boutine's body now as part of the crime scene, staring back only once at his old friend.

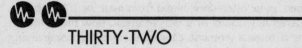

THIRTY-TWO

Four months later

On crutches, Dr. Jessica Coran worked her way through the corridors and past the cells that lined her way; she'd been pushing the healing process and so had not used a wheelchair for a week. The reconstructive surgery to her ankle tendons had worked remarkably well. She had seen some of the microscopic still shots the doctors had taken of the wounded tendons, and it amazed her that the doctors at Rush-St. Luke's Presbyterian in Chicago had been able to correct what Matthew Matisak had so blithely destroyed.

Her throat had healed nicely.

The glaring, stark white walls of the maximum security prison for the criminally insane gave it the appearance of a holy place, a white chapel or shrine, save for the gray bars.

She thought of all that Matthew Matisak had done that could not be corrected, either by surgery or prayer or the law. She thought about all of his other victims, the ones who had not lived, and she often wondered why she had been spared. She had recoiled at the gate outside and at the door leading into the cell block where Matisak now lived the life of a rather odd, unspeaking, former vampire. He was said to be engrossed in ancient works of literature from every nation, and in the Bible; word around the compound at Quantico had it that he had found numerous passages in the Bible that told men to drink the blood of others, and that his actions had been sanctioned by the highest authority, the

313

authority over all man's laws, God himself, who, as Matisak claimed, quite often drew blood from men, such as Job. She wondered how much of it was Matisak, how much rumor.

She faltered a moment, causing the guard accompanying her to stop and ask if she was all right.

"Yes, I'm all right; now, please, I want to go ahead." Her voice was a great deal firmer and stronger than she felt.

Inside she was asking herself. Are you sure you want to go through with this?

Yes, she told the voices that haunted her. Voices of the dead, Candy Copeland, Melanie Trent, Fowler, Gamble even, but most of all Otto's voice. She meant to face the vampire now caught in the net.

She hated Matisak passionately. She must go through with her plan.

Besides, the vampire apparently had dreams, and she had figured heavily in his dreams, and it was he who had requested that she come to speak with him. Could it be that, like so many other criminals trapped with only themselves and four walls to surround them, he had become repentant? Had the Bible reading softened the madman? Was there some secret he wished to convey only to her? Was there still more to learn from Matisak?

She had been called in by the new chief of the division, O'Rourke, who told her as delicately as possible that it was not an order that she speak to and record whatever Matisak wished to convey, but that it would be her decision. O'Rourke seemed genuinely to mean it. Jessica could have turned down the offer. She didn't have to be here—*except for the other thing*.

Except for the long, difficult nights in which she, too, had dreams, but not like the vampire's dreams. Hers were nightmares: nightmares of being held in bondage, unable to move, to struggle, to resist, while slowly, surely her life was drained from her; nightmares in which Matisak figured heavily, as did Otto; nightmares from which she believed she would never escape; nightmares from which she awoke screaming and bathed in sweat, her nostrils filled with the odor of blood.

The FBI had done its part, putting her on a strict regimen of work and visits to the resident shrink, Dr. Donna Lemonte. Lemonte told her she must face her fears, and he, like O'Rourke, gently urged her to hear what Matisak had to say to her.

"What could he possibly have to say that I want to hear?"

"That he's sorry," said Lemonte.

She exploded in the shrink's office. "Sorry! Fuck sorry! The bastard—"

"You need to get on with your life and put an end to this tragedy. Reliving it over and over can only—"

"But sorry isn't going to do it."

"Perhaps, but seeing him stripped of everything? Perhaps then—"

"It won't return Otto to me. It won't restore the blood he robbed from my body. It won't return—"

"You don't know what it will return, until you see him."

So she had come on the advice of her psychiatrist and at the gentle urging of the department, as psychological profiling was forever collecting data on convicted maniacs like Matisak, hoping that one day, somehow, the brain of a killer such as his could be fathomed.

She did not believe that day would ever come. They might get a few useful tidbits from a man like Matisak, and much of modern profiling techniques was built on conversations with serial killers, but Matisak was not likely interested a whit in FBI concerns.

She continued along the white corridor that led to the sealed inner sanctum where the worst offenders resided in separate cells, out of sight of the world and even one another. The walls here were so thick that even the inmates could not hear one another. It must be like living in the belly of an animal, she thought. She hoped that Matisak was suffering, but she doubted that it was enough.

It was, as O'Rourke had quoted from the agency manual, policy to speak to the criminally insane at whatever opportunity might arise in order not only to ascertain information about exactly how they went about their foul deeds but to gather their introspective reasons as to why.

All the whys were analyzed by the computers.

But they knew all about Matisak now; they had Balue-Stork records that proved him to be in every location where a young woman or man had disappeared within days of his visits. There remained, however, missing people or missing bodies, and any chance whatever of learning of the whereabouts of these supposed victims, she must take.

Indiana, Ohio and Kentucky had also been on Matisak's account list. Law enforcement agencies in those areas had been apprised, and now information on other possible Tort 9 victims was forthcoming.

But the thought of being within sight again of Matisak, of being within killing range of the man . . . it frightened her; and she was not a woman accustomed to dealing with the emotion. She wondered if she was more afraid of Matisak or herself, afraid that she would go through with her own mad plan against the madman who had taken Otto Boutine away from her.

Matisak had treated her as if she was a slaughter animal. He had drained her of her precious blood, and had fed on her blood, swallowing it.

At the courtroom door her gun had been taken from her, but she had also had the concealed one in her wheelchair. She had been brought in to point a finger at him, but she knew what she really wanted to point at him.

The courtroom appearance became excruciatingly painful and difficult for her, to have to talk about the details of his treatment of her, and she found herself physically ill at the sight of the plain-looking, ordinary-enough man in a gray suit and tie who did not look capable of the crimes she had watched him commit. He sat emotionless throughout the trials as if an observer from another country or planet, never once revealing the least emotion until he made his insanity bid.

Since the trial, she had gotten away on a much-needed rest, leaving J.T. in charge of the forensic testimony, unable to be both victim and forensic expert in the case. J.T. did an extremely good job on the stand, nailing the lid shut on Matisak. He demonstrated the spigot for the court and jury, explained how Dr. Jessica Coran had uncovered the truth below the huge throat gashes of three successive victims, and how Dr. Robertson had pinpointed the use of a sable brush used in a cosmetic attempt to cover the fact that the bodies were drained of blood.

The evidence of DNA meant another nail in the coffin over the vampire. A physical examination of the accused showed that he suffered from Addison's disease, which linked him with the cortisone capsule found at the Zion murder.

Teresa O'Rourke took the stand to explain how the psychological profiling team, using the innovative approach pioneered by Otto Boutine, had arrived at Matisak as the killer. She took too many bows so far as Jessica was concerned, but the logical, step-by-step process that led judge and jury from Wekosha, Wisconsin, across the Midwest to Chicago and Balue-Stork, was something everyone became fascinated with. They could understand this a great deal easier than the scientific aspects of the investigation.

The weakness in the case against Matisak was due to Otto's recklessness as well as her own, Jessica knew. Otto, in a highly charged emotional state, had not taken legal precautions. As a result nothing taken from Matisak's house, nor any photographic evidence from the house taken the night that Otto and Brewer had broken in, was held as admissible by the presiding judge, who quoted chapter and verse of the laws surrounding FBI and local police officials' necessity in securing proper search and seizure warrants, even in cases of probable cause where the FBI was concerned.

So the jury never heard it. This enraged anyone familiar with the case and particularly Jessica, who would have died as Matisak's final victim if Otto had waited for papers to be served. As a result none of the evidence so carefully gathered at Gamble's house by Brewer was admissible, either. The prosecutors could find no way to get this information before the jury.

This made the hair, fiber, blood and DNA evidence trebly important. Matisak was prosecuted not for killing Melanie Trent, Candy Copeland, Tommy Fowler or his many other typical victims, but for murdering Gamble, Maurice Lowenthal, Captain Kaseem, and for returning fire and killing Otto Boutine. He was convicted on two counts of murder and one count of manslaughter. Despite the fact the FBI evidence pointed to Matisak as the Chicago vampire and certain items found at Lowenthal's, such as the spigot and the designs and patent papers in his lockbox, also pointed to Matisak as the serial killer, he was acquitted of the charges of these heinous acts on the grounds of reasonable doubt and his insanity plea.

Jessica now stood before the man's cell.

She could not believe that she had made it this far. Her crutches were pinching at her underarms, and she perspired badly.

The door swung silently on an inward hinge, opening on a serving area. Matisak received his food through a tray that opened outward and moved inward electronically. At no time did a guard have to put his hand into the cell. A single chair stood in the ante-area outside the cell. This area, along with the cell itself, and the creature that stood in it, staring wide-eyed back at her, gave her the impression of a zoo, except that there were no bars here, only a thick, Plexiglas divider between them.

Matisak looked like a pathetic little man inside his cloistered, white cell behind the glass that separated him from the rest of the world. He looked like a specimen in a laboratory to be studied.

The guard pointed to an intercom in the wall beside the chair.

"You talk through there," he said.

Matisak stared at her as if she were the bug behind the glass, his blue crystal eyes never leaving her. She fought her way into the hard chair from her stilts with as much grace as she could muster, found a good place for the crutches to be leaned and then she fished in her purse for a number of items. She tried to avoid his gaze as she prepared for the interview.

As she did so, she looked into the bottom of her purse, thought about a false bottom there where she had once concealed a gun and carried it into a courtroom. The false bottom was still there. She wondered if the glass between them was bulletproof, guessing that the state would not foot the bill for such an expense. No one expected someone to come in with the intention of murdering an inmate. Perhaps the glass would deflect the bullet, however, causing her only to injure him. It might take two, three shots.

She lifted out the pad and pencil she had brought, and below this, she fished for the tape recorder.

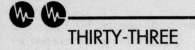

THIRTY-THREE

She showed him the tape recorder. It was her stipulation that she would come only if he would allow it. She said nothing to him, not wishing to initiate anything with Matisak. Rather, she spoke into the microphone her intentions as he leered out at her, his dark blue eyes like crystals, the only feature about him that might be called redeeming, and yet they were filled with a kind of unfathomable mad light.

"I knew you'd come . . . couldn't help yourself," he was saying as she pressed the go button on the recorder.

"Let the record show that on this day, August 13, 1992, prisoner AK2115 of the Pennsylvania Federal Penitentiary at Stony Meadow, Matthew Matisak, here on three counts each of homicide—"

"Never mind all that, Dr. Coran."

"—and serving two life terms consecutively—"

"I understand your father was also a doctor, a coroner, in fact, like you."

"—had indicated a wish to talk openly with agent Jessica Coran, also Dr. Coran, Chief Medical Examiner, Division—"

"He was a good man, your father, wasn't he?"

"—that said prisoner has agreed to this taping. Say it now!"

"I've read one of his books. Kind of obtuse writing, but very inform—"

"Say it, damn you!"

"All right . . . all right, I agree to this taping."

"Now, will you tell me what it is you wish to discuss?"

"You."

"No, no, we are not here to discuss me, Mr. Matisak. If that is all you wish . . ." she started to get up and ring for the guard.

"No, no! Don't go!" His voice was filled with a pitiable sob that seemed to her rehearsed. "I meant only to ask . . . how you are."

"How I am," she repeated, almost laughing at the irony of this man's asking her how she was. "You bastard."

He stared at her, his eyes riveting hers. "I fully understand your hatred for me."

"Good. Then we know where we stand with each other. Now, shall we continue with this . . . this interview?"

"Yes."

"Are you prepared to talk seriously?"

"Yes."

"All right. *Why?* Why did you ask to speak to me?"

"To . . . to first say that I . . . I meant . . . At the time, I was not in control of my . . . my blood craving. The doctors here understand that; they understand my physical need was quite real."

Her jaw tightened. She knew he was just toying with her again.

"And maybe . . . maybe one day I'll be a free man again . . . cured, on proper medication for my addiction. It was . . . *is* an addiction, you know."

"No one can cure you of what you *are,* Matisak. No one can. They can feed you the blood of an ox if that helps your cravings; they can ply you with proteins and hormones and medications of all sorts, but you and I know that if you had the opportunity today to do to me what you did—"

"No, never . . . never again."

She realized he was going for the model prisoner, the one out of thousands the system could help; she realized he was very adept at it. "You're incurably insane, Matisak."

"I'll be up for parole in twenty years. You'll change your mind toward me by then . . . especially if I *help* you."

"Help me?"

"Yes, help you."

"There's nothing you can do for me."

"The FBI, then."

"You don't give a damn about me or the FBI, and if it had been up to me you would not be here now; you would have been dead of electrocution."

"The FBI wants to know *why*," he said with just the trace of a grin.

She stared across the whiteness at him. The room became insufferable. He was insufferable. For a moment, she feared that the Plexiglas was not between them, and that she had been fooled into being here and that he was about to leap across the chasm between them and go for her throat. The burning whiteness of the place saw her reach to her purse and bring up the gun, which she aimed. He stood there frozen, wide-eyed, expecting the bullet aimed at his brain. She squeezed the trigger slowly, enjoying the moment, savoring the image of his brain splattering onto the white wall. She fired in her daydream and his entire body flailed and splatted against the wall of his cell, his vampire's teeth bared, in a death grimace, and she felt an overwhelming feeling of *closure,* that it was finally over. Then she looked up at the real Matisak in the real cell and found him looking quizzically at her, her dream over.

She knew what the agency wanted; she knew what Otto would want of her. She said calmly, "Let's get to the point, Matisak. You want to confess to additional killings, don't you? Some in Kentucky, Ohio? Elsewhere?"

"Perhaps," he replied, "someday."

"What, then, damn you?"

"I want you . . . I want your . . . forgiveness."

"Bullshit, and you'll never have it."

"Then at least let me explain why."

"Why . . . why?"

"For the blood . . . the addiction."

"Liar."

"I am telling you how it was."

"Liar."

"If not for the blood—"

"The *power*, you bastard. You wanted the power, to hold the threat of death over another—"

"No, I-I-I—"

"The power of feeding on another life; taking life through your mouth, down your fucking gullet. You thought it made you special, didn't you? Didn't you?"

"I was addicted."

"Didn't you!"

"I thought it made me immortal. That tells you the extent of my . . . my addiction."

"So you're no longer crazy?"

He said nothing to this.

"You're no longer going crazy?"

He refused to reply.

"Now, you're *going sane*? And we're supposed to believe you?"

"If you cooperate with me, and I cooperate with you, as my mind improves, then perhaps you can learn something about Kentucky, Ohio, other places. The question," he said, standing now, pacing in his cell, "is whether or not you want that information unlocked."

"You're in no position to blackmail the FBI, Matisak."

The madman's scars were on her body, but the deeper scars were those done to her psyche and her soul.

"There are *others,* you know," he teased.

"Other bodies, yes."

"Others like me. *Vampires.*"

It dawned on her what he was saying. "Do you really believe for a moment that the Federal Bureau of Investigation would ever in a million years, Matisak, ask you in on a case involving vampirism? Is that really what you expected of this meeting here today?"

"There are a lot of others like me, spread across this country, and when another one's craving and addiction reach the heights of mine, nothing will stop him from killing for blood, and you and your agency will come crawling to me for help. Do you hear me? Do you hear?"

"I think I've heard enough of your rantings, Matisak. This interview is over."

She clicked off the tape, stood up and rang for the guard to open the door and let her out. Behind her he said, "Look in the woods in Kentucky off I-75, about a mile from the intersection of county road 54 near Lexington. You'll find a shallow grave not a hundred yards from an abandoned old farmhouse."

Her jaw quivered where she stood. Without turning back to face him, she said, "I'll see that it is checked out."

The door opened and she hobbled out on her crutches to his final words to her. "I hope you're healing well."

The door closed with a resounding echo and his laughter. He had just posited information with her that only she knew about. It hadn't been taped. He had waited for the tape to be turned off. He had baited her intentionally. With this new information she had a choice to make. If she told O'Rourke and the others and a search actually turned up a body, then she would be sent back again to speak with this devil, and the more he cooperated with the FBI, the more likely he would be viewed by prison officials as a rehabilitated man. The body in Kentucky was most likely Julie Marie Hampton, missing for over two years, a time when Matisak took many more precautions, before he began to feel supernormal and invincible.

As she made her way back down the long white corridor she struggled with herself about what to do, knowing that in the end she must do the right thing. The Hamptons in Kentucky had to know; O'Rourke had to know, along with the others; and if she could get more information out of Matisak, then she would have to come back to this awful place again and again, consigned to this hell by her counterpart.

She could still hear his laughter.

She could imagine the official stance on this one: play out the bizarre game that Matisak had initiated . . . see where it leads. But she feared it would lead to no good. And she feared his games and where they had led in the past, and she feared that he might get what he wanted. There was nothing in this life that she wanted him to have; seeing him stripped of his personal freedom was not enough. Like the dream of carrying in the concealed weapon and blowing his head off, she feared that her cooperating repeatedly with him as he cooperated with the agency would lead to her one day carrying out that dream for real.

There would be other cases of Tort 9 level, and even some cases of a lesser degree—cannibalism, for instance— in which information gleaned from the mad mind of Matisak could help in the pursuit of an equally deadly killer that was not in a federal facility but walking loose on the streets.

Jessica had made the distance from Matisak's cell to her car in the lot with great effort both physically and mentally. She chugged the crutches into the rear seat and got into the car, where J.T. had fallen asleep at the wheel as he waited for her. He was instantly awake and when she slid into the seat beside him, he asked if she was all right.

"I'll never be all right again, but for now . . . yeah." She held her tears in check.

"What did he want?"

"He wants to use us."

J.T. frowned. "Then you were right all along. Prick bastard."

"And O'Rourke's going to want to use him."

"How can you be so sure about O'Rourke?"

"Oh, something Otto told me once about her."

"Which was?"

"That she played like him; that he admired her for being as ruthless and as tough as him."

"So where to next?"

"Lexington, Kentucky."

"He opened up about Kentucky?"

"He did."

"Holy shit, Jess. Do you know what that means? Boy, you really got to him, then, didn't you? You really got him talking. Got it on tape?"

"Let's get to the airport, shall we?"

"You're really good, you know that, Jess?"

"Yeah . . . yeah, I know, I know . . . I'm good . . . Wake me when we get to the airport."